Becoming Latina in 10 Easy Steps

Becoming Latina In 10 Easy Steps

Lara Rios

BERKLEY BOOKS, NEW YORK

THE BERKLEY PUBLISHING GROUP
Published by the Penguin Group
Penguin Group (USA) Inc.
375 Hudson Street, New York, New York 10014, USA
Penguin Group (Canada), 90 Eglinton Avenue East, Suite 700, Toronto, Ontario M4P 2Y3, Canada
(a division of Pearson Penguin Canada Inc.)
Penguin Books Ltd., 80 Strand London WC2R 0RL, England
Penguin Group Ireland, 25 St. Stephen's Green, Dublin 2, Ireland (a division of Penguin Books Ltd.)
Penguin Group (Australia), 250 Camberwell Road, Camberwell, Victoria 3124, Australia
(a division of Pearson Australia Group Pty. Ltd.)
Penguin Books India Pvt. Ltd., 11 Community Centre, Panchsheel Park, New Delhi—110 017, India
Penguin Group (NZ), Cnr. Airborne and Rosedale Roads, Albany, Auckland 1310, New Zealand
(a division of Pearson New Zealand Ltd.)
Penguin Books (South Africa) (Pty.) Ltd., 24 Sturdee Avenue, Rosebank, Johannesburg 2196, South Africa

Penguin Books Ltd., Registered Offices: 80 Strand, London WC2R 0RL, England

This is a work of fiction. Names, characters, places, and incidents either are the product of the author's imagination or are used fictitiously, and any resemblance to actual persons, living or dead, business establishments, events, or locales is entirely coincidental. The publisher does not have any control over and does not assume any responsibility for author or third-party websites or their content.

First edition: January 2006

Library of Congress Cataloging-in-Publication Data

Rios, Lara.
  Becoming Latina in ten easy steps / Lara Rios.—Berkley trade pkb. ed.
    p. cm.
  ISBN 0-425-20755-2 (pbk.)
    1. Hispanic American women—Fiction. 2. Women animators—Fiction. I. Title:
Becoming Latina in 10 easy steps. II. Title.

  PS3618.I567B43 2006
  813'.54—dc22   2005050119

PRINTED IN THE UNITED STATES OF AMERICA

10 9 8 7 6 5 4 3 2 1

To my children, who will one day grow up and wonder,
"Who am I, anyway?"
May they never be as confused as my seriously flawed heroine.
Maybe if I've done a good enough job as a mother,
the answer will be self-evident.

Acknowledgments

Writing a book really begins way before the first word is ever written. Someone says something or you experience a life event or you finally understand an important lesson, and everything that has been catalogued in your brain sort of spills out into a story. At least that's the way it works with me.

For this book, I have to thank:

My many Encantadora friends for the countless times we've talked and laughed online about what it means to be Latina. Maybe this book will help our critics realize that there is no such thing as being "Latino enough," and that we all come in different shapes, sizes, and colors. And, shhh, we can't all cook and don't all want to be mothers. Heck, we're sort of like everyone else in a lot of ways.

Theresa, for sharing some of your life stories with me. You validated the need for this book. My heroine represents all of us who are straddling two cultures. You are an awesome survivor, and I am forever in awe of you.

Caren, the coolest, most fun, most brilliant, most hardworking agent in the business. You believed in this story from the moment you read my partial, probably more than I did. Thank you for urging me for months to "finish the book." And thank you for the wonderful suggestions along the way. I can honestly say, this book wouldn't exist without you.

Cindy, I'm so grateful to have an editor who is as enthusiastic and positive as you are about this book. Your specific and detailed suggestions helped me to write a better story and to stretch as an author. Thank you.

My family, especially my husband, kids, and mother, who always understand when I can't attend a gathering because I have to write. I couldn't do it without your support. Thanks for letting me follow my dreams!

One

Wednesday, May 12

✿ Have you ever wondered if you were dropped on earth by aliens who somehow forgot to instruct you on the customs and habits of the natives?

Every time I have to spend any length of time with my family, I start to wonder, who *are* these people? Why are they so bizarre? Why, for example, does my grandmother, Lulu, insist on adorning her house with various Catholic saints, whom she trusts with her deepest secrets and counts on to deliver her every wish, yet rejects the very thought of calling a policeman when a burglar breaks into her home?

"*Hay que pedirle ayuda a Santo Jose,*" she'd say.

"But *Abuela*, you have to report the crime," I would argue, wondering how praying to the image of a saint would bring her any justice in the real world.

"Marcela, you can't trust outsiders," she'd say. "Especially anyone from *el gobierno*."

Right, you can't trust the government, but you can trust a painted figurine hanging on a wall. You see what I have to put up with? And I won't even mention the altar she has in her living room, which is supposed to be the threshold between heaven and earth that reunites the living and the dead.

But Grandma isn't the strangest one in the family. After all, she's old, and you can attribute some of her weirdness to her age. We can never *really* understand previous generations after all.

One of my favorite relatives, yet the one who makes me the craziest, is the one sitting across from me in the car, my aunt Lydia. We're driving to my cousin Amelia's bridal shower, and she can't help but remind me that I will be twenty-seven years old next week and my cousin, six years my junior, is beating me to the altar.

"So? It's not a race," I say.

"I know that. I just worry that you're not doing anything worthwhile with your life, *Mi'ja*."

Excuse me, but did she forget I'm Marcela Alvarez? A name that can be seen on at least a dozen movie credits (albeit near the end) because I'm an animator for a major Hollywood studio. They pay me an exorbitant amount of money to do something I love. I amuse children and keep them out of their parents' hair. And adults get a kick out of animated movies too, let's face it. Entertainment—what can be more worthwhile than that?

If we don't count the guy scene, I have a pretty damn good life. But in return for the nice paycheck, I've got to give the studio a large chunk of my time. *This* is what makes my family bitch up a storm. Their various complaints include: I'm never around, I'll never get married, and I'll never have children. You know . . . the end-all to being a woman.

"Worthwhile?" I ask, because I know I'm supposed to, though I know better.

"There's so much you could be doing to help others."

"Don't start in on me about my responsibilities." Although she, like the rest of my relatives, would love for me to get married and have kids, she has other ideas on what I *should* be doing. You see, Aunt Lydia is what you would call a fanatic. Her entire life revolves around various Hispanic organizations: LULAC, UFW, NSHP, NCLR, MALDEF, ACLU, NABE, NUL. To me it's all just a bunch of BULL.

I get letters from the Hispanic Chamber of Commerce all the time, asking me to join, to support my people. I should, I guess, but . . . being a successful Latina is such a burden. I'm no one's role model, and I don't want to be either. That's what none of my family members seem to understand, especially Aunt Lydia, who would love to see me become president of the next Latinos Rule the World Organization or some other ridiculous type of activist group.

As Aunt Lydia lectures me on what my life should be about, I wonder why I agreed to drive her. I focus on the road and tune her out. My mind drifts and I wonder what it would be like to be normal. To be a regular *guera*, American girl, not a Latina straddling two cultures. I've never been to Mexico, yet I feel disloyal when I feel nothing at the sight of a waving Mexican flag. It's crazy. My family makes me crazy.

As I do before most of my family events, I mentally try to fortify myself for all the comments I'm going to receive about my American way of life, about not having kids or a Mexican husband. I'll endure this bridal shower, and I'll even enjoy parts of it, but lately, I can't help but feel more at home at movie release parties than at these family events.

If I had one wish, it would be for everyone to just lay off. Let me be me and love me for who I am. I'm not a cultural tag; I'm a real person. If my family and everyone else even could finally accept that, then maybe I'd finally stop feeling Mexican in the Anglo world, and like a sell-out, a *pocha,* in my own family. I sent up a silent prayer to God to please give me a break. I'm tired of living in two worlds. *Make up your mind already—what do you want me to be?* But he didn't answer, so I shrugged and kept driving.

Saturday, June 12

❀ Rule number one about weddings: Never assume the weather will be the same where you're going as where you are. I drove from Los Angeles to Palm Springs. Yes, I know Palm Springs is a desert and it's always hotter there than at the beach, but I didn't think about it and I totally fried. My already dark skin was at least three shades darker where it was exposed, and the satiny dress I had on felt like Saran Wrap tightening around me until I couldn't breathe.

Amelia's big day had finally arrived, and I couldn't have been happier. This meant there would be no more engagement parties, or family discussions about the wedding ad nauseam, or bridal showers. At least for this particular relative. The drawback to having a big family is that you have a million and one events to attend every weekend. When someone isn't getting married, someone else is having a baby shower, birthday, anniversary party . . . you get the picture.

Amelia picked the desert because she chose a Southwestern theme for the wedding, and she wanted the natural surroundings to be, well, natural. If she'd have asked my opinion, I would have told her that June in the desert was completely insane, but hey, no one asked me.

Anyhow, the worst part about this wedding wasn't that I was dripping wet in some parts and charcoaled in others—though that was bad. The worst part—the part that sent me home like a blubbering teenage fool with mascara stains running down my cheeks—was the bomb my cousin, Sonya, dropped between the toast to the bride and groom and the lap dance Carlos performed for Amelia before he took her garter belt off with his teeth.

Sonya is a real bitch so I didn't believe her at first. She's the kind of chick who loves to stir up trouble, you know? She has no life so she enjoys bringing misery into other people's lives. I guess that way she's both entertained and she doesn't feel so terrible about herself.

So there we were, me, Sonya, Pepe (Amelia's brother, who I swear must belong to a gang. The boy is twenty-two and has more gold chains and cell phones hanging from his body than anyone I know), my aunt Lydia, and my grandma Lulu. I'm sipping on dry champagne, trying not to be bored silly. Pepe gets three phone calls in a matter of six minutes. He speaks in code—I have no idea what he says. He hangs up and offers a lazy smile. "The chicks love me," he says.

I smile back because he really *is* very cute.

"You find a good Mexicana, Pepe," Aunt Lydia says. "One who can cook and likes to make babies. None of these skinny, boyish-looking *gueras* you like to hang out with, you hear?"

Aunt Lydia is not his mother. She has no children. How could she when she's always busy volunteering in a dozen pro-Mexican/pro-Chicano groups, furthering some cause or another? Of course, her second function in life involves butting into *our* lives—telling *us* to get married and have kids while she's free as a bird.

But we all love her because we know if there's one person in our family we can count on, it's Aunt Lydia.

Today, though, Pepe isn't impressed with her. He rolls his eyes. "I do plenty of Mexicanas, *Tía,* you know what I mean? But the problem with them is that they're too hung up on family. I don't need to meet their *mamás* and stuff. I'm like a tumbleweed, *sábes*? I need to move from chick to chick. Spread my seed."

I laughed. Couldn't help it. "Tumbleweeds don't have seeds."

"Have your fun," Tía continues. "But, *Mi'jo*, don't mix the blood in the end."

Sonya frowns and stares at me.

What? I think, but don't say it.

"Don't you want to stand up for yourself and tell Aunt Lydia that a little mixed blood ain't bad? Hasn't hurt you any."

"Me?" This was the start of her bomb. "I don't have mixed blood. Both my parents are Mexican, in case you haven't noticed." I'm proud of how mature and sarcastic I sound.

Sonya smiles. A totally fake, I've-got-something-so-big-on-you smile that none of my sarcasm even makes a blip on her radar. "I'm talking about the blood you inherited from your real father."

I've only had one father. My mother has been married only once to the same man for twenty-nine years. I tell her to shut the f*@! up and that she's not being funny.

"Come on, you're twenty-seven, how long are you going to pretend you don't know?"

"Don't know what?"

My grandmother holds up a hand. "Enough."

I notice my aunt Lydia is sitting stiffer and won't meet my eyes. So of course now I'm starting to wonder what the hell is going on.

"Okay, Sonya, spill it. What are you getting at?" My parents weren't mixed, that I knew, but maybe there was a white or black or Asian ancestor in our past. So what? Good. I sure as hell wasn't planning on marrying a Latino.

Sonya shrugs like it doesn't matter, but I could tell she was dying to tell me whatever bit of smut she felt she had on me.

"No," Aunt Lydia says to Sonya in a very serious tone. I swear she was acting like Sonya had a secret that threatened national security.

"Come on, *Tía*," Sonya says. "Everyone in the family knows Marcela's real father was the *guero* her mother slept with when she cheated on *Tío* Juan."

Say what? Cheated? *Guero*? I look at my dark skin. Sonya was on drugs. There was no way I had a white father. And my mother would never in a million years have cheated on my father. "Are you trying to be funny?" I ask her, no longer willing to take her gossip lightly.

Sonya looks disinterested and shrugs again. "If you don't believe me ask your mom."

I look from Sonya to my aunt to my grandmother. No one speaks up to deny the incredible accusation Sonya has leveled at my mother.

"*Tía?*" I plead for support.

"Speak with your mother, *Mi'ja*," she says. "You're still just as Mexican to me."

Hello? Was I in the twilight zone? Just as Mexican as when? Two seconds ago? All I could do was stare at her in disbelief. Besides, I didn't give a shit about being Mexican enough for my aunt. I *did* care that I may have a different birth father than I believed for the past twenty-seven years.

So I took off to find my mother. She must have known I was upset, maybe from the distressed look on my face, because as soon as I stopped beside her at the table reserved for my family, she stood and grabbed hold of my upper arms. She angled her head and frowned. "*Qué pasa?*"

Qué pasa was that I was freaking out. If what Sonya said was true, then how *dare* my parents—my entire family—keep it from me? But I was very proud of myself. I simply said in a calm voice, "May I speak with you in private?"

Of course, private at a wedding party with eight hundred or so relatives with distant cousins so distant we had to shake hands and introduce ourselves while the bride and groom said "I do" . . . let's just say we found a barrel cactus to stand beside.

I didn't beat around the bush. This was my mom after all. I told her what Sonya said. My mother looked horrified, and I sighed a huge breath of relief and waited for the words of denial to come tumbling out of her mouth. I waited and waited and waited. "Well?" I said finally.

"It's not as bad as it sounds," she said.

I certainly hoped not.

"I was young, and I felt so pressured by marriage and all the expectations thrust upon me. But your father and I got through it. He forgave me and I love him so much. There's never been anyone else since that tiny indiscretion."

I stared at her. My mother. My sweet, giving rock of a mother whom my family counted and depended on for moral guidance. The one who advised us and lectured on proper behavior and how to follow the path God had planned for us. The one who made *albondiga* soup and taught my sisters and me how to make tortillas (still the only thing I know how to cook) while telling us how important family bonding was and not to ever forget that family was the only thing that mattered in life. I stared at her, trying to merge the image of my saint of a mother with the snake, and the cheat, and the liar who would have an affair, break her marriage vows, and then go on with life as if she'd done nothing wrong.

"Marcela, speak," my mother said.

Yeah sure, but where to start? First of all, she'd explained that she'd had an affair and that Dad forgave her, but what about the question of my paternity? "Are you saying . . . ?" I found my voice but not the right words.

"Yes, it happened. But that was a lifetime ago."

"Twenty-seven years ago?"

"A little more than that."

"Twenty-seven years and nine months?"

My mother blushed.

"Oh for Christ's sake, Mom. Who's my real father?"

"Juan is your father."

"Don't play semantic games with me, Mom. You know what I'm asking. Who donated the damned sperm?"

"Watch your mouth and have some respect."

Respect?! She wanted respect? Was that funny or what? I was practically gasping for air. "Who was he?"

My mother glanced around to make sure no one was listening to us. I had forgotten by this point that we were at Amelia's wedding and that other people were actually dancing to Shakira's latest, eating, chatting, and having a good time all around us.

"His name was Paul and he played college football and attended my prayer group. That's where I met him," she said, confidentially.

Oh great. What did they do—get it on between asking Jesus to forgive them? Ugh! The image was too ugly to picture. "He was white?"

"Yes, but very open to other cultures and especially interested in anything Mexican."

Obviously. "So what happened?" I crossed my arms. "Did you love him?"

"No. I liked him a lot, and perhaps if I hadn't been married something deeper might have grown between us. *Mi'ja*, he was a good man with a wonderful sense of humor. But I was a stupid, scared little girl, and he became an easy way to avoid my difficulties with Juan."

I swallowed, wondering if I'd inherited my own sense of humor from this mystery man.

"When your father found out, he tried to kill Paul. He was so hurt."

"What did you expect?"

"I was lucky that he was able to put it behind us and that he still wanted me."

This was when the tears started. I tried to blink them away, but it was a lost cause, so I brushed them away with my fingertips. Dad forgave her because he had a heart of gold. My father is the most wonderful, honorable man in the world. I love him with all the hero worship of a young girl still. To me, he is and will always be my only father. Whoever this scum Paul was, who would sleep with a confused, vulnerable, *married* woman, he was no one that mattered.

"*Mi'ja*," my mother began when she noticed my tears.

I took a step back; I didn't want her to touch me. Was I

wrong? I shook my head and turned around and left. I stuck around long enough to be forced to participate in the stupid bouquet toss. I didn't catch it. Big surprise there—I couldn't get a man to stick with me long enough to pop the question even if I used a hot glue gun. Then I left and cried all the way home.

I don't even know why it affected me like that. After all, nothing has changed. Juan is my dad. He raised me. He loved me. In fact, he loved me best of all. But somehow, I felt like my mother had cheated on *me*, been disloyal to *me*. And in a way, she had.

Two

Friday, June 18

❀ Man, I had one hell of a week. Had to meet with a team of Chinese animators to complete our *Land of the Firebird* project. These guys were top notch. I learned a lot about CG films from them. They could also drink like fish. I came home with a buzz every night. But also with renewed inspiration for my work. Unable to sleep, I stayed up until after 2 A.M. every morning trying to come up with a new project. I wanted to do something different, something exciting, something revolutionary. Something our studio hasn't done and redone a million times. Something that would knock the socks off our story developers. But every night, I went to bed with hundreds of roughs I ended up tossing in the morning.

As always my week flew by, and for this I was grateful. Mom called three times, but I didn't have time to return her calls. To be honest, I don't want to talk to her. I can't handle the enormity of what actually happened and how it affects me. I don't want to think about who Paul really is or that half my genetic makeup is now a mystery. I'm still me, right? That's all that matters.

So I didn't return Mom's calls. Right now, I resent the hell out of her and I don't know what it's going to take to make me feel differently.

So to feel better I did what I usually do when I feel crappy. I went out with my best buddy from work, Jackson. Nothing special, just dinner, and then we came back to my place to talk shop.

But I did something crazy—I slept with him. I'm not sure what I was thinking. One minute we're going over adding realistic movement to a dragon and the next he's got his tongue down my throat. It felt so good to be touched and caressed, so comforting, so what I needed. As pitiful as it sounds, after last weekend, being held and kissed and pleasured made me feel less lonely.

Of course, the totally insane thing is that Jackson is a friend, and nothing like this has ever, *ever* happened before. We've never even discussed our personal lives or kissed or anything. The closest we've ever gotten physically is when he rubs my shoulders at work after long twelve-hour days. He's the guy who always makes me laugh, the one I share dinners with almost every night before coming home. I *know* him, you know? But I don't know his past, his dreams, his personal life, or any of the intimate details that bind couples together, because that's not what we're about. At least not until tonight.

So, we do it on my futon, then he gets up, gets dressed, and with a gentle kiss whispers, "See you on Monday."

Here I was, naked, feeling pretty good, wondering if we ought to talk about what we'd just done, and he casually gets up and leaves. I don't know. Am I crazy to feel something was missing from that "exchange"? I wanted to curl up and cry, I really did, and I'm not a crier. In fact, I didn't. But, hell, my life feels sadly vacant lately. Here I am, weeks into my twenty-seventh year, and I'm no closer to figuring out what my life's about. To make things worse, no one seems to be who I think they are, which makes me wonder if my judgment is skewed in other areas as well. I just can't seem to make a connection. Maybe it's me.

Sunday, June 20

✿ Today started out awkward, but I ended up with a mission.

I went to church with my family like I do most Sundays, though I wasn't looking forward to seeing my mom—or Sonya.

Sonya, I managed to avoid, but my mother was a different story. She cornered me by the bathrooms and kept telling me how sorry she was and how I needed to get over it and how "that" was ancient history.

How do you tell your own mother to blow it out her ear? It really irked me how she wanted to gloss over the fact that half of who I was became a mystery to me overnight. I deserved more from her. Not sure what, but something.

"I don't want to talk about this now," I said, trying to walk past her.

"I'm worried about you." She touched my arm to stop me.

"Worried?" I swallowed a lump in my throat. "It's a little late to worry about me now, don't you think?"

"Why haven't you returned my phone calls?"

I felt hot, bubbling anger in the pit of my stomach, and I started to regret the Egg McMuffin I'd inhaled on the drive to church. "Because I didn't want to talk to you. Jesus, Mom, I can't even look at you right now."

"Don't take the Lord's name in vain."

"Grrr." I whirled, looking for something to punch, but found nothing so I turned back to her. "You have all these stupid rules. There's a proper way to say things and a correct way to act, but when it comes to being honest and open about something as important as who my father actually is, you forget all about rules, don't you?"

She stiffened and glanced over her shoulder at the pews filling up with people. "Maybe you're right. Maybe this isn't the right time to discuss this." Her hand slipped to her side.

"The right time was years ago."

"You didn't need to know about any of this. Sonya made a big mistake by telling you, and I've spoken with her."

Sonya made a big mistake? The earth might just be tipping over on its axis for me to think anything remotely positive about Sonya, but at least *she* told the truth. "You didn't think I needed to know about Paul?"

She lifted her chin. "Absolutely not."

Amazing. Who was this woman and what did she do with my mom? I have no interest in Paul, but I don't know, maybe the offer to share a picture or some sympathy for the pain she's caused me might have made me feel better. Because it does hurt. Dishonesty always hurts. Losing the blood tie to my dad also hurts.

"Well," I said, "that just makes one more thing you were wrong about."

I glanced over to the front of the church where a floor-to-ceiling crucifix looked down on the congregation. Irrationally, I wondered how Jesus could let this happen. Wasn't he supposed to lead people down a righteous path?

"You need to get over this, Marcela."

I shot her the most disgusted look I could manage and walked away. I took a seat beside my father.

I wanted to talk to him. Thank him for raising me even though he didn't have to. Thank him for loving me and never treating me any different than he did my sisters. But I couldn't do it. Silly, I know, but I kinda felt that if we didn't talk about it, maybe it would be like it never happened. Our relationship would continue just like it always had.

He reached over to cover my hands on my lap and smiled down. "You're coming to lunch, right?" he whispered.

This was our weekly ritual—lunch at my parents' after

church. I could see in his eyes that he really wanted me there, so I nodded. "Of course, *Papi*." For him, I would pretend everything was fine.

Once we all got to my parents' home, my father changed from his geeky church clothes to his geeky Sunday-hang-out-in-the-backyard clothes. Plaid shorts and some fern-looking button-up shirt. Gotta love him. As he cleaned the grill and enjoyed a beer, I noticed how much older he seemed. Even though I was a grown woman, I always thought of him as my strong, macho father. But he wasn't. He was older and weaker, yet proud enough to do things for his girls he really was better off not doing anymore—like pruning my sister Anna's palm trees every year.

Mom prepared the meat. Usually, one of us girls helped her—well, one of my sisters—I kinda suck in the kitchen, but today we all sat under the old Jacaranda tree. It was hot, very hot, and there was no breeze. Anna moaned and closed her eyes as she sat back in the chaise longue. She looked tired, but good. I hate that she's only two years younger than me, but looks five years younger. And Kate, the baby, who has always been the chubbiest, fanned her hand in front of her face, not seeming able to cool down.

I'm a sucker for punishment and can't ever let an issue drop, so I asked how long they'd known about them being only my half sisters.

I checked them out. They both had Juan's strong jaw and pronounced cheekbones. This was the first time I noticed I didn't. We all had Mom's straight hair. At 5'7" I'm taller than them both. Wonder if Paul's tall? Damn—I'm driving myself crazy.

Well, Anna shot up in her chair and Kate kinda looked down at her meaty feet stuffed into size six, black leather Kenneth Cole sandals. If Katie had grown another two inches, her weight might not look so bad. Also, if she hadn't been born the baby who everyone spoiled and rewarded with food, she might not struggle so much with her weight.

"What are you talking about?" Anna asks.

"Sonya told me," Kate admits. "But I thought she was lying. She's such a *mentirosa*, *chismosa*."

"Told you what?" Anna asks.

"It's true," I say.

"*¡Híjole!* will one of you tell me what you're talking about? What do you mean you're our half sister?"

"Dad is not my father," I whisper, and lean closer so my father will not hear. Pretty stupid since he, of all people, already knows. Then I elaborate on what I know.

Anna is shocked—truly—almost as much as I was. She can't believe Mom kept this from all of us.

Join the club.

Katie looks sad.

"So your father is some white guy none of us even knows?"

"Apparently so."

We kinda sat there, no one talking for a minute. Then Anna shrugged and said, "Well, that explains it."

"Explains what?" I ask, not knowing what she was getting at.

"Your lack of interest in anything Mexican."

I've got to admit, at least to myself, that the assessment was accurate, but I still prickled at her words. "What's that supposed to mean?"

"I don't mean anything by it, *hermana*, but maybe it's just not in your *sangre*, you know?"

"I don't see why everything has to come down to race or nationality," I protested, seeming to help make her point.

She tried to explain that genetically I just didn't have it in me to want to preserve "La Rasa." I had white blood running through my veins and so lacked the passion.

I couldn't believe my own sister was saying this. Sonya, yes, but my sister? What the hell was "white" blood anyway? Didn't we all have red blood on Earth?

"Anna, Katie, I'm just as Mexican as you. I'm also just as American as you. We grew up with the same parents, and went to the same *quinceañeras*. I made *cascarones* for Easter just like you. Got scared out of my skin on *Día de los Muertos* by Tío Paco. What does blood have to do with any of it?"

But I could see it in their eyes. I was not less of a sister to them, but somehow I was no longer their cultural equal. They were pure, better than me. I felt like a mutt all of a sudden. My pedigree had been soiled. I was less valuable.

I couldn't help it. I lost my patience and temper and stood, fuming like the cartoon characters I sometimes animate with smoke coming out of their ears. "I'm just as Mexican as you both. I just don't feel a need to shout it from my rooftop every minute of every day like Aunt Lydia."

"*Óye, qué pasa?*" My father left the sanctity of his grill and started approaching us.

"Great," Kate said. "Now you've done it."

"*Bueno?* Marcela, why the screaming?"

As much as I tried, I couldn't erase my frown. "It's nothing."

"Nothing?" He gazed at my two sisters.

"No, *Papi*," Katie said, full of guilty innocence.

Anna agreed. She always looked more serious and believable.

He caressed the back of my head, gave me a little smile, then returned to the grill.

I stared at his retreating back and wondered how life could be so unjust. How could this man for whom I had such a deep respect and love not share one speck of DNA with me? It just wasn't fair—not when I loved him so much. I ached inside at the thought of losing him.

"He always loved you best," Anna said quietly.

I blinked away tears. "How could he, when he's known the truth all along? He knows I'm not his."

"I guess in his heart you are," Anna said.

I frowned at her. "I guess I should be grateful he doesn't base his love on how much Mexican blood I've got flowing through my veins," I said sarcastically.

"Hey, I didn't mean it like that. Come on."

"Yeah, chill out," Katie agreed.

I wiped away the moisture that had collected at the corners of my eyes. "Your comments suck. How am I supposed to feel?"

"It's no secret how you feel about *La Rasa*. All I meant was that maybe now we know the reason why," Anna said, almost too casually.

"The reason why is because I'm not a superficial, racist, cliquish fool like you all."

I left without having lunch—too upset to eat. I think I had a permanent golf ball lodged in my throat. I jumped into my BMW convertible determined to show them—all of them, my sisters, my cousins, my aunt—that *I*, mixed blood or not, am just as Latina as they are.

Three

🌸 Okay, I've had a chance to calm down since the run-in with my sisters. Hell, if they want to believe I'm less Mexican than they are, then why should I care? What difference does it really make in my life?

I've chanted this to myself all morning at work, but it hasn't helped. Something inside me, maybe my hurt pride or my need to prove that I still belong in my family, dictates that I devise some kind of plan. Somehow, I need to figure out who I am. I need to prove to myself that I am my parents' daughter just as much as my sisters are. And that Paul in no way influences why I haven't embraced my Latin culture. So as of today, I start becoming a real Latina. I'm just not sure how yet—I'll figure that out later.

On another front, Jackson cornered me in the supply room, nervous and sweaty, and asked if I was going to hate him for what he'd done to me on Saturday.

I had to swallow my smile and remind the boy that he didn't "do" anything to me. *We* had sex.

He cringed at the three-letter word.

"Did you hate it that much?" I asked.

He looked horrified. "Oh, no, of course not," he said. "I really liked it, but, it's just that, well . . ." He paused and leaned closer to me. "We work together."

No kidding. Did he fail to realize this when he was pumping into me? Guys are such wimps. They all want sex without any responsibility or consequences. "Don't sweat it," I said. "Nothing's changed."

The look of pure relief on his face made me smile. Maybe he thought I'd come to work drooling all over him, asking for a ring or something. I might have just had a birthday and be well on my way toward my thirties, but I'm not a desperate female who uses sex to trap a guy into marriage. He should know me better than that. But I cut him some slack, since I wasn't quite sure how to act around him either now that we'd crossed the S-E-X line.

"Are you sure?" he asked.

"Positive."

He brought a hand up to my face and softly caressed my skin. "I wanted to call you all weekend. I felt like a dog." He closed his eyes and sighed, obviously distressed.

It gave me a sort of perverse pleasure to realize he hadn't just brushed off our sexual transgression. "You're not a dog."

He gazed at me a moment longer, then eased away as if trying to regain his cool. He smiled. "You're sure you're okay?"

Because he was being so sweet and I know he was worried, I decided to be honest. "I was a tiny bit hurt that you just got up and left right after, but I'm fine now. Let's forget it, okay?"

He nodded. "Okay? Friends?"

"Friends," I said. And to prove that that was true, we went out for lunch together and had a great time.

After lunch I called my friend Daniela. Jackson was great to share work stuff with and no one was better at giving me guy advice. But like all men, he hid behind an invisible shield when it came to anything emotional. So I didn't mention my problems with my parents to him. Daniela would be better equipped to help me and would expect to be filled in on every detail. Besides, being Argentine, and thus Latina, but having none of the baggage many of us Mexicans carry with us across the border, I decided she was the perfect person to confide in about my quest.

Daniela laughed in her easy, happy way. "Now, how are you going to become *more* Mexican?" she asked. "That's like becoming more female. You can't be more of what you already are. You can only be a better one."

And that's exactly what I need to be—better. Only, how can I be, when I don't know zip about my own culture? "That's my plan," I said. "So, will you help me?" I placed my feet on my desk and uncapped the plastic lid on the chocolate mousse pie container I brought back with me from the restaurant.

"How? What do I know about becoming more Mexican?"

"You're Latina. I need to do this with someone else who can understand what I'm going through."

Daniela promised to come over the next night so we could brainstorm and write out a plan. A woman has to have a map, and unlike a man, she consults it regularly. I figure I can probably complete this in a couple of weeks and go on with my life.

Satisfied, I dug into my dessert. I glanced over at Jackson, who was concentrating deeply on his work. He must have felt me gazing at him because he looked up, winked, then stared at his computer screen again. I smiled, then took my feet off the desk and tossed my pie in the trash. It was much too sweet.

And in case you're wondering, yes, Jackson did hurt my feelings and no, things really aren't the same—I noticed that during lunch. But I'll pretend they are because he's been my bud for years and I love the dumb jerk. Not in love, just love.

Tuesday, June 22

🍀 1. *Date Mexican men.* This was Daniela's first suggestion for my list, and I wrote it in my notepad as we made ourselves comfortable on the floor in front of my coffee table.

"I don't like Mexican men," I said. I lifted a huge slice of pepperoni and mushroom pizza from the box, careful not to let the web of cheese get on my area rug, which I picked up the last time I was in China. I paid a fortune for it.

"I know you don't, but think about this. If you bring home an Anglo as a future husband, knowing what you know now, how do you think your father will feel?"

Jeesh, I hadn't thought of that. That would be a slap in the face, wouldn't it? "He'll hate him. And the rest of my family will see it as a further dilution of my bloodline when we have kids."

"Exactly."

"Okay. From now on I date only Mexican guys." Time to put my own unfair bias aside. Not all Mexican men are macho jerks. My father isn't—well, he's macho, but not a jerk. I took another bite of pizza and stood. From my desk I retrieved an envelope. Sitting again on the floor, I opened the last letter from the Hispanic Chamber of Commerce. "I got this in the mail."

Daniela reached for her beer bottle and uncapped it. The pop and fizzing sound made me thirsty. "What is it?" she asked.

"From the Hispanic Chamber of Commerce. I guess I should join something like this."

"Hmm," Daniela said, noncommittally.

"What do you think they will want from me if I join?"

Daniela sipped from her beer bottle. "Don't know. Let me see."

She put her bottle down and studied the letter. "Probably money."

"I can do that."

"They might ask you to be a guest speaker at one of their

events, seeing that you work in Hollywood and know so many celebrities." Daniela waved her hand around as she spoke—a typical characteristic the Argentines picked up from their Italian ancestors.

Shaking clear my easily distracted mind, I refocused on my list. "Okay, done. That's an easy one." I took my notepad and wrote down my next step.

2. Join the Hispanic Chamber of Commerce.

"Next." I grabbed more pizza and my own bottle of beer.

Daniela returned my letter. "Heck, I don't know." She made a puffing sound as if to say "you silly girl." "I've never tried to be more Latina before."

I smiled. "But you've tried to *look* more Latina. Remember all that sunbathing?"

"I'm just trying to blend into Southern California culture. Not everyone is lucky enough to have been born with that nice *café con leche* color of yours."

"Nice, huh?" I always considered myself too dark. Paul sure didn't contribute much to my pigmentation. "I could start speaking with an accent," I said, my mouth currently full—and making me sound like Patrick, the little pink starfish from the *SpongeBob* cartoon.

Daniela laughed. "Sure. Go for the exotic, Salma Hayek accent. Guys really think she's sexy, you know?"

I downed a swig of beer. "Did you see her lesbian scene in *Frida*? I'll bet guys really got off on that. It might have been historical fact, but trust me, I know Hollywood, and they put that scene in for men."

Daniela snapped her fingers. "There you go. Become a lesbian. I hear the bisexual thing is big with Chicanas."

I laughed and blew her a kiss. "Volunteering to be my partner?"

She tossed a paper napkin at me. "As lovely as you are, I'm married, remember?"

"Oh yeah. Shucks." This plan was going to be harder to develop than I thought. I groaned and dropped down on my back on the cool hardwood floor. "These stereotypes are ridiculous. I'm telling you, this is why I've stayed away from these cultural tags for so long."

"Well, if you want stereotype, there's always Mexican food. We all love that." Daniela stood and took her paper plate and beer bottle into the kitchen.

"Hmm, not a bad idea." I sat up and followed her into the kitchen. After all, look at my mother and grandmother. They're excellent cooks and they are certainly typical Mexican women.

"You recycle?" Daniela began opening and closing my cabinets looking for a place to drop her bottle.

I took her beer bottle and put it in a separate trash bin. If the gestapo trashmen catch us slipping any glass or plastic into the "regular" trash, I think we get written up on the master list that goes to a special section of the government that deals severely with subversive trash violators.

"Fact is, Marcela, every good Latina wife should be able to cook. Ask my husband. I think he'd divorce me if I couldn't cook."

"Do I really have to learn to cook?"

She grinned. "I know it's a lot to ask of you, but . . . it *is* about time you learned how. And yes, start with Mexican food. It's my favorite."

We got out the phone book and searched for chefs, figuring I could use private lessons. I found a few food delivery services that bring completely cooked meals to your door. People in Hollywood don't cook. Like me, they eat out, or order in. We'll all probably die of high cholesterol, preservative poisoning, or sodium overdose, but in the meantime we're living it up. For a moment, I was tempted to go with one of those instead. Why should my future man care if *I* cooked the food or a service did?

As long as the food was hot and on the table, what difference did it make?

But Daniela interrupted my musings by speaking. "Here's a guy that specializes in Mexican food," Daniela said, pointing at the yellow pages ad. *Alberto,* written in flamboyant font and decorated with green and red chiles.

Resigned to adding cooking to my expanding list of future achievements, I jotted down his number so I could write it into my planner and give him a call. Then we went back to my living room and I wrote down my third step.

3. Learn to cook Mexican food.

Daniela stretched out on my futon. I took my place back in front of the pizza box. I wasn't finished eating by a long shot.

"Another beer?" I offered.

"No, I have to drive home tonight."

"Right."

Now, if I'm looking at my grandmother as a traditional Latina to emulate, then the next step I should have on my list involved my church. Her belief in saints, and even her altar, are things lots of Mexican folks share. I certainly don't want to fill my place up with candles and saints, but I can expand my Catholic commitment. So I wrote down my fourth step and passed my notebook to Daniela.

4. Become a devout Catholic.

"You already go to church every Sunday," Daniela pointed out, returning my list, and closing her eyes. Guess she wasn't impressed.

"Yeah, but I'm a cafeteria Catholic. I pick and choose what I like to believe and follow. I need to get deeper into my religion."

"Too late for nunhood, *piba*." She patted her belly. "I'm full. Think I'm getting fat?"

Yes, I did, but I wasn't about to admit it. Instead, I ignored the question and elbowed her hip, leaning back against the futon.

"Nunhood? Obviously, I won't go that far. But, don't you think this is a good thing to add to my list?"

"Sure."

She didn't sound convinced, but I thought it might actually be an excellent thing to do. My church regularly organizes feeding events for the poor, and in L.A. many of those were Mexican. I could participate in a soup kitchen or donate to one of the trips to Mexico. As many times as our church has gone to the orphanages in Mexico, I never once donated anything. I always tuned the priest out and left that kind of stuff to my mom. Habit I guess, because I can certainly afford it. Ever since we were kids, my parents always handled things like that. But I gave to the United Way at work. I cringed—how very American of me.

This led me to my next point.

5. *Put family first.* As I mentioned, my work has always come first, but I suppose I could rearrange my priorities now that I've "established" myself in the profession. At the beginning of my career, I had had to prove myself. People think their ethnicity is a big hurdle as far as getting hired or getting promotions. In my industry, being a woman is a way bigger handicap.

So I moved away from home, went to college, got my position at Panoply, and for the most part made my career my family. I've kept people like eccentric Aunt Lydia in an isolated compartment of my life and made sure no one at work knew what kind of family I *really* had.

"Why so serious all of a sudden?" Daniela asked, opening her eyes.

"I guess it's the thought of spending more time with my family." I smiled and took my last piece of pizza and another beer. "I figured family should be on my list."

"Hey, you're lucky. I have no one here in America. Do you know how far Argentina is? I rarely see my aunts, uncles, and cousins."

"Consider yourself blessed," I joked, because I didn't really feel that way. I love my family. And maybe when I get into our culture more, I'll have more in common with them. The biggest difference is I don't see myself as belonging to a subgroup, and they do. They'll always be Mexicans living in America. And I've tried so hard *not* to see myself that way. It's made me feel like an outsider in my own family many times.

"You don't have to do more with them, just take more of an interest in them when you *do* see them."

"Good point." Take an interest in them. My father was interested in gardens, my mother in . . . jeesh, I just realized I don't know. She's always been just Mom. So under point five I made a note to spend more time getting to know my mother. Both parents like Mexican music. In fact, my entire family gets into the whole Latin music scene. "Guess I could buy a few ranchero CDs and more Latin music," I said aloud.

"Music is important to culture. Definitely."

6. *Learn to appreciate Latin music.* Especially the funky folkloric traditional stuff that they play for Cinco de Mayo or at family gatherings.

And, if I'm going to get into Latin music, I should also learn something in the arts and history. So I added.

7. *Study our history, art, literature.*

"Okay, three more. Or should I leave it at seven?" I was starting to get tired.

Daniela shook her head. "You need ten. There are always ten steps to any program—sometimes even twelve."

Laughing, I wrote down number eight. "Wonderful. I've got my own ten-step program. Ten Steps to Becoming Latina. Think I can sell this concept?"

Daniela seemed to come alive again. She slid off the futon and took a seat on the floor next to me. "Sure. You'll be as famous as the guy who came up with the ten steps to becoming irresistibly attractive."

I laughed. "Irresistibly attractive?" Was she serious? Someone actually published that?

"You know what I mean. There are ten steps to everything."

"Sure, the guys in the office had a magazine article circulating that had the ten steps to becoming better personally endowed."

Daniela giggled. "I'll bet they did. See, if that can sell, why not becoming Latina?"

I thought about it for a moment and started laughing again. "You want me to compete with men's personal endowment?"

Daniela's laughter persisted and swelled. The more she laughed, the less she was able to stop. It was contagious and I was laughing more at her than at my ten-step program.

She held her belly now as if the laughter were causing her great pain. "Okay, okay." She waved her arms in the air, getting ahold of herself. "Toss your Latina steps in the trash, and let's write about something that can really make us rich."

I shot her my "oh, really" look. "You know something about helping men become larger?"

"Well," she said. "I haven't been happily married ten years *solely* for my cooking skills."

"Dani!" I gasped, then we both fell into fits of giggles and I felt like a teenager again. Finally, when our attack passed, I picked up my pencil again. "Okay, I've got one."
8. *Visit Mexico.*

"Hey, great idea. Now you're thinking." She wiped tears from her eyes as she regained her composure.

"Like that one?"

"Yes, I wish I could go with you."

"Leave the kids with your husband and come along."

"Yeah, right. You know the last time I took a vacation? My honeymoon."

I wrinkled my nose. Agh, great reason not to get married and have kids. I can't imagine going more than ten years without traveling. "Jeez, girl, sell your car and go on a cruise or something."

"It's not really the money. Time is the big issue. Between my job and his job and the kids' school schedule, we are never home at the same time."

"That's why you should come with me while you have a chance."

"Come on, don't bum me out. You go to Mexico and learn about your birth country."

"Hell, no one in my family has been born there."

"You know what I mean, *piba*. I like this idea."

So it was settled. I would plan a trip to Mexico.

Then we decided I'd better actually do something here in America to benefit Chicanas. It would make my aunt Lydia really happy if I went with her to some of those Chicano political organizations and learned a little about what they do. I was dreading it, but I wrote that down for number nine.

9. *Fight for the Chicana cause.* By this time, we'd been at it for three hours and were both exhausted. "I can sign up at one of the schools to mentor an at-risk Latina—kind of give a hand up to the next generation. Does that sound cool?"

"What, no giving up your plush job to work in the fields, picking strawberries?"

"This is what Chicano groups are trying to eliminate. Get farm workers out of the fields."

"You've got a point."

10. *Sign up to mentor an at-risk Latina*, I wrote, and smiled because we'd finished my ten-step program and it looked pretty good.

Daniela finally went home to her husband and three kids around midnight. I hadn't had such a good time in months.

Now as I contemplate my list, it's kind of intimidating. It's definitely going to take me more than two weeks. Hell, I should receive a master's degree when I'm finished. But it's doable, and when I'm done I'll be able to out-Mexican any of my sisters or cousins.

Now, if I can find the enthusiasm to get started, everything will be perfect. Dating a Mexican man should be fun. Of course, I don't know where to find one. And when I do, how will I get him to think seriously about me? Long-term relationships have not been my strong point. Men don't seem to be very interested in women who work twelve-hour days. I'm a workaholic, I can't cook, I don't usually put out, and I have few interests outside of animation. I'm not what you would call a *Cosmo* girl either.

While preparing for bed, I thought about who could be my first target and I remembered George from accounting. He's Mexican, I think. I'll ask him out. He's cute, single, and dresses neat. He'll count.

Four

Man, oh man, is life interesting. When I got to work today, I immediately asked George out. He acted surprised and not all that enthused actually, but he agreed. He said he was going to a Dodgers game on Friday night and that I could go with him. I felt like saying, "Gee thanks" and flipping him the bird as I showed him my swinging backside. I mean jeez, could a guy make a girl feel more pathetic? He acted like he was doing me a favor. But I didn't insult the man—I was a good girl. I smiled and accepted his "romantic" choice for a first date. After all, he's Mexican and single and good-looking—and did I mention neat? Where else was I going to find a combination like that?

Anyway, when Jackson found out I was going out with George, he sent me a curt e-mail demanding to know what I was doing. Our department is laid out pretty uniquely. Our desks are in groups of four and they face each other, kind of like leaves on a four leaf clover. This allows us to share information and talk to each other about projects. Jackson sits across from me, and the only things separating his desktop from mine are our computers. So I looked around my monitor at him and frowned.

He refused to look at me. Okaaay. "Yes, I asked George out." I typed back to him. "We're going to a ball game."

"How could you even think of dating another man after sleeping with me?" he typed back, hitting the keys so hard, I wondered if his keyboard was going to survive.

I also wondered what happened to "nothing changing between us." Since when were we an item? I must have missed the clause that said I was never to see any other man after sleeping with Jackson. "Listen, Jackson," I typed back. "Why don't we step into the sound room and talk about this?"

Without a word, he pushed away from his desk and stormed toward the sound room. I sighed and followed him.

When we got in there and the door was closed, I asked, "What's up?"

"I thought we had a thing going, you know?"

"I thought we agreed to remain friends."

"Yeah, well maybe that ain't good enough." He circled the rows of theater seats we used to preview filmed scene sequences, his eyes flashing as if he were trying to control himself.

"What's that supposed to mean, Jack?" I stood in one spot with the white screen as my backdrop.

"It means," he shouted; "that it's fucked up of you to go out with someone else, right now. Especially someone from work. What are you trying to do, prove you've moved on?"

I opened my mouth to speak, but was too baffled to say anything. "Moved on?" I said finally. "From what? We both agreed, we made a mistake. We're friends. We've been friends from day one. I don't want what happened to change that."

"What's the matter? This brother ain't good enough for you?" He narrowed his eyes. "It's the race thing, isn't it?"

"Oh, Jack." I couldn't hide my disappointment. "You know

me better than that." I moved forward and we faced each other across one plush stadium seat.

"Maybe I *thought* I knew you." He glared at me.

"I can't believe you're doing this to me. You leave me right after we're done having sex. You don't call me, so I wonder all weekend what you're thinking. You come back to work and warn me not to get any wild ideas about you and me. And now you're pissed that I'm 'moving on.' Make up your mind. What do you want?" I was yelling, screeching, probably looking like a crazy woman, but I didn't need this crap. "Forget it," I said. "Don't tell me what you want. *I* want *you* to stop this right now, before we both say something we'll regret."

I turned around and walked away from him, but he moved into the aisle in a flash and grabbed my wrist. "Is that all you have to say?"

"No," I said, trying my best to be tough. "I love you, you big jerk." I pulled my wrist free. "But if you touch me again, I might have to hurt you."

He didn't smile, didn't give any indication that he was going to let this drop. "So you still plan on going out with George," he said between clenched teeth.

"Well, yes, but—"

"Bull. I'm not putting up with that shit. If he knows what's good for him, he'll stay far away from you." And he rushed down the aisle. To accounting? To have it out with George, I presumed.

At first I didn't move. Where was this coming from? I didn't understand. Jackson was a hothead, but he was never unreasonable. And we have always been able to calmly discuss things we disagreed about. Lots of times his vision of a project didn't match mine, and we had a heated debate, but we never disrespected each other, and always went out for a beer afterward, putting our differences behind us. Granted, this was a little different, but if we were truly friends, we should be able to get past the error of our ways.

I hurried after him.

Retreating out of the art department, and winding my way around the sculpted sets and props we used to create our 3-D images and scan them into our complicated computer systems, I told myself Jackson would not do anything stupid. But just in case . . . I walked faster.

I passed the murmur of the editorial department where five editors cleaned up a storyboard sequence, making sure the timing of each shot made sense and "worked" for the length of the movie.

"Hey, Marcela," Noah, the editorial director, said, and offered a small nod.

"Ah, hi Noah," I said. "Jackson come this way?"

"More like charged through, yeah."

Wonderful. Just what I feared. "Thanks." I continued out into the hall, where the original hand-drawn comic book versions of the storyboards hung in glass-framed shadowboxes. We called it the walk of honor. At the end of the hall were the elevators. I impatiently waited for one and took it down to the business offices.

When I got to accounting Jackson had his chest puffed to twice its size and he was gesturing wildly, threatening bodily harm if George came near me.

George stayed calm. Too calm. He glanced at me and I swear, I wiggled my fingers and toes to see if parts of my body were going numb, because all the blood inside me had rushed to my face. I could tell the man was wondering why he'd gotten himself into this mess. He apologized to Jackson and informed him that our date would go on as planned.

"I don't think you heard me, muthafucker," Jackson said.

"Everyone heard you." George inhaled. "Marcela? Have you changed your mind?"

I feared for George's life at that moment, and for Jackson's mental well-being. But you know, I resented Jackson's attitude. After all, the fact that we slept together once in the heat of stupidity didn't give him the right to pull this possessive crap.

I placed a hand on Jackson's shoulder, which he shrugged off.

"You're way out of line," I said.

"Oh yeah?" he asked, anger evident not only in his flashing eyes and flaring nostrils, but in every tense muscle of his body. "Then screw you both."

After that nice line, he took off. I didn't know what to say to George.

"Unfinished business?" he asked.

"I'm sorry. I don't know why he acted that way."

George lifted a corner of his mouth in something that resembled a smile as he took a file from his desk and returned it to a file cabinet. "We both know why he acted that way."

I wasn't sure I liked George's overconfident attitude. Made me feel lacking—like he was judging me. It felt almost like George was on Jackson's side. Not that I wasn't, I mean, it bothered me that Jackson was upset. "I need to talk to him," I admitted.

George nodded.

"Do you . . ." I stumbled over finding the right words. I'd never done that before with a guy. I couldn't believe it. "Do you still want to go out with me?"

He smiled and took a seat. "More than ever," he said.

More than ever? What did that mean? I wasn't sure if this was a guy thing. He'd been challenged by another male and now he was going to go out with me come hell or high water. Or . . . not that I want to compare them to dogs, but when one dog has a bone and the other doesn't, the one that doesn't decides he has to have it, even if he didn't want it in the first place. I had become a bone. If Jackson was willing to fight for it, it must be worthwhile.

I didn't know what to say to the man, so I just smiled and apologized again for embarrassing him.

He laughed it off. "We all expect that kind of immaturity from the creative departments."

Wonderful. This guy was full of compliments. Did he forget I worked in a "creative department"? Did he include me as one of the immature ones? Was that why he'd hesitated when I asked him out? Damn, I hate when a guy makes me feel insecure. "Right. Well, I'd better go join my immature colleagues in my department and see if we can dream up new ways to make this company money."

George smiled. "You do that."

I had a bad feeling about this date.

Friday, June 25

✿ I prepared for George, ignoring the darned butterflies in my stomach. I told myself my nerves had more to do with the Jackson scene than because of George. There wasn't much to do to get ready for a ball game. I wore a pair of jeans, a spaghetti-strap top, and put my hair up in a ponytail. Then, having a few extra minutes to myself before George was due to arrive, I taped my newly typed *ten steps* on my rolltop desk in the living room. If all went right tonight I'd be able to cross off number one soon.

George showed up in jeans and a Dodger shirt and looked so incredibly hot I did a double take. Apparently, those suits he wore to work hid a nicely solid and sculpted body. Suddenly, I couldn't wait to get going. Maybe I'd get the chance to lean against him at the stadium and feel that body up close and personal.

He was relaxed and polite, but not a huge conversationalist. I did most of the talking on our drive to the stadium.

I found out he speaks no Spanish—a huge minus. He's also about five generations removed from his Mexican roots and seemed to have less interest in getting in touch with them than I did.

During the game, he was more absorbed by what was going on out on the field rather than with me. As annoying as this was, it gave me a chance to check him out without him noticing at least.

He had a great smile. And every time he liked a play, he

hooted and clapped and whistled in the most alluring way. I liked all this male enthusiasm for baseball. This was a side of George I'd never witnessed at work.

Still, after we left the stadium, I had to conclude that this date was a bust. If he preferred to watch a bunch of sweaty men run around and hit a ball, rather than talk to and look at me, there wasn't much hope.

He kinda made up for it by taking me out to a nice dinner afterward. We were a little underdressed for Houston's in Manhattan Beach, but neither of us cared.

We smiled at each other from across the table. Yep. Nothing to say. Still, he was something to look at. And now that he was actually paying attention to me, I noticed he had the most incredibly thick eyelashes I'd ever seen on a man. They made his hazel eyes look lighter, deeper . . . sensual.

I was so captivated that I didn't realize he was staring at me just as intently until he frowned as if annoyed with himself. He tore his gaze away and cleared his throat. "So, uhm, everything cool with . . . the friend of yours."

"Friend?"

"Yeah, that guy who charged into my office ready to tear my limbs off."

"Oh, you mean Jackson?" Great, choose an awkward subject. "He wouldn't talk to me."

I had told Jackson I was sorry for misinterpreting whatever was going on between us. Maybe he did want more than friendship but was afraid to admit it unless I did. I don't know. But, I reiterated that there could never be more between us than friendship for lots of reasons, but mainly because then I would lose that special guy friend every girl needs. I begged him to understand and to speak to me. But nothing. Really kills me. I never should have slept with him. Brilliant assessment, huh? Too bad it's coming way too late. I picked up my glass of water and took a sip, and smiled at George. "He'll come around in time."

"Mmm."

What did that mean? Mmm. Men shouldn't make noises that we women have to interpret. I decided I didn't want to know what he meant. "So, what's good here?"

"Everything."

That narrows it down for me. Luckily the waitress showed up— a friendly blond who was all too happy to make recommendations. George chose a twenty-two ounce porterhouse steak with a baked potato and beans.

"Me too," I said.

George lifted an eyebrow, which was also thick and nicely shaped, and ordered a bottle of wine.

"What? Why are you looking at me like that?" I asked.

"This is the first time I've brought a woman here that she's actually ordered real food."

So how many women had he brought here? Now I felt sort of pissed off. "I like to eat," I said. I wasn't one of those pencil thin girls, but I wasn't overweight either, so I enjoyed my food.

"Well, then, you're going to love this place. The food is fantastic."

More awkward silence. I finished off the water in my glass.

He waved at a guy walking by with a pitcher of water. "She needs her glass refilled, please."

"Thanks," I said.

He grinned and I had to admit that the dimples that popped out on his cheeks were adorable. Without his suit and his hair perfectly in place, he looked more approachable tonight.

"You look good in jeans," I blurted out before I realized what I was saying.

He laughed. "Thank you."

Wasn't this the part where he was supposed to tell me I looked good too? I sighed.

Our food arrived and we both got busy eating. It was delicious. The best steak I'd ever eaten. Or maybe I was just so grateful to have something to do.

"Steak sauce?" he asked.

"Sure."

He reached across and poured some sauce on my plate. Then he refilled my wineglass, since I had downed my first before the steak even arrived.

He sure was attentive. Maybe I was being too harsh on the guy. Maybe he was just a little shy.

"You know that comment I made about your jeans, it's because I always see you in suits."

"I understand."

"I wasn't checking out your butt or anything." Though I did manage a quick glance at his package—how could I not with those jeans molding themselves around him as if made to show off his goods.

He glanced at me as if surprised I'd say something like that during our meal. "Okay."

"Well." I smiled. "Maybe I *was* checking you out just a little."

He cut his meat and glanced at me again. "That's okay. I checked yours out too," he said, in way too serious a tone. Jeesh, he needed to lighten up.

"Did you like . . . you know, what you saw?"

Now, finally, he looked amused. "Marcela. You've been trying to pull a compliment out of me all night."

I gasped. "Have not."

"You should probably eat your steak before it gets cold."

I decided I might as well.

As we ate, maybe it was my imagination or wishful thinking, but I kept feeling his eyes on me. He seemed to pause a lot and forget about his food, until I looked across at him. Then he'd return to his meal as though he didn't have an interest in the world, except his dinner.

Strange man. It was almost as if he didn't *want* to like me.

When we finished he offered me dessert, which I declined. Then he paid the hefty bill and placed his arm around my back. I liked the feel of his body close to mine and found that, yes, he was solid and wonderfully warm. He smelled great too. I wondered why we weren't connecting.

When we got back to my place, I invited him in because I felt I should, even though I'd pretty much decided we weren't a match.

"Ah, okay," he said.

He sat on my futon, and stared at me as if waiting for me to entertain him or something.

"This isn't working for you, is it?" I finally asked.

"What do you mean?"

"You're not attracted to me?" I spelled it out, swallowing my pride.

"Of course I'm attracted to you."

Then why wasn't he doing something about it? In fact, he was careful not to touch me other than in the most casual way. "Oh, good," I said. Isn't that stupid? I hate a lame response.

He stood then. "Guess I'd better go."

I followed him to the door. "Thanks for . . . everything," I said.

He grinned, then sweetly angled his head and kissed me on the cheek. My heart stopped. That little nothing of a kiss sent my hormones into overdrive and my skin felt like I'd just spent five hours at the beach absorbing the hot, healing properties of the sun. "George," I whispered.

"Yep, I felt that," he said. "Interesting." And he walked out. Just like that. I was flabbergasted.

That was George.

Well, I had done one thing from my list. I had dated a Mexican man. But, I suppose I need to revise this first point. It's not really fair to cross off number one yet. I need to find a man who wants to actually hook up with me; I can't just *date* a Mexican man and say I'm done. Besides, George really wouldn't count, even using a loose interpretation of the word "date." I need a good *mojado* who doesn't speak English or a barrio boy. But where will I meet someone like that? Maybe I'll pick up a guy at the carwash. *None* of them speak English. Or a construction worker in downtown L.A. If nothing else, they have great bods. I'll have to think about this one a little more.

Five

❀ Padre Rodriguez has known me since I was six years old, so when I showed up early before mass to talk to him, he welcomed me into his office with a smile and a hug.

Becoming more involved in my faith has to be easier than finding the right man to date, so confidently and rather proud of myself, I announced to him that I wanted to do more for the church.

He nodded and continued to smile.

"So, what do you suggest?" I ask.

"You want me to suggest something?"

"Well, yeah."

He lifted a pen from his desk and twirled it around his fingers. "How can I?"

He was the boss, the one in charge. If he didn't know what I should do, who would?

"Do you read the Bible?"

"Yes. I mean, I've read parts of it. When you tell us to open to a certain page, I do."

He no longer smiled, but I could tell he was amused. Why? I don't know.

"Why don't you start by getting to know God a little better."

Was he kidding? That was a trillion times more difficult than figuring out how to become more Latina. "I thought maybe you'd tell me to join the choir or something."

"You certainly can, if you choose."

I don't choose. I can't hold a tune. "Is there anything else I can do?"

"You're looking for something to do?"

Wasn't that what I originally asked him? Padre Rodriguez is getting a little old, but I didn't think he was losing his memory. "Yes."

"Do you want to help the nuns with Sunday school?"

"You mean with the kids?" I hoped I didn't sound as horrified as I felt.

"The children are typically the ones who attend Sunday school, yes."

"I'll join the choir."

He shook his head and grinned as he stood. "I'm afraid I have to get ready for mass now. If you have a calling to sing, join the choir. If you don't, don't."

But, but, but. Then what can I *do*? I seem to remember something about not getting into heaven by works alone. "I'll read the Bible," I say, and try not to sound defeated as yet another point on my list feels like it's going to take an eternity to complete.

"You do that. And if you want to talk again, come and see me, Marcela."

"I will."

He made the sign of the cross over me and I felt properly blessed and cleansed as I walked out of his office and headed to the church to sit beside my siblings and parents whom I haven't spoken to all week. But I'm not going to lunch with them today. I'm going home. I have a lot of reading to do.

Monday, June 28

❀ At Panoply we now produce mostly feature films. We didn't start out that way. Studios used to hire us to create shorts or completely animated commercials. They were fun, and as a very young animator just starting out, I was able to learn a lot with a growing company. I got to participate in everything from initial treatment and storyboarding—and every animation process begins with a storyboard, even a commercial—to making reels of the storyboard sequences to model production, to well, actual animation.

I was so fascinated with the entire process that I had to be dragged away at night by my colleagues. Not a lot has changed since the early days. I still get lost in my work, except that I'm now one of four supervising animators and no one can tell me to go home.

We also have quadrupled in size. Jobs that we used to assign to one person are now done by three or four. We actually have a hair and clothes supervisor who dresses our characters as a fashion designer would a real actor.

This makes my job both easier and harder. I spend hours a day meeting with different supervisors and directors to make sure everyone is on target. Not to mention with my own animators who don't need me to inspire them, but appreciate it just the same when I'm around to bounce ideas off of.

Balancing the technical with the creative is sometimes difficult. And I have to step back and take some moments to visualize and see the project complete. I ask myself—what is my end result?

Sounds like mumbo jumbo, I know, but trust me, it works.

So I decided to apply the same logic to my complicated list of becoming Latina. I found a quiet spot at Panoply and focused on the end result. In the vision I'd have a fabulous guy who couldn't wait for me to get out of work so we could go out on a date. I'd be an encyclopedia of knowledge when it came to Latin music or history. I'd be able to quote any verse from the Bible. Okay, this is an exaggerated vision, I know, but visions have to be grand.

Once I could see it in my mind, I was determined to successfully accomplish something from my list. So, I cut my work day short for a change to stop by the Hispanic Chamber of Commerce on my way home.

The building is a relatively impressive one on Wilshire Boulevard in L.A. Holding my letter of invitation in my hot little hand, I entered through the glass doors and paused at the front desk where a young girl spoke on the phone in Spanish—apparently explaining that, NO, the chamber wasn't in the business of giving away money to Hispanics who want to open their own businesses.

She hung up and rolled her eyes. "People," she said. "I'm sure. Like we're just going to give away cash to every Latino who calls with an idea." She took a breath. "What can I do for you?"

Well . . . probably not much from the sound of it. What exactly did these people do for the community? Before joining blindly like I'd planned, I thought maybe I should find out a little more about this organization. I handed over my letter. "I got this."

She took it. "You must be on our mailing list. Would you like a member application?"

"Ah, sure. What are—?"

"The fees are listed on the accompanying sheet as well as the benefits. That sheet is yours to keep."

Not what I was going to ask, but I nodded and offered a tight smile. Taking all the papers and a clipboard with me, I sat in the comfortable lobby to read through the pages of information. Maybe it would tell me what they do for the community.

My benefits of membership include a monthly magazine I'll never read, a discount to their convention that I'll never attend, help with credit repair—*okay*—and vocational school financing. I suppressed a sigh and checked out the fees. Since they weren't a big deal, I started filling out the membership application.

A guy who appeared to be in his seventies walked in and chatted with the young receptionist, flirting shamelessly. He was funny and had a smooth, refined quality about him. The young receptionist laughed and flirted back in a way that you might with your grandfather's best friend.

When she took a phone call, he turned his attention to me. Uh-oh. He smiled and leaned on the receptionist's counter. "Joining?"

"I guess so," I said.

He crossed his arms and a look of concentration clouded his face. "You guess? Don't you know?"

"I'm joining."

"Why?"

"Good question. I'm not sure."

He chuckled. "At least you're honest."

I continued to write and ignored him while he continued to stare at me.

"Remember Omar Marquez?" he asked.

"No."

"Come on. Mayor?"

"Sorry," I said.

"He's my brother. We've been members since the chamber was established."

"Oh, yeah? That's great."

He nodded. "Wonderful organization. My daughter became a member as soon as she became of age. She's the owner of *Chicas* magazine."

"Really?" I wondered why he was sharing any of this with me. Maybe he was bored and needed someone to talk to.

"Ever read *Chicas*?"

I might have once or twice, but I doubt it. "Sure," I said, so as not to hurt his feelings. I signed my application and stood.

"May I?" He held out his hand for my application.

I wasn't about to hand over my personal information to a total stranger. I slipped it to the receptionist. "Kinda personal," I said apologetically.

He shrugged. "What's your name, *Mi'ja*?"

"Marcela."

"You know, Marcela, for years I had a job training agency. I got kids from high school who were headed nowhere, not college, not the military. Nowhere. And I got them trained. Made them productive members of our community."

As the receptionist took my application and entered it into the computer, I nodded at . . . "What's your name?"

"Rogelio Marquez." He held out his hand.

I shook it.

"I've seen lots of changes in the Latino community."

I bet. "Things change."

"That'll be $150," the receptionist said.

I took my checkbook out of my purse.

"Marcela," he said. "Before you write that check you should know the chamber provides education and advocacy and net-working for its members. We work alongside private and public agencies to achieve the goals of the Latino community."

Did he say we? "That's really good," I said.

He winked. "You should know why you're joining something before you do."

"She's got her checkbook out, Rogelio. You don't have to convince her anymore." The receptionist shook her head and smiled. "He's always working."

"Ah, is this your job?" I asked.

He shook his head. "I'm retired. This is my hobby."

"He's in charge of membership now. I think it's the only position left he hasn't held through the years. This place would fall apart without Rogelio."

He blushed.

"So you're the one who keeps sending me invitation letters," I said.

"That would be my department. Yep. Glad to see those letters work."

I didn't have the heart to tell him they didn't really work at all. "Well, I'm not a businessperson so I doubt my membership is that valuable to you, but—"

"Every membership is valuable. Besides, you never know, you might figure out what brought you through these doors and become one of our best members."

Not likely. I received a receipt and a packet of chamber "stuff." "Nice to meet you," I said, happy that at least I could cross *this* item off my list.

Tomorrow maybe I could start targeting my next date. But where do you go to find sexy, eligible Mexican men in Los Angeles?

Six

❀ After the uneventful Chamber of Commerce deal yesterday, I decided to spice things up. Still not sure how to accomplish this with a guy, I chose to do it with a cook instead. So when I got home I called and interviewed the personal chef Daniela and I picked out from the yellow pages.

He seemed nice enough over the phone so I invited him over tonight. He offered to do this very cool "free" presentation for me, so I was a little excited.

I imagined him cooking for me like they do on those TV cooking shows, you know, where the guy whips up this delicious meal between two commercial breaks. Maybe prepare some nice nachos with chunks of beef, homemade beans, tons of cheese, and sprinkled with jalapenos and sour cream. Yum. Or chile rellenos like my grandmother makes—the kind that are so fluffy they melt in your mouth. Oh yeah, I was wound up tight waiting for this guy.

But unfortunately, the presentation, come to find out, didn't include real food. What he actually brought were two giant three-inch binders with tons of pictures of food that I had the pleasure of looking at through a layer of vinyl while we sat at my kitchen table. Talk about disappointing. Show me *pictures* of great food and make my mouth water, then leave me with nothing but an empty stomach. This reminded me of some of my early sexual experiences—all promise and no delivery.

"We will set up weekly appointments, at which time you will learn to prepare a new dish. You should practice making it a couple of times during the week. Then when we meet again, we can discuss how you did and expand on your skills."

I kept paging through his books, shoulders hunched and stomach grumbling. "Okay."

"Do you mind if I take a look around your kitchen?" He gestured over his shoulder.

"Sure." My kitchen table is officially in my dining room, but the dining room is part of my kitchen. I love my condo, but it isn't very large and the design of the kitchen/dining room is pathetically poor. So I stood and walked two steps and, ta da, now I was in my kitchen.

He followed me, then began to open my cupboards and look at my cooking stuff, making sounds like, "ah ha," "mmm," "tsk tsk tsk." "Yes, okay, I will give you a list of items you must buy. Will this be a problem?"

"A list?"

"To cook, a chef must have the correct tools."

Sure, that made sense. "How badly is this going to hurt my budget?"

"I'm afraid you are not too well prepared to cook much of anything. How many times a week do you cook?"

"How many times a *week*?" How about once a month?

"Yes."

"I eat cereal or yogurt in the mornings, sometimes fruit." I thought harder when he began to shake his head. "Oh, wait, I eat salad a couple of times a week." I smiled, proud of myself.

He nodded in a sort of morose manner, as if he'd just learned that there had been a death in the family. "You will have to purchase quite a few items. *Sí?*"

"Okay." What else was there to say?

The real nice thing about Alberto—that's his name, just like his ad in the yellow pages—is that his specialty is Mexican food. I figured that if I'm going to date real Mexican men, I should learn how to cook Mexican food first and then broaden my menu items from there. Besides, Daniela has already agreed to be my guinea pig.

And she's right, Latin men like to be served. They want women who cook and feed them and clean for them. What a drag, when you really think about it. Probably why I never wanted a Latin man to begin with. But, I'll learn to cook—at least so I can impress my dates at first. Probably cut down on my food bill if I learn to eat a few meals at home too.

Anyway, I've done it. I've officially hired a personal chef. I feel rich. Don't only rich people do things like that? I'm actually excited. I have one week to buy the right kitchen stuff—there are thirty-three items on his list! Then we can start cooking next week. I can't wait.

Wednesday, June 30

❀ Jackson spoke to me today. I was filling my coffee mug and he strolled into our closet-size break room. I thought he was going to turn on his heels and head right back out, but he simply froze in place. We stared at each other.

"Hey," he said.

"Hi."

"Any coffee left?"

Now I felt guilty that I'd taken most of it. "I can make more," I said.

"There's enough." He reached for the coffeepot. "Excuse me."

I moved aside and gave him some space. I didn't leave. I waited patiently for him to throw me a few more scraps and continue talking. But he didn't.

"I . . . I . . ." *Spit it out.* "I'm working on a new project."

"Mmm," he said, as he sipped his coffee and tested its sweetness. Must have needed more sugar, because he opened another packet.

"Maybe when I get it more polished you can look at it. You know, before I present it to the team." When one of us supervising animators gets an idea, we always run it by each other first. If the four of us decide it's a go, we make the full-blown pitch to the development team.

"Sure," he said.

"Jack . . ."

"I'd better get back to work."

"Jeez, how long are you going to be mad at me?" The promise I'd made to myself about not losing my temper, and giving him all the time and space he needed, went up in smoke. He had no right to be pissed at me.

"I'm not mad."

"Then stop it with the cold shoulder routine. I mean, what do you want from me?"

"Nothing." He frowned. "Look, I'm cool with remaining just friends. Okay?"

"Just be honest with me. Did you . . . did you expect more?"

"Not anymore." Then he turned and walked away.

So I was right. He *had* wanted me to come back to work drooling and needy. When he dragged me to the supply room and warned me against attaching too much significance to the "event," was he hoping I had? Oh man, I totally misread his signals and now I feel stupid.

But I shouldn't, right? We're adults. He should have been up front with me. He should have come to work after that night and said, "That was great. I want you to be my girl." Then *I* could have been the one to freak out and remind him we work together and are great friends. Nothing like sex to mess up a good, honest friendship.

I took my coffee and went back to work, ignoring Jack the rest of the morning. Then about midafternoon, George called me. Surprised the heck out of me since I didn't expect him to ever contact me again. During our date, he hadn't seemed interested—and even his kiss was only on my cheek. But I must have misjudged him too, because he wants me to go to another game with him on the Fourth of July and enjoy a fireworks show afterward.

"I thought you and I . . . I didn't think you were interested in me," I said, needing to get this out in the open.

"I didn't want to be, but I am."

Didn't want to be? Why? What kind of guy goes out with a girl and hopes she doesn't spark his interest? I didn't know whether to take this personally or not. Maybe he's just come out of a bad relationship or something. One thing's for sure, he isn't much of a sweet talker.

When I didn't respond, he cleared his throat. "That didn't come out quite right."

"That's okay. Listen, George—"

"What I meant was that we work together. And we're so . . . different. But, I had fun the other night."

"Me too."

"And that kiss."

Yes, that kiss. Why was it such a big deal? It was a little peck, but I kept feeling it, thinking about it, wondering what would have happened had I turned my face and offered him my lips.

"Let's try it again," he said, his voice sounding deeper.

Part of me wanted to accept. I do like him. He's sexy, and has this quiet but strong man thing going. Nothing obvious. There's no false posturing. His strength comes from the inside, which makes him all the more attractive. And I'm sort of a sucker for powerful guys.

But he's not a real Mexican and I have to at least *try* to hook up with one. I never expected to marry a Latino, but since everyone in my family feels my blood is diluted, I should try to remedy this in marriage. Coward that I am, I gave him some excuse about being in the middle of something and promised to call him back later.

After work, I went to Williams-Sonoma with my sister Anna. I figured if I was going to buy kitchen stuff, she'd be the best one to help me pick out good stuff. She was always the one to help Mom in the kitchen.

I told her about my guy plan. I didn't go into my entire ten-step program. I just shared that I wanted to find a Mexican man to hook up with.

We browsed the store and she chose items from Alberto's list to put in my basket. "How about your chef?" she asked with a smirk.

"Naw, he's not very cute, and besides, he looks at me with disdain already, because I can't cook."

"Then he can do all the cooking in the relationship. See, problem solved."

"Actually, I was thinking of asking Pepe to set me up with one of his older friends." If anyone will know true *hermanos,* my cousin surely will.

Anna stopped pushing the cart and looked at me bug-eyed. "Are you insane? He's a gang member."

"A wannabe. Pepe isn't a gang member. Tía Yoli wouldn't allow it."

"Marcela, trust me. Tía Yoli has her eyes glued shut. She doesn't want to believe that her baby is in serious trouble."

I shrugged her worries away. I think he must be in some kind of gang too, but it's nothing serious. Probably a group of boys trying to act tough. Guys were that way today. Nothing to freak out about. "I'll talk to him."

Anna shook her head and snapped the shopping list in her hand. "Your chef wants you to buy a frying pan? Just an ordinary frying pan? You mean you don't have one?"

"Guess not."

"¡Híjole! hermana, how have you lived alone for so long?"

"I always find someone to cook for me, even if it's just P.F. Chang's."

We headed to the register. I spotted artistic-looking kitchen towels so I grabbed a handful of them. I might as well have new towels too.

"You going home this weekend?" She loaded things onto the circling belt and the cashier rang up our items.

She meant to Mom and Dad's for a barbeque and fireworks party. "No."

"You can't stay mad at Mom forever."

"I know. I'm not."

"Well, I am, kind of. She told me it's none of my business when I asked her about it, you know?"

"You're kidding?" I helped take the items out of the cart.

"Nope. She said it didn't concern me."

"See, that's the attitude that angers me most."

Anna nodded. "Yeah, she *cheated* on Dad." She shook her head. "I just can't believe it."

I took out my credit card from my wallet and handed it to the cashier. "Neither could I when I first heard it. But I'm coming to accept it. I don't know how he ever forgave her."

"Maybe she had her own forgiving to do, you know? I heard Dad was different back then."

"Different how?" I signed my credit slip and both Anna and I took the plastic bags and started walking toward the exit.

"Macho. Bossy. Unreasonable."

"Says who?" He's always been tough and in control. But men

were supposed to be that way. He was responsible for taking care of all us women, after all.

"I've heard stuff. Abuela has said, things, you know, like 'you're lucky you broke those binding chains when you did,' or I heard Dad laughing with his brothers and them joking about how he always 'kept his thumb down on her real good.' "

"Apparently his chains weren't tight enough, and his thumb must have had grease." This was bull. *Mom* was the one who screwed up. I wasn't about to start blaming Dad.

"All I'm saying is that we weren't there. We don't know what went on."

"Right."

"I'm disappointed in her too, Marcela, but she's our mother."

We got out to the parking lot and to my car. I popped the trunk and dumped the packages inside. "What's that supposed to mean? I'm supposed to accept anything she does because she's my mother?" I slammed the trunk shut.

Anna leaned on my car and crossed her arms. "She's your mother. Your blood. What do you think?"

"My blood." Here we go again with blood. I stared at my car keys in my hand, trying to keep my anger in check.

"You know what Mom always said about family. 'Without your *familia*, you have nothing, you *are* nothing.' It's true. We can't turn our back on her, Marcela."

I'm not turning my back on her. How could I when deep inside, I believe all that crap Mom fed us all these years? I'm nothing without my family, especially without Mom. She trained my sisters and me well. We need her approval, still seek out her opinions, and organize our lives to please her. My own sister would take my mother's side even if she believed her to be wrong. "What about Dad? Who stands by him?"

Anna raised an eyebrow. "He's a man. He doesn't need us like Mom does."

Not true. He needs us. And he's always been there for us—working like a dog to support us all.

"You and me and Kate—we have a bond with Mom—we're all *mujeres, sábes?*"

Since I've always felt closer to Dad than to Mom, I disagreed, but I didn't tell her how I felt. "Well, at least she's the parent we all have in common," I said sarcastically.

Anna placed an arm around my shoulder. "You'd still be my big sister, even if all we had in common were childhood memories."

I hugged her back, right there in the parking lot, never loving her more than I did right now. All the times we fought over clothes or silly jealousies drifted into the murky background of our past.

When we pulled back, we both had tears. "So you'll come spend the Fourth with us?"

"No, I've got other plans." I lied. I needed time away from all of them right now. Hopefully, Anna would understand.

"We'll miss you," she said, accepting if not understanding my decision. She climbed into the passenger side of my BMW.

I sighed and got in my car ready to drive home and put an end to this day.

Oh, and by the way, I *did* call George back today before I left the office. I turned him down. But you already knew I'd do that, right?

Seven

Sunday, July 4

❀ I'm watching the fireworks from my balcony tonight. The show from the Hollywood Bowl is visible from my place, and the brilliant colors bursting in the dark sky above the city lights look like they belong on a postcard.

Out in the warm night air, I nursed a Coors Light and listened to the pops, whistling Petes, and small explosions all around me. I could have gone out with friends, but I just wasn't in the mood.

Instead, I did something kind of screwy. I called my mom and asked her for Paul's last name. She instantly freaked out. "You're not thinking of finding him, are you? Marcela, don't even consider something that destructive. It would break your father's heart. You know how much he loves you . . . ." Blah, blah, blah.

But finally, she told me it was Peckinpaugh. Peckinpaugh? Boy am I happy she didn't leave my father and marry this guy. That last name just isn't me.

When I hung up with Mom, I did a search on the Internet for

Paul Peckinpaugh. Believe it or not, *three* popped up—one in Pennsylvania, one in Oregon, and one in California.

Hastily, I backed out of the site, thinking how stupid I was acting. I don't want to know this man. What good could possibly come of it?

None. I'm better off staring at fireworks. I know I need to let this go, but in a way, it seems to be consuming most of my thoughts. I need to focus my energies elsewhere—but where? I've got no real drive for much lately, no passion in my life, nothing excites me.

My job used to do it for me more than it does lately, I'll admit. All the scripts feel so formulaic and the idea I'm trying to develop isn't gelling. I know I want something new, but I'm not sure what that something is.

And my personal life with walk-through boyfriends definitely isn't anything to get excited about.

And my family, well, the word "disillusionment" comes to mind.

You know what's funny? I always thought that when I got close to my thirties I'd have life all figured out, and being only three years away, I'm starting to worry because I don't.

I mean, when you're in your twenties you're supposed to be messed up—people expect it. But when you hit thirty . . . you're magically supposed to have it all together: a career, a husband, kids (and if you're Latina—*¡híjole!*, you'd better *want* those kids).

This means that I've only got three years to become a millennium woman with an answer to everything. Ha! What a joke. I want to go on record as stating that we've all been duped, ladies.

Monday morning, July 5

❀Going back to work after a holiday weekend sucks. George rode the elevator up with me this morning. Well, there were others there, of course, but only George in his crisp, professional black suit, his shiny, spotless shoes, and his clean-shaven, perfectly chiseled jaw made the ride feel like a slow-motion climb up the Empire State Building. I shared with him how I would learn to make *quesadillas* tonight. I already called Alberto to proudly tell him I'd purchased everything he asked and he told me we'd start with quesadillas. Anyhow, it was a strange thing to talk to George about, I know, but I was grasping at straws.

"Does that mean you'll make me one someday?" he asked.

He was probably wondering why I had brought it up. And though I wasn't volunteering to cook for him, I said, "I suppose I could. I'll be learning how to make complete meals before too long though, so you might want to wait until I can offer more than an appetizer."

"Learning from whom?"

I told him about my chef and how I was trying to get closer to my roots. I think I actually saw admiration in his eyes. "Good thing to do," he said.

"Think so?"

"Sure. I've often thought about learning more about the Mexican culture."

Not *my* Mexican culture, but *the* Mexican culture. Guess his last name, Ramirez, means nothing to him.

"Oh? Like what?" I asked, because I think he was just bullshitting me. I don't think he ever thought about his heritage, much like me before my quest.

"I don't know. Like learning some Spanish," he said.

"Maybe we can take Spanish classes together," I blurted out before I could stop myself.

The elevator door opened and he stepped out. "I like that idea. Let's do it."

I don't need Spanish lessons. I speak Spanish. *He's* the one who needs lessons. Now my big mouth has gotten me involved in another project I have no interest in. Though I do have an interest in George, even if he is too Americanized and thus all wrong for me. I guess I could stomach a few Spanish classes.

When I got to my desk I found an old project, Elixer, returned to me for adjustments on our character. You see, each supervising animator is assigned one particular character and we're responsible for all shots with that character in it. My character is an aging scientist and the Powers That Be decided he'd look much better bald rather than with gray hair. Hair is absolutely the most difficult thing to animate because each hair has to move independently. They could have made my life much easier if they had decided to make him bald from the beginning.

Well, there goes the rest of my week.

Monday afternoon, July 5

Alberto approved of my purchases. He started by discussing the proper care of my new, shiny cooking tools. I learned about heat and how it affects food. Did you know there's a reason the flame gradually goes up and down? I always turn the heat on full blast. But no, some foods like stir-fries need full heat because you're cooking for a short amount of time in order to preserve the crispness of the vegetables, but other foods need the gentle increase of heat to keep moisture and juices from evaporating.

"You'll see that much later," Alberto said. "Today we start with quesadillas."

This is basically a bunch of seasoned cheese on a flour tortilla. Grease, fat, and oh so good. Requires an extra five miles on the treadmill, but well worth it.

He had a cute apron on and offered me one too. I slipped it on over my head. I was ready.

"Show me how your mother taught you to make flour *masa*," he said. He seemed impressed when I shared with him that I knew how to create my own masa (dough) and flatten tortillas.

"That's easy," I said. "It's kind of like playing with Play-Doh. A little flour, a little water, and you dig in." I smiled.

He didn't. "Pay attention, Marcela," he said in a very serious tone. "We never play with our food. We—"

"I was just kidding."

"Yes. What we do," he continued as if I hadn't interrupted, "is prepare it with care. Done correctly, it becomes a lovely creation, as pleasing to the eye as it is to the appetite. Like a work of art, *sí*?"

I stared at him. We were still talking about a tortilla here, right? But I understood what he was talking about. He took pride in his work, and that was good. I felt the same way about mine. I nodded.

We then proceeded to make tortilla dough together. This part was easy.

"The dough should be soft, but not sticky," he warned.

"I know," I said. I resisted the urge to squeeze my hand into a fist to make the dough ooze between my fingers. Fun as that tactile sensation would be, I knew Alberto wouldn't approve. So I used a fork until it was time to knead it, and then I used mostly my palms. After the dough was sufficiently worked, we pulled pieces of the dough apart and made balls.

"This is a good time to heat up the *comál*," he said. He placed the round frying-pan-size griddle over the fire.

"While the dough rests, right? My mom says to let it sit for about ten minutes."

"Longer if you like," he said, moving from the counter to the stove.

"Come here, Marcela." He waved me over. Alberto is about my age but makes me feel so much younger because he's got this authority thing going.

I stood by his side as he made me look at the flame.

"You want to set it at medium to high heat. See here?"

"Yes."

"If it's too hot the tortillas will cook too fast."

"We wouldn't want that," I said.

"No."

We flattened the dough balls and Alberto went into a history lesson. "According to Mayan legend, tortillas were invented by a peasant for his hungry king."

"Hmm, good invention."

Alberto smiled. "Yes. But they were made of native, dried corn kernels. Today we use either corn cooked in a lime-based solution or corn flour. We'll make corn tortillas next time."

"Good. Those are my favorite." My mom uses *Maseca*, a premade corn flour that you just add water to. It's still fresh and good, without too much work. Of course, Alberto probably wouldn't approve of anything premade, so I left out that detail.

We got all the tortillas cooked and put them into the tortilla warmer, then started shredding Mexican *queso*.

"This is the easy quesadilla," Alberto said. "We start with just cheese, but know that you can expand into many versions later. Grilled chicken and cheese, apple and cheese, ham and—"

"Let me guess, cheese."

"Right," he said and grinned. "Even veggie quesadillas are delicious, or like they serve in Mexico, quesadillas with potato and *chorizo*."

"That sounds delicious."

"Ah, to die for. The most *sabrosa* quesadilla I've ever had was sold outside a soccer stadium in Mexico." He placed the finished quesadillas on the table.

"Really? They sell quesadillas outside stadiums? Like our hotdogs?" How fascinating. Made me want to attend a soccer game in Mexico. Maybe I will, even if it's not my thing.

"Same idea." He returned to my kitchen and started cleaning up. "The only difference is that the quesadillas are sealed at the edges so the filling stays inside. They also use corn tortillas instead of flour."

I inhaled the fabulous scent of the steaming cheese and fresh tortilla. I sat at the table trying not to drool as I itched to sink my teeth into the melted cheese. I looked over at Alberto who was busily washing my dishes.

"Aren't you going to join me?" I asked. The smell was driving me crazy.

"No."

"Come on, Alberto. I can't eat alone."

He looked uncomfortable.

"Please."

Relenting, he took a seat across from me. "This isn't customary."

"To hell with customary. I can't eat all this by myself." Although I'd be willing to try. I bit into my quesadilla and . . . ah, it was a slice of heaven.

Alberto ate in silence. "Just remember," he said as he finished his small slice, wiped his lips, and stood, "being a good cook is easy. All it takes is some skill, lots of enthusiasm, and some variety."

"Sounds like the same qualities that make a great lover," I said jokingly before stopping to think what I was saying, and to whom. Alberto didn't seem to have much of a sense of humor.

But to my surprise, he chuckled. "Exactly." He took his plate to my sink and washed it. "Probably the reason why a woman who pleases a man in the kitchen finds it easy to please him in bed as well." He turned the water off and dried the plate. "Same attributes. *Sí?*"

I felt my face warm. Didn't know Alberto would end up being my sex coach too. "If you say so."

Alberto became serious again. "For this week, practice. Try different ingredients. And we'll meet again next week, same time."

I wondered when I'd find the time to do this again. "Thanks," I said as I watched him walk out my front door.

Picking up my list, I checked off number three. Not because I was done, but because I'd started my cooking adventure. To-morrow I'd go to Barnes & Noble and pick up a few books on Mexican history and literature. Then if I had time, I'd go see Pepe and ask if he can set me up with one of his buddies. I've seen some of them while visiting Amelia. Dark, muscular, hot guys who could easily fulfill a girl's wildest fantasies, not to mention a sim-ple point on a list.

Eight

🌸 Pepe thinks I'm crazy. The boy actually feels some love and a sense of duty toward his family. Who'd have thought?

I went to his house and entered his love nest (my God, I remember when he had GI Joes all over his room. Now it looks like porn heaven. I've never been surrounded by so many tits and—well, never mind). I perched myself on the corner of a rounded chair he'd stuffed with pillows. His entire room had one purpose—to seduce women. Anyhow, I told him my idea while he slouched on his queen size bed.

He stared at me with no particular emotion at first. Then he pushed his skinny, long body off the bed and started pacing and gesturing. "Are you crazy, Cuz? I mean, no, you know what I mean?"

Huh? "No, I don't know what you mean."

"It's like this. Those dudes are not good, *sabes?*"

Well, then why were they his friends? I asked him this.

"No, no *entiendes*, Cuz." He gestured even more, closer to my face. I guess this was supposed to impress upon me his distress. "They're my boys, you know. We're tight. But, you know what I mean, they ain't takin' *you* out."

"Listen, Pepe." I had to get tough with him because I needed to go out with a real Mexican guy and I couldn't stand one more second of this incongruous lecture from a boy who somehow forgot how to speak English. "All you have to do is *introduce* me to one of your nicer friends. You don't have to set up a date if that isn't cool or you feel uncomfortable. Do *you* know what *I* mean? Are you hearing me? I need you. I've never asked for anything before, so you've got to help me."

"Oh, man, *chinga*," he said, using the Spanish expletive. "Oh, man. This sucks, you know? These guys, they, you know, are machines, you know. They conquer. They take. They're masters of the bitches. They'd make you . . ." He paused and reddened. "You'd be on your knees for hours, Cuz. You'd be used and abused 'til my boys were satisfied, cuz that's the way it should be, *sabes?*"

Oh my God, I was getting a headache. Maybe this had been a bad idea, come to think of it. If his friends spoke anything like this it would be worse than any sexual torture they might think up. I drew a breath and stood. "No criminals, that's all I ask. Invite them over Sunday after church and Daniela and I will drop by and choose."

As I reached for the door, Pepe called me. "They won't go easy on you because you're my family, Marcela. You're a girl."

Hmm, so he *can* speak. "Don't you have any decent friends?"

He huffed.

"I can't just go downtown and pick one up off the street. I need someone to introduce me to some real *vatos*."

Of course I didn't have to date gang members to feel like I had a real Mexican boyfriend. When I called Daniela tonight and told her my plan, she lectured me for thirty minutes (but at least I could understand her). After calling me crazy and reminding me that most women try to escape this type of men (and when they get to my position in life, they don't look in the direction of these losers again), she asked if I was trying to punish myself. No, nothing so dramatic. I just want to see what these guys are all about. What drives them? Is it poverty? Is it a sense of not belonging to society? In Pepe's case, he has no excuse. He's looking to find himself, his identity.

This isn't a science or sociology experiment or anything. That's not what I mean. But maybe if I can date and understand a real Chicano, I can better understand my culture.

I'm starting to really want to know. What does being Mexican really mean?

Sunday, July 11

🌸 After church today, I went to my aunt Yoli's house where Pepe was hopefully waiting for me with his buddies. Daniela met me at church and we drove over together.

Pepe and "the guys" were hanging together outside, by the pool. They had swimming trunks that went down to their knees. About eight of them lounged in various spots. Two were about Pepe's age so they were disqualified immediately.

I waited for Pepe to make the introductions, but he didn't budge. In fact, I think he kinda shrunk deeper into his chair, his legs on my aunt's glass table and a cigarette hanging out the side of his mouth.

So I walked up to the guy who looked the most promising. "Hi," I said, determined to make our conversation easy and non-threatening. He looked me up and down like I was an interesting species from another planet.

"You talkin' t'me?"

Was there anyone else around? "Yes," I said.

"Wassup," he replied, and I was starting to think that indeed he couldn't speak, just as I'd feared.

"I'm Pepe's cousin."

"Oh," he said, seeming to lose interest. Didn't Pepe explain what I wanted?

"How about a beer?" I asked.

He grinned and dug deep into an ice chest as he stretched to the side to get me a beer. He opened the bottle for me, then tossed the cap on my aunt's patio. Wonderful. But he did offer me a sexy smile along with the beer.

"What's your name?" I asked.

"They call me Spike."

Spike? Well at least Spike spoke in one complete sentence this time. But I couldn't date a boy named Spike. You don't take Spike to company dinners or out with friends unless he's your body-guard. I sat beside him and sipped my beer. "What does your mother call you?"

"Asshole."

I smiled. Though this guy was rough, he had a nice face—no sharp angles, a sparkle in his eyes, a clean-shaven face. He would do. "Well, I'm Marcela. Do you have a girlfriend?"

"Many."

Okay, so he was a stud like Pepe. Got it. "Listen, Spike, I'm not in your league and I know it. I'm an animator and I live in Hollywood. I live pretty much a pampered lifestyle. I don't un-derstand Pepe's language, and probably not yours either. I don't know if we have anything in common, actually, but I'd like to go out with you if you're interested."

The boy did a double take, then chuckled as if I'd really amused him. "You want some of this, huh?" He actually pointed at his genitals. No kidding. The challenge was to say "no" with-out offending him.

Pepe sauntered over. "Hey, Cuz, get lost. Leave my man alone, you know what I mean?"

He and Spike did a complicated kind of handshake.

"She's happenin'," Spike said, which I guessed meant I was okay to talk to. "I'm gonna bag up your cousin."

Pepe didn't look pleased. "Yeah, well, you gotta do what you gotta do."

Spike got up and hooked an arm around my shoulder. "Come on."

He led me toward my aunt's house. Daniela intercepted, looking very uncomfortable.

"Where are you going?" she asked through clenched teeth.

"I'm not sure," I said, starting to wonder what exactly Spike had in mind. "This is my friend," I said to him.

He nodded. "Lay it on me."

Daniela arched an eyebrow. "Are you sure about this?" she asked me.

"Let me get the particulars of our date worked out and I'll be right out."

At this point Daniela looked at me like I'd flipped my lid. I could almost hear her asking, "You're really going to date this poor excuse for a human being?"

Spike led me into Pepe's room and as soon as we arrived he lowered his shorts.

"Whoa," I said. "Slow down."

"You wanna go out with me?"

"Yes, but I didn't say I wanted to go down on you."

He adjusted his pants. "How will I know if I want you?"

"Here's an idea." I took a seat on the cushion chair. "Let's talk."

He stared at me for a moment or two, then flopped onto Pepe's bed, propping himself up on his elbows.

"How old are you?" I asked.

"*Veinti-cuatro*."

Twenty-four and still hanging out with young boys.

"*Y tu?*"

"I'm, ah." I cleared my throat. "Older than you."

"What's this all about?" he asked, motioning back and forth between us.

I sighed. How did I explain what it was when I wasn't quite sure myself? "Let's put it this way. I've strayed from my roots. I want to date—"

"A street rat like me."

Is that what he was?

"Our roots go back to Aztec kings. Civilizations far more advanced than American textbooks will ever admit. *Nos robaron*. With guns and weapons we were too naive to create and too weak to defend against." He sat up and faced me with an angry, vicious stare. "But we're no longer naive or weak. We are taking it back using the same weapons they used against us. Is that what you want to be a part of?"

I stared at him. Wow. I had no idea. "Yes," I whispered without really analyzing what I was saying. I stood. He sprang to his feet and hooked his hands behind my head, pulling it forward and giving me the most passionate, hungry kiss of my life.

My entire body reacted to this raw fervor. Instantly, I wanted him. I wrapped my arms around his waist and ran my hands up his bare back.

He flipped me over and pushed me onto the bed.

I drew a ragged breath. "Wait."

"No," he said. "Take me inside you. Feel who I am. Know me."

My head was swimming. I'd never met a guy before who was so *intense*. "I, I, I'm not sure I want to know you that well, yet."

"Marcela," he whispered. "I don't waste time talking to bitches. If I want her, I take her whether she wants it or not."

"That's commendable."

He placed an index finger on my lips. "First rule: Don't interrupt me. Ever." He stared into my eyes, showing me the fierceness he was capable of, and I shuddered. "Second rule: I'm always right."

I didn't interrupt. I'm a fast learner.

"Now, as I was saying, I take what I want. But you're different. We can form a union. We can be one."

I didn't want to be one with him, not in the permanent sense. Could we go back to talking about Aztec kings? That was working. "Is it my turn to speak now?"

He yanked at my blouse and my tiny buttons flew off my shirt, then he bent down and bit my nipple through my bra. Blood rushed though my body and I became incredibly hot. I was breathing heavy too. I'm not ashamed to admit I was turned on, but also a bit alarmed.

"Marcela. I'm going to take you now. *Sí?*"

Sí was on the tip of my tongue, because hot, uncontrollable sex on a Sunday afternoon didn't sound all that bad. But . . . I couldn't agree to be used as an object. "Tell me your real name."

"Armando Gonzalo Hernandez Reyes."

"Wow."

He smiled and started to lower his swimming trunks again.

"Armando." I placed my hand over his. "In my world, men take you out, maybe to a movie, or out to dinner. We chat. Get to know each other. Decide if we like each other. Then when feelings grow, either emotional or sexual, we end up in the bedroom." I paused. He seemed to be listening. "I can't have sex on my cousin's bed, in my aunt's house, as if I were a teenager. I can't."

Armando blinked a few times. Then he rolled off me, looking frustrated, his rock hard erection straining against his shorts. "I don't want to be part of your world," he said, finally.

I got off the bed. "I realize that."

"But I want to fuck you."

I nodded, not sure why. "I think I want you too."

"Good. I'll pick you up tomorrow. Give me your address."

I did.

He leaned down and kissed me. "I've never had a girl like you, you know? Soft and clean and smart."

I swallowed, not sure what to say. "I've never had anyone like you either."

He frowned and nodded once. "*Mañana.*"

Tomorrow. Had I just signed a contract with the devil?

$\mathcal{N}$ine

Monday, July 12

❀ I'm having a difficult time concentrating on my work today, because I keep thinking of tonight's date. Daniela hasn't helped. She called twice to tell me to back out of it. I laughed it off, but I *did* have a twinge of doubt welling up inside. But when you think about it, it's no big deal. If things don't go well, I'll go on to someone else.

I remembered to cancel my cooking lesson with Alberto tonight. He wasn't pleased, but seemed to get his pompous feathers back into place when I agreed to pay him for the lesson anyway. From now on, I was to give him forty-eight hours notice if I wanted to reschedule a lesson. Jeesh. Why did I sign up for this again?

George surprised me by dropping by during lunch. He brought me a catalogue of the Spanish classes offered at the local community college. He seemed very excited about this. What have I started?

"Bring your lunch today?" he asked.

"Ah . . . yes."

"Want to go in the cafeteria and go over the catalogue?"

I was in the middle of something and was planning on working straight through, but . . . "Okay, give me a sec."

Jackson walked by and scowled at George.

"Hey, dude," George said.

Jackson grunted.

"No hard feelings, huh?"

Jackson dropped into his seat and leaned way back, staring at George. I hurried to back out of my computer program so I could get George out of our office as fast as possible.

"Meeting in five minutes," Jackson said to me.

"I'm going to lunch."

"Tough. Bruce said. Five minutes. Working lunch."

Bruce is the executive producer of *Land of the Firebird,* our current project. He'd probably feed us, but still, he was intruding into my time. Usually I didn't care, but right now, I knew Jackson was getting too much pleasure over interrupting my unexpected lunch date with George.

"No big deal," George said. "We can go over this later."

"No." I stood. "Tell Bruce I'll be there as soon as I can, Jackson."

"Tell him yourself. I'm not your—" He shook his head. "Shit. Can I talk to you a sec?"

"Ah, I'll be in the cafeteria. I'm kind of thirsty. Need a Coke," George said.

I nodded, and shot him a grateful look for understanding. It struck me that he was different from most men I knew who felt they had to flash that macho ego all over the place. Again, I noticed how the fact that he wasn't a tough guy made him seem stronger.

As soon as George was gone, Jackson moved in closer. "I want to talk about us."

I shook my head. "There is no us, Jack."

"Guess not."

I sighed and slumped against my desk, staring at him. "But I want our friendship back. What do you say? Can we get past what happened?"

He pulled me to my feet and put his arms around me. I hugged him back and it felt nice.

"Shit, I'm sorry, Marcela," he said against my ear.

"Me too. We made a mistake."

"I guess I kinda wanted to do it again."

I pulled out of his arms. Did I? This was the moment to go for it if I did. But no. I didn't see myself with Jackson for the rest of my life. I didn't feel that kind of chemistry with him. "You've been my friend for such a long time."

"And I've always thought you had a cute ass," he said with laughter in his voice.

"Thanks. Friends?"

He stood back, straightening his shoulders. "Yeah, and as your friend, here's my advice. Stay away from that preppy number cruncher."

"George? I like him. He's nice." Besides, all I was going to do was take a Spanish class with him.

Jackson smirked. "Nice? Don't waste your time. But if you really want to have lunch with him, I'll cover for you. Just this once."

I smiled. Things would probably never be quite the same between us, but they were at least on their way back. "I'll remember this next time you drag your butt in a couple of hours late after a hard weekend."

He chuckled. "Got me there." He patted my butt. "Mm, mm, mm, fine ass," he said as he walked away.

I hurried to the cafeteria and found George reading the catalogue, his feet up on the table.

"Got you a Coke," he said.

I took a seat across from him. "Thanks." The cafeteria was one of my favorite rooms in the building. It was a comfortable, casual place with various types of tables and seating arrangements—from picnic tables to rattan patio furniture to regular round dining tables. So no matter your mood or purpose, you had a great place to sit.

Also, at Panoply we hate blank walls, so when we got big enough to warrant an actual cafeteria, and it was built, we decided the boring white walls had to go. We figured it would be fun to "break in" to the building at night and decorate the walls. So we each brought our own cans of paint and stayed up all night drawing and painting the cafeteria walls. When you walk into the room now you're assaulted by our midnight art, leaving no doubt that you work at Panoply.

George put his feet down and leaned on the table, his arms crossed, the catalogue rolled up in one hand like a scroll. "You know what I like about you?"

"Tell me, I'm dying to know."

"Okay." He smiled. "You don't let things get to you. That guy up there acts like a jerk every time I see him and you don't seem to care."

Darn, I thought he was really going to tell me what he liked. "You don't know him. He's not usually like that," I said. And I learned long ago that head-on confrontations with men are ineffectual. In my family, Dad hollered, gave orders, acted like God, but Mom ruled the roost. I never forgot that.

"Right. And I'm sure he has a good reason for acting like a child."

Hey, this was my friend he was putting down. "Sometimes you have to loosen up a bit and act a little childish. You ought to try it sometime."

His smile slipped. "I don't think so. I'll never understand what women see in men like that."

I had this urge to keep defending Jackson, but instead I said,

"Me neither. I like mature men who can take control of . . . situations."

He got up, walked around the table, and took a seat beside me, then leaned in close. "Marcela, you like being deliberately provocative, don't you."

"I like to have fun." Though it was getting more difficult to think straight with his face, and his lips, so close to mine.

"You wanted to know why I was hesitant to go out with you."

Actually, no, I didn't want to know that.

"Because you're a loose cannon. From what I've seen, you date guys like Jackson."

Hey, what did he mean by loose? "So?"

"So, a woman who goes out with guys like that would get easily bored with a man like me. I'm not into deluding myself."

Again I got the impression that he'd been hurt in the past, and didn't want to risk his heart again on a bad bet. That was me.

"Maybe I'm ready for a change." I gazed into those light hazel eyes and the last thing I wanted ever again was another macho stud—even though, yes, that was my style. I chose boy toys because they were fun, uncomplicated, undemanding. Most didn't make it into my pants, and none squirmed their way into my life. Who wanted a permanent man?

George's gaze was sharp and somehow all knowing. "Are you sure about that?"

For some reason, he was making me nervous. All this talk about change and maturity was tying my stomach into knots. "Let's look at that catalogue," I said in a voice that sounded a bit shaky to me.

Easing back, he placed the catalogue on the table. "Looks like Monday/Wednesday classes or Tuesday/Thursday."

Both were from 6:00 p.m. to 9:00 p.m. and I really didn't want to waste that much time on either day. Maybe I should back out of this now. Way back.

"If it's all the same to you, I prefer Tuesday/Thursday. We can leave work at five and make it there in plenty of time, then we can do a late night dinner or snack afterward."

"Dinner?" Again I was caught by his eyes.

He smiled. "I know you like to eat."

His smile was pretty fabulous. Just in case you can't tell, I find this man very attractive. It's difficult not to react when he leans in close or smiles or looks at me with that soft, warm gaze. I decided that if I weren't on my quest, I would definitely pursue something more intimate with him—even after his warning that he isn't like my typical men.

"So, will that work for you?"

"Sure." Oh, hell, there goes the idea of backing out of the class. And of backing away from George.

He circled the correct Spanish session and handed me the catalogue. "You'll have to sign yourself up."

I took the catalogue.

"You'd better get to your meeting." He winked. "Thanks for sharing a Coke with me."

That wink mesmerized me, and kept me planted in my seat rather than agreeing that, yes, I'd better get to my meeting. So the big question is: Is George hitting on me? Is he interested or not? I'm so confused. Maybe he's just a nice guy who wants to be friends. Yeah right, a little voice in my head said—no man wants to be friends, even nice ones. Maybe it's only me going through hormone overload. Well, I'd better get over it in a hurry. After all, I have a date with Armando tonight.

❀ Maybe part of me felt like I had missed something by going straight from high school to college and starting a career early in life and not hanging out with a cool crowd rather than a bunch of computer nerds. Well, I certainly don't feel that way anymore.

Armando, the bastard, had swaggered into my condo last

night, checked out my place, lifting nicknacks, messing with my computer equipment, and shuffling to some rap tune in his head.

"Where are we going?" I asked.

"To eat. That's what you said you wanted, right?"

"Sure."

"Nice crib."

"Thanks."

This was how our conversation went for the first hour or so. We decided to take my BMW because he wanted to drive it and because his Oldsmobile looked like a marked car. He took me to this dive in L.A. First, I've got to say that I've never been to this particular section of the city. No one spoke English. Not the people in the street. Not the store or restaurant owners. No one.

The food was good. Mexican. The conversation not.

"Tell me more about our Aztec heritage," I said.

He shrugged. "It's our legacy." Then he shoved half a taco into his mouth and chewed.

"This—" I looked around the cramped restaurant, if it could be called that. It looked like an extra room in someone's house, and it might just be. "Isn't a way to live up to it."

"Neither is living above it all and pretending it doesn't exist."

Wait a minute. My parents worked incredibly hard so I could go to school and have what I have today. Rising above all this poverty was a better way to live up to our heritage than clinging to cultural customs that keep us enslaved. But I didn't voice my opinion.

He shoved the rest of his food into his mouth and reached across and took my hand. "Let's go."

I wasn't finished, but that was okay. We went to a club next. The music was deafening. We took up a quarter inch of the dance floor. Armando had the moves. When he was through, I was sure he'd touched every intimate place on my body. But just in case he hadn't, he led me to a back room where couples were engaged in all sorts of sexual activity, including full-scale intercourse.

Armando invited me to undo his fly. I looked around self-consciously. No one noticed us. I suddenly felt too old for this. I wanted to go home. There was no point in speaking, though, because we wouldn't be able to hear each other.

When I ignored his request, he started licking my jawline and my ear. He spoke into my ear, telling me all the disgusting things he wanted to do to me.

I shook my head, but his hands paid no attention. I tried to get into it. Maybe I was being a prude. Maybe I was getting *too* old too fast. I kissed him. I touched him how he asked to be touched. But when he backed me against the wall and drew my legs up, I knew this just wasn't going to work. Too many other people around. Music was too loud. Guy was too wrong. I struggled to get loose. He shoved me hard against the wall again and gripped my face painfully, digging his fingers into my flesh. "Don't fuckin' move," he warned.

So I kicked him in the balls, then kneed him in the face before running out as fast as I could. What else could I do? A mock rape (or would that have been considered a real rape) was not my thing.

When I got to my car, a young girl, maybe thirteen years old, was spray painting gang shit all over the side. I yanked the spray can out of her hand. "What the fuck are you doing?"

Instantly—I didn't even see it happen—she pulled out a switchblade knife. I dug into my purse and called 911 as she flung every insult ever invented at me. Before I was finished with the call, Spike was behind me grabbing me by the hair. "You bitch. You messed with the wrong *vato*." Blood ran out of his nose. He pulled out a gun and I saw my life flash before my eyes. Even the young girl with the knife stood frozen in place.

"Calm down. I don't want to screw you in a club full of people. Okay?"

"You do it when I say and how I say," he shouted.

"Wrong." I didn't care if he *did* have a gun. No guy was going to talk to *me* like that.

He cocked the gun.

Ah . . . maybe his having a weapon did give him more power after all. Would he really shoot me between the eyes because I wouldn't sleep with him? Definite emotional issues going on.

With a smirk, he lowered the gun. "Not worth wasting a bullet on you, bitch."

The police arrived then. Most of L.A.P.D., I think. Spike hid his gun and the young girl started running.

"Get her," I shouted.

She was easily apprehended. Spike was on the floor with four officers holding him down and cuffing him. And me? For the first time in my life, I was shoved up against a black and white and rudely forced to wear the coldest, ugliest bracelets of my life. "But I made the call," I protested. No one listened.

It seemed like half the club was evacuating. There were Mexicans running in all directions. This was a nightmare, and somehow I was in the middle of it.

Once we got to the station, I was able to sort the details out for the police. I explained how I'd called them after finding the teenager tagging my car.

They all seemed to get a laugh over my parking a BMW outside a club in East L.A. "What's a girl like you doing out there anyway?" one beefy police officer with messy brown hair asked. His name tag identified him as Officer Martinez.

I'm an idiot, what can I say? "My date brought me."

"That fine gentleman who was carrying a concealed weapon and had fifty bags of coke on him. That your date?"

"Yes, sir."

"Yeah, well, this is his third strike so he'll be locked up for a long time. You'll have to continue your relationship over a phone line."

"I don't plan—"

"And as for you. I'm in a good mood and I'm going to have my hands full tonight, so I'm gonna let you go without charging you with disturbing the peace, disorderly conduct (I'd put up a little bit of a fight when they were taking me in without listening to my side of the story), and intent to sell narcotics."

"I wasn't—"

"As long as," he raised his voice, "you leave, and promise never to come down to my jurisdiction again."

I nodded. No problem there. I'd never go to that part of town again in my life. Ever.

"Good." He said something to the officer beside him. Then they slipped a sheet of paper in front of me. "Sign to press charges against your auto detailer."

I picked up the pen and started signing, but then a thought passed through my head.

"What? Why are you stopping?"

"What's going to happen to her?" I asked.

"Juvie, she's a regular troublemaker on the streets."

I stared at a man who was probably a good person, but who seemed burned out or jaded. He seemed to have no emotions, no compassion.

"Can I see her?"

"What the hell for?"

"I just want to before I decide if I want to press charges."

He huffed. "Suit yourself. Come on." He motioned for me to get up.

My head hurt, my eyes stung from crying (yes, I cried when I realized I was on my way to jail), and my muscles were sore from fighting off that jerk my cousin set me up with.

The officer led me to a small detaining room that smelled like a sweaty gym. The young girl was slouched in a chair, her elbow resting on the edge of an eight-foot-long wooden table, which just might have been around since the 1950s. Her eyes raked over me like I was gutter scum.

I stood on the opposite side of the table. "Why did you trash my car?"

No response.

"I'm going to have to have it repainted now. My insurance probably won't even cover it."

"Think I give a shit? *Pinche vendida.*"

Sell out? Me? Her venomous response made me cringe. How did such a young girl have so much hatred inside her? "No, I can tell you don't. Did you just mark up my car because it's a nice car?" Jealousy, envy, maliciousness had to be at the root of it. Artistic inspiration didn't play much of a role here.

She glared at me without a response.

"I've worked hard to get what I have. I don't need some punk kid who is too lazy or too stupid to realize she should be studying rather than hanging out in the street, messing things up for me."

"Fuck you." She jumped to her feet.

The officer standing to the side touched my elbow. "Hey, keep the insults to yourself."

I ignored him because I was on a roll, and because I realized that maybe this could be my number ten on my list—mentoring an at-risk girl. Who could be more at-risk than this kid? Of course, I'd pictured myself volunteering to help a ten-year-old with homework, not a hardened teenage criminal with shark eyes. But I'm no wimp. I could handle this.

"If I press charges against you, you're in Juvie. You not only ruined the paint on my car, but you threatened me with a knife."

"Should have gotten you while I had the chance."

"Maybe." We stared each other down. "Okay, here's the deal. You work for me and pay off what it's going to cost me to repaint my car and I won't press charges."

She frowned. Tears made her eyes glisten.

"I'll pick you up once a week. You help me out at home and I'll pay you."

"Probably not a good idea," the officer interrupted.

"I ain't doin' shit for you," she said.

"Fine. Enjoy your stay in Juvenile Hall." I faced the officer. "I'm ready to go."

He shook his head as if saying, why did you even try?

I glanced at her once more and she stood stone-faced, her eyes red from unshed tears, staring straight ahead. "If it were me, I'd agree and get my free ride home in the police car tonight."

Her glare contained a mixture of anger and fear.

"I'm trying to give you a chance here."

"Why?"

"I don't know. Maybe because if I were in your shoes I'd appreciate some slack. A break."

With a barely perceptible nod, she agreed.

"Where should I pick you up?"

"School. East L.A. Middle School."

"Got it. See you on Friday after school. I'll be right in front." I frowned, trying to act tougher than I felt. "You know my car."

So now I've got a girl to mentor. If she doesn't rob me blind or slice my throat with her knife, it might turn out okay. Actually, my fear is that she won't show at all. I can't hold her to anything. I didn't press charges, and I can't go back and do it after the fact if she doesn't hold up her end of the deal. I feel ambivalent about the whole thing. Part of me wants to help her, and part of me wants to pretend we never met and go on with my life as it was before Spike and my quest.

But there is no going back. I'm on a wild ride now, and I can't get off until it's over. I just hope I don't barf when I hit the steep drops.

Ten

Tuesday, July 13

❀ By the time the whole fiasco was over, it was early morning before I got home, exhausted beyond belief. Having no choice, I dragged my butt in to work. Jackson noticed that I was practically falling asleep at my computer, then overheard me telling Daniela about my date from hell and asked if I was okay as soon as I hung up.

Genuine concern flashed in his eyes.

"Yeah. You heard the whole story, huh?"

He nodded. "So what were you doing going out with a guy like that. Are you crazy or something?"

"I knew he was edgy, even had my suspicions that he was a gang member, but I didn't think he was an insane criminal."

"Girl." He frowned. "You've got to have your head examined. If he's a gang member what did you expect?"

"Excitement. He seemed like a guy living on the fringe. Revolutionary type." I moaned. "What really worries me is that my cousin is hanging out with guys like this. I'm going to have to talk to my aunt."

He stood and walked around our desks. "I hope you pressed charges against this asshole for assault."

"He was busted for carrying a concealed weapon, for resisting arrest, and for dealing drugs. They're going to put him away for a while without any help from me." Last thing I wanted was Spike coming after me again when he got out.

But by the look on Jackson's face I knew he didn't agree with my decision.

"He wouldn't have shot me. He was trying to scare me, show me he meant business, rescue his pride after getting kicked in the balls."

"He tried to rape you, then threatened you with a gun. You're fearless and not afraid to defend yourself, but what about the next girl who doesn't fight back?"

See, where was George? This was the Jackson I loved. He was right. Last night I was tired and wanted to go home and I wasn't thinking straight. "I'll press charges."

"Good." He smiled. "I've gotta go downstairs for a while. Stay away from gang members, okay?"

No problem there. I'm not going through that again. I'll have to find my Mexican man elsewhere. The search can go on, or not. Maybe that isn't such a great point. After all, a Mexican man isn't going to make me more Latina. I have to concentrate on changing myself. And maybe, as the police report at the station referred to her, Lil' Teddy, aka Lupe Perez, aka number ten on my list.

I reached for the phone and dialed my aunt's number. She needed to be clear on what her little boy is mixed up in before it was too late.

🌼 George and I attended our first Spanish class, but our conversation was a bit strained. I wondered if it was because we really didn't have anything in common. I tried to joke with him and tease him, but I couldn't break through his shell of politeness, so I finally gave up and listened to the instructor explain her syllabus and what she expected we'd know by the end of the semester.

She had us practice saying our names and asking a partner their name. Pretty basic. George had terrible pronunciation. I tried not to laugh, but finally couldn't help myself.

He ended up smiling back. "Pretty bad, huh?"

"Yes."

He shrugged and continued smiling. "You're lucky that your family taught you some Spanish."

"My family is the original *Viva La Rasa* family."

"*Viva La Rasa?*"

"You know, pro-anything-Mexican. Our language is sacred, our culture is derived from ancient tribes more advanced than Bill Gates. Our *frijole* is the seed of our power and wisdom."

George laughed.

We got a frown from the instructor.

George leaned closer, letting me get a whiff of his delicious cologne. "Sounds like a fun family."

They are, I had to admit. I loved my family. Even with the stain I now carried with me. My parents had always been good to us, raised us with morals and ethics. The kind of things that seemed to be missing from the current generation. Look at Spike and Lupe for goodness sake. "What about yours?"

The instructor stood by our table with a smile. "*Vamos, vamos. Yo me llamo . . .*" She paused and waited for George to insert his name.

"George," George said, complying.

"*Y como se llama usted?*"

"*Y como se llama usted?*" George parroted in his thick American accent.

"*Muy bien. Otra vez. No hablen mas en ingles, entiende?*"

"*Ah, sí,*" George said, probably not realizing he just agreed not to speak anymore English in class.

The woman reminded me too much of my high school teachers and was making me wish I'd stayed out of this class. She turned her gaze to me.

"*Entiendo*," I said. I understand. No more English. Darn. I was just about to get to know George a bit.

We didn't get a chance to chat again until after class.

"That was fun," he said. "Thanks for doing this with me."

"Hey, no problem." I kind of liked staring at George's embarrassed face as he tried to speak or understand his historic tongue. "I need to brush up myself."

"No." George shook his head and eyed me. "You don't. Why did you suggest we do this? Your Spanish is impeccable."

"How do you know? You're not exactly a good judge."

We walked toward the parking lot. He brushed his shoulder up against mine every once in a while. We were the same height. "I can tell," he said.

"Well, maybe I just wanted to see how pitiful your Spanish really was."

"Where's your car?"

I pointed in the general direction where I'd parked my rental car. I wasn't about to drive my tagged vehicle around city streets.

George headed toward it. "Maybe you wanted to spend some time with me."

Well, that was an arrogant, full-of-himself kind of statement. "Yes, actually, I had been hoping that during our break we could find a quiet corner on campus for a hot quickie."

He angled his head and grinned. "You mean I sat stuffing my face with Oreo cookies for fifteen minutes when I could have been having sex with you?"

"Don't you feel stupid?"

He chuckled. "Very."

We reached my rented Mustang and stopped walking. "Well, here I am. I guess I'll see you tomorrow at work."

Staring at me with sexy, half-closed eyes, he said, "You didn't answer my question."

"I don't remember hearing a question."

"Do you want to spend time with me?"

Yes. A resounding yes. With George I could be just me and that seemed to be enough for him. No pretending. No trying to be fun or exciting or interesting. In fact, when I tried that, he ignored it. So in a strange way I found myself relaxing with him, and it felt wonderful. But I said, "I . . . I can't." Because I was in a state of flux and I didn't need any more confusion.

"Is it because . . . because you're still sleeping with Jackson?" he asked in a kind of embarrassed way.

"No. I mean . . . he's just a friend."

He arched an eyebrow. "I'm not an idiot. He didn't pull that possessive crap because you're his friend."

"George." I didn't know how to put this. Any way I said it, I came out looking like a sleaze. "We did. Once. But it was a huge mistake," I added quickly.

"Why?"

"Why was it a mistake or why did I sleep with him?"

He shrugged. "Both. Either."

"I slept with him because I was lonely." Suddenly the night seemed too quiet and I felt too vulnerable. "And he's a friend that I love and trust, so I accepted—no, I initiated the physical contact." And I had. I shook my head at the memory. I'd leaned against him, put my arms around him, teased him with seductive language. When he finally jumped me, it was probably because he couldn't take any more.

"But it was wrong for the same reasons," I continued, wishing I could take that night back. "You don't sleep with your friends. I've never wanted to date him. I want to confide in him about my dates like I've always done, and have him tell me I'm way too good for any guy."

George gazed into my eyes and I felt like he was looking right through me, like he could see things I wasn't ready to reveal about myself.

I smiled, feeling foolish for opening up like this. "Why is it women have to bring all this angst into sex? We should be more like men. In. Out. Over. Next."

George reached across and brushed some of my hair off my face, tucking the strands behind my ear and gently running the side of his index finger along my jaw. "Men get lonely too. And we have sex for the wrong reasons. And we regret it."

I swallowed. Couldn't have said a word if I tried.

George moved in close. I thought he was going to kiss me, but he didn't. "I took this Spanish class to get close to you. To have a reason to spend time with you."

I gazed into his dreamy eyes. I licked my lips when his hot breath touched my mouth to see if I could capture his taste. My God, he could turn me to Jell-O without even trying. "Me too," I admitted.

He continued to stare at me: my eyes, my mouth, my eyes again. I saw the temptation in his gaze. I saw the need in there too. The same need he'd stirred in me.

But I broke eye contact. He was stirring a different type of need as well. A need that was deeper, more emotional, scarier than the physical. If I wasn't careful, I'd find myself entangled in some-thing much more dangerous than facing a man with a gun.

He cleared his throat. "Good night, Marcela."

As he eased away, I wanted to yank him back, but I didn't. George was the type of guy who played for keeps. And I . . . wasn't. I'd never thought about it before, and it made me feel sort of cold inside to realize that perhaps I am somewhat like a man. Sex I can handle, as long as it's not with a friend, but a relation-ship with demands and expectations and responsibilities and hurt feelings—why bother? I had to make sure George remained a friend. Just a friend. Nothing more. At least, not yet.

Eleven

Friday, July 16

When I pulled up to Lupe's school, I didn't expect to find her out by the curb waiting for me. I barely stopped the car and she jumped inside.

"Go," she growled.

She acted like she was running from the police. I looked out the window and noticed a bunch of girls, probably her friends, staring at my Lupe-decorated BMW. (I left my rental car at home and brought the BMW so she would recognize it.)

"Go already," Lupe yelled.

"Okay, okay." I peeled out into traffic. "What's the big hurry?"

"I just want to get this over with."

I pushed my sunglasses to the top of my head and glanced at her the best I could while keeping my eyes on the road. "You're going to have to help me more than one day, you know?"

Lupe stared out the window and seemed to be tuning me out.

"Did you tell your parents you were going with me?"

More silence on Lupe's part.

"Maybe we need to stop by your house and have a talk with them."

Lupe's incredulous look told me maybe that wasn't such a great plan. "Are you stupid or something? My brother's in the mix. He'd probably shoot you on the spot."

Oh? Another upstanding citizen? "If you're going to be spending time with me, I feel an obligation to let your parents know."

"Well, don't. My mom works in a sweatshop downtown. I don't see her until after 8 p.m. usually. She don't care what I do."

"And your dad?"

If Lupe's eyes were weapons, I'd have lacerations all over my body. "The same. In a tire shop."

"So you're basically on your own all day?"

"How did you get so fuckin' smart? Shit, you're like Einstein or something, huh?"

Well, at least she knew about Einstein. And she had sarcasm down to a science. I drove in silence the rest of the way home. Then when we arrived, she followed me to my apartment. I had no idea what I was going to do with her once we got inside. I didn't really want her to clean for me or anything. I had to think of a job she could do that would also teach her a skill.

"Make yourself at home," I said as we walked in.

She looked around, then crossed her arms and stood rooted by the door.

I listened to my messages. My mom reminding me of my cousin's baby's first birthday party tomorrow and hoping that I was "okay." My sister wanting guy advice—as if I were qualified to give her any. And my chef confirming our next lesson for Monday night. The disturbed part of me was a little disappointed that there were no calls from George. We had another nice night during Thursday's Spanish class, although he remained strictly friendly. And today at work, I didn't even see him. No surprise, since I rarely see anyone from the business offices, but . . .

What was I expecting? George was no fool. I'd turned him down already. He wasn't about to keep asking me out.

While I thought of something to assign to Lupe, I asked her to water my plants. I gave her a watering can, pointed out my plants, and turned her loose.

Then I took out my laptop and pulled up my dream project. I've been playing with a character, hoping a storyline would jump out at me, but I was basically writing the same story that we'd produced the last three times. Something was missing, but what?

I noticed a shadow behind me. Lupe was watching me. "Done?" I asked.

She shrugged. "I guess."

"Have a seat." I patted the futon beside me.

"Yeah, like I want to sit that close to you."

I smiled. If I had ever been this obnoxious to my parents, they would have hung me from the backyard tree. "Suit yourself. Then my toilet bowl needs cleaning. Down the hall, first door on your left."

"Dream on," she said.

I stood. "You know, you can drop the attitude. It's not going to get you anywhere. You're here to make amends for spray painting my car. You either cooperate or I take you back to the police station and press charges." Not that I thought I could at this point, but Lupe hopefully didn't know any better.

Lupe's face turned red, the she plopped onto the futon. "Let's just end this torture soon, so I can go hang out with my *carnalas* before it gets too late."

Grateful that she'd told me about her plan to get together with her street friends, I decided to keep her busy the rest of the evening.

I showed her how I create movement for static three-dimensional figures.

"Cool," she said.

"Ever work with Photoshop or any type of Web design program?" I closed down my work.

She shrugged.

Did that mean "no" or she didn't know? "How would you like to design your own website?"

I saw a spark of interest in her gaze, but she shrugged again.

I pulled up a basic copy of Photoshop. "First thing we're going to do is create stuff to put on the website. Ever hear of digital graffiti?"

She moved in closer to me and stared at my screen. "No."

Oh, but she wanted to. I resisted a smile and typed in LUPE'S CRIB. "Now, you're going to turn this boring text into something worth looking at. You're going to warp it to make it look like it's got movement. You're going to decide on colors, angles, softness, lighting, intensity. Basically, you're going to make it look cool."

She nodded.

I angled my head and gave her a quick look before turning my most valuable possession over to her—my computer.

We changed places and I began my instruction. Once I explained the features and I saw how fast Lupe caught on, I let her go, let her experiment.

She worked on my computer for hours. Not only had she transformed the title into wild script, but she had created a dazzling background by layering faded rap lyrics over a picture I had of the sun coming through tree branches. It was impressive, and I decided Lupe was one smart kid.

I made some phone calls and got some of my own work done while she kept busy.

When I noticed my stomach rumbling, I opened up a can of tuna fish and we had sandwiches. I figured the night had turned out all right after all.

As I dropped her off at home, I noticed that even after nine at night, kids hung out in the street. "Same time next week," I said.

"Right."

And she was gone.

Saturday, July 17

❀ Just as I was about to spoon up some moist *pastel de leche* and savor the sinfully sweet cake, little Jason stuck his dirty little hand right on my plate and splattered frosting all over my new Ruby Rox dress.

"*Ahi, Mi'jito,*" his mother, my mom's cousin said, sending me an apologetic glance.

He laughed as if defying his mother and ruining someone's dessert were the funniest things in the world.

I grabbed his wrist and shook his hand to try to get the frosting off.

"Hey," my cousin said. "What are you doing?" She pulled him away from me and held him close to her side, as if he were the one who had been wronged.

"Just trying to help."

She grabbed a napkin and frowned at me as she walked away, wiping his hand.

I took a few napkins myself and tried to dab the green colored frosting off my red dress. Great. Ready for Christmas in July.

Damn, I'd better go wash this off. I tried to avoid the screaming and crying toddlers who littered the grass as I made my way to the house. Kids! Why do single adults get invited to children's birthday parties anyway? It's not like there's anything for us to do. It just becomes another opportunity for parents and grandparents to remind you that your eggs are rotting inside you, and that you'd better get busy looking for a husband.

"Oooh, what happened?" Katie walked out of the house I was about to enter.

"Damn, Jason. The little monster did it on purpose."

Katie laughed. "He's only two. He doesn't know any better."

"Yeah, right."

Katie moved aside and let me enter, then followed me inside. "You didn't call me back."

"Sorry, I got in late last night. Besides, I'm not qualified to give guy advice." I found the bathroom and turned the water on full blast in the sink.

"Yes, you are. You have more experience. I mean, you must have slept with like thirty guys in your lifetime."

My jaw dropped open. "Thirty?!" What kind of slut did she think I was?

"Okay, twenty."

"Tell me about this guy," I said, not sure if I should provide a number for her.

"Okay," she said with a huge grin. "His name is Gilbert and he's super nice—"

"Mexican?" I interrupted.

"Huh?"

"He's Mexican?"

"Yeah," she said, as if that were a stupid question. "Anyway, he's older than I am, and I'm wondering—"

"How much older?" I asked, wondering if Katie had hooked up with one of her college professors or something.

"If you stop interrupting, I'll tell you."

I nodded and looked in the mirror at the faded green stains probably permanently bonded to the fibers of my dress. Damn kid.

"He's smart, has a great job, nice house—"

"How old?"

"Eleven years older than me. Do you think that's too old?"

Katie is twenty-two and a little naive. "That depends."

"On what?"

"A lot of things. Does he want you for sex or marriage? And has he been married? Does he have kids? You realize he's older than me?" Now why can't I find a Mexican guy my age who has a good job, nice house, and so on?

"Well, right now," she said with an evil grin, "sex is about it. Morning, afternoon, and night."

I frowned. This was my baby sister. I stopped messing with

my dress and took her hands. "Katie, sex is great, but . . . well, just take it easy."

"Take it easy? What kind of advice is that? Is that what you would tell one of your friends? Is that what you would do?"

"Yes. Listen, I haven't had that many sexual partners."

"You lie."

Yes, but I was feeling myself jump into protection mode here. I wiped at my dress again, not meeting her eyes. "Sex shouldn't be just about sex."

Katie laughed.

"What?"

"Come on, I'm not a kid. Anyway, forget that. Do you think he's too old for me?"

If he can have sex three times a day, apparently not. "As long as he makes you happy, Katie."

She smiled. "Wanna meet him?"

Definitely not. "Just keep him to yourself for a while."

"How about a double date?"

"There's only one problem with that idea." I squeezed past her and went to the closet to get my purse.

"What's that? And where are you going?"

"I'm outta here. I made my appearance, brought a gift, I'm done." I gave Katie a hug. "And when I find someone to go on a double date with, I'll let you know."

I escaped with only minimal damage. Whew. One more family event over and done with.

At least that was what I thought. Should have known it was too good to be true. My parents stopped me on the way to my car.

"Your father and I thought we needed to have a talk, just the three of us."

But Dad didn't look very excited about this talk, and I wasn't either. I've done a good job of making excuses about how busy I am at work and ignoring Mom's invitations to dinner. But I couldn't graciously get away now, could I?

"Sure," I said. "If you want. I'll come over soon and we'll do that." Well, I could try to postpone the inevitable.

"*Mi'ja,*" my father said, "nothing gets better by running away from it."

From the look in his eyes, I realized he was speaking from experience. I held his gaze just long enough for him to know that I wanted to talk to him, but just couldn't.

"Well," he said, "we don't want to keep you. You probably have a big Hollywood party to go to tonight." He stuck his hands into his pocket and puffed out his chest.

"But, we need to resolve—"

"Quiet, Marta," my father said. "Marcela said she'll come home soon. Let her be."

I felt the tension between them and knew my mother would back down. She always did. I frowned and wondered if I hadn't learned to do the same with the men in my life. Perhaps I did that, at times, but I always thought I was more like my father. In control—I respected him for his strength. But right now, at this moment, even though he was on my side, I questioned if giving orders and brushing aside the opinions of someone you loved was truly an admirable quality.

I leaned across and kissed Mom good-bye. A new kind of female bond made my heart ache just a little for her and I felt my anger slip. I wanted to talk to her. I wanted to know about her relationship with my dad. I wanted to know *her*. But, I couldn't. At least not today.

I gave my father a quick peck and hurried to my car.

Twelve

Thursday, July 22

❀ This week is flying by pretty much uneventfully. I've been swamped with work, and made it home late every night, but that's nothing unusual. Spanish class has been the one fun part of the whole week. I can't believe I'm actually enjoying it. The teacher has figured out that I'm basically there to offer George moral support and uses me to help out other students. George has started to call me "teacher's pet." I can't believe we've worked together for four years and I've never gotten to know him before. What a nice guy. He buys me dinner after class each time, and then sits and listens to me talk his ear off for a good hour. Tonight I even asked him if I was talking too much, but he just shook his head.

"Would you tell me if I was?" I asked.

"No, I'd just stuff an eggroll down your throat."

Since he didn't do that, I have to assume I was okay.

I keep trying to get him to talk about himself, but the only thing he opens up about is sports. The man loves just about every sport. He has season tickets to the Dodgers and the Lakers and he's memorized every boring statistic related to those teams. But I didn't tell him it was boring, because when he talked about it and I watched the little boy enthusiasm on his face, I wasn't bored, just fascinated.

"What about you?" he asked.

"What about me?"

"Where do your passions lie?"

That was a loaded question. I smiled. "You know the answer to that one."

"Tell me it's not your work."

"Would it make me too much of a nerd if I said it was?"

We got the bill, which he snatched. As he took out his credit card and kept his eyes locked to mine, he said, "Just means we'll have to work on expanding your interests, won't we?"

Will we? Okay, I'm intrigued.

We left the restaurant together, and walked out to the parking lot. The night had gotten chilly and I shivered. The top I'd worn to work today had criss-cross stings running along my back, which basically left it exposed.

Immediately, George pulled off his coat and hung it on my shoulders.

"Thanks," I said. I snuggled into his lingering warmth, wearing it like a cape. Mmm, it smelled so good.

"You're easy to please," he said, and I noticed he was watching me with this affectionate intensity that I liked.

I laughed. "Simple minds . . . I enjoy lava lamps too."

He shook his head. "You just always seem so happy."

We got to my car. "Guess I am." I started to shrug out of his coat, but he placed his hands on my shoulders.

"Let me." He slid it down slowly, exposing only a fraction of a centimeter of skin at a time, running an index finger down my bare back, along my spine, and around my shoulder blades.

I shivered again, but this time it had nothing to do with the cool air touching my skin. My body tensed and all of a sudden the light, easy evening took on a different mood. I looked over my shoulder and watched his furrowed brows as he focused on what he was doing.

Finally he looked up and met my gaze. "You've got the most beautiful, delicate back I've ever seen."

I began to warm up fast. Maybe the whole friendship thing was all wrong after all. Maybe this was about sensual touches, and major attraction, and out of control passion. Maybe it didn't have to be more than that.

I turned around and ran my hands down the expanse of his chest. "Didn't think you noticed things like that about me."

He took my hands in his. "Are you kidding?" He inched a step back. "I notice everything about you."

So why was he pulling away?

"You like cars?"

Frowning, I nodded.

"I'll have to take you to the races one day. All that speed and danger. You'll love it."

Yes, I would. I smiled, realizing he was wisely putting the brakes on our quickening libidos. "You *have* been studying me."

He walked two parking spaces away and opened his car door. "That okay?"

More than okay. Especially now that he'd moved from studying to touching. "As long as you're having a good time, George, anything's okay."

He shook his head and chuckled.

We got into our separate cars. Nights like these that I spend with George make me wonder what it would be like to do less things separate in life, and more together. This was why George was so dangerous. He makes me want . . . things I never wanted before. Romance. Stability. Attachment.

And I've got no time for any of that.

Friday, July 23

❀ I am making progress on my list, though it might seem as if I'm not. I'm learning about Mexican cooking. Not only the couple of meals that I actually cooked—this evening I made Mexican rice, which Alberto taught me how to make last Monday—but also a little about which spice or herb to use on certain foods and why. For example, *perejil*, which is Mexican flat-leafed parsley, is usually added at the end of cooking stews, soups, and green mole sauce, because it acts as a digestive cleanser. Who'd have thought? I usually just moved it aside. I thought it was a nice, green decoration. I didn't know I was supposed to eat it.

I'm also actively working on Lupe. Tonight, I made arrangements with a convalescent home about a mile from my house to come by with Lupe and clean the graffiti off the building. I had originally called them to see if we could stop by and help wash dishes or something. But when they mentioned they had graffiti on the north wall, I figured that was perfect. We'd clean it up and paint over it. Great lesson for Lupe. Hopefully it will make her think twice before marking up other people's property.

So she did her homework and worked on her website while I practiced my cooking skills, then we ate and drove to the convalescent home.

"This isn't fair," she complained as we carried buckets of soapy water and bleach outside.

"You're right. It's not fair that these people have unwanted markings on their building thanks to kids like you."

"I didn't do it."

I dipped my sponge in the bucket. "Would you like to go point out the ones you did do, and we can go clean those up instead?"

Lupe cursed and tossed a sponge in her bucket, making a large splash. But reluctantly, she started cleaning.

I wasn't exactly thrilled to be out there washing up someone else's mess either. This wasn't what I envisioned when I thought of mentoring someone. Besides, I'd much rather be out with friends or working on my computer at home. But I told myself this was for a greater good. And it did feel kind of nice to do something for my community.

"Do you know who might have done this?" I asked, to make conversation.

"How should I know? This ain't my turf."

"Thought you might be familiar with what this stuff means." Some of it appeared to be names, but other stuff just looked like strange code words. What is it with gangs and scribbling their names all over buildings? It seemed so primitive—something cavemen did back when they didn't know any better. So who says the human race has evolved?

Lupe gave me an angry glare and wiped hard, spraying water all around her. "You're so stupid. It doesn't 'mean' anything, just that this is their territory."

Two could play the glaring game, so I gave her one of my mean looks. "Excuse me, but I'm not well versed on gang procedure and what the names on the walls mean, so you can cut out the insults."

"Whatever." She dipped the sponge in the bucket again, then hit it against the wall, this time spraying me with the water.

"Lupe, do it right," I snapped, angry because she'd gotten me wet, but mostly at her attitude and the way she spoke to me.

"I'm doing it how I want. If it's not good enough for you, Your Highness, then take this sponge and shove it up your ass." She held the sponge inches from my face.

I swear, I wanted to take her sponge out of her hand and use it to clean out her mouth. "Maybe we need some rules. Like every time you use disrespectful language you get a fine and the money you owe me goes up."

"You can't do that."

"Oh, yes, I can," I shouted, losing my temper.

She took the sopping wet sponge and threw it at me, getting the whole front of my shirt wet. Took me a second to react, but I picked mine up and threw it at her retreating back.

"Shit," she screamed.

I almost laughed, because this struck me as ridiculously funny, but I was too angry to laugh just yet. "Get your butt back over here and finish."

After a momentary stare-down, she marched over and picked up her sponge. I braced myself for another soaking, but she got to work on the wall. Her eyes were red and I saw the frustration she felt at being forced to do something she didn't want to do. I quickly pulled my own frustration in check.

"Sorry I threw that sponge at you," I said. "I shouldn't have lost my temper." Stooping to her level wouldn't teach her anything valuable.

"I'm only sorry my sponge didn't hit your face," she said.

She hadn't aimed at my face, but I didn't point that out. We worked without talking for the next couple of hours. When we'd gotten most of the dirt washed off and paint scraped off, we called it a night.

My back ached and my feet hurt. As I looked over at the angry young girl beside me, I wondered if she appreciated what I was putting myself through for her. I trudged away with heavy buckets and a sore body, and realized that this mentoring business was serious stuff. I'd definitely taken on way more than I had bargained for when I wrote that point on my list.

I looked over my shoulder at her. She slouched against the clean wall with her arms crossed, making no attempt to help me pick up. I suddenly felt ashamed for ever thinking that helping another person could ever be a point on a list to improve myself. At this very moment, Lupe became real to me, and to be perfectly honest, I was scared.

Saturday, July 24

❀ I dropped by my grandmother's house early this morning, because she said she wanted to talk. Feeling bad for neglecting her lately, I readily agreed. So I got up early, shrugged off yesterday's Lupe frustrations, and picked up some donuts to share with Grandma over coffee. Little did I know that she had invited me over to have the death talk.

This is one we've had many times before about what she wants me to do when she's gone. "*Abuela*," I said with a sigh, "you're healthier than me."

"That's because I don't eat these terrible dough things full of unhealthy fat."

So much for bringing her donuts. "So you agree. You're going to live to be five hundred."

"Of course not. Now, remember, I want you to clean my desk out and take all my ink pens. You're the smartest one in the family and you'll probably get the most use out of them. Shred all my papers. My bills. Anything with my identity on it."

"I remember, *Abuela*." Everyone in the family has their one last chore. This one just happens to be mine.

"The last thing I want while resting in the grave is to be worried that someone will steal my identity. How can a person rest in peace if a crook is walking around using her name?"

Let's see. Since you'd be dead . . . who the hell cares? But I can't say that to my grandmother. She has her beliefs and her way of doing things and you just can't argue with her. "I'll take care of all your records."

"Ah." She brightened. "Records. That reminds me." She stood up with a definite spring in her step. "I've got a surprise for you."

"Really?" Now she had my interest. I popped the rest of my donut in my mouth and followed her into the living room.

"I have a secret to tell you. This is what I wanted to talk to you about."

"Okay."

She opened up her beautiful old walnut cabinet. Inside she had dozens of old records, and an old Victrola.

"You see here? Stand closer."

I peeked inside the cabinet.

"In this album." She picked up one of her records—78s.

These records are the coolest things. They are about a quarter of an inch thick and weigh as much as a large magazine. This particular album was a Glenn Miller fox-trot.

"In here," she continued, "will be where I'll leave your inheritance." She smiled.

I stared at her then glanced to where she was pointing—the inside jacket of the album.

"What inheritance?"

"I'm leaving a little something to all you grandkids, of course."

"So we each have our own secret hiding place?"

She giggled. "Only you will know where to look. Isn't that brilliant?"

I can just see us all when she dies, ransacking her little house, each going to our own secret place to claim our ten dollars. "Well . . ."

"That way you don't have to pay taxes or deal with any government interference."

"Yes, but *Abuela,* if you invest it in mutual funds or something—"

"No. No way am I putting my money in a bank."

"Doesn't have to be a bank, but—"

"It's safe right here, in my house."

"But it isn't growing. And I'm not so sure it's really safe."

"Marcela, I know what I'm doing. When I go, you come and check in here. Okay?"

There's no getting through to this woman sometimes. Her bizarre ways drive me crazy, but I love her. So I nodded. "Okay."

After all, it's not worth worrying about her investing what little money she has managed to save.

After I reassured her and enjoyed a nice morning drinking coffee with her, I left to run some errands before going home to get ready for our yearly company party.

Should be fun. Can't wait.

Thirteen

❀ Usually, Panoply has their annual company picnic at one of the exclusive country clubs along PCH overlooking the beach. But this year, they decided to try this new "silent" club. In order to communicate with your friends, you have to write on notepads. Panoply executives thought it would be fun, kind of like in school when you passed notes to communicate. Of course, this group used pictures rather than words.

I arrived at A Tale of Two Nightclubs late, scanned the room and noticed almost everyone already here. Even George had beat me and now sat at a table all alone. He saw me come in, but only acknowledged me with a slight nod of his head. I lifted my left hand to wave and smiled, thinking he might return it.

He looked interested and it appeared that he might offer me a seat at his table. But just as he lifted an arm, Jackson and the rest of the art department guys waved and jumped up and down, silently calling for me to join them.

I laughed because it must have been pure torture for those guys to have to do something quietly. I headed to their table, more than willing to wind down and have some fun.

Out of the corner of my eye I saw George slouch in his chair as if he were incredibly bored. He seemed to be nursing his drink, watching everyone around him draw furiously and laugh, while he remained an outside observer. Sometimes I wondered if he thought he was too good to hang with the rest of us. Other times, I felt he was just shy.

I ordered a martini and started drawing on my notepad. Then I flagged down a waiter and asked him to take my note to George, who was uncrossing his legs and straightening in his seat while searching for someone to bring him his tab.

He opened it. Inside I drew a picture of a hand with a finger crooked, and it said, "Come on over." I knew he didn't think much of the creative department, but maybe if he got to know us better . . .

I smiled when he glanced at me. He took a notepad and wrote something, then asked the waiter to be his delivery boy again.

I opened it and it said, "I can't draw."

"So what?" I wrote back and drew a picture of him sitting at his desk with numbers floating around his head. "We all have our own gifts. Can I come sit at your table?"

"Only if you draw me a picture of yourself," he wrote. This time he ordered a second drink, so I knew he'd decided to stay a little longer. Either that or he was afraid the waiter was getting tired of being the go-between.

I stood and left a table full of coworkers who acted disappointed. They silently protested with sad faces and sheets of paper with ghosts and the words "boo" on them.

Still, I walked to George's table and sat across from him. For a couple of seconds we stared at each other, me offering him a soft smile. He returning it and adding a wink.

I took a sheet of paper and started to draw a picture of myself.

When I finished, George looked at it and chuckled. The caricature didn't resemble me much. Well, a comic version of myself maybe.

On his own sheet of paper, he wrote, "This doesn't look like you."

"What do I look like?" I asked in writing.

George gazed at me, seemingly taking in every intimate detail. My eyes, my face, my lips, my neck. He stopped short of letting his gaze travel down my body. "Beautiful," he wrote.

I lifted an eyebrow and leaned back in my chair. "G-r-a-c-i-a-s," I wrote, one letter at a time, and slid the paper across the table at him.

We didn't "speak" for a few moments.

"Let's save the Spanish for class," he wrote, and passed the note back to me.

"Why? Aren't you enjoying the language?"

"Yes, but I make enough of a fool of myself twice a week. I don't need to do it again tonight."

"I like the way you speak Spanish. It's cute."

He chuckled. "And you're just being nice."

"True." I smiled as he read the note, then quickly scribbled a second note and passed it to him. "Okay, no Spanish. I didn't expect to see you here tonight."

"Why?"

"Because, you don't seem to 'mix' all that well."

He arched an eyebrow. "You mean us left-brainers don't know how to have fun."

"I mean, you don't seem to like company events."

He studied the note before answering. "And you do?"

"I love this company. Been with it practically since its inception."

"Is that why you don't leave for bigger studios? I hear you're pretty good."

I chuckled, wrote my response, then leaned across the table

and placed the folded paper in his empty glass. When he pulled it out and opened it, it read, "I'm very good. Interested in finding out how good?" Hey, he left himself wide open. I couldn't let that comment go by without teasing him a bit.

This time he openly glanced at my breasts, which felt like they were swelling under his scrutiny. Then he leaned back in his chair and crossed his arms.

Were we done talking?

I glanced around the bar, waved at a few friends, then returned my attention to George, who still stared at me.

"You're creeping me out, Georgy. Stop staring."

A corner of his lips hiked up and then as if it took great effort, he reached out an arm and picked up his pencil. "I don't get you," he wrote.

I didn't want this to turn into another dissection of me and my mistakes. "Do you want to get me?"

His eyes narrowed. "Part of me does, and another part is telling me to run like hell."

I laughed. Smart man. "Is that why you haven't asked me out again?"

He looked bothered. "I did ask you out," he wrote. "On the Fourth of July and at school, but you turned me down both times."

He didn't ask me out at school; he asked if I wanted to spend time with him. I didn't. I don't. It's just that I'm attracted to him. "Do you have a fragile ego?"

"Yes."

I chuckled. "I'm sorry if I bruise it. Considering we work for the same company, it's probably better this way, huh?"

"Maybe," he wrote back.

"So . . . ," I wrote.

"So . . . ."

We drank our respective drinks. Every instinct inside me was telling me to get up and go talk to someone else. Stop this flirting. This would be another mistake, like Jackson. Hadn't I decided he should simply remain a friend? So what was I doing?

But instead of walking away from George, I asked, "What do you say we continue this discussion at my place?" I was walking head-on into a charging freight train, but I couldn't help myself. Once I finally found the perfect Latino for my list, my dating days would be over. Didn't I deserve one last fling? Even a woman on death row was offered her last meal. And George would make a tasty morsel.

With a frown, he wrote something on his sheet of paper and passed it to me. But before I could read it, he reached across and took his note back. He crumpled it up, and said, "Let's go."

I opened my eyes wide as if he'd committed a major sin by speaking. At my reaction, he smiled.

Once outside, he took my hand and led me to his car.

"What about my car?" I asked.

"We'll come back for it."

Once behind the wheel, he turned to me. "How do I get there? I can't remember."

I gave him directions.

When we got to my apartment, I started talking and talking. I couldn't stop.

He didn't seem to notice my nervousness. He strolled through my living room and looked at my framed posters of animated characters, and toys on the shelves.

"Colorful furniture," he said, more interested in me and my place than he had been the first time he was here.

My place was kind of art deco, and yes, colorful, but comfortable, and I loved it. "Drink?" I asked.

"No."

"Food?"

"No."

"Me?"

He chuckled.

"Okaaay. I'm out of ideas."

"Don't you ever just relax?"

"Rarely," I said, and sat on my lime green futon, crossing my legs and tucking a hand behind my head as I propped an elbow on the back—the optimal picture of a relaxed woman, when inside volcanic eruptions were going off. "I feel like if I keep going then maybe I'll end up doing what I'm supposed to be doing. I'll get it right by trial and error."

"What are you supposed to be doing?" He circled my living room one more time.

"Don't know." I shrugged.

"Give me a for instance."

"Well, right now, for example, I've decided to take Lupe under my wing. Maybe that's one of the things I'm 'supposed to do' in my life. Who knows?"

"Lupe?"

"A young girl I'm mentoring who most likely belongs to a gang. But she drives me insane." I straightened from my relaxed pose. Just thinking of Lupe makes me tense. "She's so difficult to reach."

He looked surprised. "Didn't know you did things like that."

I didn't. Usually. "Is it so hard to believe that I want to help out in my community?"

He studied me, slipping his hands into his pockets. "Yes, and no. You're an animator who works, in effect, for children, so your interest in kids doesn't surprise me, but I don't know where you find the time. You live at work."

Hmm, he'd noticed how much time I spend at work? And my wild streak, and how my bare back looks. What else had he noticed about me? "I don't really like kids all that much."

"Then why are you mentoring this kid?"

"Because I'm insane and need my head examined," I said.

He grinned. "No." He pulled his hands out of his pockets, and started looking around my living room again, picking up a photo of me and my two sisters. "It's never a bad idea to help someone."

I shrugged. "The opportunity presented itself and I went for it. Trust me, I'm no saint."

He lifted his eyes away from the photo and gazed at me pensively. "Maybe you don't have to be a saint, just someone who cares a little."

Maybe. Problem was, I was neither.

He placed the picture frame back gently, then paused at my rolltop desk and noticed my list taped inside. Crossing his arms, he leaned closer.

"Hey," I said, "that's personal." I wondered if he was nervous. Why else was he all the way on the other side of the room, touching my personal belongings rather than me? This was especially strange since the first time he was in my apartment he barely gave it a second glance.

"What is it? A list of your goals?"

I sighed and pushed myself off the futon. Then I fit myself between the desk and his hard, warm body. My hands rested on his broad shoulders. "Did you come over to be with me or snoop inside my desk?"

I felt his erection immediately spring to life in his pants. He eased his hips into mine, and watched for my reaction. "You can learn a lot about a person by what's on their desk."

"What would I learn about you?" I didn't move my hips away, because the pressure felt nice. Tonight wouldn't be a mistake, I promised myself. This wasn't like Jackson. As much as I tried to convince myself George could be a friend, he wasn't. No, this would be about fun. About sex and passion and . . . something we could both walk away from with a smile on our faces when it was over.

He angled his head and inhaled just below my earlobe. "That I make bad decisions," he murmured.

As I pushed closer to him, he groaned.

"Me too," I said. Like bringing him home—bad decision? Encouraging him—bad decision?

But, if he wanted to take this any further, he didn't give me any indication. His body was taut like he was trying his darndest to control himself. Finally, he ran his hands down my butt.

"George?"

"Hmm?"

"Will you kiss me?" Another bad decision, but at this point, I might as well go for three and oh.

He pulled back and brought both hands to my face, taking his time and looking into my eyes with a sexy, lazy gaze. "Do you know you've got some blue in your eyes?"

Blue? I felt like I was coming out of a dream. "What?"

"Mostly gray . . . but a hint of blue."

I frowned. What the hell was he talking about? I shook my head and pushed on his shoulder just a touch, sliding away from him easily. He didn't try to restrain me. "I know. Isn't it crazy? I've always wondered where the hell that came from. Then a few weeks ago I found out. At least I think I found out. My real father must have had blue eyes. No one else in my family does."

He followed me to the futon with a look that said, "What the hell is she talking about?" "Real father?"

"Found out my mom cheated on my dad and got me as her . . . what would you call it, reward, or punishment?"

George sat beside me and pulled me against him. "You could never be anyone's punishment."

"Don't be so sure." I twisted and lay on my back with my head on his lap.

He lifted me a bit and lowered his head and kissed me like I haven't been kissed since probably high school. Sweet, tenderly, lovingly.

I wrapped my arms around his neck and kissed him back. Oh my God, I wanted to lie there all night in his arms. I wanted to close my eyes and shut out everything except the warm glow I felt inside at this moment.

"Oh, Marcela," he said, when the kiss ended to allow us a second to take a breath. "I didn't think . . . I mean, I wasn't planning on . . ." He quickly managed to change positions and lay above me. "But I'm going to."

I caught my breath, then smiled. "It's okay, I'll still respect you in the morning."

"This isn't a joke. Can't you take anything seriously?"

Taken aback, my smile withered. "Seriously? What's so serious about having sex and having some fun?" And to make my point, I reached down, unsnapped his pants, pulled down the zipper, and touched him. "That is what we're going to do, right?" Yes, I'd lost my head. I no longer cared whether this was a bad or a good decision—because I needed him.

"Ohhh, man," he said. Then he kissed me again as I continued to fondle him.

"Oh, Marcela. I'm yours. Just keep touching me and I'll do anything, anything you want."

Anything? I had some laundry that needed to get done. Since he wanted me to be serious, I thought I'd better not mention that.

He reached for my pants. "Should we go to your bed?"

"Doesn't matter," I said.

"Where is it?"

"What?"

"Your bedroom."

"Let's just stay here." I attempted to lock onto his lips again.

"Why?"

I shrugged, not exactly wanting to go into why I didn't let men into my bed. "It's my bed. Kind of . . . personal."

He laughed. "I'm about to strip you naked and make love to you. That's pretty personal, don't you think?"

"Yeah." He had a point. "It's just that . . . that's my personal space."

"Can't I be a part of it? If we're going to do this, I want to be part of all your space. I want to know you."

"You can get to know me right here, babe." I caressed him some more.

He kissed the side of my neck. "Let me make this something you'll always remember."

That was sweet. But . . . this wasn't about creating lifelong memories. It was about experiencing, feeling, mutual enjoyment.

"Look, Marcela—"

"Fine, fine. Let's go." I scooted off the futon and stood, thinking maybe we were doing too much talking when we should already be naked.

He reached for me, wrapping an arm around my waist as he sat on the futon and looked up at me. "You act like you just want to get this over and done with."

"Don't you?"

"Well . . . yes, but—" He cut himself short. "No, I don't want to get it over with. I want to enjoy it and you. I want to kiss you and caress you and make love to you all night, again and again."

He made me smile, and he made me want him all the more. "That sounds fantastic, George." My fingers wove through his thick hair.

"Thank you."

"What else do you want?" I asked, using my most seductive voice.

"I want your legs to shake when you see me walk in the room. I want you to call me at home in the middle of the night because you can't sleep without first making love to me. I want tonight to mean something to you. I want this to be the start of something special."

"Wow." I stared at him, then sank down to my knees, feeling overwhelmed. "George, I . . . how do I put this?"

"What?"

"I'm not looking for a relationship."

"You're not? But I thought you said—"

"It's a bad time for me. I . . . like you. I really like you." I lowered my gaze, sad that he wasn't the guy that would satisfy my list. If he was a little less American, maybe spoke with an accent, he would fit the bill.

"So what's the problem?"

"I . . . I need to continue dating other men."

George stiffened. He stared at me for what seemed like an eternity, making me feel small. I wasn't sure if the look in his eyes meant he was surprised, angry, or what. But when he pushed me away, stood, and zipped up his pants I got a clue he wasn't pleased.

Quickly, I stood as well. "George. Don't go. Let me explain."

He looked like he wanted to call me all kinds of dirty names that I probably deserved, but he kept his mouth shut. He pulled the keys out of his pants.

"George. Come on."

He turned his back on me.

"Hey, what about my car?"

Again he acted as if he hadn't heard me.

I touched his shoulder. "I'm sorry."

Almost reluctantly, he looked at me over his shoulder.

"I'm so very sorry. I thought you wanted to have a good time. I'm not ready for more."

As he gazed at me, his angry expression softened. "I'm not Jackson. I'm not going to fu– . . . sleep with you on your futon and pretend nothing happened."

Tears touched my eyes.

"You said you were ready for a change. I thought that meant you were ready for a serious, adult relationship."

I wanted to say, "I am," but what he considered an adult relationship was obviously different from what I did, so I lifted my chin and stiffened my back.

"Get your act together, Marcela. You deserve better than what you're willing to accept from men, don't you see that?"

Maybe it was the look in his eyes or the way he said what he said, but I lost it and cried. I can't believe that I cried. Tears just flowed out of my eyes like someone had switched on a water valve in our props department.

"Man, I always pick the wrong woman," he said. "That's the second thing you'd learn about me. I make bad decisions and I pick the wrong women."

When George walked out of my apartment, I felt like the worst piece of trash in the world.

I fell against the door, tempted to go after him, but instead I leaned my back against it and slid down, dropping my forehead onto my knees.

He got it right when he said to get my act together. I'm a mess. I'm getting older and I'm still a mess. How sad is that?

I don't sleep around. Not like some women. Jackson was an aberration, and George . . . I've never wanted a man more. But he was talking permanent. Not dating, but a relationship. And I can't start something serious with George when he so obviously isn't what I want to take home to my family.

George is sweet and sexy but way too Americanized. He wouldn't wow my family with revolutionary talk of Aztec kings like Armando would have.

I laughed at myself like a crazy person, my strangled voice sounding pitiful in my lonely apartment. Yeah, Armando was a real prize. For a few moments, as I made my date with the creep, I tried to convince myself he was the young male version of my Tía Lydia. Guess I always knew better.

Just like I knew George's last name didn't make him Latino. Just like I knew he'd want more than casual sex. But I ignored my better judgment because I liked him so much and I wanted to pursue this wild chemistry between us.

So, looks like I'm back to square one.

I wiped my eyes angrily. *Stupid.*

Call Mom, a voice inside my head said. She'll help you straighten all this out. I pushed myself off the floor. "Yeah, right. This is all her fault."

I walked into my bedroom knowing that it wasn't her fault. But for tonight, it was easier to blame her.

Fourteen

❀ The verdict was that everyone seemed to like the silent club, for a while, then they all apparently left and hit a few "real" clubs.

"You should have been there, Marcela. Chuck downed five screwdrivers within an hour. He went home with a hag that looked like Phoebe from *Friends*."

I frowned, trying to figure out what was wrong with a girl that looked like Phoebe.

"Except she looked like she'd gained fifty pounds, and got hit in the face with a pizza roller from all the pockmarks she had," Steve said and laughed.

I turned on my computer and popped in the new CD I bought over the weekend—Jennifer Peña's latest. Jennifer was the little girl who had played young Selena in the movie about the ill-fated Latina singing star eight years ago. Now she was becoming a hot artist herself and would soon cross over into English, according to my sister Kate.

"Hey, you brought some culture, huh?"

I wasn't much in the mood to be teased by my colleagues today, and just because the music was in Spanish didn't make it culture. Blacks and whites could be totally clueless about Latinos. In fact, I think none of us really understand each other.

Jackson walked by and rustled my hair, then took a seat in a rolling chair beside me. "Where did you disappear to?"

"When?"

"After the company party."

"Oh." I didn't want to talk about it. "I went out with George."

"What's with you and George anyway. That guy seems so boring."

I brought my work up on my computer, and tried to concentrate on what I was doing. "He's not."

"Shit, he never even cracks a smile." He flashed a superior smirk. "Guy wouldn't know a good time if a stripper jumped out of a cake and planted herself—"

"Look. I didn't ask for your opinion, and if you're going to—"

"Don't bite my head off."

"Well, lay off."

He glared at me. "Don't tell me it's serious."

"It's nothing, okay. Nothing. So leave me alone." I got up and left as the guys all gawked, open-mouthed, at me. Damn Jackson and damn George.

Jackson caught up with me as I reached the hallway.

"Hey." He took my arm to stop me. "What's wrong?"

I yanked my arm free and glared at him, but when I saw the look of concern on his face, all the fight drained out of me. I wanted to tell him the whole ugly story, but I couldn't talk to him. Not like I used to. So instead I told him about what happened with my mom, and about my plan to improve myself.

He scratched the back of his head. "Sounds . . . like a lot of work for no reason."

"I need to do this."

He narrowed his eyes. "Wait a minute. I get it. George fits. He's Mexican. That's why you want him."

"No, actually, he doesn't fit. That's sort of the problem. I wish he did. But he's so many generations removed from his Mexican ancestors that he'd probably have to look up the word immigrant in the dictionary to understand what it means."

"You are one crazy chick. Do you realize how insane all this sounds?"

"No."

"Marcela. I don't like the guy, okay? He looks down his nose at us. Thinks what he does is superior to what we do. But if you like him . . . what the hell difference does it make if the man just crossed the border yesterday or if his family's been here for twenty generations?"

"It just does." I stepped away from him. "Thanks, Jackson, but I need to go see him."

Jackson crossed his arms and shook his head like he felt sorry for me, or like he thought I needed serious psychiatric help or something. Maybe I do.

I went down to the business department to see George. Somehow, I figured if I talked to him, I could set it all right again.

He took his eyes off his computer only for a fraction of a second, then continued working. I wished I had his power of concentration.

"We need to talk," I said.

"I'm working."

"Just for a—"

"I'm working. And besides, we've said all there is to say to one another."

"Is that so?" Why did I have this urge to slap him?

"Yes, that's so."

"That's it. You're finished with me?"

His jaw clenched and he seemed to lose his precious concentration for a moment. Then he hit his print button and stood. As he passed by me, he simply said, "Good-bye."

He was being unfair. And not very understanding. Yes, we were at work and this wasn't the best place to talk this out, but he could have at least given me a chance to explain.

I decided he would come around. I needed to give him a chance to cool down. After Spanish class, we'd be away from the office, and he'd come around.

"All right, George. I'll leave. And just so you know, I had to call my friend to drive me to get my car Saturday morning. So I'm a little pissed at you, too."

I went back to my cubicle to work. And I got my wish; everyone left me alone.

Thursday, July 29

❀ I was wrong. George didn't speak to me Tuesday or tonight in Spanish class.

During break, I gave it one more shot. He put money into a vending machine and picked out Oreo cookies, which fell with a thump in the bin. I reached down and took his snack.

He gave me a startled expression that quickly turned to annoyance when he realized it was me.

"How about you share these with me and we chat?"

He drew in a sharp, irritated breath and looked away. "Keep them." Then he dug in his pocket for more change.

"I'm sorry for what happened," I said, suddenly feeling like I was spending too much time apologizing to men.

"No problem." He dropped coins into the machine, ignoring me.

I hate being ignored—it drives me nuts. I stood in front of the vending machine, forcing him to look at me. "George. Seemed to me you were pushing things into fast forward a little early in this relationship. I mean, come on, as sweet as all that talk was about weak knees, you couldn't really expect an exclusive relationship."

"You know, I was right about you all along, Marcela. You fit into the Hollywood crowd perfectly. Congratulations."

What did that mean exactly? I could hardly be lumped into the Paris Hilton crowd, if that was what he was insinuating. "Can't we just have a good time, and see where it leads us?"

He smiled, but I wasn't fooled, because the rest of his demeanor remained cool and detached. "We did. It led us nowhere. Now if you'll excuse me." He waved his hand and indicated the vending machine behind me.

I felt sad, rejected, hurt. "Here." I placed his Oreo cookies in his hand and left. I didn't want to sit in Spanish class anymore. And I didn't want to think about why it mattered to me if George liked me or not.

As I walked to my car, I took out my cell and called Aunt Lydia. One of the points on my list that I hadn't yet touched was to get more into the Chicana cause. If anyone could steer me in the right direction, it would be my aunt.

"*Bueno,*" she answered.

"Want company?"

"Marcela? I'd love to see you, *Mi'ja*, but I'm on my way to a meeting."

"Great. Can I go with you?"

After a momentary pause—she was probably picking herself up off the floor from shock—she promised to wait for me.

When I got to her place, she didn't even invite me in. "*Vamos, vamos*, I'm late." She ushered me to my car. "You drive."

"Sure. So where are we going?" I asked as we put on our seat belts.

"I'm speaking to young business executives. I'm on a panel."

"Really? Cool."

"I'm so glad you're going to be in the audience." She beamed.

"Me too, sounds interesting."

She scoffed. "Marcela, I know you don't find my work the slightest bit interesting."

"No, really, I do." We stopped at a red light. I glanced at my aunt and she gave me a "get real" kind of look. "Okay, maybe I haven't in the past, but I'd like to get a little more involved now."

"Seriously?"

I nodded. The streetlight turned green so I stepped on the gas.

"Well, what do you want to do?"

"Why don't you start by telling me what the Chicano movement is all about?"

"Oh, *Mi'ja*," she said with laughter in her voice. "That's a huge topic."

I had the time. "Okay."

"Well, it began in New Mexico with Reies López Tijerina and the land grant movement, then Rodolfo "Corky" Gonzales picked it up in Denver founding the Crusade for Justice in 1966. You've heard of him?"

"No."

She shook her head. "His poem 'I Am Joaquin'?"

"Ah, no."

"*Ahi, niña*. You have to read it. The roots of Chicano nationalism, our cultural identity in Aztec myths, and Aztlan—the mythical Chicano homeland—all grew out of Corky's poem."

My interest sparked at her mention of Aztec myths. Maybe Spike had been onto something. "I'll read it."

"I've got about a dozen books you can borrow. But take good care of them and don't forget to return them."

I followed her directions, getting on the 5 freeway.

"Then you've heard of Cesar Chavez?"

"Yep. He's even on a stamp now."

Aunt Lydia didn't appear impressed by my knowledge. "The importance, here, Marcela, was that these people saw injustices and fought to remedy them where they could. Some were successful. Others weren't. We continue to press for further changes and to make sure no one forgets that this is our homeland."

She wasn't going to get agreement from me on this point.

That California was once part of Mexico in the early 1800s had little to do with our life today. To me this was *my* homeland—mine and all my friends of every race that lived here. It's part of America—my country.

We arrived at her meeting place in Santa Ana, just in time for her to take her seat on stage. I took mine in the audience. An interesting turn of events was that that guy from the Hispanic Chamber of Commerce was on the panel with Aunt Lydia. Remember him? Rogelio.

After an interesting discussion on how young businesspeople could benefit by hiring Latinos and amazing statistics on what a powerful workforce Latinos were, they took questions and then ended the formal guest speaker part of the meeting. Everyone milled around chatting with each other.

I approached Rogelio. "Remember me?" I asked as I tapped his shoulder and scooted around so he could see me.

He gazed at me for a few moments, probably trying to place me. "Hey, *sí, sí*. I remember you. At the chamber, *verdad?*"

I smiled. "Yes."

"So, are you a member here too?"

"No, no, I'm here with my Aunt Lydia." I pointed to the stage where a couple of young, good-looking guys seemed engrossed in whatever she was saying.

"Lydia is your aunt?" Rogelio looked surprised and excited. He clapped his hands together. "You know, that makes sense. I'll bet you she was the one who gave me your address so I could add you to our mailing list at the chamber."

"You're probably right." Aunt Lydia probably had us all targeted for propaganda. "I enjoyed listening to you up there."

"*Gracias, Mi'ja.*"

Rogelio's kind eyes made me want to spend more time talking to him. "You're like a walking data bank. I wasn't familiar with a lot of what you said up there—about the number of Latinos in America and stuff."

"We are a powerful force, and we are a young group." He chuckled. "Well, some of us more than others." He rubbed the top of his gray hair.

I laughed. But his statistics made me think of my project and the very real possibilities of targeting Latinos for Panoply's next film. But could I sell it to my colleagues? I've never been one to shove my ethnicity down anyone's throat, but perhaps I could simply share it.

Just as I was thinking I had better go rescue my aunt from those gorgeous hunks, she walked up beside me. "Rogelio, I sure hope you're not making a pass at my niece."

He laughed. "Me? You know I'm a faithful husband to my beautiful wife, God rest her soul."

Aunt Lydia caressed his shoulder. "She was a lucky woman. So, you met my Marcela?" Now she turned her adoring attention to me and I felt special. I was finally becoming the kind of niece, the kind of Latina, she'd always hoped I'd become. Maybe my plan was starting to work after all. For once, I felt accepted by one of my family members—my favorite one at that.

"I knew this lovely young girl had to be related to you, a lovely woman."

"*Ahi*, Rogelio," Aunt Lydia laughed. "You're such a flirt." She placed her arm around my waist. "We should go."

"We should," I agreed. "Take care," I said to Rogelio.

"You take care of yourself, *Mi'jita*, and come visit me some day."

"I will," I said, though I doubted I ever would.

As we walked back to the car, I asked my aunt about those handsome men she was chatting with. "I should have had you introduce me."

She made a face. "They're white."

"So?"

"Forget it, Marcela. If I were going to introduce you to a man, he wouldn't be an Anglo."

A lightbulb went off in my head. I don't know why I didn't think of this before. Who knew more Mexicans than my aunt Lydia? "Okay, how about you introduce me to a Mexican man."

She placed a hand to her heart. "First you come with me to one of my meetings, and now you'll go out with any man I choose?"

I laughed. "Sure."

"Marcela, you've just made my year."

I got in my car. "Stop being so dramatic."

"I'm so proud of you, *Mi'ja*."

Anyone would think I'd decided to give my body to science or something. Jeesh.

"I've got the perfect man for you!"

"Great, set it up for this weekend."

"I will."

So, now I've got a blind date with a Mexican guy this weekend, who my *tía* said I will love. I'm glad she's ecstatic about it, because though I did my best not to think of George tonight, as I lay in bed trying to fall asleep, I wished I were going out with George instead.

A little voice inside me whispered that if he was a man who would willingly turn down a guaranteed one-night stand with a woman who didn't expect him to commit, then perhaps I'd made a big mistake. I'd turned down honor and a man of character for an unknown Chicano who fit a label.

I buried my head under my pillow and told the voice to shut up.

Fifteen

❀ Daniela and I went to see an exhibit by a California artist named Simon Silva. He paints very colorful Mexican scenes. I bought a couple of his prints for my house. It also gave me an idea on how to approach my new project.

After listening to Aunt Lydia and Rogelio's panel discussion last night, at work today I kept trying to figure out how I could target the Latino market. How do I give my project a Latin twist? None of the animation studios have attempted it yet. Feature-length animated films include movies about Native Americans as in *Pocahontus*, Chinese as in *Mulan*, Greek as in *Hercules*, even *Tarzan*, but where were Latin myths and stories celebrated?

My excitement grew and I couldn't wait to get home and play with my ideas a little more.

Daniela chatted with Simon Silva and had him sign a children's book that he had illustrated. I was happy to shake his hand and take home his paintings.

"All right, let's go." I hurried Daniela toward the entrance.

"What's the rush?"

"I'm not rushing." But I was. When I get an idea, I can't wait to get on my computer and begin working.

"Let's go get dinner."

Damn. "Okay."

We went across the street from the exhibit to a bar where we ordered mixed appetizers and martinis.

Daniela chewed on a dumpling. "Mmm, good. So, how is the dating game going?"

"Lousy. Don't ask." In fact, I wasn't sure how any of the points on my list were going.

"Well, I've got an admirer," she revealed.

Okay, she got the expected reaction from me. I put my shrimp back down on my plate and stared her down. "Excuse me? You're married. Or has that little fact escaped your memory?"

She waved her fingers in dismissal. "So is he. He's a young dad who takes his daughter to ballet. While my seven-year-old is in one room his three-year-old is in the next."

"And?"

"We talk, that's all."

That wasn't all or she wouldn't have brought it up. "Good, because you've got a great husband."

She growled. "I suppose. But it's nice to have a guy flirt with you again," she said with a dreamy expression.

I wondered why people ever got married. After a few years, they inevitably got tired of each other and wanted out. "Isn't it nice to have a loving husband and a dedicated father for your children?"

"Yes," she admitted. "Like I said, all we do is talk." She sipped her drink and when she came up for air she smiled. "Listen, I have a favor to ask you."

"Sure, anything." Except cover for her if she was going to cheat on Fabian.

"Come with me to the Argentine club next weekend." Her parents make her go once a month, and she's never very thrilled by it.

"I don't know. I've got enough of my own cultural events to attend."

"Hey, didn't I bring my kids and husband to that party from hell your aunt threw last year?"

I groaned. Party from hell was an understatement. Aunt Lydia was supporting a Chicano political candidate and rented an entire restaurant on Olivera Street. She invited the media, so my sisters and I helped her get as many people to the party as possible. That way it would look good on TV. We managed to get about five hundred people to attend. But these radio shock-jocks showed up and riled the group into a frenzy, and Tía's nice little political party spilled out into the street where a mini-riot broke out.

"Okay, when's this Argentine gathering?" I asked.

Daniela gave me a satisfied look. "A week from Saturday."

"I'll be there. Any reason why you need company this time?"

"Yes. Two reasons. The first is that Fabian can't make it, and I don't want to drive with two kids on my own. Second is that I want to introduce you to a nice guy."

"Daniela," I warned.

"What? I'm trying to help you fulfill the points on your Latina list. And if I can't have any fun myself, I want to live vicariously through you."

I laughed. "He's not the ballet dad, is he?"

"Of course not." She looked horrified. "He's mine."

I raised an eyebrow. "Yours?"

"You know what I mean."

I didn't want to know.

"No, he's a nice Argentine," she continued. "Latino, right? Won't he do?"

"Not exactly."

"Well, you might have to be flexible here. And not so cliquish. You Mexicans act like you're the only Latinos in America."

I laughed. "Girl, I don't even want to date Mexicans, okay?"

"Then this is perfect."

"I don't want any Latino, but if I'm going to marry one eventually, he should at least be Mexican to make my family happy."

Daniela shrugged my protest away. "Your family's crazy. And now you're getting crazy too."

I was. "But you still love me, right?"

"*Sí, sí.* I love you. But you can't marry me, I'm already trapped, remember? So, you'll meet my friend?"

I shook my head in defeat. "Why not?"

And that was that. Two mystery men to meet in the next couple of weeks.

To put a perfect seal on my day, before collapsing into bed after reading up on Mexican myths until three in the morning, I got more information on the three Paul Peckinpaughs. It can't actually hurt to find out more about this guy. At least, I should find out his medical history. You never know when that will be of use. Right?

Saturday, July 31

✿ I think I'm making some progress with Lupe. We went back to the convalescent home to finish up our paint job. After the first time when all she did was bitch about having to scrub the "damn side of a building," I expected more of the same. Her attitude needs major work. But she was better, kind of resigned to the fact that I'm serious about her working to pay off what she's costing me on my car—almost five thousand dollars! I'm "paying" her twenty bucks per hour. At this rate, she should be working for me until her twenty-first birthday. I'll have to call it a wash after a few months, though I'm more than willing to continue seeing her if it makes a difference.

I actually think she secretly likes having someone care. The staff made a really big deal about how the outside wall looked when we finished and ordered pizza for us to share as a celebration.

Lupe sat surrounded by elderly ladies who cooed and praised her for all her hard work. "It isn't every day you see young girls helping out, taking time from their schedules to help others."

"It's nothing," Lupe said with a blush.

"No, it means so much to us, sweetheart."

Lupe shyly took a bite from her pizza, and smiled.

"Wasn't it horrible what they wrote on our home?" they talked among themselves. "We have so little extra money to clean up things like this. We can't thank you enough," they repeated to Lupe.

"You're welcome," she said, looking as if (I may be reading more into this than was there, I realize) she felt guilty.

I watched. Lupe was polite, and when the women babied her a bit, serving her more pizza, offering her a napkin, pouring her Kool-Aid, she allowed it without protest.

I cleared the table and tossed the paper plates in the trash, then stood by the wall to watch Lupe more openly without her noticing. I crossed my arms and leaned on the wall. On days like today, Lupe looked young and sweet and I wondered what it would take to see this side of her more often. She's still totally hostile with me, but what the heck, you can't ask for miracles.

Sunday, August 1

🌸 I went out with Luis—my blind date. I could see why my aunt likes him. He's loaded, rich, *muy importante*. Picked me up in a limousine. Can you believe that?

He conducted at least five business deals during the first two hours of our date. He's got some kind of import–export business. I got to hear all about the history of his company and how he built it from nothing and invested his last ten thousand dollars in his dream. I kept thinking that if he had ten thousand dollars, he didn't start with nothing, but there was no need to point that out.

He comes from a well-off Mexican family. Though he's not annoyingly into the Chicano movement and he said he's Mexican, not Chicano, he still supports organizations like LULAC, which is probably another reason my aunt thinks he's a prince.

All this I learned on our way to Morton's Steak House in Palm Springs. When someone else is driving and you're drinking cocktails in a limo, I guess it doesn't matter how far you have to go.

He bought a three-hundred-dollar bottle of wine and I tried not to be shocked. No man had ever spent this kind of money on me. I also started to worry. What does a man who picks you up in a limo and spends a half grand on dinner expect in return?

"So," he said, "tell me about yourself."

I was a little surprised he asked since up to this point all he'd done was talk about himself. "Well, what do you want to know?"

"Your aunt said you make movies. She also said you're gorgeous and I have to agree with her."

"Thank you." Okay, he was winning a few points back. "But I don't *make* movies. I'm an animator."

"Do you get to meet the actors who do the voices?"

"Yes." People always asked that. "Personally, I feel a bit insulted that we do all the work and an actor comes in and reads a few lines and gets all the fame and money. But that's life, I guess."

He frowned. "But you get paid well, don't you?"

"Sure."

"Because your aunt said you're well-off."

What did that matter? I mean, he couldn't want me for my money; he's loaded. I suddenly got this immense fear that he was going to stick me with the check. "I do okay. Can't complain."

"Oh good." He looked relieved. "You know, I met Harrison Ford once."

"Really?"

Then he went on for the next forty-five minutes talking about himself again and his chance meeting with Harrison.

When we finished our meal, I was ready to call it a night. Unfortunately, I had to endure another two-and-a-half-hour drive back to Studio City. I think I emptied his scotch bottle.

At the end of the date, he had the limo driver pull up to the curb and I thought he was going to try to get romantic. But he actually pulled out his planner to see when we could go out again. This guy is way too busy for me, not to mention boring.

"I don't have my planner with me," I said sarcastically, "so I'll have to give you a call."

He smiled, oblivious to my jab. "I look forward to it. I think you and I might be a good match."

How he figured that, I didn't know. I smiled back.

"People spend way too much time dating and looking for romance," he said, closing his planner and shifting to face me. "That's not what makes relationships last."

"What is?" I asked, even though I knew better than to prolong this date. The quicker this night ended the better.

"Common culture. Common beliefs. Compatible life goals."

"I'm sure all that helps." And with a sinking feeling in the pit of my stomach I realized this was exactly what I was looking for. He was the perfect Latino. So why did he feel so wrong?

"You and I are both professionals. I don't expect nor do I want a traditional woman who stays home and raises kids. I want a woman who is a mover and shaker, like me. Our lifestyles match. Our culture matches. And I'm sure we'll be sexually compatible."

I tried not to choke on the alcohol fumes coming from my stomach. "How can you be sure?"

He ran his eyes down my body. "You're very attractive."

Sure, that made sense. Sexual compatibility is always based on physical attractiveness. NOT.

So, I told him I'd call him and stepped out of the limo. As he drove away and I watched the taillights flash, I groaned. I don't want to call him. I don't want to call him. I don't want to call him.

But how could I not? He was Mexican. He was politically involved in La Rasa enough to satisfy my family, but not to annoy me. His career was his life, so he wouldn't demand that I alter my life much. He was perfect. But he left me cold inside. He saw me as another acquisition at worst and as a business partner at best. Was that what I wanted for the rest of my life?

I had to struggle not to hunch my shoulders in defeat as I turned around to go into my apartment. Finding a man CAN'T be this hard. Can it?

Sixteen

Wednesday, August 4

❀ I guess I've been pretty grumpy lately and no fun to be around, because my entire department decided to play a practical joke on me. They do that every once in a while. We've gotten everyone at least once, and we all have a good laugh afterward.

I got to work and they told me that the props department decided to change some of the props for *Firebird*. Where our fire monster knight was to drop balls of slime on a city to save it from destruction, they now wanted to use water balloons.

"We can't use water balloons," I said, irritated, because we'd gone over this a million times. "Do they want to fill the balloons with slime?"

"No," Jackson said. "Water."

"That won't work." As they knew I would, I stomped away and headed to the props department.

There Henry and Bill waited for me, and straight-faced told

me we'd do a demonstration, promising me that the water would work better.

"Bill, water is too wet, it will destroy the cardboard buildings."

"So will the slime. We shoot once and hope it comes out right. We're not going to be able to reuse the city no matter what medium we use, and water is much more realistic looking."

"I know, but water will make the cardboard wilt and will make the city look fake."

"Let's do a test."

"Test?"

He handed me a small cardboard box about as big as a microwave and told me to hold it, and not move. Then just as I realized what he was going to do, he dumped about twenty gallons of ice cold water on me and the box.

I screamed and shuddered. The box in my hands lay at my feet, completely abandoned in a soggy pile.

The entire crew, including my fellow animation buddies, if they could still be called that, burst out laughing.

"Ha, gotcha," Jackson said, coming forward with a giant beach towel.

I snatched it from his hand as he snickered and backed away.

"I can't believe you all did that, you low-lifes. I don't even have a change of clothes."

"You can work in that towel. None of us will mind," Jackson suggested with a much too innocent look on his face.

"Gee, thank you." I walked out of the room after patting myself as dry as possible. Then I picked up my purse and keys and headed to my car. I'd have to go home to change and then come back.

On the ride down in the elevator, George walked in. He did a double take when he saw me with my hair plastered to my head and my clothes molded to my body. I looked down at my feet where a small puddle was forming. He didn't ask. In fact, he didn't even say a word. He got in and turned around to stare above at the declining red numbers.

I wondered where he was going, but when we got to the lobby, I headed to the parking garage without speaking to him either. Two could play at this game.

❀ At home, I changed clothes and dried my hair. I also took the opportunity to call my grandmother to see if she needed anything. Lots of times I stopped by on the weekend and took her grocery shopping or to the mall. But since I planned on skipping Spanish class tomorrow, I thought I might see her instead.

"*Mañana?*" she asked. "If you want to come and eat a good meal for a change, then come, but I don't need to go anywhere."

"I don't want to make you work." I strolled to my desk and sat.

"Taking care of my granddaughter is not work. But I thought you told me you were taking Spanish lessons or something on Tuesdays and Thursdays."

How she managed to remember everyone's schedule was a mystery. The woman had the sharpest memory. "I was helping out someone I thought was a friend, but he's not. So I'm done going to those classes."

"Ah, too bad. Brushing up on Spanish is good for you."

But sitting in the same class with George wouldn't be good. I pulled my list off my desk and stared at number one. "*Abuela,*" I said, "how do you know when you meet the right guy?"

She laughed softly. "When it hurts more to imagine life without him than with him."

Her answer made me frown. Sounded like the best of two evils. "What about love?"

"Where do you think the pain comes from? Are you in love?"

"No, no. But I chased someone away for all the wrong reasons, and I'm feeling bad."

"*Dios* forgives, maybe your friend will too."

I smiled. *Dios*? God may forgive, but George was plainly human. "I apologized but he refused to accept it."

"Try again, but this time be honest—admit to your faults. We are not perfect."

She could say that again. "I'll try. See you tomorrow?"

"No, go to class. Face your problems."

When I got back to Panoply, I planned to go straight to George's office to tell him the truth. Grandma was right. George deserved the truth even if he hated me more after listening to it. But as I pulled into my parking space in the underground garage, he was leaning against the post beside where I park.

I got out of my car and just stood there.

"I was hoping you weren't gone for the day. It would've been a heck of a wait until morning."

I blinked. He was talking to me, and he even made a joke. This was a good sign.

"I want to apologize for being so hard on you. I've had a lot on my mind, and . . . I had no right to expect something from you that you weren't ready to give."

He expected me to be a normal woman who would want a relationship to grow and flourish. "You have nothing to apologize for."

"Yeah, well, I'd like to just the same."

To be honest, I wasn't used to men apologizing to me. I didn't know what to say. I shrugged. "Well, knock yourself out then."

He cracked a small smile. And there was something else in there too, something warm and inviting, and it gave me courage.

"Considering we work for the same company and are bound to run into each other, I thought it would be a good idea to clear the air, is all," he said.

I could feel him slipping back behind his polite, professional shell.

He took a step back.

"Ah, wait." I dug in my purse and pulled out my list of ten items. "Here." I handed it over to him.

He glanced at it and frowned.

"This is why I didn't want a relationship with you. I'm working on this list. The one that was on my desk. The one you were looking at that I didn't want you to see."

He read through it then shot me a perplexed look.

"I only went out with you at first because you're Mexican. Well, because I thought you were really Mexican. And I need to date Mexican men."

He lifted an eyebrow as he stared at me. "Are you trying to flatter me?"

I sighed. I'm handling this all wrong, I know. But I can't stand him being mad at me anymore and I'm nervous. "No. I'm trying to tell you that I'm sorry—again."

"Marcela, you don't have to. Really. It's okay."

"No, it's not okay. I miss talking to you. I dated you because of my list, but I . . . that's not why I want to keep dating you."

He closed his eyes for a second and drew in some air. Then his gaze connected with mine and he looked sad. "You're gorgeous and funny and I hoped we could—"

"George, listen. I'm a little screwed up right now. I'm trying to figure out what I want, and I didn't want you to get hurt. You started talking this stuff about us being permanent and all, and I panicked. I didn't want . . ."

George stared at the list in his hands. "And you didn't want to be stuck with me while you searched for your real Mexican guy."

"I'm a jerk. You don't have to spell it out. But, I don't care about that point on my list anymore."

He folded the paper in half, all the while staring at me, probably wanting to say something really mean. I couldn't blame him if he did. "Man, Marcela. What am I supposed to say now?"

"I don't know." I felt miserable. "Maybe that you accept my apology and you still like me—just a little?"

"What's with this to-do list anyway?" He snapped the folded paper onto the open palm of his empty hand as if he were swatting a pesky fly.

"Remember I told you I found out my mom cheated on my dad and I actually have a different birth father?"

George shrugged. "Vaguely."

"Well he's white, and my family thinks I'm no longer as Latina as I used to be, and . . . I need to show them I am. Hell, it's complicated."

With a frown, he continued to stare at me.

At least he didn't tell me I was crazy the way Jackson did. "Well, I just wanted you to know how I really felt." I turned around to walk to the elevators.

"Wait." He took a step closer to me.

I stopped and turned to face him.

"I'm still not sure how you feel, but . . . maybe we can find out."

I breathed a sigh of relief. "Okay."

He moved almost in slow motion, and came to stand in front of me. "Remember I said I make bad choices with women?"

"Yes," I said, my voice barely above a whisper.

"Twice."

He'd gotten burned twice?

"I've worked in the entertainment industry all my life. And the women I've dated have been . . . superficial, interested mostly in their careers, party girls. I was stupid enough to fall in love. Two times."

I nodded. "And you don't want to do it again."

He smiled. "I do. But this time, I want someone who will fall in love back."

"Oh, George." My heart skipped a beat and I wanted to wrap my arms around him. "I'm really bad at serious stuff."

He reached across and took my hand. "Then maybe we should stop this before one of us gets hurt."

I squeezed his fingers. "No."

He pulled me with him toward the elevators and hit the button. When the doors opened he hurried us inside. All in one swift motion he hit my floor then tipped my chin and angled his head. The kiss that followed was no more than a caress, a promise.

His eyes were dark with passion when he lifted his head. "I don't want to be another of your throwaway men."

My heart was beating like crazy. He wasn't even close to the type of man I usually dated. And apparently I couldn't throw him away—something about him kept drawing me back. Maybe because he *was* so different. I wanted to look at him, touch him, talk to him, be with him.

The elevator doors opened. He pushed the "open door" button to keep them open. I noticed we were on my floor. I should have stepped out, but all I could do was stare at him. He'd brought me back to work. Why hadn't he pulled me into his back seat?

"Hey, Marcela. You're back," Steve said with a chuckle as he strolled past. "You can come out. We'll be good."

I forced a smile and dragged my attention off George to look at Steve. "Payback is going to be a bitch. You know that, don't you?"

He walked away pretending to shake in his shoes.

"I'll talk to you later," I said to George.

He nodded.

"I'll call you."

"Let's sleep on all this. Now that we both know where the other stands."

"Okay." I stepped out of the elevator. The doors closed. And George was gone.

I'm starting to believe that you can't plan who you're going to fall in love with. Not that I'm in love with George, but I could fall in love with him. We don't fit in any of the ways that would satisfy my list. But he makes me feel cared for, special, beautiful—and not just for my body.

Dating a man just because he's Mexican makes no sense. What was I thinking? How am I going to fall in love with a label? Happily, I decided I wouldn't call Aunt Lydia's Mr. Perfect back. I was going to give George and me a chance instead.

Saturday, August 7

❀ Part of my list included doing more family stuff, even though I always seem to be doing something with one of them. But I agreed to help my mom clean out her garage. This whole love thing had me wondering about her and my dad, and Paul, and I figured I might be able to work in some questions.

As I opened a box, I yawned for the twentieth time.

"*Que pasa, Hija*? Why are you so tired?"

"I spent last night at the movies with Lupe, then stayed up working until early this morning."

"Lupe is the girl who spray painted your car?"

"Mm hmm."

"I'm very proud of you, Marcela. God will bless you for helping that poor lost soul."

Poor lost soul? I'm actually starting to think Lupe is a demon in disguise. Last night at the movies she purposely spilt her coke on the girls sitting in front of us, then when the girls jumped out of their seats and demanded she be more careful, Lupe outright punched one of them in the mouth. This without provocation, without reason. I felt so bad for the girls, I offered to buy them all new movie tickets for another night and gave them enough money to cover their snacks. Then I dragged Lupe out and shoved her into my car. I swear, I felt like smacking her. I gazed at my mother who wanted to make this kid out to be an innocent victim. "Think so?"

"*Si, Mi'ja*. Not everyone is lucky enough to have the life your father and I provided for you. So we have an obligation to be compassionate to those who are obviously lost."

Compassionate was one thing, but maybe Lupe needed discipline more than compassion. I took down three boxes full of Christmas decorations. Mom wanted to toss what she no longer used. I opened one box and found the little puppet elves she always propped up throughout the house.

I gazed at my mother. I've been pretty hard on her lately. Yes, she screwed up with Paul, but hell, that was before I was born. She's been an awesome mom. "You want these?" I asked.

"No," she said.

"Can I have them?"

"Sure."

In silence, I continued to empty the box. "Lupe hates me." When I got in her face in the car, she pulled out her knife again. This time, she didn't scare me. I told her to give it to me or I'd dump her in the street. I wouldn't have really dumped a thirteen-year-old in the street, but it was a good bluff. She called me about a dozen names, but handed over the knife.

My mother used a spray bottle to cool herself down, then dabbed a towel on her neck. "No, that girl doesn't hate you. She's just never had anyone care about her before, and doesn't know how to accept help."

"I'm not sure I really care."

"Then why are you doing this?"

"Because I should."

"*Mi'ja*, this girl doesn't need someone treating her like an obligation. She needs a friend, a guide."

"I'm afraid I'm not a very good role model." And I don't feel sorry for her. She's a brat. She's mean. She's dangerous, and she doesn't want my help.

My mother stopped sweeping and placed a hand on her hip. "You are an excellent role model." She pointed at me. "You are intelligent, honest, kind, loving. Marcela, no one is perfect, but you have a lot to offer others."

Aren't moms great? They never see your faults. I placed some items she no longer wanted in the trash.

"Bring her over for dinner next weekend."

Not in this lifetime. "I don't know, Mom."

"Bring her."

"Okay." But if the little monster does anything to my family, I won't be responsible for my actions. As I wiped dirt off my forehead, I crouched down beside my mom to help her untangle Christmas lights. My mother thinks the world of everyone, how could she understand a girl like Lupe? As I glanced at her, I felt the same warmth and love I had had for her as a child, and I felt guilty for all the awful feelings I'd been having toward her lately. "I've been really pissed at you."

"I know."

"You act like you don't feel bad about what you did."

"Marcela, that was so long ago. I felt bad for years. Your father reminded me daily what I owed him, and I became a virtual slave, running around doing what I could to make it up to him. But finally I decided nothing would make it up to him. I couldn't take back the past, and I couldn't continue to be reminded of it and punished anymore. Sometimes we have to forgive and go on. If he had chosen not to forgive I would have had to leave. Neither of us wanted that."

"But—"

"But nothing. I was wrong, I know, but I can't relive the guilt and pain. Not even for you."

"It's all new to me, you know?"

"I know."

"Then why do you act like I should just get over it?"

"Because it doesn't change anything."

That's where she was wrong. It changed a lot. It changed me. "Do you . . . do you have a picture of Paul?"

She sighed. "No. Are you kidding? I threw everything out." She tucked my hair behind my ear. "You're planning on finding him, aren't you?"

"Probably not."

"Do it, if you feel you have to."

I nodded.

"Oh, *Mi'ja*." She smiled lovingly at me. "My first precious baby. I'll never tell Juan this, but I can never completely regret what I did." She caressed my face. "How could I when I know that if I hadn't been with Paul, I never would have had you?"

I hugged my mother and squeezed the tears out of my shut eyes. I tried to understand what it was like for her to be married at such a young age. By the time she was my age, she had three girls already. She did better than I would have done. The woman in me completely understood and forgave her. The little girl hurt like hell.

$\mathscr{S}$eventeen

Saturday evening, August 7

✿ Daniela's Argentine club was . . . fun. And cute in a corny kind of way. I was relieved to learn that Mexicans aren't the only Latinos with fanatical patriotism. This club was a shrine to Argentina. Argentine flags everywhere, pictures and paintings of Argentine scenery and points of interest. Tango music flowing from the speakers. And dozens of Argentines speaking in rapid-fire Spanish.

Daniela laughed at my observations. "And if you ask any of these Argentines why they're living here rather than in the best, richest land in the world, they'll tell you they're going back in a few years. No one is here to stay."

I smiled. "Richest?" Argentina may be a nice place, but every nation south of the United States is miserably poor.

"As in natural resources. You know how it is, our *mamis* and *papis* see it how they wish it were. It's why I indulge them and come to these get-togethers. Come on."

We found a table to plant ourselves. Daniela's kids took off to play.

"Okay, when Enrique shows up, this is what we'll do—"

"Really, we can skip this part. I don't want to be set up with—"

"Give him a chance. He's a nice guy."

Yes, but my heart seemed to have set its sights on another nice guy who I'd kind of promised to chuck that item on my list. Even if George wasn't exactly a recent immigrant, we did share the same background, sort of. And besides, I get this weird feeling inside every time I see him. It's strange. It's never happened to me before.

"Just promise you'll be nice to him."

"Of course I'll be nice. I'm a nice person, aren't I?"

Daniela didn't answer. Probably better that way.

As the club filled up and the delicious aroma of barbequed beef filled the air, I started to relax and enjoy myself. They even had a stage and some entertainment. Not the best singers in the world, but not bad either.

Of course, Daniela didn't give up, and when Enrique arrived, she invited him to sit right beside me. And guess what? He was gorgeous—the bluest eyes you've ever seen; short, brown, curly hair; and an awesome smile with perfectly straight white teeth. Wow.

Daniela didn't have to twist my arm to talk to him. In fact, I had to remind myself not to gawk.

She elbowed me. "Didn't I tell you?"

"Okay, I owe you one," I whispered.

"*Querés bailar?*" he asked.

Sí. I *quiero* whatever he wants me to *querer*. But, I'm not a tango dancer, and I told him so.

"I will help you," he said.

So I gave it a try, and we got a good laugh at how terrible I was.

Afterward we returned to the table and finished our fabulous meal. The beef was so juicy and tender it melted in your mouth. The internal organs I could have done without, but I'm willing to try anything and it wasn't half bad. You just had to pretend you didn't know you were eating intestines, kidneys, and blood sausages. And the wine . . . well, I think I emptied a bottle all by myself.

At the end of the evening I gave Enrique my number at work, and agreed to go out on a private date. The skeptic in me needs to take a breather. This turned out pretty well, even if a little voice inside me is still saying, "He's not Mexican."

Monday, August 9

❀ Enrique called and invited me out tonight. A little soon, plus I have a cooking lesson that I don't dare cancel, so I told him I'd meet him for a drink. What the heck.

As I hung up, George walked in. "I brought your list back to you."

I took it, feeling a little embarrassed that he'd had a few days to study it. "Thanks."

"That's some list."

I laughed. "Yep."

"Kind of made me wonder though."

"Wonder what?"

He folded his arms across his chest and ran his hand along his chin as if scratching a nonexistent beard. "If there isn't more to being Latina than what you eat, the music you listen to, or the men you date."

"Of course there's more."

"Right. I mean, you could theoretically accomplish all those things and not be any more Latina than you are right now."

That couldn't be true. I sat back in my seat and crossed my

legs, studying George closely. Mr. Analytical. "How would *you* go about it?"

He lowered his arms and braced them on my desk. "I'd take all the combinations and permutations that make up a Latino, specifically a Mexican Latino since this is what you're aiming at, and combine them to come up with a stereotypical Mexican. Sort of what you've done. But the end result is exactly that, a stereotype."

He was right, of course, Daniela and I had sort of taken cliches and built our list. But we had to start with something.

"Think about it. You're an animator. How would you create a Latino for a movie?"

"Well." Funny that he asked since this is exactly what I've been thinking of doing. "If I were going to create a character for an animated movie, I would take prominent features and gestures and exaggerate those components to create a person that could represent that subculture."

He nodded.

I nodded. Was that what I'd done? I was becoming a cartoon character? I laughed.

He shrugged and stood upright. "I just think you need to be careful and think this through a little more."

"I have." And I am, every day. "I've done more than build a cartoon character. I'm trying to learn, to become more informed. Yes, maybe a couple of those points, like say the first, aren't the best, but others will help me know my people better."

"Like taking a trip to Mexico?"

"Yes."

"That's a good one." He smiled. "Actually, it's your best one."

George had a great smile, and for a second I allowed myself to get lost in that smile. "Thank you."

"Okay if I tag along?"

"You want to go to Mexico with me?"

"I do."

I smiled back, liking how those two words sounded coming from his mouth. "Really?"

He laughed. "Sure. It'll give me a chance to immerse myself in the language."

"Okay."

"Let's plan it for the next month or so."

"Great."

"I also came by to see if you'd like to go to a game with me tonight? Dodgers are home. We can start over. If you're ready for that after what we talked about the other day."

Oh, hell. I had just promised Enrique I'd go out with him. "I, I can't."

"Oh." He took a step back and nodded. "Okay, I understand."

No, he didn't. "Ah, wait. Can I have a rain check? I really would like to go with you. And I'd love to start fresh."

After a moment's consideration, he said, "If you want to play hooky from Spanish class on Thursday night, they have another game."

"I'd love to."

That earned me a grin, and that grin made my day. What is this man doing to me?

Tuesday, August 10

❀ Aunt Lydia called to tell me she's very disappointed in me for not hooking up with Mr. Full-of-Himself. I agreed to go to another one of her meetings. This seemed to satisfy her.

My cousin Pepe called to tell me I'm no longer his cousin. His mother makes him check in with her every day after school and he's not allowed out after 8:00 p.m. Which is just as well, he says, because his buddies don't want to have anything to do with him anymore after I got Spike put into jail. I felt like cheering, and telling him it was best for him not to be associated with those losers. But since he was already irate, I decided to skip my opinion.

Alberto called to give me my shopping list for next week. He usually leaves it on Mondays before he finishes his lesson so I have a whole week to get what I need, but last night he forgot. Ready for this? I can make tortillas, Mexican rice, shredded beef, beans—real beans, not the ones from cans—and I'm going to learn to make *taquitos* next week. Can't wait.

And Enrique sent a dozen red roses to thank me for last night's date. All I did was have a few drinks with him. We didn't even share a kiss. Mostly we talked about our families and our countries. Well, he talked about his. I told him I planned to visit Mexico for the first time soon.

When George stopped by my desk to see if I wanted to ride to class with him tonight, he spotted the roses. "A secret admirer?" he asked, sitting his cute butt on my desk. "I'm jealous."

I groaned, wishing foolishly that he hadn't seen those, but happy that he'd admit to being jealous. "I hope not. I did my friend Daniela a favor by being nice to this guy and . . ." I laughed. "You don't want to hear this."

"Well you must have accomplished your nice mission to deserve such a grand gesture." He reached across and pulled a rose out of the vase.

"I think he's the grand gesture kind of guy."

"Maybe you earned them."

I gasped and my eyebrows hiked up of their own accord. If Jackson had said that, I would have laughed it off, but with George, I realized I was flushing. "I did not, you pig," I said, trying to act as I would have with any other man from my office.

He laughed. "I didn't mean it like that." He stood. "I'm going to take this foot out of my mouth and go back downstairs. We riding together?"

Though I was having fun driving the rented Mustang while

my car was in the shop, I still would rather ride with George than drive by myself so I said, "Absolutely."

With the red rose in his hand he swept the soft rose petals along the side of my face, caressing me as if he were using his fingertips instead of the flower. "Well, then I'll *absolutely* wait for you downstairs." He dropped the rose on my lap.

❀ After class, I invited him to dinner.

"I'm tired," he said, starting his car.

"You're not mad at me again, are you?"

He frowned. "About what?"

"Because I went out with Daniela's friend. It wasn't really a date. She asked me to—"

"Marcela, you can go out with whomever you want."

"I know but—"

He reached across and put a fingertip to my lips. "I'm really just tired."

I stopped him from putting the car into drive. "Ask me not to see any other guys and I won't."

"Why would I do that?"

"Because . . . you want me for yourself."

He grinned and leaned closer to me. "Whether I do or not isn't the issue. If you want to stop seeing other men, you will. I shouldn't have to ask you to stop. You don't really want me to tell you what to do, do you?"

"You're right." Again, he struck me as so different from most guys I hooked up with who would most definitely have told me what to do, right after they pouted and pulled a bunch of possessive shit. Did that used to make me feel wanted? I could call a radio psychologist and ask her to tell me why I gravitated toward those type of men. She'd probably tell me it was because of my dad. And maybe she'd be right.

I lost my train of thought then because George kissed my lips, lingering only slightly, then gently eased my hand away and put the car in gear.

"George?"

"Hmm?"

"I won't see any other men."

He maneuvered onto the freeway and rested his wrist on top of the steering wheel.

"Because I'd like us to date and see if whatever is going on between us is something or not."

He drove without comment and I couldn't guess what he was thinking.

"Okay?"

"Hmm."

Was he ignoring me? Didn't he get it that I don't deal well with being ignored? I sighed and leaned my head back on the headrest. "I think I've figured out what I want. I'm ready to try this serious relationship thing."

He continued to drive in silence.

"Do you have anything to say?"

He reached across and caressed my face with the back of his fingers. "Are you going to call your birth father?"

"What?" Where did that come from?

"I think you should. I think you've got some questions about him, and it's going to bug you until you get them answered."

What the hell business was it of his? "What does that have to do with me and you?"

"I'm your friend, right? Giving you my opinion as a friend."

"I don't want your damned opinion and I don't want to be your stupid friend. Weren't you listening to me?"

"Yes, I was. I heard everything you said." Then after a few moments of silence, he turned on the radio.

When we pulled into the Panoply parking lot, he parked beside my car. Then he reached across and lifted my chin. I gazed at him.

"You haven't figured out what you want. It takes longer than just a couple of weeks."

"Okay, I don't know. At least not yet. But I think I want you."

He smiled. "Oh you do, huh?"

"Yes."

"You're ready to try a serious relationship now, even though it's not your thing?"

"Yes."

"And you don't see the obvious problem with that any longer?"

"What problem?"

"I don't go for this whole Mexican American thing. My family has lived in the Southwest since the time it was still part of Mexico. After the war, they simply became Americans. They didn't care as long as their lives weren't affected and they got to keep their land. I guess I'm pretty much the same. I'm too far removed from Mexico to really care that my ancestors once came from there. So, you see, I'm not the long-term guy you're looking for."

As I stared at him, he looked exactly like what I didn't know I was looking for. "But finding a Mexican man had to do with my family. I've never really cared about that. I hoped it would make me more of what they respect. But it's not me. What I really want is someone like you. Someone who speaks English, and is not a gang member, and doesn't really care about ethnic politics, and loves animation."

"I hate animation."

"You do?" I tried not to look horrified.

He laughed. "Still like me?"

"Well . . ." I eased forward in my seat. "No one's perfect, I guess."

"I've got to go," he said, still smiling. "I'm really beat."

"Baseball game on Thursday?"

"Yep."

"George?" I reached across and ran my fingers through his hair, right above his ear. I wanted him to kiss me again. I wanted him to tell me that he wanted me. Okay, I admit it, I wanted him to jump me.

"Marcela," he warned in a low rumble. "Stop tempting me."

"Listen, George. I . . . I want to call Paul, you know, the guy who donated the sperm to make me. And I was kind of wondering if maybe . . . you might . . . you know, be there with me when I do." Out of all the things I wanted to say to him, this seemed the safest.

His expression softened and the glazed look in his eyes disappeared. "You name the date and time, and I'll be there."

"Thanks." That meant more to me than he could ever know. I'm not afraid to call Paul or anything, but if the guy hangs up on me, it might be nice to have someone there to tell me I wasn't a total fool to call.

He nodded. "Marcela?"

"What?"

"Are you sure you won't get bored with a guy like me?"

"You're not boring." I leaned closer to him. "Not to me."

He looked unsure, which surprised me because he was always the one who was in control, mature. This tiny unveiling of his insecurity was so endearing I wanted to pull him close and hold him.

"You're so creative and lead a pretty intense life. You've got parties, take all sorts of exciting trips, have a million friends. . . . I'm, what do your friends call me, a number cruncher?"

"George, when you walked away from me that night in my apartment and told me I deserved a better guy . . . no man has ever done that to me before. I was hurt and angry with you, and then I realized you were right. I do deserve a better guy. And you *are* a better guy. You're not boring. You're kind and respectful and . . ." I stared at him. "You make me feel . . ." Maybe that said it all.

"Okay," he said, apparently satisfied. "Maybe I can try to loosen up a bit, and you can try on this 'serious stuff' for a while and see how you like it."

I pulled him close into to a sharp hug and as I held him and he held me, I was a little scared. This was new territory for me. Opening up, letting someone in. I'd have to take it slowly.

I pulled away from him. "Okay, okay. I'm leaving, before I start blubbering all over you."

I heard him chuckle as I scooted out of his car. "Good-night," he called after me.

That night as I drifted off to sleep, I wondered why I wanted George so badly. Was it because he saw me just a little better than I even saw myself, and didn't let me get away with any crap? Maybe. And maybe it was because with George, I didn't feel like a girl. He treated me with respect and dignity and for the first time ever, I felt like a woman.

Eighteen

Wednesday, August 11

❀ Some weeks it feels like every project you've ever had gets piled onto your desk at the same time. Projects that need to be edited. Projects that need new scenes. Sketches that somehow no longer fit someone's new vision of the movie. Add to that an interview I need to give for the DVD version of *Firebird,* meetings for new storyboard brainstorming, and a boss who is currently yelling at me over the phone, and you have an accurate picture of how my day is going.

As I sat behind my desk and swatted the only bit of hair not being held up by the four butterfly clasps on my head, I was horrified to see Enrique, the Argentine god, walk into my office.

"Hi," he said.

"I'll get back to you," I said to my boss as he continued to yell while being hung up on. "Enrique. Hi." *What the hell are you doing here?*

He had flowers in his arms and extended them out to me.

"Ah, thank you. How did you get in here?" Past the guards who are supposed to announce guests and keep ordinary looky-loos away.

"You mean on the lot? Well, I told them I was your fiancé. Actually, that I was here to surprise you with my proposal."

I dropped his flowers on my desk. He wanted to marry me? He must be kidding. "You lied to get in. Well, that was creative." Let's pretend here. Maybe I heard wrong.

"No, I didn't lie. Marcela, I want to marry you."

"But, but I barely know you."

"I know, but—"

Footsteps behind Enrique interrupted him. "Marcela, I . . . oh, excuse me. You're busy," George said, eyeing Enrique as he strolled into the art department.

"No, I'm not. Enrique was just leaving."

"Enrique?"

"Her fiancé," Enrique clarified.

George's eyes didn't exactly pop out of their sockets, but they came pretty close.

I kind of laughed in a very nervous, hysterical way. "Ah, no, no, no."

"I came to ask her to marry me."

"You're going to pop the question now?" George asked, still looking shell-shocked.

Enrique frowned, apparently trying to understand that figure of speech, and I used his moment of confusion to come around my desk. "No, he's not."

"Yes, I am. Marcela, listen to me for a moment."

"I'll leave you two to do this in private."

Enrique took my hand and dropped down to his knee.

I shook my head like a crazy woman with my mouth open yet unable to speak. George was abandoning me and Enrique had lost his mind. "Excuse me," I said finally and shook my hand free. "George, come back here."

He shook his head and continued to walk away. "Send me an invitation to the big event."

"You spineless wimp. Come back here and fight for me."

He laughed and waved a hand as he disappeared out the door.

Damn him. I turned toward Enrique, really angry now. "Get up," I snapped.

"I didn't expect to do it like this."

"Look, Enrique, I'm not going to marry you. I don't even know you."

Before he could reply, Jackson walked in. "Hey what's this about you getting married?"

I dropped onto my chair and looked up to heaven to see if I could get some help here.

"George said some guy was in here proposing." He frowned at Enrique. "You don't have time to get married. We're waiting for you in the storyboard room."

I counted to ten, trying not to blow up. I even smiled as sweetly as I could. "Jackson, give me five minutes, okay?"

"Five. Then I want your butt in the meeting. You're holding us up and I have other things to do."

I turned to Enrique. "Enrique. I don't know what this is all about, but—"

"I shouldn't have done this where you work."

"Probably not. But it isn't just that. Why would you want to marry me when we've only gone out on one date?"

He looked uncomfortable. "For immigration purposes."

Great. Just what I need—to be someone's ticket to America. "No."

"Please. I will be a good husband, and—"

"I'm sure you would be, but—"

"I need your help. If you just think about it for—"

"Enrique. Slow down. I can't put my life on hold for you and commit a felony, by the way. I'm sorry."

He looked disappointed, and I felt bad for him. Just like I felt bad for all immigrants looking for a better life. It always seemed unfair to me that through the luck of birth one person was born in a place with all the opportunities in the world, and another where he had to fight for survival.

"You're a nice guy, Enrique. I'm really sorry."

He smiled sadly and with that he was gone.

That was it. The last straw. No more dating Latinos. I'm officially crossing that number off my list.

Ignoring all the work on my desk, I went to my meeting.

❀ "Okay, I'm ready to go to the game," I said as I walked into George's office that evening.

"Game?"

"Are you playing dumb?" I was in no mood after the day I'd had.

"No." He shook his head. "I figured that was cancelled, considering you're getting married."

"I can't believe you left me alone with that guy."

"That guy? You mean your fiancé?"

"You know what, George? Go to hell."

I heard a deep laugh as I turned my back on him. Deep and male and sexy, and something I wanted to hear more of, I realized. Then George must have literally jumped over his desk, because he was by my side reaching for me before I could take one step away. "Hold on there, you little firecracker."

I glared at him, mostly for effect.

"You can't blame me for being a little upset. After all, I'm supposed be the only sucker dating you from now on, and suddenly you've got a fiancé."

He deserved to have that smirk slapped right off his face, didn't he? "Think you're funny, huh?"

He shrugged. "So what was that all about?" he asked, sounding a little more serious and nudging me toward his desk.

"He . . . " I didn't want to go into the whole Enrique story, so I decided not to. "I got rid of him."

"Because you'd rather have me?"

"Yes, you egotistical jerk."

Again I was treated to that rich male laughter, and I decided I liked this new George who had decided to loosen up.

"So there will be no more fiancés in your office, or ex-boyfriends threatening to kill me in my office from now on, correct?"

"Yes," I repeated through clenched teeth.

"Good." He walked behind his desk and opened one of his drawers where he pulled out a gift wrapped box. "I got you this."

He bought me a gift? I met his sexy whiskey-colored eyes. "A present?"

"Not a big deal. Open it."

I did, and inside I found a Dodger cap. I smiled.

"Ah, sorry it's not diamonds or a box of chocolates, but I thought if you're going to hang out with me, you need your own cap. Do you like it?"

I leaned across his desk. "I like it."

He glanced around the room, probably worried someone would see us.

"And I like you," I told him.

He leaned forward and gave me a quick peck on the lips. "I like you too, and I want to take you home with me."

I could do nothing but arch an eyebrow.

He chuckled. "I need to stop by my place and change before the game," he explained.

"Fine. I can't wait to see . . . your place."

❀ The second the door closed behind us in his house, George pulled me into his arms. He kissed me. Very, very nice. I started to feel light-headed and flushed, and as his hands roamed my body I thought about how I wanted this to work. I hadn't had a real relationship with a guy since high school. I wanted a boyfriend, someone who actually cared about me.

I caressed the side of his face and pulled back. If this was truly going to be different, then everything had to be different, which meant I would absolutely *not* have casual sex with him. We had to build our relationship first. "So," I said, "nice house."

"Want to walk down to my bedroom?"

"Why, George, you sure do know how to proposition a woman," I joked with him.

He took my hand and led me to his bedroom. "I need to get out of this suit, and we'll be on our way."

I wasn't sure where to look as he began to strip.

"Am I making you nervous?"

"No."

In nothing but his long briefs—you know, the type that hug a man's butt and crotch, but extend down his thighs like shorts— he walked over to me. "Liar." He hooked a hand behind my head and planted a soft kiss on the side of my neck.

I shuddered, and wrapped my arms around his waist. Darn it, this no sex thing was going to be hard.

But he didn't make any moves that might suggest sex was on his mind. He only held me.

"You're really beautiful, Marcela. Do you know that?" he whispered.

I eased back and swallowed the lump in my throat. "You're not so bad yourself."

"I mean it. You're gorgeous. I can't blame those guys for wanting you."

No one really wanted me. Not Jackson, and not Enrique, not the other jerks I've dated lately. They didn't want *me*. They wanted something *from* me. Only George seemed to want the real me. "Are you trying to sweet-talk me into bed, stud?"

He chuckled. "Oh, yeah, I forgot you can't be serious."

I slipped out of his arms. Maybe I couldn't be serious. Old habits die hard. "I seriously need a Dodger dog, so get dressed. I'm starved."

He pulled a pair of jeans out of his closet and jumped into them. "Hey, Marcela?"

"What?"

"Are you okay?"

"Of course." Actually, I was a little shaken anytime I was in his presence, but even more so to see him in his underwear.

He slipped on some socks and shoes. "Good, because this relationship stuff isn't anything to worry about. Just open up a little and trust me." He tossed a shirt over his head, grabbed a baseball cap, and winked. "Ready?"

I trust him. It's the opening up part I don't really know how to do. "Sure," I muttered, and as if walking on clouds, followed him out of his bedroom.

$\mathcal{N}$ineteen

Saturday, August 14

🌸 Today, behind the wheel of my car, I was one of those annoying, angry drivers that cuts everyone off and always thinks she has the right of way. This because Lupe sat beside me in the passenger's seat and we were on the way to my parents' house.

"One false move and we're through."

"You promise?" Lupe asked.

"I mean it. If you get out of line or open that garbage mouth and disrespect my parents just once—"

"Chill. I'll be nice to your precious *mami* and *papi*. You're such a whipped baby. I swear."

I continued to drive, glaring at the road in front of me. "I care about my family."

"Yeah, well I care about mine too."

"If you cared about your family you'd study and try to make something of yourself. The only way you're going to help them is by succeeding."

"Oh, hell, here we go again."

"Damn right, until you get it through your thick skull."

"Shit." She shook her head. "Why did I agree to spend any time with you? I should have just gone to juvie."

I glanced at her. "You don't mean that."

"Yeah, I do."

She'd rather go to jail than spend time with me? "Why do you hate me so much?" I pulled up to the curb of my parents' house.

"I don't."

"Yes, you do. Why?"

She wouldn't answer.

"I want to help you. I really do."

"You can't."

"Why?"

She huffed, then turned to face me. "You don't know how it is on the street. I have to learn to survive, and you can't teach me that."

"But school—"

"Is a joke. They don't teach me shit of what I need to know. You wanna help me? Buy me some chrome." She jumped out of my car.

"Chrome?" I asked over the hood of my car.

She stuck out her index finger and thumb and pointed at me. "Yeah, *un quette*, a strap. You know, a gun? So I can live."

I stared at her for a moment, feeling miserable. Maybe she was right. I was deluding myself. How could I even hope to understand the kind of life Lupe and her family led?

Feeling way less confident after each meeting with Lupe, I trudged to my parents' house.

My mother welcomed Lupe as if she were a long lost niece. She got her some *agua de zandia* and placed a plate of Mexican bread in front of her. Was she trying to make her feel at home? When was the last time Mom had bought Mexican bread or made watermelon juice?

"Mom, back off. She probably eats this stuff all the time," I said.

"You back off," Lupe said. "I love these *panes*."

"See?" my mom said.

"Fine." I walked out to the backyard patio. Excuse me for living. I sat on a lawn chair and held my head.

"Rough week?" My dad's voice came from behind a bush.

I looked at the bush. "What are you doing in there?"

"Looking for a nest. Darn birds wake me up every morning." The bush was right outside his bedroom window. He backed out of it and shook dead branches and spiderwebs from his hair.

"Find it?"

"Nope." He sat beside me. "*Como estas, Hija?*"

"I'm okay."

"Haven't seen much of you lately."

"I've been working a lot." And I feel guilty for wanting to look up Paul.

"Do you know Katie is dating a man eleven years older than her?"

I'd heard more than I wanted to hear, but it surprised me that he'd heard. "It's nothing serious, *Papi*."

He grumbled. "Eleven years. *Viejo, pendejo.*"

I tried to hide my smile. My father was essentially calling this guy a stupid old prick, though the literal meaning of *pendejo* is strand of pubic hair. Hmm, what an image.

"A man his age has no business going out with a young girl like Katie." He sat beside me.

"Daaad, he's not old. Jeez, he's in his eartly thirties."

"You talk to her, and tell her to find someone her own age."

"Guys her age are jerks. They're immature. All they want is sex."

"Don't say that word around me. *Ahii.*" He shook his head. "Girls. Why couldn't I have had boys?"

I rolled my eyes.

"And what about you?"

"What about me?" My family didn't know about George. For now he was going to remain just mine.

"Dating Pepe's friends. Little boys." He sounded disgusted.

"Who tells you these things?"

"I hear." He pointed to his ear. "You girls think I don't, but I do."

"Well, that date was a mistake."

"Find a man who will take care of you. One who will love you. Stop playing with boys. You work with boys, you date boys, you . . . need to grow up."

"I'm happy on my own, *Papi*." I'm happy with George too, but that will probably be over once he gets to really know me. He's almost too good to be true, and I find myself thinking about him way too much.

He placed his big hand on my neck. *"Mirame."*

I looked at him.

"I don't care if you ever get married. That's your mother's thing. If you're happy, I'm happy for you."

"I am."

"Then why go out with Pepe's friends?"

"Just a crazy idea I had. He seemed cool, talking about Aztec gods and stuff."

"Aztec gods?"

"Forget it." I stood.

"Marcela, don't let your aunt fill your head with crazy stuff."

"I won't."

"I've always been proud of you just the way you are."

"I know." I went back inside to get away from him. Another result of my mother's affair was that I now felt uncomfortable around my dad. I know he wanted to talk about it, and I couldn't, so it was easier to avoid him. In the kitchen, I found my mother and Lupe huddled over the kitchen table with my childhood photo albums. Great.

"Mom, could we help you make lunch?"

"You? Help me cook? Are you kidding?"

With that attitude, no wonder I never learned how. "I'm taking cooking lessons, you know?"

"This here was when she learned how to ride her bike. She cried for two hours over that skinned knee," my mother shared with Lupe.

Lupe gazed at me with a smirk. "I could see her doing that."

I pretended to glare at her.

Lupe stood. "I'll help with lunch. I can cook, and I don't need a chef to learn how."

"Isn't that sweet?" my mother said. "But no, Lupe, go out with Marcela and have some fun. You're not here to work."

"Funny, that's all Marcela wants me to do."

Because she was supposed to be paying off the paint job on my car. Did she forget that? She made me sound like a slave driver. "Not today," I said. "Mom's right."

"So we're going to have fun?" she mocked me and my mom.

"Sure," I said, wanting to wring her neck. "Come on, let's go up to my room." I still had sketch pads on easels, and games and paint programs installed on my old computer.

She reclined on my bed as I turned on the computer.

"You're such a nerd," she said. "Your idea of fun is working on a computer all the time. How sad."

I looked over my shoulder at her. "You want to do something else?" Sometimes I do get overly focused on my work, and I think everyone will find it as fascinating as I do.

She pulled something out of her backpack-looking purse. "How about we smoke one of these?"

"A joint?" I tried not to panic though I looked out the window to make sure my dad or a cop wasn't out there peeking in.

Lupe grinned. "So, you do know what it is?" She took out a lighter.

"Of course I know what it is. Put it away."

"Ever smoke one?"

"No." I know, I'm the only one in America who's never gotten high. So maybe I am a nerd, but so what?

She lit the thing.

"I said put it away."

But it was too late. She'd already lit it and was sucking on it, inhaling carcinogens and toxins.

"Mmm," she moaned.

"Lupe," I said, feeling sad for her. "You're only thirteen."

"So?"

"Give me that."

"Gonna join me?"

"I'm going to flush it."

"Then hell, no, I'm not giving it to you."

I sprang from my seat and yanked the offending cigarette out of her hand. "Damn it, you don't know when to back down, do you? I said no and I mean no."

She looked startled for a fraction of a second before she frowned and put the tough kid mask back on. "I don't have to listen to you."

"You do when you're in my home or my parents' home. I've put up with a lot of crap from you, but I *will not* put up with disrespect anymore."

She lifted her chin in defiance. "Fine."

"Now if you have more of these give them to me." I held the joint up, trying to keep the ashes from falling on the carpet.

Her mouth opened wide. "No way."

"Fine. Grab your backpack and I'll take you home. We're finished."

"Shit. Why? This isn't fair."

She looked young and innocent and I knew that if I didn't stick to my guns this time, she'd never learn to respect me. "Life isn't fair, you should know that."

"I hate you," she said.

I tried to hide the fact that her hatred bothered me. I was trying to save her life and the kid couldn't stand me.

My bedroom door opened and I immediately hid the joint behind my back. Katie frowned and stared at me.

"Hi," I said.

"Getting high in mom's house?"

"No," I said, feeling guilty for no good reason. I pushed past her and went to the bathroom where I flushed the joint.

Katie eyed me suspiciously when I returned.

"Look, get that look off your face, and stop dating older men."

"What? You said it was a good idea."

"Yeah, well, Dad gave me hell for not advising you correctly."

"I'm not dumping Gilbert."

"Dump him." I opened a window to air out my room and gazed at Lupe. "Are you going to give me the rest of them or are we leaving?"

"You mean you'll leave me at home and you'll never pick me up again. I won't have to see you anymore. That's your threat?"

This was a risk, but I had to take it. "That's right." She was either going to play my way or I'd have to give up on her. I hoped she cared enough about herself to make the right choice.

"I don't want to dump him," Katie whined behind me as Lupe and I stared each other down.

Lupe frowned. Then reached into her backpack and pulled out a little sandwich baggie with about five joints and handed it to me.

"Thank you," I said.

"I'm only doing it 'cause I like your mom. She's cool."

Right, save face kid. "Yes, she is."

I turned to Katie. "You know what you have to do."

"But you haven't even met him. He's really great."

"And I'm not going to."

She narrowed her eyes. "You know, you really suck." Then she left my room.

Great, someone else who hates me. It's absolutely no fun to be mature and responsible.

I turned on my computer for Lupe. "Ready?"

"I guess. There's nothing else to do."

I explained a world-building simulation game and she got to playing. I know she enjoys computers. She doesn't have one at home. And even if she doesn't want to admit it, she's good at educational, creative games. The kid has a brain.

Lupe played on my computer and I took a nap until lunch time. I dreamed of seducing George.

Twenty

❀George is coming over for dinner. I'm cooking for him. Then I'm going to call Paul. Big night.

My chef taught me how to make shredded beef tacos. They were tasty and not so difficult to prepare. You grab a huge chunk of beef brisket and toss it in an ovenproof pot. Then you sprinkle onions, garlic, salt, pepper, chili powder, and tomato sauce on the meat and let it sit in the oven for like three hours. When you pull it out, the beef is so tender that it falls apart.

So, I'm making quesadillas as an appetizer and shredded beef tacos with rice as the main course. I'm very excited. I never thought I'd be able to prepare a meal for someone. Okay, it's not a seven-course meal, but it's a start.

I took a shower and used extra care getting dressed, misting myself with perfume, rubbing lotion on my skin, choosing a soft feminine silk top and a short skirt. I wanted to knock George's socks off. I've been such a flake with him that I want to show him that I can be a normal girl too.

As I was finishing, the doorbell rang. The clock on my wall said George was an hour early. Did I give him the wrong time? I opened the door, grateful that at least I was dressed, but found myself staring at Lupe.

"Ah, what are you doing here?"

"I need to spend the night." She pushed inside my apartment. "Why do you stink?"

"Lupe." I tried to be patient. "You're not spending the night. And how in the world did you get to my place. We're miles from—"

"I hitchhiked. How do you think I got here?"

Say what? "Hitchhiked?! In Los Angeles? Please tell me you're kidding."

"I'm not kidding. Look, my brother is fucked up again, to-tally high and his friends are there. Last time I was alone with them . . . I just need to stay one night. By morning everything will be fine."

I stared at her. Why did this girl always have stories and prob-lems so far-fetched, I felt I was on an episode of *Cops*? "I've got plans tonight. You can't just drop by whenever you want."

Lupe gave me a disgusted look. "Fine." She headed to my front door.

"Wait." I grabbed my purse. I had no choice, I'd have to give her a ride back home.

She glared at me. "Wait for what?"

"I'll take you home."

"Like hell you will."

"Let's go." I placed a note on the door for George to come in and make himself at home. I left my key with my neighbor. With any luck, I'd make it back within an hour.

We climbed into my car and after we were both buckled in, I

peeled out of my parking space. "I'm getting sick and tired of your crap," I said.

She pouted and looked extremely young at the moment.

"You're going to end up behind bars or dead one day, if you don't shape up."

"Shut the fuck up."

"Don't tell me to shut—"

"Keep your eyes on the road."

I hit the brakes before slamming into a white refrigeration truck. The freeway was at a dead stop. Great. "Hitchhiking is dangerous and stupid."

"Like you care. You said you cared, but you lied. You're just like everyone else."

I pushed hair out of my face and counted to ten. She was impossible. We didn't speak again until we pulled up to her home.

"I'm not staying here."

"Yes you are. Let's go talk to your brother."

"Marcela, trust me. You don't want to talk to him. Just go home to your perfect life and leave me alone."

I headed to her house. Lupe sighed and followed me.

I knocked but the rap music was so loud, probably no one heard me.

"Here, get out of the way." Lupe walked in. "I'm inside, now go."

A guy dressed in low slung jeans and a tank-tee peered around the corner. "Where the fuck did you go?" he asked Lupe.

"She came to see me."

His bleary eyes focused on me, or at least tried to. He rubbed his eyes and nose. The guy looked like he hadn't bathed since last Christmas. He also looked unsteady. But with a smile, he asked, "What did you do? Bring me a present, Lupe?"

"No, she's leaving. Go on. Get out of here," Lupe yelled, and tried to close the door in my face.

Her brother stumbled forward and completely unexpectedly slapped Lupe across the face.

"Hey," I yelled, and pushed my way inside.

"You no good little cunt." He shoved her against the wall so hard that she bounced off it.

Lupe pulled out her switchblade knife, but her brother hit it out of her hand and sent it flying across the floor. Then he slammed her against the wall again, this time squeezing his hand around Lupe's neck and lifting her off the ground. She gagged, trying to pry his grip loose.

Oh my God. What was he doing? "Let her go!" I pulled on his arm with all my strength, but couldn't get him to let go. Lupe's face turned red.

"She can't breathe," I shouted.

He didn't seem to hear me or maybe he didn't care. As if captivated, he watched Lupe's eyes bulge and smiled at her frantic fight to gasp for air.

Fear unlike any I've ever felt pierced my heart and permeated every cell in my body. I pounded his upper arm to try to make him release her. Didn't work. Then I kicked his leg as hard as I could, but nothing seemed to faze him. Oh God, please help me.

Finally he let her go of his own free will, tossing her on the floor like a rag doll. Then he turned to me.

"Oh, shit" is a little mild, but oh, shit. I swallowed. "Lupe, go get back in the car," I said as calmly as possible.

She coughed and crawled across the floor.

He turned around and kicked her in the ribs, as if she were nothing but a stray dog.

"You asshole," I said, and shoved him with all my strength. What kind of animal inflicts that kind of pain on a little girl—on his own sister?

He grabbed me, tearing my elegant silk top. I screamed and squirmed away from him. Desperately, I ran to the front door. Before I could yank it open, it flew open on its own, and I ran straight into the chest of a police officer. He wrapped an arm around me, turned me around, and snapped handcuffs on my wrists.

About a dozen other cops charged the house, rounding up everyone—about five guys I hadn't even known were in the house.

I knew better than to fight this time around. I looked for Lupe. "It will be okay," I said.

She closed her eyes; the corner of her lips were stained with blood. When one of the officers approached her, she looked at him like a frightened, cornered animal and swung her arm at him.

He cried out and placed a hand to his face. Blood oozed out. Somehow, she'd gotten ahold of the knife again and slashed the officer's face.

Oh, no. "Officer?" I said to the one holding me.

"Shut up," he said, and led me to his car.

"She's scared. Her brother just beat her up."

"Neighbors said you all have been partying for hours and threatened them bodily if they complained about the music again."

"Lupe and I just got here. I had no idea."

"That's obvious, *hermana*," he said, speaking the Spanish word for sister with a heavy gringo accent. He shoved me into the backseat of his car, and his eyes raked over me like I was worth nothing. His eyes accused me of things his badge probably prevented him from verbalizing. Was I just another dirty Mexican to him? Was he cleaning the streets? Getting rid of the Spanish trash?

Lupe was tossed in after me.

"You okay?"

She favored her left side where she'd been kicked. "You couldn't listen to me, could you? I told you not to go in there."

"You were right," I admitted. "I hoped I could persuade your brother to keep better tabs on you."

"Oh, he keeps tabs on me all right."

I glanced at her. "What does that mean?"

"Nothing."

"Lupe. Does he hit you all the time?"

She frowned and looked down at her lap.

"Do your parents know?"

"They can't control him. Look, forget it. It doesn't matter."

Of course it mattered. No one should be subjected to such brutality on an ongoing basis. "We need to do something."

She laughed harshly. "Oh? What do you want to do, Ms. Fix-it?"

"Talk to your parents. Get your brother out of the house."

"Sure, that will help." Sarcasm.

"We'll get a restraining order and keep him out."

"Look, don't get involved. You want to end up raped or something?"

"Raped?" I searched her face. "Has he . . . ?"

"I'm used to it. It's just his friends that . . ." Tears rolled down her face.

My mouth opened as I tried to get words out, but my voice had disappeared. I wanted to kill that bastard. I wanted to pull Lupe against me and hold her, but with my wrists in cuffs, I couldn't. "Lupe."

She angrily tried to wipe her tears on her shoulders.

"You're not lying to me, are you? Because this is serious."

"Why would I lie?" Moist eyes flashed at me.

"I don't know. You haven't been the most honest person in the world to me."

"I've been totally honest."

Yes she had. She'd never lied. She'd been up-front about everything she'd done and wanted to do. "I'm sorry," I said.

"About what?"

"I'm sorry you've been handed such shitty cards in life."

She snorted and shook her head, staring out the window.

"Look, forget the whole thing about paying me back for my car. I really want to help you, Lupe."

"Oh, now you suddenly care?"

I scooted closer. "Yes. I care. Look at me."

She glanced at me, then turned to the window again.

"I'm sorry. I haven't really understood. I haven't gotten you. But I'm starting to. Just give me a break. Give me a chance."

Lupe shrugged. "What have I got to lose?"

Nothing. Sadly, nothing.

Twenty-One

When I walked into my apartment, a cloud of smoke greeted me. "What the . . . ?" George was asleep on my futon. Leaving the front door wide open, I ran through my living room into my kitchen where my shredded beef was burned to a crisp. I dropped the roasting pan in the sink and ran the cold water, then between coughs and gasps opened my window.

The noise must have awoken sleeping beauty, because he stumbled into the kitchen. "What's going on?" He looked around the apartment, sudden alarm bringing creases to his forehead.

"Our dinner is ruined, damn it." I waved a grocery bag in the air, trying to direct the smoke out the window.

He rubbed his eyes, probably more from smoke irritation that from sleepiness. "Don't you have a smoke detector? I could have been killed."

I placed a hand on my hip. "Yes, I have a smoke detector, but the battery was low, and the darn thing was beeping, so I took the battery out."

"I guess replacing the battery didn't occur to you?" He walked over to the sink and turned the water off. "It smelled really good in here when I walked in. I thought maybe you went out for beer or something." He lifted the roasting pan out of the sink and looked inside, wrinkling his nose.

"I wish." I took the roasting pan out of his hands and tossed the whole thing in the trash—pan, meat and all. I turned to face him, totally worn out. "I'm sorry."

He opened the fridge and took out a flour tortilla. He heated it on the flames of my stove, then rolled it up and took a bite as he gazed at me. "What happened to your shirt?"

Oh yeah, my torn blouse. That was the least of my problems. Officer Martinez had not been happy to see me again, and he'd laid into me pretty heavily. He didn't believe that I had nothing to do with the drugs in Lupe's apartment. Too much of a coincidence, he said, that I should be picked up again for being in the presence of a drug dealer. I was fingerprinted and charged. He didn't hold me because his cells were full, and I wasn't dangerous or likely to disappear. Otherwise, I probably would have spent the night behind bars until Aunt Lydia could spring me. But Lupe was a different story. With her history, he had no option but to detain her.

"Well, is there an explanation?"

I tried to think of how to explain tonight to George. Where to start? But something strange came over me and I could no longer hold it together. I walked into his arms and started to cry.

"Marcela," he said, his voice full of concern. He caressed my back. "Shh, it's okay." He held me and kissed the top of my head, and I felt safe and secure for the first time all night.

"You probably hate me," I cried.

"I don't hate you."

"I burned your dinner."

"It's okay."

"Lupe. She came by. And I tried to help her, but—" My own sobs interrupted my incoherent explanation.

"Your mentee?"

"She tried to tell me she was in trouble. But I wouldn't listen. I'm so damned arrogant. He beat her up, and he tore my shirt, and the police came and saved us, but now I've got to go to court, and—"

"Whoa, wait a minute." He pulled me away from his chest. "Who tore your shirt?"

I saw male protectiveness in his eyes. We didn't want to go there. I wiped my eyes. "Lupe's brother. He abuses her. Physically and sexually. George, she's living a colossal nightmare. No wonder she's so messed up. And now I'm afraid she's headed to Juvie. What am I going to do?"

Concern written all over his face, he nodded and led me to my futon. "First of all, you're going to calm down. You're going to eat something and get a good night's sleep. Then we're going to talk about this tomorrow when your brain is a little clearer."

"I'm not hungry." The rest of it sounded good.

I collapsed on the futon. He closed my front door, then sat beside me and brushed my hair back. I could see the worry on his face. Poor guy probably didn't know what to make of me anymore. His fingers ran down my silk blouse. The weight of his hands on my body felt amazing. "You look beautiful," he said.

I laughed, because though I might have started out the night ready to knock his socks off, I knew right now I was a mess. "I wanted to look really good for you."

He bent forward and kissed me softly on the lips. "You do," he whispered. "You're the most beautiful woman I've ever met."

"Thanks, George." I rested my head on his shoulder and closed my eyes, feeling much better.

"You're welcome," he said, sounding far away.

When I awoke some time in the middle of the night, George was gone. I climbed into my bed wishing he'd stayed.

Thursday, August 19

✿ Number four on my list of becoming a real Latina involved the church. The only progress I'd made on that front was to use my checkbook more often and in larger amounts. After the four gospels, I gave up on trying to understand the Bible on my own. But when I walked into our family church on this midmorning weekday, it wasn't to satisfy my list. I stood surrounded by empty pews. Rays of sunlight passed through stained glass windows, creating warm, inviting colors, and a feeling of peace. I stared up at Jesus on the cross and became overwhelmed by emotions so strong that I sank down to my knees and started crying. Loud sobs spilled out of me, and they seemed amplified as they echoed in the large church. My shoulders and my back shuddered with the overpowering release that came from somewhere deep inside.

Once I had drained my tear ducts and cried for everyone from Jesus to Mom and Dad to Lupe, I picked myself up and went to see Padre Rodriguez. I don't know why it was he, of all people, I needed to talk to. Maybe it was because he was an outsider. He didn't want me to join any organizations or to understand and accept the past or to spare his feelings.

I spilled my guts about Lupe. "I'm scared. I don't know what to do. It's so hopeless."

He sat across from me in a section of his office where he had two comfortable, stuffed leather chairs. "Nothing is impossible if you believe, my child."

I hate when religious types say things like that. Maybe I lack faith, but us mere mortals on Earth need more than flighty spiritual sayings. "Padre, believe in what?"

"In yourself. In knowing that there exists an open door or window. In God who will lead you to that opening."

I sighed in frustration, needing something practical. "They're probably going to lock her up, which is bad enough, but when she's released from Juvie, I can't allow her to stay in that home with her brother."

He leaned forward and clasped his hands together. "I believe our state has government offices that can deal with issues such as Lupe's. You have a choice to use these services."

Social services? What, call and report her family to child protective services? So Lupe can be taken and put into a foster home with more adults who don't care about her? That didn't strike me as a good choice, though if I couldn't think of another, it would be better than where she was at now.

"Trust yourself. God will show you what to do. After all, he has led you to this crossroad."

I looked into Padre Rodriguez's kind black eyes. Had I been led to Lupe? In the last couple of months my life seemed to have become total chaos. Thinking back to the day of Amelia's bridal shower, I hazily recalled my prayer to God. I groaned. "Oh, why did I complain? I had had it so good."

"I beg your pardon?" Padre Rodriguez asked.

I shook my head. "Nothing." I stood and kissed Padre Rodriguez on both cheeks, surprising him. "Thank you."

He crossed himself. "God be with you, my child."

"And also with you." I gathered my purse and was about to walk out when a thought crossed my mind. "Padre?"

"Yes."

"As you know, I've wanted to do more for the church. Would it be possible for me to start a group or something for children like Lupe?"

"What kind of group? We have Sunday school."

"No not like Sunday school. I mean to help kids who are in trouble. Kids who need life skills. Kids who now have nothing to lean on but a gang in the street."

"Kids who need to be introduced to our savior?"

I smiled. "What do you think?"

"I think it would be marvelous, except the church doesn't have the resources for something like that."

"If I fund it myself . . . ?"

"You can use the church grounds, yes."

"Great. Thanks. I'll get back to you on that."

I exited through the church and looked back up at Jesus. "Thanks," I whispered, and crossed myself as I exited the church.

❀ George handed me a business card.

"What's this?"

"Lawyer. Call him."

"Why?"

"From what I gathered about last night, you're going to need one." He took my elbow and invited me to lunch.

"I've got tons of work. I got in super late this morning." Since I'm never late, no one questioned me, but I've got people breathing down my back to finish the scene I'm working on.

"It'll wait. I want to hear all about last night."

As we shared hot dogs and fries with ice-cold beer, I filled him in on all the details.

"So this Officer Martinez didn't believe you had nothing to do with the drugs and weapons in the house?"

"He was pissed because he let me go last time and told me to disappear and I showed up again."

"Should be pretty easy to get you cleared of all charges."

"I know." I sighed. "I'm not worried." I took a fry and dipped it in ketchup. "I just wish I had listened to Lupe when she came to me for help. I should have let her stay at my place, but all I was thinking of was that you were coming over and . . ." And I was hoping for a romantic night in his arms.

He reached across the table and caressed my hand. "Don't beat yourself up."

I dropped the fry. Even with ketchup it didn't look appealing. "Anyway, I'm now implicated in the drug charges as well as corrupting a minor."

"Call the lawyer."

"Yeah." I looked across at George. "Thanks."

"I haven't done anything."

Yes, he had. "This lawyer a friend of yours?"

"Works with Panoply's business attorneys. I know he's good."

"Think this guy will represent Lupe too?"

"Can get costly. She won't be easy to represent. Sounds like she's guilty. She attacked the officer."

"I'll cover the costs. And I don't think she even knew what she was doing, George, or who was coming after her. You should have seen her. Her eyes were clouded with fear."

He leaned back in his chair, looking disturbed.

"What?"

"Nothing."

"What are you thinking?" I leaned across the table.

"Hell, Marcela. Just be careful. She's got parents. She's not an abandoned child. You've got no rights here, okay?"

"I know. I've got to talk to her parents."

He frowned. "Don't go to that home alone again. Ever."

"George," I said with a smile. "Ordering me around already? You're not even officially my boyfriend yet."

He took out his wallet and dropped a few bills on the money tray. Then offered me his hand. "Let's go, and you can tell me what I have to do to become 'officially' your boyfriend."

❀ I prepared a small salad and worked on my spec project. A quiet night at home was just what I needed. No dates. No Lupe. No Chicano movements.

Lupe had been detained overnight and a juvenile petition was filed with the DA's office. Because so many beds were filled to the max at Juvenile Hall, the probation department released Lupe to her father early this morning. Her trial date has been set for next week and when I talked to Lupe today, she agreed to take me to the clothing factory where her mother works. I need to talk to her about hiring a lawyer to represent Lupe. I was also going to try to convince her to get her son out of the house, but Lupe informed me that when he was arrested last night, unlike us, he hadn't been released. With three warrants and the bust last night, he'd be locked up until his trial and hopefully a lot longer. That done, tonight I'm taking a breather.

I've been driving myself crazy trying to come up with a good Latin character. Pancho Villa? No. There's Joaquin Murrieta, who was sort of a Robin Hood. He could make a good character for an animated movie geared for children. But there was too much controversy about him. I could always do a re-creation of Zorro. It's been years since Disney's version was released.

I worked for about three hours then needed a stretch. Out on my balcony I inhaled the warm night air. The drawback to living in a city is that you smell nothing. No flowery scents, no salty sea air, no evergreen smells. Nothing. Truck and bus exhaust every once in a while floats up to gag me, but that's it. At Mom and Dad's house you have the orange blossoms and jasmine smells in the spring and summer time, and lavender and spearmint in the fall and winter. Even the trees have their own distinct scent.

Of course, if I lived in the suburbs I'd have to drive an hour and a half to get to work. So I could live in a scent-free world—small compromise.

I fingered the lawyer's card in my pocket and without considering the time, I went back inside to get my cordless then returned to my balcony. Might as well get this over with—still can't believe that jerk cop pressed charges against me.

The call was answered on the third ring. Unfortunately, it was answered by an answering service. No, I don't have an emergency. Yes, I can leave a message and have Mr. Sullivan call me back in the morning. Sigh.

Maybe I should go inside and do some Internet research on Mexico. Pick out a hotel and some fun sights to see. I walked back in and locked my slider. I returned the receiver back to the cradle and noticed the numbers for the three Pauls on my desk. Just where I'd left them so George and I could call.

Picking up the sheet of paper, I considered calling. I don't really need George here. I'm a big girl. What the heck. Without dwelling on it any longer, I dialed the California Paul first, but got a busy signal. So I hung up and dialed the number for the Paul in Oregon.

"Hello," said a woman's voice.

"Hi, may I speak with Paul please?"

"Who's calling?"

"Marcela."

"Just a minute."

"Hey," he said a few moments later when he got on the line.

"Ah, hi, you don't know me but—"

"Sure, I remember you."

He did? I shook my head. No, he didn't. "Actually, we've never met."

"At the DuckStop right?"

"No. I'm Marta Alvarez's daughter. Does that name mean anything to you?"

"Ah, I don't think so."

Man, this was hard. "You were in the same church group about twenty-eight years ago."

He laughed. "Is this a joke? I'm only twenty-four years old."

I let myself breathe. Didn't even realize I'd been holding my breath. "I'm sorry. I guess I've got the wrong Paul." I quickly hung up.

My hand shook and I wondered if I had the nerve to try this again. After sitting and holding the receiver in a choke hold between my legs for a couple of minutes, I tried the Paul in California again. Since the third was in Pennsylvania, I figured with the time difference, it might be too late to call him.

"Hello," a man answered.

"I'm looking for Paul," I said.

"You found him. How can I help you?"

He probably thought I was selling something. Either that or he was not very friendly. "Have you ever known a woman named Marta Alvarez?"

"Who are you?"

"I'm her daughter."

"Is your mother lost or something?"

"No, sir. I'm looking for a man who knew her twenty-eight years ago. Who was in her prayer group."

"Can't help you."

What did that mean? Did he know her or not? "Ah, Paul, this is important. You see, you could be my father."

"Your father?" he shouted. "Listen, lady. I never knew your mother."

"You're sure?"

"Of course I'm sure. I don't need any more kids. Good-bye." He hung up.

Okay, maybe this hadn't been such a good idea. I was shaking all over, damn it. I slammed the phone down and drew a deep breath. Why am I doing this to myself? Why? I've got a perfectly good father who loves me. I crumpled the paper into a ball and tossed it into the trash.

I grabbed my keys and headed to my car, not knowing where the hell I was going.

Twenty-two

I got to Aunt Lydia's house in record time. Just my luck she was having a group gathering, and Sonya was there waiting for our aunt to help her out with a resume or something.

"Sit and chat with your cousin," Tía Lydia said. "We'll be done with our meeting in about ten minutes."

"Hey, Marcela."

"Hi," I said.

"You still pissed at me?"

"No. I wasn't pissed."

"Yeah, right."

"Actually," I said, "I should thank you. I needed to know the truth." Though it hadn't gotten me anything but trouble since I found out. I got a glass of wine from my aunt's fridge and downed the entire thing. Then I poured a second.

Sonya seemed at a loss for words. "Poor Tío Juan," she said.

I laughed.

"What's so funny?"

"You." Bitch. All she ever wanted to do was stir up trouble.

"If I were in your shoes, I wouldn't be laughing."

"What would you do?" I crossed my arms, still holding my wineglass, and smiled at her.

"Hard to say. Your whole family lied to you. And the guy you thought was your father—"

"Fuck you, Sonya. He *is* my father."

She smiled.

Damn it. Why was I letting her get to me? Why of all nights did I have to run into her tonight? All I wanted was to talk to Tía Lydia and see why she never told me about Paul.

"Well, he raised you. But he's not your father."

I finished my wine. I hated her. She obviously had no concept of what made a man a father. "Come to think of it, there *is* one good thing about Juan not being my genetic father."

"What's that?"

"You and I aren't really related." Since her father and my father are brothers, that would mean she and I shared no blood link. Of course, since Aunt Lydia was our father's sister, it also meant I wasn't genetically linked to her, and that was too painful to contemplate.

I left the room before I broke the wineglass over Sonya's head for making me analyze all this.

I sat in the living room listening to a group of political activists discuss the Immigrant Children's Health Improvement Act, which would lift the ban on legal immigrant children's access to state and federal health care.

"No, instead of bringing this to the floor, they waste our tax dollars with that *pinche* Rohrabacher bill," one of the guys said passionately.

"Well, it didn't pass," Aunt Lydia said. "We should be grateful for that."

"What bill was that?" I asked, wondering what evil they thought our government was trying to inflict on us poor Latinos.

All heads turned my way and critical eyes pinned me in place. I felt like hiding behind something. Why did I open my big mouth?

"This is another of my nieces, Marcela. She's very concerned about Chicano issues."

And about global warming.

"*Bienvenido*," they all said.

I nodded.

"The Rohrabacher bill would have forced doctors and nurses in hospital emergency rooms to target possible undocumented immigrants and gather identifying information such as their fingerprints and photos for the Office of Homeland Security."

"Man. Really?"

"If they wanted to qualify for uncompensated care, they would have had no choice but to comply," my aunt explained.

"Homeland Security," an older gentleman grumbled. "Sure. It's just another anti-Latino bill. That's what it is."

There was a murmur of agreement in the room.

"Its provisions would have even allowed them to deport women in labor," said a woman with long, black hair and braids, disgust evident in her tone.

The U.S. government isn't stupid. If they could get the baby to let out its first scream on the other side of the border, it's one less Mexican American they have to worry about. Same reasoning the Mexican moms want the babies born in America. What a sad game we all played with people's lives. I started to get a headache.

"Okay." Aunt Lydia clapped her hands. "Let's focus on the ICHI Act, and see what support we can build for this bill. We need to call our senator and every elected official in each district. *Sí?*"

Again a murmur of agreement.

"*Muy bien*. Until next week."

They all stood and folded their notebooks. Some had nice briefcases or laptops. This group was obviously well-off. Professional, well-educated, influential Latinos. I had to mentally erase my prejudiced thoughts of Chicano groups, because the two I'd had the chance to meet have been pretty cool. Guess they weren't all weird *locos*.

My aunt then happily invited me into the kitchen. She poured me some coffee, and placed a plate of coffeecake and other pastries in front of me. Looked good.

"Now, Sonya. Let me see your resume."

Sonya looked uncomfortable, but handed Tía Lydia a manila folder.

"No, no, no," she said. "*No te dije*, you don't list McDonald's and Taco Bell."

"But I worked there."

"*Mira*, Sonya. You want to be taken seriously, no? List your college activities. What other work have you done?"

I paused from sipping my coffee. "Nothing. Even at McDonald's all she ever did was eat their burgers."

My aunt lowered her reading glassed down her nose. "That's not helpful."

"And I'm not fat," Sonya said.

"Didn't say you were." I chose a pastry, though for the first time ever, I wondered if I should stop eating so much crap.

"Can we get back to this?" Aunt Lydia asked. "Get rid of the menial stuff. Show your education."

"I can list the job at the doctor's office, but it was just cleaning up and filing and stuff."

"Great. You were a doctor's assistant."

I coughed, pretending to choke on my pastry, then chuckled.

"Marcela, please," my aunt said. "I'm surprised at you."

I'm surprised at myself too, but Sonya has gotten on my nerves too many times lately.

"You know," Tía Lydia brightened. "You have an opportunity to help your cousin out."

Help Sonya? I'd rather drink arsenic. I swallowed the pastry and it went down like cardboard.

"How about a job recommendation?"

"She's never worked for me. What are you talking about?"

"I'm sure you can come up with a good job title for her and write up a wonderful recommendation."

"You want me to lie?" I couldn't believe what I was hearing.

"If we don't help each other out, who will?"

I looked at Sonya. She was mean, lazy, and I couldn't stand her. No one could. "You need my help, cousin?"

"Ah, no, that's okay."

I shrugged. "Okay."

Aunt Lydia placed the resume on the table and slapped Sonya on the shoulder. "Yes, you do."

Sonya made a face like she had stomach cramps.

I smiled. *Go for it. Ask me for a favor.*

"If you want to write something up for me, I'll accept it."

I dropped what was left of my pastry on my plate and placed my weight on my elbows as I leaned forward on the kitchen table. "I don't want to write something up for you, you lying, manipulative, two-faced *bruja*."

"Marcela!" Aunt Lydia said.

I held a hand up to quiet her. This was between me and Sonya and it was a long time coming. "But I'll tell you what I'll do, because we're blood, right? Even if you consider mine diluted, you sack of crap. I will arrange for you to get the worst, lowest-paying position at Panoply that's available. But you will work your ass off and prove yourself or I'll fire you myself. Agreed?"

Sonya was beet red. She gathered her papers and stood. "You think I need you? I don't need you!"

"You were fired from McDonald's for sitting on your butt and eating hamburgers. You worked at the doctor's office for what—

two months max? Couldn't handle the pressure. All you're good at is gossiping." I shrugged. "You've got nothing else going for you. I guess I don't blame you."

Aunt Lydia stood back, probably realizing it was better to let us go at it.

"You'll be sorry for this, Marcela."

"Yeah, I'm shaking already."

She stormed out of the kitchen, and there was silence until Sonya slammed the front door.

"Happy with yourself?" Aunt Lydia asked.

Hell, yeah. "Think I was too hard?"

Lydia shrugged and sat across from me. "I'm sure she deserved some of that."

Yes! Go Tía Lydia. "Much more than that."

"But remember, she's only twenty-three and trying to learn who she is."

"Tía, if she sees who she really is, it will scare the hell out of her. Even her own family hates her."

"Don't say that." Aunt Lydia loved all her nieces and nephews, so she was probably the only one who liked Sonya.

"Fine. Let's not talk about her. I want to know about Paul anyway. That's why I'm here."

"Paul who?"

"The man my mother had an affair with."

"Oh." She looked all over the table. Anywhere but at me. "I don't know anything about him."

"Never met him?"

"Never." She brushed crumbs off the table.

"Do you know what happened to him once they stopped seeing each other?"

"Why don't you forget about him?"

"Why is it that's the only answer you all have for me? This man is my father."

"No! Juan is your father." She stood. "My brother has worked all his life to take care of you girls. He's the only father you have, and you owe him."

She was going to be no help. "My mother is your best friend. I don't believe you don't know anything about Paul."

"Your mother made a grave error. Don't make the same one. Let it go."

I stood too. I'd already decided to let it go, but I wanted to know why in the hell no one had shared this bit of information with me. I always thought I could trust my family. We live in a heartless world, but at least we should be able to put our faith in our family. But I was wrong. I should have known better. "It's late. Sorry I came."

I got as far as the door frame, when she said, "He had dark hair. Nice personality. Friendly. Always had a smile on his face. *Mi'ja*, how will this help you?"

I frowned. That grumpy guy from California couldn't have been *the* Paul, then—he didn't know the meaning of the word friendly. He must have been telling the truth.

"He was my friend," Aunt Lydia continued. "I introduced them. Never dreamed they would get involved. Do you know how I felt when I found out what they did together—how my two friends betrayed my brother?" She shook her head. "An affair. My God, with a *guero* of all people. I still don't know what your mother was thinking."

Aunt Lydia introduced them? Wow. This was a new development. I didn't even know Aunt Lydia spoke to white people. Okay, I'm exaggerating, but just a little. "You don't know where he is?"

"Now? Of course not. That was over twenty-some years ago. He could be dead."

My whole body tensed at her last words.

"I'm sorry, *Mi'ja*. I didn't mean anything by that."

"It's okay. I'm tired. I should go."

"Marcela, you're a good girl. You were raised by two parents who love you. Isn't that enough?"

"Sure." And it was. But I couldn't help myself. Even though no one in my family seemed to understand, I was curious about Paul. Though I truly wished I wasn't.

Twenty-three

Friday, August 20

❀ Before I realized what time it was, I'd put in a sixteen-hour day. I shut down my computer and groaned at the stiffness in my back. Not a soul was left in the building. Even the die-hards had left by 8 p.m.

I waited for the elevator and wondered if I'd make it home without falling asleep. Maybe I should just curl up by my computer and let the soft hum lull me to sleep.

The elevator door opened and George stood inside gazing at me. "Hi."

"You're still here?" I said.

"Just coming up to get you." He stepped off the elevator. "We were supposed to meet for dinner at El Torito tonight, remember?"

I groaned. "I forgot. I'm sorry."

"When you didn't show, I thought you were late. After an hour, I got worried. After two, I thought you were out getting arrested again."

I smiled. These days, that could be a possibility, I guess. Then a second thought came to me: he'd waited two hours?

"I called the office and didn't get an answer so I thought I'd come by, and lo and behold there was your car still in the parking lot."

"I'm sorry. I forgot we'd agreed to have dinner together."

"You don't get paid any more for extra hours, you know?" He moved in closer, then lowered his head and kissed the side of my neck.

I wrapped my arms around him. "Mmm, George." I love how he does that.

"Marcela, it's ten o'clock. What are you doing here so late?" His hands slipped under my top and his fingers did wonderful things to my sore back.

"Just got caught up." I pressed against him.

He continued to kiss my neck, then followed my jawline to my lips. We shared a soft, sexy kiss that made me want to melt into him completely.

"Caught up, huh? I don't believe you for a second. What's wrong?"

I told him about my Paul calls, and admitted how hurt and confused I was, and how I didn't want to think about it anymore. "At least when I'm working my mind is occupied."

He held me tighter, but the embrace had changed from sexy to comforting. And I needed that.

"Why didn't you wait for me to be with you? I didn't want you to have to make those calls alone."

This man was so sweet and wonderful, and the only person who seemed to understand what I was going through with regard to Paul. "You're here now, and I feel better talking to you about it."

"We'll call the last guy together."

I shook my head. "I can't pursue this anymore."

He pulled his hands out of my shirt and hit the button on the elevator. It opened, and we stepped inside. "You can't *not* pursue it. Your family will eventually understand, Marcela."

His eyes held me just as close as his arms had and I smiled at him. "I know," I sighed. "It's just me. I don't understand any of it. I hate that my mother did this and I wish all of it was just a bad dream. I don't want Paul to even exist. But he does and, damn it, it changes everything."

George nodded and pulled me into his arms.

I let him hold me. "I'm acting stupid, huh?"

"Of course not." We approached the end of the elevator ride and he kissed my temple and let me go. "After all these years, you just want to know the truth. It makes perfect sense."

The elevator doors opened and we walked out into the lobby. I wanted to thank him for listening, but words just weren't enough.

"Not to change the subject," he said, "but did you call Sullivan?"

The security guard opened the glass doors for us. We said good-night and headed out to the parking lot.

"I did, and he thinks he can get all my charges dropped. Both mine and Lupe's statements match and even her brother admitted that he didn't know who I was. I didn't have any drugs on me. I wasn't high. They had no grounds for arrest other than I was in that house."

"Good." George walked me to my car.

"Yes, and he's going to Lupe's pretrial date next week, to try to get the charges dismissed or reduced. I'm praying things work out for her."

"Me too."

"After her trial, if it goes that far, I want to take that trip to Mexico. Think you can take off in a couple of weeks?"

"Take off?"

"You still want to go?"

He seemed to be doing mental calculations in his head. "Sure. I'd have to make some arrangements here at work, but sure."

"I need to wrap things up here too. And I've got to be here for Lupe. I'm going to see her mother on Monday."

"Want me to come?"

I shook my head. "I'll be fine."

"Call me after you talk to her. I want to make sure you get home safely."

"Can I call you when I get home tonight?"

"For what?"

"To say good-night." I can't believe I'm even saying these syrupy, lovey-dovey things. I'm not the sentimental type. But George makes me feel different. I want to share stupid phone calls with him when we have nothing to say to each other.

He ran the backside of his fingers down my face. "You can come home with me and say good-night from across the mattress."

"I know." I smiled. "But if I did, I'm afraid we'd mess this up."

"This what?"

"I don't know. This." I pointed from him to me.

"Is this becoming real?" he asked.

Real? What did I know about real? "Do you want it to be?"

He hooked an arm around my waist. "I want you."

We kissed again, but this time it was much more than a hello kiss. My body overheated big time as his tongue entered my mouth and demanded a response. But I was also nervous. Sex with George would actually mean something. It would change things, and neither one of us was really ready for that yet. Well, at least I wasn't.

I backed away. "I'll call you."

He chuckled. "Okay."

Monday, August 23

❀ What I saw when I walked into the decrepit, old building in downtown Los Angeles with Lupe by my side was beyond description. I've always considered myself an informed person. I'm not into politics or a particularly active person in my community, I admit. But I thought I knew what L.A. was all about. I thought those few homeless individuals I pass in the streets were an aberration. I thought that mistreatment of immigrants was one great myth spread by people like my aunt who want to pile more and more rights into our large Latino political bank. If anything, I figured problems existed in D.C. or New York, not California.

I was so wrong.

Lupe warned me that her mother worked in a sweatshop. I didn't know she was being literal. On a day when the weather was reaching 100 degrees, I found a group of about fifteen Hispanic women working in an unair-conditioned warehouse. The temperature in the building must have been about 120 degrees. No one complained. They worked and wiped the sweat off their foreheads periodically.

"Where's your mom?" I asked Lupe.

She pointed her out to me and waved at her so she'd come over to us.

Lupe's mother had to beg for permission to speak to me and was told by the woman in charge (another Latina) that she'd have to stay after hours to make up the time. Since it was after six at night, I wondered how late she expected this woman to stay.

The woman barely met my eyes. I explained the problem with Lupe and she broke down and started to cry. "Please don't take her from me," she begged in Spanish.

"No, no, you don't understand. I'm not with the police or the state. I'm Lupe's friend."

She gazed at me with distrust. And I understood. After all, why would a twenty-something-year-old woman want to be friends with a thirteen-year-old? I explained about the lawyer, and she agreed to let me hire Mr. Sullivan to represent Lupe.

Then I broached the subject of her son and his abuse of her daughter.

Her eyes flashed at Lupe. "Why do you say such dirty things about your brother?"

"It's true, *Mami*."

"No," she shouted. "He takes care of you, and you are always in the street getting into trouble and doing God knows what, you little *puta*."

Lupe was about to bolt, I could tell. Though I was shocked at the mother's outburst, I placed my hand on Lupe's shoulder and stepped between mother and daughter.

"She's not lying," I said as gently as I could.

"*Mire, señora*, you don't know my daughter."

"I saw your son beat your daughter. You have to permanently get him out of the house when he's released from prison."

She lowered her vision. "We will not. He will get out of jail and come home where he belongs."

"See," Lupe said in English to me. "What did I tell you? She's not going to throw him out. After all, they benefit from his drug money."

So she would sacrifice her daughter? Let her be abused by her son? No wonder Lupe spent so much time in the streets. She didn't want to go home. I made a decision that perhaps I shouldn't have, but at the moment, I had to.

"She will have to be out of your house until her case has gone to court," I lied. "We need to show that Lupe is in a safe environment, and that she will be in school and not on the streets anymore."

Lupe's gaze held a question.

I avoided her eyes momentarily. "I need your permission for Lupe to stay with me."

Both Lupe and her mother looked surprised. "You want her to leave my home?"

"Only until after the judge has cleared her case. If not, she could be taken away permanently."

Though she was willingly feeding her daughter to her wolf of a son, she obviously didn't want to lose Lupe. She nodded, agreeing. "I must get back to work."

"I understand. Thank you for your time."

Without a good-bye, without a hug or warm word for Lupe, she returned to work.

"Come on," I said to Lupe.

"You don't want me living with you," she said as we walked to my car.

"Yes, I do."

"Liar."

I glanced at her. She looked terrible, with bruises on her face and along her neck and a purple top lip, but she smiled.

"I don't mind, Lupe. Do you? I guess I should have asked you first."

"Whatever."

When we reached my car, my four tires were slashed. "Shit. I can't believe this!" I kicked a flat tire. "What is it with you people?" I felt this incredible rage and this sense of hopelessness. How was anyone going to get ahead in this neighborhood, when these people sabotaged each other?

Lupe looked at me and I think she felt sorry for me. She also looked guilty even though she hadn't done anything. "I can get my *carnals* to get you new tires, but you probably wouldn't want me to."

Turning to her, I suddenly realized the hilarity of the situation. I had somehow managed to get on her side, and now she was going to rip someone else off to help me. "You mean you can have your gang friends steal some tires for me?"

She nodded.

I laughed. "No. I'll call triple A. But thanks. I think." I got my cell phone out of my purse and dialed.

"You too. Thanks."

I hooked an arm around her neck and gave her a hug as we leaned against my car. "No problem."

Now all we had to do was hope we didn't get jumped before a brave tow truck driver arrived to get us out of this hellhole.

Twenty-four

Thursday, August 26

🌸 Living with a child requires a huge adjustment. One I was ill-prepared to make. This I realized by the end of the second day. I couldn't get to work early, because I had to drop her off at school. I couldn't stay at work late, because I had to be home for her in the evening. Not to mention having to stop work in the middle of the day to go pick her up. For a workaholic, this is torture.

Once at home we did okay. We worked on the computers together—she building her website, me on things I brought from work. We cooked together. Lupe is pretty handy around the kitchen. We watched TV and, interestingly enough, our taste in programming is similar. Probably because I'm in animation, I tend to like lots of the MTV stuff, reality shows, and situation comedies. It almost felt like I was having a slumber party every night.

Tonight we had a slight problem when she blasted her rap music to an ear-splitting pitch. Not wanting to squelch her teenage rebellion stage too much, I simply put on earplugs and worked on my computer. But my earplugs didn't help my neighbors, and I had them banging at my door. Of course, we didn't hear them until the music was turned off.

I pulled off my earplugs and ran to the door, when Lupe signaled me that I had company.

Three of my neighbors: Mr. and Mrs. Reynolds who are childless and workaholics like me, Mrs. Martinez who is a sixty-something divorcee who looks remarkably good for her age and usually entertains quietly every weekend, and a brand new couple with a young baby, all yelled at the same time: can't hear themselves think, waking the baby, obscene language, etc., etc.

"I'm sorry," I said to them all. "Won't happen again."

They stormed away, and I closed the door and faced Lupe. "Wear headphones."

"Headphones are for geeks."

"News flash. Geeks are cool. Wear the headphones."

She grumbled but kept her music off, so we managed to get along fine the rest of the evening. Mostly because she slumped on the futon and ignored me. Sometime later she went into my kitchen, found something to eat, returned to the futon, and turned on the TV. She stayed put until she fell asleep a few hours later. I turned the tube off and placed a blanket over her. Then I picked up her glass of soda and the bag of chips from my coffee table. Great, brain food. Do you tell a thirteen-year-old not to eat junk food? How about making her brush her teeth and wash her face before bed? Like I said, I've got a lot to learn about this kid stuff.

Before going to bed, I made an arrangement with my mother. I'd drop Lupe off at school and she'd pick her up and keep her there until the evening when I got off work.

Friday, August 27

❋ I worked straight through lunch so I could get as much done as possible. I took about three dozen phone calls, and had to sit through two meetings. George checked in with me. "I kind of missed you in Spanish class last night," he said.

"I miss Spanish class too," I said. I was no longer attending. Too many other things going on right now.

"How about me?"

"Ah," I stalled, in a singsong manner to tease him. "Yeah, I kinda miss you too."

He chuckled. "How's it going with Lupe?"

"Not bad. But I'm way behind on work."

"I'll let you go."

"Sorry, George."

"No problem. I'm taking off early to go golfing today. Looking forward to having you all to myself in Mexico."

I haven't had a chance to work on that. I needed to make arrangements. "I'll call you this weekend. I promise."

I made the same promise to Daniela when she called to chat about her ongoing flirtation with ballet dad, and to my sister who couldn't bring herself to dump Gilbert, and again to my grandmother who I hadn't seen in two weeks. I was starting to feel pressured and overworked by the time I glanced at the clock to go home. After six.

When I realized what I'd done, I bolted out of my seat. "Shit." I dialed my parents on my cell. "Mom, I'm so sorry. I know I'm supposed to pick up Lupe, and I lost track of time, but I'm on my way."

"Marcela," my mother's voice was cold. "You can't forget a child."

"I know. I'm sorry." I rode the elevator down.

"Listen, I've been thinking. She's done very well here today. Maybe she should just stay until the court date."

"I can't ask you to do that." I reached my car. "I'll be there in forty-five minutes, an hour tops."

"Really, we don't mind. Let her stay. How can you take care of her when you work such ridiculous hours?"

I sat behind the wheel of my car. Was I being crazy? How did I actually expect to take care of a kid? My mom was probably right. "She's my responsibility," I said without much enthusiasm.

"You have a good heart, and lord knows you did the right thing offering her a place other than her house to live. But you can barely be responsible for yourself. What will Lupe eat? Restaurant food every night?"

"Actually, I can cook quite a few meals now."

Marta laughed. "Come on, Marcela."

"I can. Really."

My mother scoffed and it kind of annoyed me. "And I can leave work early and work from home next week."

"Marcela. You can't manage both work and a child."

I was getting tired of her always telling me what I couldn't do. "I'll be there in an hour." I hung up. Lupe was my problem. Correction, my mentee, and I would take care of her. I made a commitment to Lupe and then dumped her on my mom. No more.

Sunday, August 29

❀ When my family attends church services on Sunday, they take turns driving Grandma. Lupe and I picked her up this Sunday. I figured since I owed her a phone call I'd do one better and see her in person. We had a nice drive chatting about everything from how thrifty it is to reuse nylons that have runs in them (as long as you wear pants or long enough skirts) to simple recipes to add to my collection of newly acquired cooking skills. She also informed me that Amelia was pregnant and we'd have to start planning a baby shower.

"Pregnant already? She just got married."

My small grandmother beamed. "These things happen quickly."

"Apparently so."

"Someday, when you get married and get to know a man intimately, you'll see what it's like."

I'll see what what is like? Pregnancy? Sex? Since I really didn't want clarification, or to have to admit that I knew what part of it was like already, I smiled and nodded.

"It's such a blessing to have a family," she said with a faraway look in her eyes. She had quite a clan. Grandkids, great grandkids. It must be something to be able to look back and see the tribe that you created—the mass of humanity taking up space because of you. Something akin to revulsion turned my stomach. I think I'm not cut out for marriage and family.

I glanced at Lupe in the backseat. She gave me a conspiratorial oh-brother look. I winked. Finally—someone on my side.

I pulled Katie aside when we got there. Her eyes were swollen and she looked like she hadn't slept in days.

"What's wrong?"

"I broke up with Gilbert."

"I'm sorry," I said.

"No, you're not. You wanted me to do it."

Hell, not if it was going to make her miserable. Not if she really liked this guy. I put an arm around her. "Kate. Dad and I were only thinking of you. Gilbert seemed too old for you."

"He cared about me. He made me happy. Did that matter to you?"

I couldn't answer. I wish I hadn't offered any advice.

She shot me a disgusted look and stalked away.

Lupe, who was standing to the side but well within hearing range, stepped up beside me. "Should I introduce her to one of my brother's friends?"

"Not funny." I'd have to call Kate later and have a talk with her. Maybe I should have met the guy when she asked me to. Maybe I should have taken more of an interest in my baby sister's life. Damn. "Come on. Services are about to start."

After Mass, Aunt Lydia and Rogelio agreed to take Grandma home so I could chat with Padre Rodriguez. I wondered if Rogelio and Aunt Lydia were becoming an item. Rogelio was a nice guy, but way too old for her—easily by more than twenty years. Oh well, not my business.

Lupe and I met Padre Rodriguez in his office. I introduced him to Lupe. Without me having to tell him, he knew who she was.

He smiled and shook her hand. "I'm happy you were able to attend Mass with Marcela."

Most likely, Lupe wasn't a regular churchgoer. She acted sort of intimidated, stayed by my side, and didn't speak during the entire service. But now in this simple office, she looked more relaxed. "I used to go to church with my mom," she said, not looking Padre Rodriguez in the eyes. "She still goes sometimes."

"Good. If you keep God close to your heart, he can work the most amazing miracles in your life."

Lupe's eyes narrowed, and this time she did meet his gaze. "I think God forgot about my family."

"Maybe your family forgot about God."

Lupe shrugged.

I decided to interrupt, feeling a little uncomfortable that Padre Rodriguez was being so direct with Lupe. "Padre, about the group I'd like to start. Do you have a place in mind that we could use?"

"We have the classrooms. They can be used after school, or perhaps the auditorium. You can take a look. But remember, I cannot supply you with any help. The church cannot pay for staff or any materials you might need."

"I understand." How much could it cost? I could afford it. If not, I'm sure I could get some type of business loan or something.

Rogelio might come in handy after all. Maybe he can steer me toward a good way to finance this project.

Lupe and I went to check out the classrooms.

"What are you going to do?" she asked, lifting a piece of chalk and scribbling her street name on the board.

I told her my plan, as I picked up an eraser and erased her tag. She didn't look impressed with my idea or with my erasing her work of art.

"What?" I asked.

"Nothing."

"No, tell me. What do you think? Too corny?"

"You trying to get gangbangers to this 'club'? Street kids? Who?"

"Anyone who needs help. Like you. You needed a place to go to get away from your house, so you resorted to hanging out in the street. If you had a place like this to go, wouldn't you have preferred it?"

"Get real." She shook her head with a smirk on her face.

"I am being real. You wouldn't have come?"

"No."

"Why not?"

"To a church? You've got to be kidding."

"But why not? I could bring in computers. Teach skills like—"

"Animation?"

"Yes, and other stuff too. I'm not trying to set up a counseling center or anything. Just a type of educational rec center to learn something other than how to write your name on walls."

She rolled her eyes. "You think you can save people like my brother?"

Probably not. "I don't want to save people like your brother. I want a place for kids that are stuck in a bad situation, but who are actually good. Like you. Am I being naive?"

She considered it. "I think it's cool. But no one is going to come to a church. And besides, this is too far from East L.A. What are you gonna do, bus us in?"

"Good question."

If not here, then where? I suppose I could think bigger and rent a location in L.A. Actually hire employees, life skills coaches. Hmm. I'd have to give this more thought.

"Okay, one more question," I said. "Will you help me? Will you be involved?"

She leaned on a table and crossed her arms. "You gonna pay me a consulting fee?"

I grinned and nodded. "Smart girl."

Pleased with herself, Lupe nodded. "Does that lawyer think I'm gonna be around to help you?"

Sullivan attempted to work out a resolution through a private conference with the judge, but because her offense was against a police officer, they denied it. He attempted to get the DA to dismiss the case but this was denied as well. She'd have to go to trial. I was definitely worried, but I didn't share my concerns with Lupe. "You'll be around. And I'll need your input. Otherwise, I might choose something educational, like . . . English grammar for you all to learn."

She responded with a somewhat weak nod. We'd work on this idea. After her court date, after life got back to normal—if that was ever possible.

Twenty-five

❀ Juvenile court is conducted in a manner similar to an adult trial, except that there is no jury. But it's just as intimidating and just as nerve-racking. As a witness for the defense, I was allowed and expected to attend. I sat beside Lupe's parents.

The prosecutor presented his evidence and called his witness—the officer whom Lupe attacked. They described her as a vicious teenager who maliciously went after the officer's face in order to resist arrest.

My mouth dropped open at the unfair image they'd created of Lupe. It hadn't happened like that at all. Lupe didn't "go after" the cop. She could barely move after the kick she'd received to the ribs. She had simply reacted and attempted to protect herself. I was sure that in her mind she didn't look at a police officer and see a friend.

After proving beyond a doubt that Lupe was guilty, the prosecutor brought in other "evidence" such as her prior delinquen-

cies, her school records, her family history. He then ended this
nightmare by recommending Lupe serve time in Juvenile Hall.

Then it was Lupe's turn to defend herself. Sullivan called me
as a witness. He asked me the few questions he'd warned me he
would ask. Basically, I pleaded with the judge to understand
Lupe's emotional state that night, and how she'd feared for her
life. She hadn't meant to hurt the officer, but had actually picked
up the knife to defend me against her brother. When she lashed
out at the officer, she hadn't even remembered she had the knife
in her hand, but had been desperate to escape. I felt like I'd
poured my entire heart out trying to paint a sympathetic picture
of Lupe and her crime.

Afterward, the judge recessed to study the evidence, and we
waited. I smiled at Lupe when she looked over her shoulder.
Wanting to encourage her, I lifted my thumb up.

The lawyer explained to Lupe's parents what was happening
and the court-appointed translator translated.

When the judge returned about fifteen minutes later, I
couldn't breathe normally waiting to hear his decision.

"I've reviewed the evidence and am prepared to give you my
decision. Miss Perez, unfortunately, you have not been in a family
environment that fosters either safety or proper nurturing. And
for that, I sympathize with you. You were compelled to make
choices for your well-being, which children shouldn't have to
make.

"However, they *were* choices. And there were several you could
have made. You could have called Ms. Alvarez to come and get
you from a friend's house. You could have walked to a police station and reported what was occurring in your home. You could
have chosen differently, but you did not. You chose instead to attack an officer of the law who was there to help you." He paused.

I didn't like the direction of his monologue. The officers were
there to arrest everyone in that home, not to help anyone. And it
was my fault that Lupe returned home. She didn't want to be

there. Didn't the judge understand that she was frightened? Lupe was thirteen. Thirteen! And she had been beaten by her drugged-out brother.

"And I see," the judge continued, "that this has not been the only time you have made an unwise choice. You have been picked up and released five other times for assault, defacing public property, vandalism, and truancy.

"That you are now living with Ms. Alvarez does not help your case, because, in my opinion, she is not the best guardian." He shifted his gaze to me. "You have not set proper examples for this young lady, Ms. Alvarez."

Wasn't our lawyer going to object or something? "Your Honor," I said.

"Don't interrupt. You're not required to speak."

"But I think I should—"

"No, you shouldn't."

"But, Your Honor, I think you're missing some important facts. Lupe has changed a lot in the last few months—"

"Ms. Alvarez."

"She's going to school. She's helped clean up graffiti by painting the outside of a convalescent home—"

"Ms. Alvarez! Mr. Sullivan, counsel your witness to keep quiet before I'm forced to have her escorted out of court."

Sullivan turned around with a frown and signaled me to shut up.

"I'm sorry," I said.

The judge cleared his throat. "As I was saying, I would not recommend that you live with Ms. Alvarez. If I believed her to be a proper guardian, I might have considered probation under her care, but unfortunately I don't see that as an option. I also find returning you to your home not a suitable solution. Therefore, I am sentencing you to three months at camp—"

"Oh, no," I called out loud, not able to control myself. Lupe's parents immediately wanted to know what was going on and turned to their translator.

"The juvenile detention camp will provide you a safe and structured environment," the judge continued to address Lupe. "There you will be encouraged to take responsibility for your behavior and personal development. You will attend school classes, drug counseling, and be taught life skills. I will recommend that you also are exposed to anger management classes and have the option for religious training."

Lupe had sat upright, back straight, as the judge spoke to her, but now I could tell she was crying. She sniffed and brought her hands up to her face.

"During the time Miss Perez is detained, Mr. and Mrs. Perez must prove they are able to care properly for Miss Perez, or she will be placed in foster care upon release from camp." He hit his gavel and stood.

Lupe wiped at her eyes with angry, short gestures. I was shaking all over. A court translator was explaining the sentence to Lupe's parents, who looked distressed. The room felt like it was spinning. How could this happen? Lupe was just a child. How could they lock her up?

She was taken away then. I clutched the back of the bench to steady myself as I watched her disappear. She looked back at me. I could do nothing but stare at her and watch her bow her head as she accepted her fate. *Do something!* a voice inside me screamed. But there was nothing I could do. Her parents were allowed to talk to her. Lupe didn't seem to be listening. She nodded, glanced at me once more, and then let the bailiff led her away.

I stumbled out of the courtroom. Outside the doors two strong hands gripped my shoulders.

"Hey."

I looked at George's face, but I was still too stunned to speak or to ask what he was doing here.

"Hell, it didn't go well," he said.

I shook my head, still in my state of catatonic disbelief.

He placed an arm around my shoulders. "I'm sorry, Marcela. Damn."

Sullivan walked out of the courtroom. "Marcela. She'll be fine."

I whirled at the sound of Sullivan's voice, snapping out of my daze. "How can you say that?"

"Because, he could have sentenced her longer or turned her over to the California Youth Authority, which is the juvenile equivalent of going to state prison. He didn't. Because of her age she got a break. Camp might be good for her."

"Whose side are you on?"

"Hers of course. But let's face it, she'll be supervised better in a state camp. She'll go to school everyday. She'll learn coping skills and then maybe she won't end up in Juvenile Hall when she gets older."

"I wanted her with me."

"That was obvious."

"Well, you didn't say a damn thing." I felt like a tea kettle, losing more and more steam before completely letting go and screaming like a maniac.

"And you said too much." He exhaled and ran a hand through his hair. "Look, three months is not bad. Hopefully, her parents will get their act together and she'll be back home soon."

"And if they don't, she goes into the foster care system?" I shrieked. "You've got to get that changed."

"Let's work on her home life."

"And just what do you think I can do about her parents?"

He gave me a look that calmed me down and scared the crap out of me at the same time. "I hope you can do something to get through to them that they're going to lose their daughter unless they prove they're providing a safe environment." He shrugged and placed a hand on my shoulder. "I'm sorry, Marcela."

I nodded. "I'll see what I can do." At least her brother had been arrested the same night we had, and had recently been sentenced to fifteen years in jail for various drug and shooting crimes. He'd probably only serve less than a third of that, but by then, Lupe would be about eighteen and would be able to move out. Her parents could claim Lupe would be safe. That would be a plus.

George caressed my back. "Let's go."

He walked me to my car. "Will you be okay to drive?"

I didn't feel okay. In fact, my stomach heaved as we reached my car. I bent over, gripping the side of the car door, and vomited right beside the driver side, and right on George's left foot.

"Ah," he said. "You're not okay."

"I'm sorry." Tears clouded my eyes.

He shook his foot. "No problem."

I opened my car door and reached for some tissues. "Here, I'll clean it up."

He took the box of tissues and put a hand to my shoulder. "It's okay. I got it." He lifted his foot, took some tissues, and swabbed off his shoe. Then he tossed the used tissues in my car wastebasket.

I felt about as small as a cockroach. "What am I going to do, George?"

He stood there looking strong and capable of handling just about anything, but he sighed. "There doesn't seem to be much left for you to do." He patted my back. "You've done your best."

Had I? "Yeah. Look, I've gotta go." Tomorrow I'd go see Lupe's mom.

"I'll follow you to your place."

As much as I've come to appreciate having George to lean on, right now, I needed to be alone. I needed to think. "No, don't. I'll be fine."

"Are you sure?"

I nodded and pulled my car door open. Then I reached across and touched George's arm. "Thank you."

His only response was to pull me toward him just enough to kiss my forehead. Sweet and comforting.

Friday, September 3

❃I marched into the factory where Lupe's mother's worked, found the foreman or supervisor or whomever she was and slipped a one hundred dollar bill into her hand. "I need Mrs. Perez for thirty minutes."

The woman looked at the money in the palm of her hand and then back at me and nodded stiffly. She called Lupe's mother and ordered her to go with me.

Mrs. Perez didn't look happy to see me, but she followed me outside.

I was planning on keeping an eye on my car this time.

I spoke to her in Spanish. "I'm sorry about what happened in court yesterday."

"It's her own fault."

No, it wasn't. Didn't this woman realize that? "If you keep shutting your eyes to what's happening under your own roof, you're going to lose her for good."

"My son is in jail and my daughter in juvenile detention. What else do you want from me?"

"For you to intervene. Lupe should never have been allowed to hang out in the streets at all hours of the night. She should have been supervised better."

"Look, Miss, my family is just trying to survive."

"I understand that, but it doesn't take much to show your daughter you love her, to demand she be home when you get home from work. To show an interest in her studies."

Mrs. Perez lowered her gaze. "I don't know anything about school. I can't read. I can't help her. She lies to me. She's out of control."

Lupe was out of control, but I know she was getting better. I *was* making a difference, no matter what that judge said. "If you'll let me," I said, "I'll help you."

She studied me. "And why do you care? What's in it for you?"

Good questions. "I care about Lupe. She's a good kid. She's smart. And I couldn't live with myself if I knew I didn't do everything I could to give her a chance to get out of . . ." I stared at her, not wanting to insult her. "If I didn't help her find a better life."

A spark lit Mrs. Perez's eyes. "I'm trying to do that too."

"I know." I shrugged. "But it's okay to accept help from a friend."

"You are not my friend." She stepped back. "I come to this country and I lose my family. My son poisons himself with drugs. My daughter has no respect for her family. And with your help, she will one day leave me altogether."

I frowned. "She won't leave you. She'll leave the ghetto. She'll learn how to have a better life than you have. Don't you want that?"

"No."

"I don't understand. Why not?"

"She is already a stranger to me. She is ashamed of me. That's what girls do in this country. They are ashamed of their *mamis* and *papis* who work to support them. I am not ashamed that I work for a living."

So, what, she wants to keep her daughter poor and uneducated so that she will not look down on her mother? I don't get it. "Are you saying you don't want me to help Lupe?"

"We don't need you meddling in our lives."

"I don't want to meddle in your life. I just want to be there for Lupe if *she* needs me."

"She does what she wants. If she wants to visit you and spend time with you, I can't stop her."

Precisely the problem. She, the mother, doesn't feel she can stop her thirteen-year-old daughter. "Thank you for talking to me."

"I had no choice."

"I'm not the enemy, Mrs. Perez."

"You pressed charges against my boy. You *are* my enemy."

No need to argue that her "boy" was a violent, drugged-out child abuser who probably would have done terrible things to both of us that night if he'd had a chance. "I'm sorry," I said, and turned away.

I got back in my car wishing things could have been different between us. But I realized we were from way different worlds. And maybe she'll forgive me one day, but I'm going to do everything in my power to make sure Lupe gets as far away as possible from her world.

Twenty-Six

🌸 I had lunch with Jackson, and came back to three phone calls from George.

"Jeez, three calls. That man's too overbearing."

"He's worried about me. I was a mess after that court hearing. If you had been there, you would have been worried about me too." I picked up the phone and dialed George's office.

"Guy's a control freak. You'd better listen to me before it's too late."

George answered and I turned away from Jackson. "What's up?"

"Hi, Marcela." He sounded distracted. "I was calling because I have good news."

"What's that?"

"It's about our vacation," George said. "What do you say? Mexico time?"

"Mexico?" I didn't feel like going on vacation now.

"You need to get away."

I stared at my computer. "Maybe, but—"

"Come on. I asked for the time off and got it. You gotta work on your list, remember?"

"I never made reservations. Never booked airline tickets."

"Well, didn't you want to see as much of the country as possible? Let's drive."

Yes, I did want to see as much of Mexico as I could. I wanted to experience life the way most Mexicans did. Driving was a great idea. "All right." We'd leave for Mexico, this weekend. Why not? I did want to keep working on my list.

When I hung up I turned back to Jackson who was watching me with a strange expression.

"I'm going to Mexico with George."

"You're getting too serious about this guy. You realize you haven't gone on one date in weeks?"

"I'm happy just dating George." And I was.

He shook his head. "You're asking for heartache."

Was I? Was this getting too serious? If it was, I couldn't help it. I didn't want to stop seeing George, and I couldn't wait to spend some time alone with him.

I picked up the phone and called Katie. I had to tell her I'd made a mistake by suggesting she break up with Gilbert. Who was I to say who was right for whom?

Sunday, September 5

❀ Crossing the border into Mexico was like crossing into a new world. To describe the difference is almost impossible. On one side of the border there is order. Streetlights govern the flow of traffic. Homes and businesses exist in their proper zones and the separation is clear. There is a general feeling of cleanliness and safety. On the other side it is pure chaos. Cars going every which way, swaying around potholes. Massive amounts of people on cracked, broken-down sidewalks. Homes and businesses coexist-ing side-by-side within buildings that are often painted, it would seem, from a six-pack of paint cans.

I scooted closer to George.

He reached over and patted my shoulder. "Doing okay?"

"Sure."

"So. Where to first?"

"I thought we'd see Encenada first, then make stops at each major city on the way to the capital." Once we got to Mexico City, I had a list of cultural and historic places I wanted to visit.

"Okay. Let me see the map." He pulled over and studied the map.

Immediately, two guys started to bang on the window, speak-ing in an angry tone.

George eyed me, then rolled down the window.

"*No pueden parar aqui.*"

"What's he saying?" George asked.

"You can't park here."

"I'm just reading the map," George told the guy, pointing at the map stretched out on the steering wheel. "I'll leave in a sec-ond."

"*Aquí esta mi tienda. Salganse ahora. Están justo donde paran mis trokas.*"

"What?" George asked, seeking my help.

"I think we're blocking his store."

"From what?"

"I don't know." I leaned across George.

"*Necesitamos direcciones para Encenada.*"

"*Ah, Encenada. Sí. Sí.*" He immediately began giving me di-rections, becoming instantly helpful.

"*Grácias,*" I said. "Give him a tip," I told George.

"A tip for what? He won't even let me read my map in front of his store. What a jerk."

"Trust me."

George sighed, but reached into his pants and gave the man a five-dollar bill.

"*Grácias señor. Grácias. Que tengan buen viaje, Señora. No hay prisa. Váyansen cuando esten listos.*"

I smiled. "There. He said to take your time. You can read your map now, though I know how to get there. His directions were easy."

George folded the map and shot me an annoyed glance. "No one likes a smug copilot." But he followed my directions and we drove along a beautiful highway along the coast and watched the sun set into the ocean.

We made it to Encenada by nightfall, where we got a room.

As we walked in, he dumped our bags on the bed and moaned as he stretched. The long drive had us both feeling a little stiff.

"Ah, this room only has one bed," I said.

He shrugged. "So?"

"I don't think it's a good idea for us to share a bed."

He chuckled and reclined onto the bed. "Am I that irresistible, that you don't trust yourself to sleep in the same bed with me without attacking me?"

"Very funny." I walked to the window and looked out at the happening nightlife. "I'm starving."

"Good. Me too. Dinner?"

"Let's go. And when we get back, we flip to see who gets the bed."

He stood, then leaned over and slapped my butt. "I'm sleeping on the bed. You sleep wherever you want."

"George," I warned him. His little joke had been only partially funny. I don't think I could sleep with George next to me in bed. After all, the guy *is* sexy and male and I'm a needy woman.

"Just ignore my erection when you feel it and go to sleep," he teased. "Unless you don't want to ignore it."

My stomach tightened. "This is going to be a long trip."

He kissed my temple. "Just keep reminding yourself I'm not a real Mexican, and you won't have any problem resisting me." He eased away. "Come on. Let's go eat."

Okay, I deserved that. I followed him out, needing food more desperately than I'd thought. And a few beers.

Encenada was great. The place was one huge party town. And it was full of Americans. We found a cool club that had two-dollar tacos and a waitress that George said was sexy, and who happily brought beer bottle after beer bottle for us to enjoy.

I lost track of how many we drank. Then I dragged George out to the dance floor. He complained that he wasn't a good dancer, but he was not bad. His eyes were glued to my body. He seemed to have lost his normal inhibitions. I hadn't had such a great time in years.

By the time we stumbled back to our hotel room, I didn't care that we were going to share the same bed. After all, George was trustworthy. In fact, I took off my top and walked around in my bra while George pretended not to notice. Guess the beer lowered my inhibitions too. Then I slipped into the bathroom, and changed into my Disney cartoon short and t-shirt set, before he got the wrong idea.

"Traitor," George said.

I smiled. "Some of my best friends work for Disney," I defended, and climbed under the covers.

George had changed into a pair of loose cotton shorts. He turned out the lights and climbed in beside me.

"Good night," I said.

George tucked his hands behind his head. Muffled music from the clubs across the street drifted into our bedroom. "Wonder if that noise is going to last until morning."

"I don't know," I mumbled, already feeling the heavenly cloak of sleep.

Sighing, he turned on his side. With my eyes closed, I couldn't tell if he was facing me or away from me until he reached across and I felt his caress on my upper arm.

"Mmm, you smell good and you're soft and warm."

Caution flags began to fly behind my eyelids. George wasn't going to make a move on me, was he?

"Maybe you should take that pajama off."

I laughed. "You're drunk."

"So are you."

"Yep."

George let his hand slip to my breast. "Come on, Marcela. Take it off," he said.

The caress was sweet and sensuous and I didn't want him to stop.

He slid closer. "Let me touch your bare skin. Let's get rid of all barriers between us." One of his legs covered one of mine.

"Ah, George. Wait."

But he didn't wait. In the dark, he found my lips. His kiss intensified my drunken state and I couldn't think straight. I kissed him back. Mexican music filled the room, but it became dim background noise dulled by the sounds of our heated breath.

Both his hands now searched to slip under my top.

My God, was I going to sleep with him on our first night together? It's not that I didn't want to. I did. But not when he might not even remember it in the morning.

His erection pushed against my belly. "Marcela, I want you so bad."

"Wait. George. Slow down."

"I'll go slow," he promised.

I eased both his hands away and gently pushed him off me. "I mean really slow. Like let's stop and think about this before it's too late."

"What's there to think about?"

"I don't know, maybe about what this will mean."

"Aren't you the same woman who wanted to get it over and done with on your couch?"

Pushing hair out of my face I sat up. And contemplated his question. Was I? "No. I guess I'm not. I don't want just sex. Not with you."

"What the hell is that supposed to mean?" He looked offended.

"I want you to care about me."

"You think I don't?"

"I want . . ." What did I want? Love? I shook my head. "I want you to be sober."

"Marcela, I know what I'm doing."

"I don't. Please, just go to sleep and keep your hands off me."

He acted annoyed, or was that sexual frustration I saw in the shadows of his face? Then he chuckled. I wondered if he was laughing at me or at himself. He reached for me and scooted closer until his crotch pushed against my hip.

He nuzzled my temple. "How am I going to sleep with this hard-on?"

I swallowed an internal groan. George needed to learn about the fine art of seduction. He wasn't sweeping me off my feet here. I slipped out of bed and turned on the bathroom light. From my toiletry case I took out a tube of lubricant, and handed it to him.

"What's this for?"

"Go take care of it so we can both sleep."

George stared incredulously at me. "You want me to give myself a hand job?" he asked. "No way."

"Fine, then keep it away from me."

"Fine," he said, and plopped back onto the mattress, definitely irritated and indignant now.

I wondered if it was wise to get back in bed with him, but where else was I going to sleep?

As I sat on the edge of the bed, he reached for my hand. I met his eyes. He winked. "You are one tough woman," he said, sounding just a tiny bit impressed.

"Mad at me?"

He chuckled and let go of my hand. "Furious."

We fell asleep together, each facing the opposite wall.

Twenty-Seven

Monday, September 6

❀ George pounded on the bathroom door. I shut the water off in the shower and wrapped a towel around my wet body. I opened the door and peeked out. "What?" I asked in my most annoyed voice.

"Where's my wallet?"

"How should I know?" I can't believe he got me out of my shower to ask me for *his* wallet.

He ran a hand through his hair and walked away. "It's gone."

I walked out of the bathroom, holding the towel around my breasts. "What do you mean, gone?"

"Gone."

"Where did you put it?"

"My back pocket. Where I always put it."

He wore a fresh pair of khaki pants. No shirt. Did he mean he had his wallet in his back pocket last night? "Did you take the wallet out of your pants when we got in last night?"

"I dropped my pants on the floor, and tried to figure out how to get into yours. I didn't take anything out of them."

I disregarded his remark, because right now, the important thing was that George had lost a couple of thousand dollars. Not good.

"This is unbelievable." He raked fingers through his hair again and paced. "Someone must have picked my pocket."

"Look, it's okay. I have plenty to last us a couple of weeks." I pulled out my ATM card. "Besides, I have this."

"Great. Not only do you make more money than I do, now you can pay for my vacation too."

Did it bother him that I made more money than him? That was a bit of a shocker. "Under the circumstances, don't you think it's kind of stupid to let your ego get the better of you? What you'd better do is call your credit card companies and report your cards stolen."

He gave a humorless laugh and yanked his bag. "Come on. Let's get out of here."

George's mood only lasted for a while, and then he seemed to accept that stuff happens, and he started to loosen up again, practicing his Spanish with me.

We drove for a day and a half, stopping only to sleep and eat until we reached Mazatlan.

Wednesday, September 8

❧ The Mexican coast is beautiful, and I found myself relaxing and de-stressing.

I called home to make sure everything was cool. My mom had spoken with Lupe's mother and said Lupe got settled into camp okay and that she could receive phone calls on Sundays. I'd call next weekend. Dad said to be careful and grunted something about it being crazy to attempt this trip by myself. I didn't tell him about George. Even though I'm an adult, and even if I pretended there was nothing going on between George and me, Dad would still freak out about my traveling with a man. He's old fashioned that way.

In Mazatlan we got a hotel again. "Two beds," George requested.

I smiled—smart move. I took out my credit card, handing it to him.

"I'll pay you back," he said.

I caressed his strong back. "My treat."

Our eyes connected momentarily, and I understood without him saying anything that the kind of treat he wanted wasn't in my wallet.

I eased back and strolled the lobby, generously decorated with flowers. A warm breeze kept the open, mission-style building cool.

"Ready?" George asked, placing his hand on my lower back.

I nodded and let him lead me to our room. On the way, we passed the hotel store, and I stopped to buy a white cotton dress that would be great for touring the city.

George waited patiently.

In our room, he took a shower then dropped onto his bed with the TV remote.

"What do you want to do tonight?"

"I'm doing it."

"You're kidding? We're in Mazatlan. There's so much to see."

"I'm broke. You go do whatever you want to do."

I sat on his bed beside him and he eyed me from the corner of his eyes.

"It's not going to be any fun vacationing with you if you're going to keep worrying about the money you don't have." I emptied my wallet on his bed. "There, it's all yours. Now you have money and I don't."

He pursed his lips and shook his head. "Marcela, it doesn't work that way."

"Yes, it does. It's yours. You earned it."

He smirked. "Not yet, I haven't."

"For driving." I slapped his arm.

"Hmmm." He clicked the TV remote until he found CNN.

I took the remote out of his hand and turned the TV off. "Give me that."

"No. I want to go out." I hopped off his bed.

"Well, I want to stay in and relax. Give me the remote." Sitting straight up in bed, he held his hand out.

I shook my head.

"Marcela," he warned.

I sat on my bed and crossed my legs, doing my best to pretend I didn't hear him.

"All right," he said. "You asked for it."

I looked up, thinking he would get dressed so we could go out, but instead saw him lunging at me. I screamed and tried to hold the remote high above my head, out of his reach. He landed on top of me and wrestled me for it. Unfortunately, he had no trouble prying it out of my hand, leaving me pinned under him and out of breath.

He smiled down at me.

"You're not really going stay here and watch TV, are you?"

He lowered his head, his lips hovering above mine. "Yes, I really am . . . unless, you have a better suggestion?"

I raised an eyebrow and glanced at his lips.

They quirked upward and moved closer to mine. "Do you?"

I parted my lips to answer him but he dipped his head, closing the distance between us in a long, languorous kiss, which he ended by gnawing on my lower lip—an erotic, sexy move that made me forget what it was he asked me.

When he pulled back, he gave me a deep, searching look. "What happened the other night?"

"What do you mean?" Suddenly, my heart was beating too rapidly.

"Marcela, I want you. I want to spend hours holding you, touching you, making love to you."

Making love. I'd had sex before, but you know what, I'd never made love. "Okay."

He chuckled. "Why do you sound frightened?"

I shook my head against the mattress. "I don't."

"You do. Talk to me."

I looked into his eyes and felt both adored and trapped. I pushed against his shoulders. "Let me sit up."

He rolled off me.

"I want you too, George. But I . . . didn't want to do it the first time while we were drunk."

"Okay." He nodded. "You're sure that's all it was?"

"Sure." Though I wasn't exactly sure. I *was* afraid. But of what? That if he made love to me I'd fall in love with him? That maybe I sort of already was heading in that direction? That maybe Jackson was right and I was letting George get too close? I wanted to explain what I felt to him, but I was having a hard time understanding my own feelings.

"I don't have to tell you how much I care about you, right? You know. I'm crazy about you."

"I know." And I did.

He reached across and ran his thumb along my bottom lip. Then he leaned across and took my lip between his own again, running his tongue along it and moaning. "And you're so sexy I can barely stand it," he whispered.

Shit, he was starting to convince me that staying in was a good idea after all. "You really think I'm sexy?"

"Oh, yeah." He grinned and his dimples winked at me. "Do you really want to go out?"

I did. "Just for a while."

He growled and threw himself onto his back.

I took my purse and put my wallet back inside, leaving him

the cash. "It's okay, George. Stay and watch TV if you really want to. I can go alone."

"Sure you don't mind?"

"Well . . ." I sort of did, but then again maybe it was a good idea to put a little space between us or we might never leave this bedroom for the rest of our vacation. "No, I don't mind."

I changed into my new white outfit and got my hotel key. "I'll be back in a while."

His gaze left the TV and roamed my body. "Jesus, you're going out in public dressed like that? I can see right through that outfit."

I smiled. "Looks nice, huh?"

"If you want every pervert on the street chasing after you."

A few months ago, having hot men from Mazatlan chasing after me wouldn't have sounded half bad. But somehow, in the last few weeks, George had become the only man I wanted. "You can always come after me to protect me," I said, and threw him a kiss as I walked out the door.

❀ Across the street from our hotel was the Monumento al Pescador, Fisherman Monument, which the concierge said I had to see, because it is the best-known monument in the city and a symbol of Mazatlan. With that recommendation, how could I refuse? Besides, it was on the beach and the ocean beckoned me. I crossed the street and circled the interesting monument of a lighthouse, a buff-looking fisherman and a beautiful naked woman. The Spanish plaque gave me the details of how Mazatlan began as a fishing village, and outlined what each piece of the monument represented.

I took a moment to admire the city behind me. Beautiful. Sure didn't look like a fishing village anymore. And the ocean was too gorgeous to neglect. Kids played at the water's edge. Adults stood nearby keeping an eye on the children. Others walked or jogged along a path. Deciding a stroll would be perfect, I headed that way, though I wanted to walk on the sand, not a concrete path.

I took my time, enjoying the heat of the midafternoon sun high over the ocean. The misty breeze touched my face and kept the heat from getting overbearing. The sounds of crashing waves gave me an unfamiliar sense of peace and contentment.

Funny, how I lived so close to the coast in L.A. and never managed to get out there. I made a mental note to take my sketchbook to the beach every once in a while, and spend some time thinking and drawing. As I inhaled the fresh, salty air and absorbed the beauty and wonderment of nature, I began to feel inspired. Maybe I'd buy a sketchbook now. Why wait until I got home?

But this invigorating feeling didn't last long, as someone kicked up the sand beside me.

"Señora," George said.

I smiled, thrilled beyond belief that he had followed me out. "Señorita," I corrected.

"That's right, you're not married."

Amen.

"Can I join you?"

"Depends."

"On what?"

I lifted my sunglasses so he could get a good look at my attempt at sultry eyes. "How willing you are to walk quietly beside me and absorb the energy of the ocean and the pulse of the city?"

"Hmm." He narrowed his eyes pensively. "I think I'm willing to do just about anything you want me to do."

I lowered my sunglasses back onto my nose. "Well, then follow me, you foolish man."

Twenty-Eight

❀ With just a hint of a smile, he walked beside me as I kept strolling down the beach, wondering how this relationship that had started out so awkward had managed to get so wonderfully fun and sexy. I suddenly realized that I was happy. Just walking beside George on the beach, I was deliriously happy. And if Jackson was right and things were getting too serious, I didn't care.

I reached across and took his hand.

After hundreds of silent steps, George cleared his throat and asked. "Can we stop and sit for a while?"

"Sure."

The sand was warm beneath us.

George put an arm around my back. "Man am I glad I was smart enough to come after you because this is a million times better than TV."

I gazed at his handsome profile. "What changed your mind?"

"I realized—real quick—that I'd foolishly let a gorgeous

woman walk out of our *shared room* dressed in flimsy, almost see-through cotton in Mazatlan. And I jumped out of bed as fast as I could to look for you."

"So you could protect me from other men?" I nuzzled his neck. "My hero."

He chuckled and squeezed me tighter against him. "No, so I could enjoy staring at you in that outfit."

"Lucky for you that you found me."

"Yep, thanks to the concierge guy who watched you walk away."

I decided this was fun and wondered how long I could keep dragging compliments from him. "He did, huh? He must have liked what he saw if he remembered what way I went." No need to tell George that I had *asked* the man where I should go, and that he had directed me so he knew exactly what way I was heading.

"Long legs." He reached down and ran the back of his hand from my ankle to high up on my thigh—almost high enough to make the sexy move indecent. "Exposed back, gorgeous caramel-colored skin covered in white." He leaned back and dropped a series of kisses down my spine. "Who wouldn't notice?" He took my elbow and guided me down onto the sand.

My arms wrapped around his neck and I pulled him over me. He was enticing me or I was enticing him. I don't know which, but I did know that I wanted him.

I buried my fingers in his hair and kept his head in place as I devoured his mouth. His hands impatiently traveled from my breasts, down my rib cage, and over my hips, then back up again.

We broke for air. "Oh, George."

He was flushed and I wasn't sure that he even knew where we were anymore. His eyes were unfocused. "I need to buy some condoms," he said.

"Excuse me?"

"I don't have any."

"Oh."

"And you want me to use them, right?"

"Ah." Was he asking me if I wanted to have sex or if I wanted protection? "I'm on the pill."

"Good." He kissed my chin. "Then forget the condoms. I don't need one. I mean, I'm . . . safe."

I eased away from him and sat, touching my flushed face. Safe? Did he mean disease-free? I really didn't need a reality check—this cold end to the fantasy going on in my head.

"Marcela?"

I smiled at him and caressed his face. "You won't need the condoms any time soon." I stood.

"Hey." He frowned. "Did I say something wrong?"

I shook my head. "George, you always say everything right. You always have everything calculated and analyzed and catalogued. You never just go with the flow."

"I don't understand."

"I mean, it's sort of like throwing a bucket of ice water on a girl to start talking condoms and disease when you're thinking of making love to her."

And would this have bothered me with any other guy? No. We would have whipped out the condoms and had sex. So why was I on George's case?

"I'm sorry." He reached over and cupped my shoulders. "Look, I'll make you a deal."

"What?"

"Tonight I'll do whatever you like. I won't analyze a damn thing. I'll give you creative control."

I laughed. "You'll do whatever I want?"

"Sure."

"And what do I have to do?"

"Forget about that ice water moment and go back to touching me and looking at me the way you were before I opened my big mouth."

"Deal. I know just what I'd like us to do."

He smiled and just as quickly, he frowned. "Wait a minute. What do you want to do?"

It's always a good idea to make a guy worry a bit, so I ignored him and started walking down the beach again. He followed me.

❀ The third floor of the hotel was dedicated to the fitness center and the palatial spa. I entered the coed steam bath searching for George. He rested his back on the redwood wall looking like he'd run a couple of marathons. His eyes were closed and his head tipped back. With only a towel around his waist he looked magnificent.

I sat beside him. "George," I whispered. "You sleeping?"

He opened one eye and looked at me. "Go away. I hate you."

I laughed. "Didn't you enjoy your massage?"

He straightened a bit. Both eyes open now. "Massage? Is that what you call that?"

"I ordered you a deep tissue massage. Most guys like that one the best."

"Marcela, I thought that woman was trying to kill me. I can't move. Can't feel my body."

I reached across and caressed his upper arm. Well I could certainly feel his body and it felt damn good. "It's supposed to relax you."

His eyes grew more focused and he looked down at the towel I had wrapped around me. "What are you wearing under that towel?"

"Same thing you're wearing under yours."

"Really?" Now he really looked interested.

"Did you like your facial?" I asked, deciding I'd better change the subject.

His forehead became a blanket of wrinkles. "You mean having someone coat my face with thick mud, having it harden, then letting her scrape it off? Then when I'm thanking God it's over, having her pour stinging acid on my skin?"

I laughed. "George, you're such a wimp. It's supposed to feel good, and it wasn't acid she put on your face."

He nodded. "She did, then she wrapped a hot towel around my face and left me there to suffer. I can't believe you women *like* that."

I shrugged and rolled my eyes at him. "Sorry you were so miserable. My treatment was great."

"And now we're supposed to steam until what . . . we turn into cooked lobsters?"

His skin was already pretty red. Was that from the massage or the hot steam? Poor guy. Maybe I should have ordered him a gentler massage for the first time. He did say he'd never done this before. My mistake.

"Like what you see?" he asked.

Was I staring?

He pressed the palm of his hand on his moist, sexy chest and wiped a drop of sweat that would have run down past his belly button and under his towel.

"I guess we'd better get back to the room. I ordered you a tux. We have dinner plans."

He frowned. "Now I'm supposed to stuff my red, hot, sore body into a tux?"

I laughed. I couldn't help it. He looked so horrified. "You did promise you'd do whatever I wanted."

He groaned and stood. "Right." Then he walked out of the steam room in slow, measured steps as if he were one hundred years old.

By the time I got into our room, he had showered, cologned himself, and changed into his tux. Wow. My own perfect, dark Ken doll. I wanted him. He glanced at me for a second then back to the mirror where he continued to work on his bow tie.

"Can I help?" I walked over and moved his hands away. I

wasn't sure if I was seducing him or seducing myself, but I was way past aroused.

He stood still, staring at me as I worked on his tie.

"You're so amazingly beautiful, Marcela," he said as if in awe.

I glanced at his face and froze at the intense gaze and focus of his eyes. Maybe I wasn't the only one wondering why we were putting clothes on instead of taking them off.

His hands cupped my face and his lips touched mine in a soft, gentle caress. I closed my eyes and enjoyed the feel of his fingers on my hot skin, even if it wasn't nearly enough to satisfy the fire inside of me.

"I wanted to pull that towel off you today," he whispered. "But I couldn't lift my arms."

I smiled as my eyes fluttered open. "Why didn't you ask me to do it for you?"

He lifted an eyebrow. "You mean you would have?"

"You never know. A hot, sweaty man who just endured hours of pain only to please me is a pretty big turn-on."

He shook his head. "Great. I've got a kinky sadist on my hands." He playfully slapped my bottom and turned back to the mirror. "Hey, nice job with this bow tie." He turned away and sat on the bed to put on his shoes and, for just a moment, I couldn't take my eyes off him.

❀ Dinner became a perfect close to the evening—at least my version of a perfect close. Candlelight, outdoor tropical paradise, soft music, filet mignons with lobster tails, wine. George ate like a man who'd been shackled to a cave for years and has just been released.

"Not enough food for you?" I asked as he buttered his fourth piece of bread.

"Huh? No, it was fine."

Why is it that most men are happy with two half-pound garbage burritos and a beer?

"Fine?" I asked, a bit disappointed with his response.

He bit into and chewed his bread. "Mmm, I mean really good."

Okay, now he was trying to be nice. I folded my hands together and rested my chin on my fingers as I watched him. In that tux he looked like he had just walked off an old Humphrey Bogart movie. Elegant. Classy. Sexy. But the truth of it was that I had created that image. It wasn't him. He was a simple, analytical guy who was perfectly happy behind his mathematical figures, or sitting at a sporting event in jeans and T-shirt. "What are you doing here with me, George?"

He stared at me with a frown. "Eating?"

"Here in Mexico."

"Vacationing?"

"Seriously." Did he just hope to get lucky? I had this great need to explore Mexico, to learn about my people, but he, why was he here?

"Seriously, I'm here because a vacation in Mexico with you struck me as appealing."

"Why?"

He swallowed his last bite of bread and wiped his mouth with a white linen napkin. Then he reached across for my joined hands. "To let you in on a little secret," he whispered. "I kind of like you."

"You came for me?"

"I came to have fun with you." He gave my hands a little squeeze then released them as he straightened in his seat and looked around for the waiter. "So," he said, "are you having fun?"

"Yes."

George ordered us both some coffee then gazed at me with a content look on his face. "Me too."

We stared at each other for a few long seconds.

"Where to next?"

Did he mean tonight? No, he meant on the travel agenda. "After another day or two here, onward to Mexico City."

"Ah, your real goal. All this relaxation and pampering is really a sidebar, isn't it?"

"No. I want this too. I want to see and do all of it."

"Are you finding what you're looking for?" He drank from his coffee cup.

"I'm not looking for anything in particular."

He chuckled. "Now you be serious. You're looking for your roots or something. Am I right?"

He was kind of right. "No matter how far removed we think we are, our ancestors came from here. I only want to get to know this country a little better."

George sort of frowned. "Can I offer an opinion even though you didn't ask me for one?"

"Sure."

"I totally support what you're doing here, but just remember that nothing you find here in Mexico will make you you, Marcela."

"I know."

"Do you? Because whether you're Paul's daughter and you're half white or—"

"I'm not half white." If I kept denying it maybe I could make it untrue.

"Hear me out." He held up a hand as if to keep my temper down. "Nothing you discover in Mexico or you learn from Paul when you find him is going to change who you are."

"I've already changed."

"No," he said gently. "You've got a new wound, and it's made you grow up a bit and become a little less naive about the perfect world you thought you lived in, but no matter what race you want to embrace, it's not going to change who you are inside. You know that, don't you?"

Of course I did. Wasn't that always what I told my family? What a sad way to define yourself if you are simply your race. I smiled at George, because though we were complete opposites—he was right-brained, I was left; he enjoyed hot sweaty sports while I liked nice, cool, artistic museums—somewhere deep inside where it mattered most, we connected.

I nodded and we finished our coffee in silence.

The waiter brought the bill and placed it beside George. He looked at me and twisted his mouth. "Should we save your cash and use credit?"

I reached across and looked at the ticket. "I can always get more money with my ATM, just use the cash."

He nodded. "I could get used to having a woman take care of me," he joked. "You've bathed me, clothed me, and fed me. What else are you going to do with me tonight?"

Love you. The thought flitted through my mind and I quickly shoved it aside. What was I thinking? "You've fulfilled your end of the deal. You're free to do what you want the rest of the night." Though there wasn't much night left. "What is it you want to do, George?"

For a few moments, he gazed at me pensively, then a soft smile grew on his lips before he stood. "Let me show you."

Twenty-Nine

❀ Häagen-Dazs bars. He bought us a couple of ice cream bars and took me to the rooftop garden to eat them. Here we were, dressed to the nines and eating ice cream on a stick under the twinkling stars to the sounds of the rhythmic ocean waves. Not what I wanted and, I had the feeling, not what he wanted. After hours of sexual innuendos, dozens of hot kisses, and a romantic dinner, the expectation of what was sure to follow was so close it hung between us almost uncomfortably.

We both knew it, but it was as if neither of us knew how to make the first move. After all, he'd rejected me rather harshly that time in my apartment and I'd rejected him just recently. So . . . I gazed at him as he stared out at the black ocean.

I decided I was bolder than he was, so I'd better be the one to take what I wanted. "Is yours good?"

He'd chosen the ice cream with almonds; I'd chosen dark chocolate.

"Mmm," he said, taking another bite and nodding.

I walked around and stood in front of him. "Can I take a bite?"

He licked vanilla ice cream off his lips. "Of mine?"

"I'll let you taste mine if you let me taste yours."

His Adam's apple bobbed up and down. His gaze was smoldering as he angled his ice cream bar toward my lips.

Keeping my eyes locked to his, I opened my mouth and wrapped my lips around a corner of his bar, letting the chocolate and vanilla melt in my mouth. Then I pulled back and sucked on my bottom lip—the one I knew he liked so much. "Mmm, you're right. Delicious."

He drew a deep breath.

"Your turn," I said.

He inched forward so I could feed him, but I shook my head. Instead, I decided I needed to leave him no doubt as to what I wanted him to do. Taking the dress off my left shoulder, I lowered it and pushed it down past my lacy bra covered breast.

I let him take a good look before unclasping the front snap. Then, though it was colder than hell, I rubbed my ice cream bar along my nipple until it was almost numb and dripping with sticky ice cream. "Wanna taste?"

He didn't hesitate. With one arm wrapped around my waist, he pulled me toward him and closed his warm mouth around my nipple.

"Oh," I sighed. This was pure heaven.

He licked and sucked and nibbled as I caressed his head with one hand. My ice cream bar was long forgotten in my other, dripping down my forearm.

He took his ice cream and found my other nipple, drawing the cup down and exposing my right breast. Then repeating what I'd done, he slathered my right nipple with vanilla ice cream before feasting hungrily on my hardened, frozen flesh.

I tossed my ice cream on the floor knowing some custodian

was going to hate me, but I couldn't help it. I had to brace my-self, so I clamped onto his shoulders.

When he'd licked me clean, he gazed up at me. "I love giving you creative control."

I laughed and decided he still had too many clothes on, so I quickly freed him from his tie and began unfastening his shirt buttons. "Give me your ice cream; I sorta dropped mine."

Without questioning me, he handed me what was left of his melted bar. "I have to return the favor," I said as I let vanilla drip onto his bare chest.

He gritted his teeth and looked up to the stars, and when I brought my mouth to his own erect, masculine nubs, he groaned in satisfaction.

He allowed me the freedom to pleasure him for far too short a time before he became impatient and pulled my head up to take my lips in a passionate kiss.

He pushed me back onto a reclining deck chair.

I reached for his trousers and worked on his belt and zipper.

Somehow, without my noticing, he had my dress pulled up and his hands were all over my thighs and hips and . . . oh, yes, there too.

I wrapped my hand around his stiff erection and moved up and down the length of him, marveling at how great it felt to finally be here touching each other.

But his caresses and his touches became too intense, too inva-sive, and I knew I couldn't take much more.

I tried to shove his hand away before it was too late, but he wouldn't allow it. His fingers delved deeper. His tongue plunged into my mouth and my hips rocked against his hand.

I couldn't help it; I let go and allowed the intense feelings to overtake me into the most glorious climax I could imagine.

Only then did he ease up. He pulled his hand away, and his kisses traveled down my jawline to my neck.

As I lay there with George above me, I realized neither of us had said a word.

I shifted under him, wrapped my legs around his waist, and guided his penis toward me.

He stiffened.

Please, don't bring up the condom.

He lifted his head and gazed into my eyes.

I lifted my hips, making his tip enter just a bit.

"Please," I whispered.

His arms were shaking and beads of perspiration blanketed his forehead.

I ran my hands up his strong arms and across his shoulders, still covered with a shirt and coat. I knew he didn't want our first time to be like this. My George was a romantic. This was too much like *just* sex. But sex was exactly what I needed to block out these crazy feelings I had for him in my heart.

"I need to feel you inside me, George. Stop thinking and do it."

And he did. He thrust inside me so hard and so deep, I actually screamed. His mouth covered mine and he eased up, working into a rhythm that quickly drove me toward a new fevered climax even more delicious than the first.

George was right with me, but at the moment of ejaculation, he pulled out and left a nice mess on my dress.

I was too winded to speak. So was he.

Silently, he stood, and adjusted his pants. Then he helped me up.

Dawn was starting to break. "Want to watch the sun come up?"

"Sure," he said.

I pulled a leaf off a plant and tried to clean my dress off as much as possible and make myself as presentable as I could under the circumstances, when what I really wanted was to run and jump into a shower.

We both sat side by side, staring and waiting for the sun to make its appearance over the ocean.

Why wasn't he saying anything? Did he like it? How was he feeling? Okay, now who's the one overanalyzing?

"George?"

"Hmm."

"You okay?"

"Sure. You?"

"Yeah. Great."

"Good." He nodded, and continued to look away from me.

Shit. "Why aren't you looking at me or talking to me?"

He glanced quickly my way then at his hands on his lap. "I'm afraid to say something wrong."

I smiled. "What could you possibly say that's wrong?"

"Oh, believe me. You'd hold up your dress and run if I said some of things I was thinking right now."

Okaaay. Now he was starting to worry me. I'd run? My stomach suddenly tightened into a knot as large as a baseball. My mind started scanning every possible horrible scenario. He wasn't married. I knew that. He hated making love to me. No. He didn't want me anymore now that he'd conquered and won. Get real, Marcela. Okay, so what? Let's see, he didn't come inside me. He wanted a condom. Why? "Oh shit, tell me you don't have AIDS or something?"

"No." He looked horrified. "No, no, no." He stood and shoved his hands into his pockets.

"Stop acting so fucking weird."

"Okay. You're right. I'm thinking that I want to hold you naked in my arms. That I want to really look at you without all those clothes on. That I want to spend the day in bed. That I want to tell you how wonderful you look and how much I adore you and that I feel like I want to be inside you again because it felt so damn right—like that's where I belong. I want to say all kinds of possessive shit that will freak you out. That's why I don't want to speak."

Relief washed over me like some kind of soothing balm. "George, it's okay." I stepped closer to him. "Don't you think I *need* to hear a few sweet words from you after what we just did?"

"I don't know. With you, I just don't know."

I wrapped my arms around his waist and let myself collapse against him. "Forget the damn sunrise and let's go back to the room. I'll take all these clothes off and you can look and touch until your heart's content."

His arms crushed me in a clearly possessive embrace before taking my hand and leading me back to our room. Once inside, he stripped me slowly, kissing every inch of me. Then we made love. He was gentle and whispered sweet words of encouragement that made me blush, not because of their sexual connotations, but because of how loving they were and how much they touched my heart.

By the time I fell asleep in his arms, he was right, he'd frightened me a little. I wasn't used to being told how special I was or how perfect my body was or how weak I made a man feel. I was used to being told I was a good fuck. Tears squeezed out of my eyes and I snuggled closer to George.

"You okay?" he mumbled.

"I'm sore, you animal," I whispered hoarsely and laughed so he'd know I was teasing him.

He kissed the top of my head. "Get some sleep. I'm not done with you yet."

I hoped not. I really hoped not. I could get very used to making *love*. And that scared me most of all.

Thirty

Thursday, September 9

We awoke sometime in the early afternoon, showered, ate, made love again. Took a nap, and repeated all of the above.

"I need to get out of this room," I told him by late afternoon.

He sat on the bed, leaning against the headboard. "You want to go see a bullfight with me this afternoon?"

"A bullfight?" I tried to hide my horror at his suggestion, but pretty much failed.

He was reading the things-to-do section in the entertainment magazine, and held it up so I could see. "They have a bull ring about three miles away."

"That doesn't mean we have to go see it."

"Are you kidding? I'd love to go."

"Well . . . ?"

George jumped out of bed and slipped an arm around my waist. "Please."

I chuckled. "All right. All right. Let's go."

*   *   *

❀ I like sports. I don't participate in many and I don't particularly like watching them on TV, but I like the *idea* of sports. Exercise, fresh air, competition—it's all good.

However, and this is a big however, someone needs to explain bullfighting to me. Where is the sport? George and I sat in this huge arena where both men and women cheered, first for lesser-ranked bullfighters who cruelly threw spears at a defenseless animal until it bled, became infuriated, and charged at anything that moved in the ring. Then when the scared and bleeding bull seemed drained of all energy, the glorious matador walked out, basking in audience applause, and took his turn at tormenting the animal.

I swear I was wishing that bull would turn around and shove its horns up that matador's rear end.

Most of the time I hid my head in George's chest. I think he thought me cute, but this had nothing to do with girlish squeamishness. I was simply thoroughly disgusted and angered.

When I moved my face away from George's chest (since I needed to breathe every once in a while, I had no choice), I tried to focus on something other than what was going on in the pit below. The architecture in the arena, the ads wallpapered to the side walls, the Mexican flags waving along the edges of the stadium. And to be fair to the matador, he himself was somewhat of an artistic piece. Dressed in a gold costume and performing a sort of balletic dance while the monstrous beast charged at him and he dodged the sharp, lethal horns.

George seemed entranced and along with the crowd breathed a sigh of relief every time the bull just missed its target. He appeared to be having a good time. But even he cringed when finally the bullfighter drew a sword and waited for the bull to make what would be his last charge at the matador's cape. The matador plunged the sword into the unsuspecting bull's heart and lungs, and the audience cheered wildly. I think I stopped breathing.

The mortally wounded bull tried to fight back while foaming at the mouth and coughing up blood, but he stumbled to the ground and broke into spasms. I closed my eyes and shook my head, unable to witness the last heartless, ceremonial stab of the sword into the bull that died moments later.

The whole thing was so distressing, so unbelievably cruel that I couldn't move. I had never witnessed anything die in my life, and I felt something innocent inside me fade away. How could people enjoy such violence? As we left, I went to the bathroom and splashed cold water on my face, trying to wash away the last couple of hours.

"Wasn't that awesome?" George asked as we walked out of the arena.

"Awesome," I repeated.

"I've always wanted to see one of those live." He took my hand and we walked toward the waiting taxis.

"Mmm, well, now you have."

Angling his head and squeezing my hand, he asked, "You didn't like it, did you?"

Understatement of the year. "I think I was rooting for the wrong team. Mine lost."

"Sorry." George chuckled. "You're turning into a real softy."

"Let's go back to the hotel and discuss my softness."

He lifted an eyebrow. "You're a walking talking male fantasy, you know that?"

"Yep."

He laughed and took my hand, a definite spring to his step. "Let's go buy some ice cream."

Sunday, September 12

❀ We drove about eighteen hours straight toward Mexico City when we left our love nest in Mazatlan. Our plan was to make it to Agua Calientes without stopping, then spend one night there before driving the rest of the way to the capital. On the drive, I called Lupe.

"You surviving?" I asked in a lighthearted way so as not to upset her.

"I've got school every day, which totally bites, and hours of physical fitness, but I'm still alive if that's what you mean."

"Yeah, I know. What's wrong with the system trying to make sure you stay healthy and get a good education? Who knows, you might actually need all that knowledge one day."

"I doubt it. Teachers are such losers. A bunch of geeks that don't know anything about the real world."

"Give them a break. Most haven't lived the type of life you have, okay?"

"No kidding."

"Have you seen your mom?"

"No."

"Do they allow visitors?"

"On Sundays."

But her mother hadn't shown up. That just killed me. "I'll come see you as soon as I get back." I'd told her about touring Mexico.

"No, it's okay."

I didn't sense she wanted my company. Or maybe she was acting. It was hard to tell over the phone. "I'm sorry I left you right now, Lupe. I feel selfish."

She laughed. "I'm fine. Really. They treat me better here than my parents do at home. How's it going with your boyfriend?"

"He's not my—" How did she know about George? "I never told you I was traveling with anyone."

"I'm not stupid. I figured you went with a guy."

I had to keep reminding myself Lupe was only thirteen. "Just a friend," I said.

"Whatever."

I sighed. "Okay, whatever. I'll see you soon, okay?"

The phone got passed to someone in the institution who thanked me for calling and hung up.

Then I checked in with my mom and told her I was having a great time. Then I spoke with Dad, then my sister Anna. Once I was finished talking, I needed to recharge the battery on my phone. You'd think I'd been gone a month rather than a week.

George drove silently, checking a map every once in a while, and listening to all my conversations.

"Anyone you want to call?" I asked once I hung up.

"No, thanks. I found a shortcut coming up. I'm going to take it and see if it saves us some time."

"Fine." His curt "no, thanks" bothered me. Didn't he have family members he was close to? "This lonely, mysterious man impression of yours kind of worries me. Those are the kind of guys that one day flip out. Ever work for the post office?"

He rested one hand on top of the steering wheel and reached over to play with my hair with his other. "I'm not lonely or mysterious. I just have no one to check in with."

"Tell me about your parents."

"What's to tell? He was a man. She was a woman."

Smart-ass. "Was?"

"Dad died. Mom still is."

"Does she live in L.A.?"

"My mom lives in Arizona with my sister." He took the turn off the main road.

"Oh? So you have a sister."

"Carmen."

"Younger?"

He smiled and let my hair slip through his fingers, placing both hands on the wheel as he straightened. "Older."

This was like pulling teeth. If he didn't want to talk about it, fine. Just seemed strange to me.

No one spoke for over a mile, so I jumped when he said, "There's not much to tell."

I looked at him and waited to see if he was going to say more.

"My grandfather and Dad built a stonecutting business from the ground up. Backbreaking. A bitch of a business, but it was successful. I had no choice but to work with my dad while in high school. Then I decided to go to college and not take over the business like he expected and all hell broke loose."

"He didn't want you to go to college?"

"Nope. Forbade it."

"And you went anyway?"

"Yep."

End of story? I kept watching him. He drove without expression for a few more miles.

"He told me never to come back home, so I didn't." Again more silence. "My sister tracked me down when he died and I guess my mom took it hard that I left, so I call her every once in a while."

Just every once in a while? Man. He was cold. "Too bad."

He shrugged. "You can't live someone else's dream. You have to follow your own path."

Again, this struck me as cold. "At a huge cost," I said.

He glanced at me, but said nothing. Maybe it wasn't a huge cost to him. Maybe he'd "followed his own path," as he had said, and was happier for having done so. Not everyone was so easily led by his or her family. I placed my elbow on the window edge and my chin on my hand, staring out at endless fields and shrubs. Maybe I was simply a wimp.

The next second, I don't know what happened, the car jolted and the entire front of it exploded. All we saw was black smoke. George fought to keep control of the car and pulled it over to the side of the road.

As we stood on the side of the road, the hood open and both of us staring at the smoking engine, George said, "Engine blew."

"Did it overheat?"

"Looks that way. Gauge must not be working, because it gave me no indication that the engine was getting too hot."

"Great," I said, and walked to the side of the dusty road. I picked a spot, sat down, and leaned my head back, letting the sun beat on my face. What the heck, I'm old enough to start collecting wrinkles.

After a few seconds, something blocked my sun. I opened my eyes and looked up at George.

"Are you just going to sit here in the middle of nowhere?"

"Have a better suggestion?"

"Yes. Let's start walking."

"Walking? Where?"

"I don't know. Back to the main road. At least there were occasional gas stations. Maybe we'll find a house or store or something. We can't just sit here."

"If we wait, someone is bound to drive by and help us."

He held out his hand. "Get up."

I groaned, but accepted his help. Retrieving my purse and cell phone from the car, I said, "Maybe we can call for help."

"Call whom?"

"I don't know." I dialed zero for an operator, but the damn thing wouldn't work. No signals out here. Great.

George had started walking without me. I jogged to catch up with him. Silently we walked. And walked. And walked. An hour and a half later we were still walking, and I'd had it.

"This is stupid." I was hot, tired, and cranky. "We don't know how far the main road was. You drove for what, thirty minutes along this shortcut? Let's just go back to the car."

George pulled open a map he'd brought with him. "Look, there's another small road coming up. We must be getting close. Looks like there's a gas or food store."

Out of frustration, I yanked the map out of his hands. "I've walked too many long, dusty, hot, muscle-cramping, miserable miles already. I'm not moving another inch."

"Marcela, be reasonable. Do you want to spend the night alongside a road?"

"No, I want a warm bath and a bed." I sat on the dusty road.

He sighed and sat beside me. "Me too. In fact, I'd like to give you that bath."

That made me smile. "Now you're talking."

Tenderly, he touched the side of my face. "Do you want to wait here and I'll walk to this next road on the map and get help."

Did I want to be left alone? No way. "I can keep going."

He helped me up. "Don't worry. We'll be fine."

I wasn't so sure. We seemed to be in the middle of nowhere, but it was nice that George was acting so brave and in control. "I'll just walk behind you, so I can stare at your cute ass," I said.

He shook his head and smiled.

We walked for about another thirty minutes and then out in the dusty distance, I thought I saw something moving. A vehicle of some type.

"What's that?" I asked.

George froze.

"I hope someone kind and friendly, because we're out in the middle of nowhere and at their mercy."

Thirty-One

We both jumped up and down and waved our arms, making as much noise as we could. Since we were the only humans out here, the guy in the pick up truck couldn't miss us.

He slowed as he approached us and stuck his head out the window. *"¿Que pasa?"*

What's wrong? I explained what happened with our car.

The man looked from me to George, then shook his head. *"No hay nada abierto hoy, saben? Si quieren pueden quedarse en mi ranchito hasta mañana y los llevo al próximo pueblo cuando salga el sol."*

I couldn't help feeling elated and wanted to hug the man, but I nodded and smiled instead. *"Sí, grácias. Grácias."*

"What? What did he say?" George asked.

"He's going to let us spend the night at his place tonight and give us a ride to the next town in the morning. Nothing is open today, he says."

George frowned. "Maybe we can call a tow truck from his place."

"Maybe."

"*Subansen*," he said indicating we slide into the truck.

We drove deeper into empty countryside until the driver turned onto the small road George had seen on his map. After about twenty minutes we reached a small dilapidated, old, shed-like structure.

The man stopped the truck. "*Aquí estamos.*"

We're here? Here where?

Behind the barn-like thing was a small house that didn't look much better.

Four kids came running out and threw their arms around the man who seemed to be their father. He kissed the tops of their heads and gave them each a little tube with a jelly-like substance—something they seemed to enjoy very much if the way they squealed meant anything.

He told us to follow him inside. Two women, one younger and one older, smiled and nodded as he explained that he'd found us.

The older woman offered us a chair and a drink of cold, flavored water, which we thankfully accepted. I was dying of thirst.

The man smiled at George. "My mother," he said, pointing at the older woman. "My wife." He pointed at the other woman who continued to cook after the introductions.

George nodded. "*Bonita*," he said.

The man grinned at George's compliment of his wife's beauty. "*La suya tambien.*"

George frowned and looked at me for a translation.

"He said your wife is pretty too."

"My wife?" George chuckled. "He means you?"

I smiled. "You're quick today, George. Just thank him." No point bothering to explain that we are currently traveling and living in sin.

The man took George out to feed the horses some of the hay he had in the back of his pickup truck, and I stayed and watched the women work. The children, who seemed to be curious about these strangers, stared and giggled from the small living room.

I offered to help set the table or something, but the two women wouldn't hear of it.

They asked me instead to tell them about America. I wasn't sure what to say. My world was so different from theirs that I didn't think they could relate.

George and our rescuer came back some time later with a chicken—one with blood-stained feathers and no head. He handed it to the older woman who took it outside.

"I think we're sleeping in the barn," George whispered.

"You don't have to whisper; they don't understand you."

"Right. He showed me a spot on the hay and handed me some blankets. My Spanish is bad, but I'm pretty sure that's what he meant."

Since this seemed to be a one-bedroom house and there were four kids and a grandmother aside from the couple, I wasn't surprised. Where else would they put us?

Grandma came back in with a plucked chicken, which she scrubbed clean in the sink. I hoped to hell she wasn't planning on feeding us that chicken. I had just decided to become a vegetarian.

We spoke a little longer about the United States, and I shared with them that I was traveling through Mexico in search of my roots.

They smiled and nodded a lot.

We all had dinner and I learned that they'd slaughtered the chicken in honor of us. I silently apologized to the dead bird. I forced myself to eat a small piece and loaded up on homemade tortillas, beans, and pozole instead. Everything was fabulous.

After dinner, the women cleaned up and the children studied. Then everyone gathered in the living room to chat. They offered George and I the place of honor on the couch. We were lucky to find these nice people who, despite their poverty, appeared happy and obviously shared a lot of love.

❀ Once we retired to the barn, I was exhausted. Inside there was a small counter with items I didn't recognize. The rest of the building had bales and bales of hay. Off to the side were a couple of horses and a cow.

I sat on a bale of hay where George had spread out a blanket, and nothing had ever felt so comfortable. "Ahhh, I never knew hay was so wonderful and cushy."

"Glad you like it."

I didn't want to move anymore. I dropped back and closed my eyes.

A few minutes later George was shaking my leg. "Hey, wake up. Marcela." He chuckled and stretched out beside me. "You can't pass out on me yet."

"What?" I rubbed at my stinging eyes.

"I thought you might want to have some kinky sex on the bales of hay."

I looked across the barn into the eyes of a smelly cow. "Yeah, right." I pulled myself up on my elbows, feeling self-conscious. "That cow is staring at me."

George laughed some more. He slipped a hand under my top and unsnapped my bra. "Do you know how sexy you look right now all sleepy and tousled?"

"Geooorge," I said, pushing his hand away. "Come on, cut that out."

He nuzzled my neck. "I want to have some hot, sweaty, earthy sex. Please."

I gazed into his heavy-lidded eyes. "Are you serious?"

"Oh yeah," he said into my ear.

This was the first time George had asked for sex. Usually he wanted to have long lovemaking sessions where we worshipped each other for hours. Nice, but sometimes too intense. This sounded like fun. "Okay." I started to undress.

As I stripped, he watched me and occasionally reached across and touched. I sank my knees into the hay and watched him do the same.

I admired his flattened, tight belly and my heart skipped a beat at the trail of dark hair that led to his ready erection below it. "You look so good."

The only lighting came from a couple of lamps hanging crudely on the wall. It was dark and warm inside the barn and I was quickly getting in the mood.

He lay on his back, his hands cradling his head, looking up at me. "Thought I'd let you take control."

I leaned over him. "Sure, make me do all the work."

He gazed at me with a wicked grin. "Show me what you got, honey."

I sat up and straddled him, caressing his smooth chest sprinkled with hair at its center. "Honey, huh? Well, this honey is going to make you beg for mercy so watch out."

I kissed his chest, moving down his body until I reached his waiting erection. "Oh, hon-ee. You are a work of art."

He gazed down at me and laughed sort of nervously. "Oh yeah? From an artist, I'll take that as a compliment."

"I want a little taste. That okay?"

Poor guy gulped and nodded. Couldn't even speak.

I smiled and took him in my mouth.

He cursed and tensed.

I guided my hand up and down as I indulged a little at a time.

I loved the sounds of pleasure escaping from deep in his chest. I felt decadent and naughty doing this practically outside, in a dirty barn. The cow mooed. I opened my eyes and looked at it from the corner of my peripheral vision. *Please stop staring at me.*

I closed my eyes and concentrated on George, who was oblivious to the world around him. But suddenly, he pulled me roughly up and away from him as the feelings apparently became too intense.

He wrapped an arm around me, and pulled me in for an erotic kiss. Then he flipped me over and took to my breasts, devouring the sensitive tips. His hand, his fingertips, ran from between my breasts down over my belly and stopped at my belly button.

"George?"

"Shh," he whispered. "Don't stop me."

Stop him? Was he crazy? I wanted him to keep going. I couldn't get enough. A couple of hours ago, I had been dead on my feet, and now I was wide awake, burning up inside, wanting George to climb on top of me and ease the ache that he'd created.

He cupped my waist as his lips followed the path his hands had marked.

I arched my body as he reached the spot between my legs. "Oh, yes." Within moments, even though there was a solid roof on the barn, I saw stars.

As soon as I was able to catch my breath, I pushed him off me and again maneuvered over his erection and let it slide into me. "Ahh. George, this feels so good."

He lay there, drinking me in with hooded eyes. I paused, letting him get a look, giving him the opportunity to touch, which he did. His hands covered my breasts. He cupped them, and held them in his warm hands. A thousand tingling sensations traveled down my body. Then he fanned his fingers out, moving one at a time over my nipples. The friction made them swell to twice their size.

My heart tripped all over itself, as I covered his hands with mine. I guided one of them down.

I moaned as he rubbed, knowing exactly what I wanted him to do.

The cow mooed again. I opened my eyes and glanced down at George. We both stopped moving and burst out laughing.

"I wonder if this is what it's like for Old McDonald," George said.

I lowered myself forward and kissed him. "If she insists on watching, let's give her a great show. What do you say?"

He rolled me onto my back and in the next few minutes, I forgot about the cow and the hay pinching my ass through the blanket, everything except the gloriously wild ride George took me on. I never wanted this to end.

But it did and, oh, what an ending.

❀ Afterward, I sat down petting Bessie's nose as she indulged in bites of hay. All she wanted, after all, was food. Guess she figured if humans were in the barn close to so much hay, they should pass some her way.

George sat across from me, sated. He ran his hand rhythmically up and down my back. "When we're old and gray, we'll look back on this and laugh."

"Mmm, or shake our heads in mortification."

"I won't. It'll be something we can joke about while our kids and grandkids look at us as if we don't understand what it's like to be wild and crazy."

"Kids?" I shrieked. "Grandkids? Have you been smoking some of Bessie's grass?"

He gave me an amused look. "You don't think we'll have any?"

"We?" I continued to stroke the cow's soft nose. "Maybe you will. Me, I don't know."

"I see how this is panning out. Use me for sex without any thoughts of commitment."

I smiled. I hoped he still understood that I was about as committed as I planned on being for a very long time. "You aren't complaining are you? About being used, I mean?"

"Not me." He sat looking very pensive for a while, then he stood and reached for his briefs and pants. As he dressed he gazed

at me with a sleepy smile. "Do you know what you look like sitting naked petting a cow?"

I became self-conscious. "Ridiculous, I'm sure."

"No." He stepped forward. "Delicious." He bent down, took
my hand, and pulled me up. His mouth descended onto my
breasts, kissing and licking and biting.

"I never knew that hiding behind that suit and all those numbers was a sexual stud." I wrapped my arms around his head, holding him exactly where he was.

He tilted his head up, letting my nipple slip out of his mouth.
"Oh, you knew it. That's why you pursued me so ruthlessly."

I laughed. "Oh, I pursued you?"

I felt a small sting to my backside as he slapped it playfully,
before pulling out of my arms. "Question is, now that you've got
me, what do you plan to do with me?"

I followed him. "Keep you as my boy toy of course."

He crouched and remade our bed, then held out a hand to me.
"I'm no boy, Marcela. You've always known that."

"Hold on, let me get my clothes."

"No." He took my hand. "I want you to sleep naked."

Who was I to deny him what he wanted? I took his hand and
lay on the blanket.

Dropping down beside me, he held his head up with one hand
and played with my breasts with the other. Did he realize he
couldn't do that for long before he drove me totally crazy?

"You know you're going to have to take those pants back off."
I swirled my fingers in circles around his chest.

"And you know you're going to have to offer me more than sex
to keep me around on any kind of permanent basis."

I tried to ignore the challenge in his eyes. What more could I
offer him? And who said I wanted him on any kind of permanent
basis? But just as that thought crossed my mind, I felt an unfamiliar tug to my heart at the idea of him not being around. "Baby,
you name it and you've got it," I said.

"I want you. All of you."

"Take me then, I'm here only to please you, babe." I batted my eyes and I kissed him then to stop him from talking.

He lost his pants, and sex seemed like more than enough for him tonight. Who said I had to give him more?

Thirty-two

Monday, September 13

We were awakened by the sound of loud Spanish male voices. I scrambled out of George's warm arms and frantically wrapped myself in the blanket. He tried to help me by pulling the blanket up over my breasts and managed to expose himself instead.

The two men who entered the barn looked surprised and alarmed as they saw us half-naked on the piles of hay struggling with a blanket. They stood there speechless, gawking at us. Finally one of them spoke. "*Quienes son ustedes?*"

Who are we? I explained that we were spending the night as guests of the owners.

They apologized and left us to get dressed. George chuckled and took me in his arms. "We've done it now. They'll never invite us back."

"Oh, I don't know. I'm sure it spiced up their day to be flashed by a couple of Americans before they start their workday."

He cupped my face. "You know what spices up my day?"

"Yes." I ran my hand over his firm, naked buns. "But I can't have sex with you right now. Let's get dressed."

"I was going to say waking up beside you. It's pretty darn great."

Because he was so sweet, I kissed him. After all, I know what I look like in the morning.

🌸 We joined the family inside the farmhouse and the farmer's wife showed us to the bathroom so we could clean up.

After literally rolling in the hay with George half the night, I needed it, and thankfully accepted the use of the shower. I washed up as best I could, but unfortunately had to put on the same dirty clothes. Yuck. I couldn't wait to get back to my suitcase.

After a quick cup of coffee, we waited outside while the men got the pickup truck ready for the trip into town.

"*Señora*." One of the small girls tugged on my pants. "*Me empuja?*" She pointed to a swing they'd made from a piece of wood and some rope.

She wanted me to push her. I threw George a "why me?" look, but he laughed and refused to come to my rescue. "Go for it. Make a friend," he said.

I smiled at the kid and nodded. A bundle of excitement, she ran to the swing and climbed on. I figured she must be about four years old. She was adorable as heck with little curls all around her head and the biggest smile I'd ever seen. She giggled and squealed with delight the higher I pushed her.

She made me laugh.

George came to stand a few feet beside me. "Cute."

"Yes, she is."

"I meant you. Pushing her."

I pushed even harder and the little girl screamed and laughed.

"You're going to make a great mom one day," George said.

I turned to look at him, wondering where all this talk about kids was coming from. But before I could say a word, I felt a blow to my head and heard George call "watch out" at the same time.

I was knocked onto my back, and for the second time in twenty-four hours I saw stars. But this time it wasn't at all pleasurable.

"Are you okay?" George lifted my head off the ground.

I blinked my eyes and put a hand up to my forehead. "I think so."

Our farmer friend and his two buddies came running over, circling around me with concerned looks on their faces. All four men were talking to me at once.

The little girl broke through the barricade and shook her head as she looked down at me. "You're not supposed to let the swing hit you," she said in Spanish. "You've got to stand back."

Thanks for the tip, kid. I stood unsteadily, but George was right by my side with his arm around my waist. We walked to the pickup truck.

"You'll ride inside with me, and my men will ride in the bed of the truck with the bales of hay," the farm owner explained, again in Spanish.

I felt bad putting his workers out like that. "We can ride outside."

I explained to George and he sort of agreed, though he suggested he stay outside while I ride inside.

"I'm not riding inside without you."

"I don't like the idea of you riding on loose bales of hay, especially after hitting your head."

"I'm fine."

He shook his head as if convinced I was beyond help. "Whatever you decide is fine with me."

"Good. Then if *you* don't mind riding in the bed of the truck, let's go for it."

"After all that walking yesterday, I'll ride anywhere."

"Got that right. I'd ride bare-butt on the back of a donkey if it meant I didn't have to walk." I climbed onto the truck and hoped I didn't topple over and break my neck once we started driving.

But all three Latin men looked horrified and shook their heads and demanded I climb right back down. No girl was going to ride up there where it was dangerous. Especially a California city girl.

My head was already pounding and all the shouting was making it worse. I looked to George for help, but he shrugged.

"Okay, okay." I put my hand out to shut them up. No point in arguing with them. This wasn't the time to let them know women could do anything men could do. Besides, who really wanted to? I'd much rather ride inside; I was just trying to be polite. So I allowed them to be macho and gallant and thanked them profusely as I slid into the cab of the pickup truck.

George slid in beside me with a smile.

"What?" I asked.

"Nothing."

"What?"

"I kind of like this male-dominated society."

I leaned my pounding head back. Damn, I really took a hit. "It only appears to be dominated by men, babe. After all, I'm sitting inside."

George softly pushed my hair back and looked at my forehead. "You sure you're okay? You've got a lump developing. I should get you some ice."

"I'm fine," I repeated.

He laughed. "You're such a commitment phobic that any mention of a serious relationship lands you on your butt."

It was the swing that knocked me on my butt.

George pointed at the kids. "Do they really make you that nervous?"

"Kids?" The young girl in curls had recruited her older brothers and sisters and they were all pushing and hanging onto the ropes of the swing and having a great time. I stared at them. "Only the thought of having my own makes me nervous."

"Why?"

I shrugged. "You're trapped after you have them."

"Trapped?" He arched an eyebrow in question. "In what?"

"Just trapped. People become trapped in jobs they don't like, in marriages they want to leave. Because of the kids." I shrugged.

"Does that mean you don't ever want any?"

I shook my head. "I didn't say that. I just like my freedom."

"See what I mean? Commitment phobic."

"You know exactly what I want and where I'm at in my life. It has nothing to do with phobias."

"No, I don't know what you want. Why don't you fill me in?"

He knew about my list and what I needed to do.

"Tell me where this is leading." He pointed to me and back to himself. "Because you're starting to worry me again."

"After the last few nights together, you don't know where this is leading?"

"Where? To another night of great sex."

"Is there a problem with that?"

"No." He shifted in his seat. "I mean, yes. I've done the fooling around thing in my twenties. I played the dating game, and did the bar scene, and I'm done with all that. When I go out with someone now, I want a relationship."

Don't I know it? I turned to face him. "I can do that," I said. I AM doing it, aren't I? We've fallen into a girlfriend/boyfriend relationship. And I *want* that—I'm thrilled to be an "us," but I sure as hell don't want to talk about kids or think about forever.

He sighed and opened the truck door. "Let me go get you some ice. Your head is looking worse by the second."

He jumped out of the truck and hurried into the farmhouse, leaving me alone with my aching head.

🌸 The farm owner dropped us off at an auto repair shop in a small town outside of Agua Calientes. I offered him fifty bucks for gas and food and for giving us a place to sleep for the night. Fifty would more than cover all that, but I figured he needed it more than I did.

"*Grácias, señora, grácias.*" He offered a wide grin.

George shook his hand to thank him as well.

"You'd better watch the cash. It's all we've got, and I don't think this town will have an ATM on every street corner," he said to me.

"We've got enough for now."

We knocked on the door of the auto shop and our friend explained what had happened and asked the man to help us.

Sí, sí, esperen un momento. He led us to a waiting room while he got his tow truck ready.

"Marcela." George leaned his shoulder on a wall and looked down at me to where I'd sat on a bench. "I understand that you're looking for someone more Mexican. If you want me to embrace more of my Mexicanness, I will. You can introduce me to your parents as your Mexican boyfriend. I've got the last name."

The ice had helped the swelling on my forehead, but not the throbbing on the inside. I lifted my pounding head and stared at him. I couldn't tell if he was teasing me or if he was serious. I didn't care about him being Mexican enough anymore and he wasn't going to fool my family with a last name. "I don't—I mean, I just want you to be you."

He pushed off the wall and knelt in front of me. He ran his fingertips carefully along my forehead. Then he stretched up and kissed the spot that was probably turning purple by now. "You want me to be me?"

"Of course." I straightened my back and ran my fingertips along his growing whiskers. He looked damned sexy.

"Marcela," he said. "I don't want to spook you, but I have to tell you something."

I'm not sure I like it when someone starts with something like that. I glanced out the window. "We should go find the tow truck driver, don't you think?"

"Wait." He frowned. "I've got to say this." He took both my hands. "I'm falling in love with you, Marcela." He said it almost as an apology.

Oh no. He didn't just say that, did he? I stared at him, unable to speak.

"The more time I spend with you, every time I hold you or kiss you or make love to you, I feel like my heart is completely full. You make me laugh and remind me of what it's like to really live life. And all I want is more of you. I'm hooked," he said with a shrug.

I smiled and searched my brain for something light-hearted to say, but nothing came to mind. I sighed. I should feel elated that someone as wonderful as George could think he loves me. But I was frightened. This was serious. Love. Wow.

"Say something, please," he said.

Oh God. I'm so damned confused. I want him, but I just don't think I'm ready for anything permanent. Let's face it, I'm married to my job. Then my family takes up a huge chunk of my life. I don't want any more changes. I like being alone, living alone, dating here and there. "George, I . . . don't know what you want me to say?"

"You don't?"

My heart slammed into my chest, because I feared I did know. "No."

"Do you want me in your life?"

"Yes," I said immediately. "Of course I do."

He stared at me and acted like he wanted to say more, but he took pity on me and let me go. He stood. "You're right. We'd better go get our car. We can talk more about this when we get settled somewhere."

He left.

"Shit, shit, shit." I slammed my forehead with my hand, forgetting the welt already there. "Ouch. Shit." I bent at the waist and held my head in my hands.

How could I let him walk away? How could I not give him a better response after he poured his heart out to me? Because I'm an idiot, that's why.

I hurried out to find George and the tow truck driver. Which I managed to do amazingly easy since they were right outside the door getting ready to call me out.

We climbed into the truck and headed out to get our car. But when we got back to where our car had broken down, we found a huge problem—there was no car. It had been stolen.

Thirty-three

🌺 For the first time, I saw George really distraught. "How are we going to get back to civilization? Do you know what the rental car company is going to say?" With both hands behind his head, he stalked the area where we'd left the car, kicking up dust. Then he paused and inhaled deeply. He turned his attention in my direction as if waiting for me to answer his question.

Getting back to civilization wouldn't be a problem. The car rental company might be a little ticked at us though. And I wasn't thrilled to have lost my luggage with all my clothes and shoes. "We have insurance," I said, for lack of something more helpful to say.

"Fuck the insurance. First my wallet, now our car."

I felt bad and guilty like I'd done something wrong. Stupid, I know, because it wasn't my fault the car broke down and got stolen. Maybe because I felt his temper and anger were fueled more by my lack of response to his declaration of love than because of the stolen car. The car seemed to give him an appropriate avenue to vent, and he was taking full advantage of it.

"Hey." I stood in his path. "Come on. We work for a movie studio. Doesn't this remind you of a bad Western or a Bob Hope comedy?"

"There's nothing comedic about getting your car stolen in an isolated part of Mexico, and don't you dare make a joke. Let's get out of here."

Jeesh. Okay.

We accepted a ride back to town from the tow truck driver. At least there we could rent a place for the night and make arrangements to get another car.

We found a small motel, which seemed more like a bed and breakfast. George checked us in while I went to a general store and bought a couple of generic pants and tops with pretty much the last of our cash. But, I desperately needed to change out of my clothes.

We got our own room, but had to share a bathroom with other guests. I wasn't too happy about that, but after sleeping in a barn this felt like heaven.

We climbed the stairs to our room. George immediately collapsed onto the bed.

"I'm going to go take a shower," I said.

"Okay."

It felt sooo good to wash off the grime and dust accumulated in my pores. The quick wash up at the farmhouse helped but didn't come close to the soaking I needed. I stayed under the spray of water until it turned cold, then went back to my room to change.

George was not in the room; he probably went to see about getting another car.

❀ I dressed in the simple outfit I bought and realized it wasn't half bad. At least it was comfortable and it would do until we got to Mexico City.

I decided to call for help, so I picked up the phone and placed a call to Panoply—to Jackson. I told him what had happened.

"What do you want me to do?"

"Wire me some money to the Hotel Ritz in Mexico City. We'll be checking in there tomorrow, and they are large enough to be able to accept the transfer."

"You got it."

I gave him the address. "There's more."

"What?"

"George told me he loved me."

"Whoa. Our man, the number cruncher, trying to get into your pants, is he?"

"Gee, thanks a lot."

He chuckled. "Didn't mean it like that. You're totally loveable. But . . . sure it's not a line?"

"Trust me, it's not a line."

"Man. What did you say?"

"Nothing."

"Nothing? Dude tells you he loves you and you say nothing?"

I groaned. "You know me. I'm totally ill-equipped to handle matters of the heart."

George walked in then and my first instinct was to hang up on Jackson. Those two still couldn't stand each other.

"Girl, I told you he wasn't the guy for you. You should have listened."

"I should have."

"He's not the love 'em and leave 'em type of guy; he's gonna wanna stick."

George dropped his pants, his shirt, then his briefs. He took a towel and wrapped it around himself. "I'm going to go shower. Who you talking to?"

"Jackson," I said.

His face darkened and his jaw tightened. "I see."

"What?" Jackson asked on his end.

"George just walked in and asked me who I was talking to."

"Oh, loverboy is in the room, huh? Guess you can't talk anymore."

"That's right," I said.

George walked out without another word.

"He left," I said with a sigh.

"Well, listen," Jackson said. "If you don't love him, then tell him. Send him home. End it now, before things get worse."

"What if I do care about him?"

He was quiet. "Enough to change your whole life for this guy? Come on, Marcela. You ready to settle down?"

"No."

"Then be fair. Get rid of him."

I ended the call and sat alone, contemplating what I should do. I didn't want to get rid of George. He was the best thing that ever happened to me. But I also didn't want to make any drastic changes to my life.

George walked back in, smelling clean and looking gorgeous.

"Jackson says hi."

"I'll bet he does."

He was pissed. No doubt about it.

"He's going to wire us some money."

George whirled on me. "The last thing I need is one of your ex-boyfriends bailing me out of trouble."

"He's not an ex-boyfriend, he's my friend, and we're going to need some money."

"Then I'll call *my* office and have *my* secretary wire us the money."

"Great," I shouted back.

He dressed in angry jerks, then stalked over and dropped on the bed beside me.

I placed my hand on George's stomach, caressing him gently through the material of his shirt. "Are you angry because I asked Jackson to send me money or because I was talking to him period?"

"I'm not angry," he denied, but he stared up at the ceiling and his words were short and clipped.

I felt awful. Not only because I'd failed to graciously accept his love, but also because I had expected this trip to be a little more glamorous and it was turning out to be a disaster.

"You know he's just a friend. And we work together and we're going to talk and see each other."

He didn't look at me, didn't respond.

"You can't be jealous of him, George. I swear, you don't have to be."

"You could have called someone else."

"I called work. They can send me money. Jackson can talk to our producer and authorize a money transfer."

"So can your bank." He turned his head and looked at me. "You didn't call them though, did you?"

He had me there. "Maybe I needed to talk to him, to check in, to connect with my job."

After a long, hard look, he turned his head away. "Things getting too hard to deal with here? Ready to go home and stick your head back in your work where you're safe?"

I pulled my hand away from him. "What the hell is that supposed to mean?"

"I mean, you're a workaholic and you use work to avoid dealing with real life."

"Give me a break, George. I love my job; that's no secret."

The word "love" hung between us.

"Yes, you do. Good to know you can commit to something."

"Shit." I stood. "I don't need this. You know that?"

He glared at me, but I could also see the pain in his eyes. Why was I lashing out at him? All he'd done was tell me he loved me. The bastard.

Standing and walking around the bed, he came face to face with me. "You don't know what you need." He hooked a hand behind my neck and pulled my head and my lips toward his. "Or what you want."

"I want you," I whispered against his lips. "I do."

His mouth covered mine. The kiss was like magic, like each time he touched me. I knew I was home. I didn't want to lose him. I had to make it clear to him that I cared about him even if I wasn't able to say that I loved him.

He walked me back to the bed then eased down and placed his weight on me. Purposefully, he slipped the top I'd just put on over my head. He stared at my breasts and released the front clasp of my bra. Gazing at me through sizzling eyes, he drew a breath. "Is this what you want from me?"

"Yes."

His eyes locked with mine. "Is this *all* you want?"

Honestly, I didn't know. I think I always assumed I'd end up like Aunt Lydia—being my own woman, in control, free. But George was complicating things. He made me . . . want more. When I hesitated, he pulled back.

"George." I held onto his shoulders. "Make love to me."

I couldn't deal with questions that delved excessively deep right now. I had too many other things on my mind that I had to clear up first, before I could explore how I really felt about George and what that could possibly mean in my life. "I . . . I need you," I said.

His hungry gaze held a hint of disappointment, but he nodded. "Come here then," he said.

He kissed me hard with incredibly intense pressure, parting my lips and plunging his tongue through. His hands ran up and down my body, hastily.

As my breasts flattened against the rough texture of the fabric of his shirt, I scratched at his back, wanting it off. I wanted no barriers between us. I wanted to feel him inside me. I could feel him slipping away from me, and I wanted to draw him closer, show him how I felt about him, at least physically.

He stripped himself and me naked as we battled on the bed like two wrestlers.

He pinned me. I rolled on top of him.

He licked and bit and tugged.

I gripped and squeezed and pulled.

We made love.

And it was explosive.

❀ When it was over, I knew I'd made a huge mistake. Not because I'd slept with him in order to end our argument, but because I didn't say the words he needed to hear. Hot sex, which we both needed, was great, but a total lack of connection was not. No sweet words like in the past. No afterglow caresses. He'd given me sex, but he'd held back all his love, and I missed it.

He sat on the edge of the bed with his back to me, staring at the sunset out the window. I reached across and caressed his perfectly tanned, smooth back.

He looked over his shoulder and smiled. The moment was right. The man was more than right. It was now or never. I had to say it. He obviously needed to hear it. I cared about him, so why not say it? Three simple words that would make my man happy.

"I . . . I'm sorry," I said.

His smile faded. "You are?"

"*No*, I'm not sorry we did . . . we had sex. I'm sorry if . . . I can't . . . If I don't . . ."

"Love me?"

"No, that's not what I meant to say." I sat up and got on my knees. "Damn."

He stood. "Forget it."

"I don't want to forget it. That was incredible between us. It's always incredible."

"I agree."

"But it's still not enough for you. You're still not happy."

He slipped on his pants. "I am."

"I have to do this my way, George."

"Fine."

"No, it's not fine." I grabbed a pillow and hit it. "Stop saying that you agree with me and that everything is fine."

He paused in mid-buttoning, and his look seemed to ask if I'd gone crazy.

"You just don't understand how it is with me. My whole life my family has been telling me what I want and what I need, what's good for me, what's right for me." Tears stung my eyes. "But I don't know. When it comes down to it, I don't know if marrying a Mexican man and having twenty kids is really what *I* want or what they want."

I sighed and leaned on the headboard, watching him, feeling drained. I couldn't say the love words, because I wasn't sure what those words meant to him. To me they meant I wanted him—I wanted a relationship. But forever, I don't know. With George, knowing the speed he seemed to travel, he'd be buying wedding rings before the end of the year.

He frowned and approached the bed, then dropped down to his knees and tentatively placed a hand on my thigh, as if frightened I might break. "Hey, come on. It's okay."

I stared down at my hands on my lap. I fingered a piece of thread on the pillowcase.

"I didn't mean to make you miserable by telling you I loved you. I just needed to tell you how I felt. To let you know I'm out for more than a fling."

I met his gaze.

"I hoped you were feeling the same, but . . . I think I need to give you more time."

I placed a hand over his, and Jackson's words about being fair and letting George go echoed in my head. "You're just not giving me a chance to catch my breath. I need time to—"

"You've got it." He smiled sadly. "You need to know exactly what you want." He exhaled heavily. "And I'm only in your way." He stood and picked up his shirt.

"Where are you going?" I asked.

"Going to call for a car to come and get us." He put on his shirt. "Take us to Mexico City." His shoes were next. "I'll get you there, then I'll fly home."

"Without me?"

"Looks that way."

I couldn't believe it. Just like that, he was leaving me.

Thirty-four

Tuesday, September 14

🌸 After riding all night in a Lincoln Town Car, we arrived and settled into the plush Hotel Ritz in the heart of Mexico City's historic center. We showered, changed, did some shopping, ate, and slept. But mostly we ignored each other.

What the hell happened? All I wanted George to do was to move slower and give me time to make the needed internal adjustments for a permanent relationship. I didn't want him gone all together. And now he was leaving. He called and made arrangements with the airline to leave, then watched sports programs on TV.

I tried to pretend I was cool with all this. While he watched TV, I spent hours on the phone talking with my animators, having useless discussions because they had everything under control.

Once they booted me off the phone so they could actually get some work done, I called Daniela and had a marathon conversation with her. Her husband had taken the kids on a fishing trip and she stayed home to clean and relax.

"I had to go to Adriana's ballet class, of course, to tell the instructor she would have to miss class."

Didn't make sense to me, because she could have called, but I was desperate to keep her talking so I asked, "What kind of ballet is it again?"

"What kind? It's ballet. Who cares? The thing is, I stayed and chatted with my friend, you know, ballet dad," she said conspiratorially.

Ballet dad? She'd lost me. "And?"

"Well, I told him about how Fabian remodeled our living room and put in a fireplace. He wanted to see it so I invited him over tonight after work."

Oh, now I remember. Ballet dad. Daniela's innocent flirtation, which sounded like it was moving past the flirtation stage. "Be careful, Dani."

"What?" she asked, full of innocence.

"Come on. What are you doing?"

"Just being friendly."

"Your husband's away and you invite another guy over?"

"Maybe I shouldn't be telling you any of this. You're my friend. I thought you'd understand."

I don't understand infidelity. "I'm your friend, girl. Just remember there are things you can't take back, okay?"

"Yeah. Okay. I'd better go."

I didn't want her to go, but I agreed. "See you in a week or so."

With no one else to call, and nothing to work on, I sat on the balcony and stared out at the city for hours, questioning myself.

Should I let George go? With all my family obligations and work, maybe this would be for the best even if it didn't feel like it right now.

Or maybe I should go home with him. Maybe I was looking for something too intangible to ever find. Maybe Daniela and I had gone about my quest the wrong way. Maybe there was nothing

I could *do* to become more Latina. Or maybe my family was right about me and I just wasn't Latina enough and never would be.

Here was my opportunity, right under my nose, to embrace a real relationship—one that could lead to marriage and children. A Mexican guy who would willingly embrace his Mexicanness for me and my family. This was it—my chance to prove to my family how much I really did belong . . . and I couldn't close the deal.

I watched George read a newspaper while he waited for the right time to head downstairs and catch a cab to the airport.

"Sure you don't want me to go with you to the airport?"

"I'm sure," he said.

His flight left in four hours. I didn't think I could take another two hours of staring at him and having him pretend I wasn't in the room. I'd already endured two days of this.

I paced from the French doors leading out to the balcony to the front door. Back and forth. Back and forth. Then finally I stopped. "I'm going to miss you," I said to the man behind the paper.

He didn't respond.

"George?"

"Hmm."

"Can you put the paper down and talk to me?"

He let a corner flop down and looked over the top.

"Thank you."

Still he didn't speak.

What did I want to say? What did I want from him? "Please don't leave."

He inhaled. "We've been through this. I'll see you when you come home."

I felt a sudden stirring of hope. We'd take a little break, then I'd get home and we'd take up where we left off. I smiled. "One week then. I'll see you in one week?"

"Okay." He went back to his paper.

But something inside told me that if he left, we would never be able to pick up from where we left off. I walked over and eased his paper down, and sat on his lap. "I'm sorry," I said, caressing his face. He'd come to mean so much to me and I didn't want to lose him.

"Don't be. We tried."

"Don't say 'we tried' that way. I'm not finished."

He sighed.

"Please, George." I felt like I was sinking.

He caressed my back, his fingertips moving up and down my spine. "You really need to be on your own for a while longer. You told me that, and I pushed. I didn't get it. I do now."

I shook my head. "What I need is you." I lowered my head and kissed his lips.

But George turned his head. "Marcela, don't make this any harder."

I moaned to keep from crying and rested my forehead on his shoulder. "I've never felt like this about anyone, don't you understand? Don't leave me, George. *Please.*"

"Hey," he whispered. "Come on. You're killing me here. I'm trying to be smart—to be strong." He continued to caress my back in a gentle, reassuring rhythm, using his whole hand now. "I'm not *leaving* you. I'm giving you time. Space. It's what you said you needed."

I did say that, didn't I? "I . . . I meant emotional space, not physical. You don't need to go."

"I don't know what that means. I love you. I can't be with you and pretend I don't. I just can't do this relationship thing on my own," he said. "It may sound weak, but it hurts. When you're ready, maybe . . ."

My pain was quickly turning to anger. I bolted off his lap and wiped my eyes of tears, which had started to collect and blur my vision. "I'm ready damn it. I'm here with you; I made love to you. What else do you want from me?"

He stood. "Your heart."

I closed my eyes for a moment and shook my head, feeling

lost. This was all new territory for me. "I thought I *was* opening my heart to you."

"Marcela," he whispered. His crooked index finger tipped my chin up and our gazes locked. "Take some time. Figure things out. Don't ask me to stay because you're afraid of losing me."

"If you leave me now, George, it's over. I mean it."

"I'm trying to help you out, can't you see that?"

I looked around the room for my purse. I needed to get out of here. Shopping. I needed more clothes.

"Hey," he said.

I picked up my purse. "Have a good trip home."

He clasped my arm. "One day, you're going to thank me for leaving. You're going to know I loved you enough not to crowd you; not to take advantage of your fear of being alone to trap you into a relationship you're not ready to commit to yet."

I stared at him. A part of me absolutely knew he was right. I thought about our studio mantra when a story just wasn't coming together—sometimes you have to go backward in order to go forward.

"Are you okay?" he asked.

No, he was breaking my heart, couldn't he tell? I tried to pull my arm loose, but he held on. "Let go."

He let my arm go and shoved his hands into his pockets. "That's what I'm doing."

"Yeah. I know." And it hurt so badly. I didn't want to be let go. I wanted him to cling to me and tell me he would convince me to love him out of the sheer force of his own love. That he'd never let me go. That he'd love me no matter what. But who was I kidding? This wasn't a Lifetime movie. I walked out of our room without looking at him or touching him.

I left the town center and headed to where the concierge said I'd find the Plaza de las Estrellas Galleria mall. With over two hundred boutiques and restaurants, I figured there would be tons of stuff to take my mind off George, but as I wandered through the busy, noisy mall crowded with people, I realized that staring at clothes didn't interest me. I walked around feeling like a zombie.

I didn't return to my hotel until I knew George would be long gone. A huge part of me hoped he'd still be there. That he'd changed his mind, and that we'd spend the night making love and forgiving each other. And maybe I could even tell him I loved him, because right now I'd say anything to keep him.

But my hotel room was dark and empty when I walked in that evening. I didn't bother getting out of my clothes. I curled onto the first bed in a fetal position, and wondered what was wrong with me as I cried myself to sleep.

Friday, September 17

❀ It took me a couple of days to get over my slump. I slept on and off throughout the day, watched Spanish soap operas, and cried about everything—even laundry commercials where the grandmother got the stain out of the granddaughter's favorite shirt. A bustling city was right outside my window, but I didn't have the energy to go out. Maybe because I wasn't eating.

But, after two days of imprisonment, I told myself I either had to get out or go home. I forced myself to shower and dress and go downstairs for dinner. As I ate all alone in the hotel restaurant, I realized that maybe being alone was what I really needed after all. This trip to Mexico was for me. It should never have been a romantic getaway with a guy.

The next morning, I took care of the issue of the stolen rental car and filed the appropriate forms. Then I called my cell phone company and told them that my charger had been stolen, and they advised me where to buy a new one so I could recharge my phone.

Once that was taken care of, I called home and checked on Lupe. Mom said that from what she knew, Lupe was fine, but that her mother had been unresponsive when she called. Damn the

woman. Once I returned home, I'd have to have a serious talk
with her. She could tell me it's none of my business, she could ignore me, but she couldn't ignore her daughter anymore. Lupe
needed her mother. I could be her friend, but the judge had been
correct, I couldn't be a parent figure.

Then as an afterthought, I called work and joked around with
Jackson for a while, and realized I missed being there. Panoply
was home. I belonged there. I fit in. There's something to be said
for fantasy. And I'm good at it.

"You doing okay?" he asked as our call wound down. "George
came to see me today."

I tightened my grip on my small cell. "He's back at work
already?"

"He looked like shit. Told me to call you and make sure you
were okay."

"Were you going to?"

"Going to what?"

"Call me."

"No. I knew you'd phone if you wanted to talk. So, do you
want to tell me what happened?"

"No." I looked out at the plaza. "I can't talk about it. He
touched something inside me and I don't even feel like the same
person anymore. Does that make sense?"

"Not really."

"It doesn't to me either."

"When you get back, we'll go out and get drunk together and
you'll be back to your old self in no time."

"Sure." Though that sounded like a horrible idea. "Take care,
Jack." I closed my phone. For some crazy reason, I felt like I was
saying good-bye to him for good. Had I outgrown our friendship?
Or had I killed it months ago by sleeping with him? Maybe both.
In any case, there would be no more late night bars for me.

Finished with my calls and my lunch, I tackled the town.

Mexico City is a town of contrasts. Ancient ruins sit alongside modern buildings. A dynamic business metropolis buzzes with energy, power, and money, while incredibly poor slums cry out for help in the same vicinity.

The city's history called out to me, so my first stop was the Metropolitan Cathedral that sits in the very heart of downtown Mexico City on what was once the Aztecs' holiest sites. Their Templo Mayor, or Great Temple, once stood tall with all its splendor until it was destroyed by the Spanish to build instead a symbol of the Catholic faith.

I walked the footpath around the site's ruins, reading how construction workers accidentally uncovered the remains of the temple in the late 1970s. Amazing that it was hidden for so long. I bent down and touched the stones, wondering how a culture that was supposedly primitive could have built such an amazing structure.

My mind worked in images and they now began to roll—almost like a movie reel. I pictured how stunning and exotic the temple must have looked to Hernán Cortés and his men when they rode into the Aztec city of Tenochtitlan almost five hundred years ago. The pictures in my head became vivid and I imagined them with color and music and motion. Getting a jolt of adrenaline rush, I found a corner to sit in and turned my brochure over to sketch this scene as it played in my mind.

At the end of the tour, I entered the museum, where representations of the temple in all its various stages of construction were depicted in paintings, drawings, and models. I became absorbed by what I saw and read.

The temple was built in this location because it was the site where the Aztecs received their prophetic vision of an eagle perched upon a prickly pear cactus devouring a snake—still depicted to this day on the Mexican flag.

A place of religious significance where ritualistic sacrifices were performed for the Aztec gods, the temple was described by the Spaniards as reeking "like a slaughterhouse." But to the Aztecs the sacrifices had deep religious meaning and were performed to satisfy their gods. Death was necessary for birth.

I couldn't sketch fast enough. I bought a notepad and drew everything I saw. I bought books and postcards of recovered artifacts. I spent the whole day in the museum. And when I left, I went straight back to my hotel.

As if suddenly possessed, I stayed up all night drawing and recreating the entrance of Cortez into the world of the Aztecs. The battle on the steps of the temple—swords and firearms against sharp obsidian arrows; white men in red and gold uniforms riding on four-legged, sweaty beasts fighting against dark-skinned warriors with only their brawn and their bravery to defend them. The defeat of one of the greatest pre-Columbian empires in the Americas. By five in the morning, when I finally collapsed into bed, I knew I had my next project. Even if I had to take it to Disney or finance it myself, this would become my next movie.

I spent the rest of the week at a mellower pace. I toured the city, visiting Frida Kahlo's Blue House where she had lived with Diego Rivera for ten years; the Palacio de Bellas Artes, because I loved paintings; and continued my research on Cortez and the Aztecs with a visit to the National Palace once occupied by Cortez.

Then I took a forty-five minute excursion to the three pyramids: one to the Sun, another to the Moon, and lastly, one to the Feathered Serpent. They still stand tall outside Mexico City. I climbed to the top and with each breathless step, I felt freer and more liberated. I felt like a conqueror myself and like everything was possible. Mexico stands above sea level and maybe I was simply getting light-headed. I thought better to descend before my mind really got carried away.

During the evenings, I strolled downtown and ate incredible meals. Though I was all alone, I was happy. But I missed George, and wondered how much better this would have been if I had been able to share it with him. Impulsively, I slipped into a restaurant and found a table on the outside patio. I dug my cell out of my purse and called him.

His deep voice answered the phone.

"It's me," I said.

"How are you?" He sounded relieved.

"Fine." Was he worried about me? I ached inside because I wanted so badly to be with him. "I . . . I've figured out my next pitch to the studios."

"Oh yeah? That's great."

"Yeah. Really great. It's going to be awesome." I paused and he was quiet. This was bullshit. Neither of us wanted to talk about something as idiotic as my job. "I found what I came to Mexico to find, George."

"What's that?"

Yes, my movie—the workaholic in me couldn't deny the importance of what this creation could mean for my career and the satisfaction I'd get from seeing this story told on the big screen. But equally important, I found myself feeling more grounded. A calm, peaceful mood was starting to settle in my heart. "Answers."

The more I soaked up Mexico, the more I saw a beautiful country with a rich history, but the less I identified it with Latinos back home. We *were* different. Perhaps the immigrant journey or the American influence had changed us, but though we maintained certain elements, we were a new breed. My aunt wasn't fighting to be Mexican. She was fighting to be accepted into American society. I realized I didn't have anything to fight for, and my guilt at not being Latina enough began to fade.

I was ready to go home.

"I want to share those answers with you. If you're still willing to . . . see me."

"I'm willing."

But I felt the distance—the barrier he'd put up to protect himself from me. Another stab to my heart.

"Thanks, George."

"For what?"

"You said I would thank you, and you were right. I needed this time alone to do what I came here to do." When he was around he absorbed my every thought, my every feeling. I had nothing left to devote to my work or to myself.

"You're welcome," he said.

I wanted to give him something back, but I still couldn't give him what he wanted, so maybe I should do what he did for me and let him go. "You had me figured out from the beginning, didn't you? I wasn't the relationship kind after all."

"Marcela, come home. Call me when you get back. We'll talk."

I squeezed my eyes shut, trying to clear the blurriness. "Goodbye." I closed the phone, not waiting for his reply.

I ordered a fruity drink and sat in a plaza with lights twinkling and crowds of people walking and talking, and placed a hand to my heart. The pain was real and sharp, and I drew a deep breath, trying to figure out what was wrong with me. Then I remembered what my grandmother said about love. You know you're in love when it hurts more to imagine life without someone than with them.

Oh shit, I think I'm actually in love with George. Now what?

Thirty-five

Saturday, September 18

❀ The bolt clicked as I turned the lock. I pushed the door open and stared inside my apartment. Drawing a breath, I walked inside. *Home.* Seeing my familiar apartment made me feel both like a soldier returning from war where everything that once mattered now seemed trite, and comforted to be back on familiar ground.

I kicked my foot backward and shut my front door, then dropped my bags. Now what?

Monday I'd return to work, and this weekend, I'd go visit Lupe at camp. I'd pick up from where I'd left off. But today, right now . . . what?

Turning right back around, I grabbed my purse and my keys and went grocery shopping. At the store, I filled my basket with fruit, peppers, onions, green chiles, a beef brisket, corn tortillas, sour cream, cheese . . . I just kept throwing stuff in. Pretty soon, my basket was so full I had a hard time pushing it to the checkout line.

I took home my twenty bags of groceries and filled my fridge, leaving out only the items I planned to use. Then I started cooking. I made everything I'd learned from Alberto: rice, a bowl of beans, chile rellenos, tostadas. I cooked for three hours straight, then sat down and had a great meal all by myself. I had a little of everything and it was marvelous.

With a full belly, and a feeling of satisfaction, I waddled to my desk and hit my answering machine. I had ten messages. The first five were from salespeople, the sixth from my dry cleaner telling me I forgot to pick up a couple of outfits, the seventh from Rogelio inviting me to the chamber for a new member welcoming party. I smiled. That guy was persistent. The eighth call stopped me cold. It said, "Hi, this is Paul Peckinpaugh. You, ah, called me a few weeks ago. Remember me? Well, I told my dad about the strange call, and he, ah, knows your mom. I got your number off our Caller ID box. I didn't tell my dad I had your number, but maybe you'd better call back. You might actually be my half sister if what you and Dad say is true. Well, later." He paused. "Call me."

My wonderful dinner felt like a brick in my stomach. Half brother? Thoughts and images and colors flashed through my mind. I hadn't even considered siblings. Oh my God. *Oh my God!!* As if struck by a whip to my butt, I dropped down to the waste can beside my desk. I turned it upside down and searched for the crumbled piece of paper with Paul's number. Sighing a breath of relief, I found it. Thank goodness, I hadn't emptied the wastebasket before leaving for Mexico. I could have always gone back to the Internet, but right now, I was too agitated to be able to search properly.

What do I do? Do I call this guy back? He was the one in Oregon. The first one I'd called. The young guy I had spoken to. *My brother*.

I had to call back. I had to know.

Picking up the phone, I dialed the number with shaky hands. The ringing terrified me. I was shaking. What would I say?

"Hey," a voice on the other side said.

"Paul?"

"Yep. Who's this, Brittany?"

"No. Marcela. I'm calling about my mom, Marta, and your dad. You called me back and—"

"Ohhhh, yeah. Right."

Neither one of us said anything for a few seconds, but it felt like an eternity. I didn't even move, just stood motionless in the middle of my living room.

"Your dad thinks he knew my mom?"

"Said he was in love with a woman named Marta once. They had a thing, but she dumped him because her family wouldn't have accepted him."

I sucked in some air, because if I didn't breathe, I'd pass out. Paul hadn't admitted to his son that he'd had an affair with a married woman. Marcela didn't blame him, why hurt the kid? "I'm sorry," I said.

"Hey, for what?"

"I don't want to cause your dad or your family any trouble."

"Yeaahh." Paul said. "This could get a little sticky. I wondered if I was actually being smart by calling you back. But I figured you can't hide from the truth." He paused. "So, you think my dad might be your father too, huh?"

"I think so."

"Well, if he is, he is. And he'd want to know. This was before he met my mom. Shit happens, you know?" Then as if realizing what he said, he corrected himself. "I mean, life is full of unexpected turns. It's too bad your mom didn't contact my dad while you were still young."

I couldn't believe how *nice* this guy was. "Well, he might *not* even be my birth father. We don't know."

"Guess we'd better find out."

"How?"

"Let's arrange a meeting. Get some tests done."

Travel to Oregon? "I think it would be best to talk to him first. He might not want—"

"Marcela. If I had a kid out there somewhere, I'd want to know. My dad's a good man. His only regret will be that he didn't know about you earlier."

I nodded. "You're okay with all this?" I was scared shitless.

"Not really. My mom probably won't deal too well with it. But it's not like he cheated on her or anything. She didn't even know my dad thirty-two years ago."

But my mom *did* cheat on my dad. Jeez, what a mess. I could hang up and forget the whole thing. I didn't want to hurt any more people. Even if Paul was indeed my sperm donor, what difference did it make? I didn't really want a relationship with the man. But what about the younger Paul? What if he was my brother? "Paul?"

"Yeah."

"Do you have any brothers or sisters?"

Soft laughter touched my ear. "My sister Diana is twenty-two. My brother Kevin is nineteen."

I felt dizzy. Reaching for my chair, I sat at my desk.

"Instant family," he said.

"I can't handle this," I admitted.

"Marcela, it won't be that bad."

"Yes, it will. Look, forget about me. Don't tell your dad or your siblings that we talked again. I'm sorry I called you."

"Forget? How can I do that?"

"I'm sorry."

"I've got to give my dad your number. He deserves to know if you're really his daughter or not."

I was hyperventilating. "What if he's not the Paul my mom . . ." *Had an affair with.* "Knew?"

"Then it would be a pretty huge coincidence that my dad just happened to have been in love with a woman named Marta thirty-two years ago. Hell, you're my half sister. We should meet."

I held my forehead in my hand and shook my head. "Let me think about this a little while."

"You take your time and think. I'm telling my dad that I talked to you and that we're thinking about where and when to meet."

"Okay. Fair enough. Take care," I said.

"Hey, wait a second."

"What?"

"You married? Have kids?"

"No," I said quietly, almost as if I were secretly sharing privileged information with an enemy. "You?"

"No. I go to Oregon State. Agriculture major. We own an organic farm out here."

"Oh. I'm . . . an . . . ah." I tried to clear my head. "I work for an animation studio in Hollywood."

"Cool. What do you do?"

"Animation."

He laughed. "Wow. Well, nice to meet you."

"Thanks. You too."

"One more thing."

"What?"

"If my dad does turn out to be your father . . . I don't know how to ask this, so I just will. Do you plan to ask to be included in his inheritance? I'm just asking because—"

"*No*, no, I hadn't thought about money or inheritances or . . . any of that. Honestly."

"Sorry, it's just that as the oldest kid, Dad promised me the farm and I'm the only one who is really interested in the business anyway, and—"

"Paul, I don't want your business."

"Okay, okay." He sounded nervous.

I felt bad for him. How unfair for an outsider to show up and become a threat to what you always expected would be yours. "I only want to know the truth. For years I thought I knew who I was, and . . ."

"I understand," he spoke warmly. "Let's meet. Let's get to the truth."

"Okay."

We hung up without saying good-bye. This was only the beginning. I just hoped it wasn't the beginning of a huge mistake.

Uneasily, I stood and backed away from my desk. I had an incredible need to call George and share this with him. I needed him to hold me and tell me everything would be okay. George was good at that. I stumbled into my bedroom and collapsed on my bed. "No," I said to myself. I could handle this on my own. I had to. Until I was ready to offer him more of myself, I couldn't lean on George anymore.

Sunday, September 19

❀ Somehow, I managed to focus on my work over the weekend. I began initial storyboards and text treatment on my computer so I could present my idea to my team. My excitement grew as I saw my vision begin to take shape. I hadn't been this absorbed by a project since the first one I worked on for Panoply eight years ago. I only stopped to go visit Lupe since Sunday is the only day she is allowed visitors.

Although this camp was minimum security, it was still surrounded by a barbed wire fence. I had to go through security, then was escorted to a library-type meeting room. Lupe sat at a table scribbling something on a sheet of paper. When I got close, I noticed she was drawing.

Her eyes registered surprise when I sat across from her. "Hey, I didn't think it would be you."

"Hi Lupe. Expecting your mom?"

"Sort of."

"How are you?"

"How do I look?"

She looked okay. This wasn't a country club, but it wasn't as horrid as I'd pictured either.

"What? You have nothing to say? No words of wisdom?"

Was she mocking me? "Sorry Lupe."

"For what?"

"The judge was right about me. I'm no role model."

She gazed at me. "Here," she said, pushing the notepad across the table.

She'd drawn what looked like architectural plans.

"Some ideas for your center." She pointed as she talked. "Here's a comfortable hanging-out place with TVs and headphones. Over here's a game area. Computers in this corner. Keeps the flow of quiet areas off to the sides."

"You're designing the community center?"

She shrugged and tried to look disinterested. "Just thinking about it. To help you out." She took back her notepad and leaned into her chair. "Nothing else to do around here."

I had been thinking of abandoning that idea. I had no experience running something of that magnitude, probably not enough money, and no business taking responsibility for young kids. "Where would we put something like this?"

"All over L.A.? But you can start in my neighborhood."

I nodded as our eyes locked. Okay. If she was still willing to work on our relationship, I was still willing to do my part.

"This," she said, gesturing around the room, "wasn't your fault, Marcela."

I reached across the table and took one of her hands in mine. Here was this kid trying to make *me* feel better. "Hell, I'm sorry about everything."

She pulled her hand loose from mine. "Sorry enough to forget about the money I owe you?"

I already had, but I got the feeling she didn't want me to forget about the debt. She was too stubborn or proud to admit she wanted to continue our friendship. Working for me gave her a good excuse. "Not on your life. You've got tons of hours to put into this center."

"Child labor is against the law. I learned that in here."

Smiling, I said, "Then what do you say you just hang out at the center? Keep an eye on things for me."

"As long as you're not there all the time telling me what to do."

How could I be? I had a career that already took up most of my time. I needed help and advice. I needed Rogelio. I guess I'd be going to his welcoming party after all. "Okay, it's a deal. I'll put this together. You help me run it. I'll keep my distance."

She nodded. "I'll be out in a little over two months. But . . ."

"What?"

"Will they let me go back home?"

I sure as hell hoped so. "Your mother loves you too much to lose you. She'll make sure you return home."

The doubt in Lupe's eyes was painful to watch. But no matter what happened I'd stick by her. This I'd already promised myself.

Thirty-Six

Monday, September 20

❀ Monday morning when I got back to the studio and the initial hellos were over, as well as the obligatory questions about my trip, I settled behind my desk to tackle all that I had missed while on vacation.

For once, I had few interruptions.

Probably the hardest part of being back at work was to know that George was downstairs and I couldn't see him or talk to him. In Mexico, I was able to rationalize the relationship away, that it wasn't really love, that I was just lonely, but now that I was back home, I still missed him. How was it possible to want someone so much, and yet not be able to commit to him?

Then later in the day, I faced my second challenge—what to do about Paul? I called the airport and booked a flight to Oregon. Then I called the young Paul and told him I'd be there to see him next month. He sounded pleased, but butterflies bumped into the sides of my stomach—probably trying to avoid the burning acid bubbling in there at the thought of actually meeting this man who had created me.

Thursday, September 23

❀ I strolled into the welcoming party Rogelio was throwing for new members of the Latino Chamber of Commerce. The room was large enough to fit about fifty people. Only about half that many were attending today. People milled around and chatted, so I did the same. Met an interesting guy who owns a car dealership, a lady financial planner, and a few others. Finally, Rogelio asked everyone to serve themselves from the buffet table of sandwiches, potato salad, fruit, and cookies and take a seat.

Standing at the podium with a smile on his face, he looked like a man who loved his job. He made a pitch for more money, a plea for us to hire Latinos whenever possible, and a promise to expand services and benefits to us, Latino business owners and entrepreneurs.

But after he finished his speech, I cornered Rogelio about opening up a center for kids. "Think I'd be able to get help setting up something of this magnitude?"

Rogelio made a less than encouraging face. "Nonprofit is noble, but no one wants to put their money down for something like that."

"I do."

"How much do you have?"

"Enough to lease a building for a year or two. But, you see Rogelio, I can't run it. I don't know anything about running a good, inspiring, educational place for teens. I need someone who can manage it, and people who can advise me on how to best get financial help in the future if I can't fund it on my own."

He placed a hand on my shoulder. "You want to bring money and jobs into a Latino community, then I want to help you." He gave me the number of a man who would be able to set up a non-profit corporation for me, and the name of a bank manager who could help me with the bank loan. "I know some people who might also donate some money to help you get started. And if you need volunteers, I can suggest some names."

I was overwhelmed. I took all the names he gave me, and grew increasingly more excited. Me own a nonprofit organization? Wow. All I wanted to do was have a place for young kids to hang out, stay off the streets, and learn something fun and useful.

"Thanks, Rogelio. I appreciate it. Really."

"Ah," he said. "Don't mention it. You remind me of myself when I was young and started my job-training program. My goal was to place every kid into a job. Yours is to make sure they have a life. A worthy and honorable goal."

I felt myself blush. "Thank you."

"I'm having dinner with your *abuelita* tonight, by the way. Why don't you stop by and we can talk more about your plans?"

He was seeing my grandmother? That was a shocker. "I didn't know you knew my grandma."

"Lydia introduced us. Lulu is a great cook." He patted his rounded belly. "And I'm not one to turn down good Mexican cooking."

I laughed. "Tell her I love her and will stop by and see her later this week. I'll call some of these people you've suggested and maybe we can get together afterward."

"You bet, *Mi'jita*." He patted my back and went off to chat with other members.

And I went to bed that night dreaming of the possibilities.

Friday, September 24

❁ Ready to pitch my movie idea to my team, I gathered them in the storyboard room. I was armed with my drawings, each with its own beat outline that would map out the actions and emotional changes in the characters. Adrenaline pumped through my body. They had to love it. I loved it. It could be the best movie animation Panoply ever created. But I had to sell it first to my team, before we developed it and pitched it to our director.

Just as I got started, our department assistant, Amy, poked her head into our room.

"Sorry," she said. "Call for you, Marcela."

"Take a message. Please," I remembered to say, even as distracted and eager as I was to get started.

"Ah, it's urgent. I wouldn't have bothered you otherwise."

Urgent? I frowned, wondering first if something had happened to my grandmother. At her age, I always expected the worst. But it could be a problem with Lupe, my court trial, or any number of things. I put down my sketches. "Excuse me," I said to the guys gathered in the room.

Hurrying to my desk, I questioned Amy. "Who is it?"

"Daniela."

"Daniela? Did she say what was wrong?"

"She was crying. Wanted to talk to you. Said it was an emergency." Amy sounded apologetic and a bit out of breath as she took quick steps to keep up with me.

"Thanks," I said as I reached my desk. I picked up the line. "Dani?"

"Marcela." She sniffed. "Oh, thank God."

"*Que pasa?*" I switched to Spanish and I'm not sure why. More intimate? I didn't want anyone to overhear—though no one was in the room.

"It's Fabian. Oh, Marcela." She cried and sounded as if her heart was being ripped out of her body.

"Shh, hey, Dani. Tell me what's wrong." I was freaking out.

"He was shot. He's in emergency."

Shot? Emergency? The hospital. Okay. "Where are *you*?"

"I'm here. I'm waiting. But you've got to get the kids for me. Can you pick them up from school and take them home?"

"Yes, of course." By "here" I assumed she meant she was at the hospital. "Give me the names of their schools." Two were in elementary school, the other one would be in preschool.

She rattled off the names.

"Okay. Don't worry, sweetie. I'll take care of them."

"*Gracias*, Marcela."

"How in the world was he shot?"

"All I know right now is that he went to the liquor store next to his office, probably to get cigarettes, and there was a holdup and he was shot. I'm so scared, Marcela."

"He'll be fine. Hang in there. I'll go get your kids."

I hung up and stood there for a few moments. "Hell," I said. Then went to cancel my meeting.

"Everything okay?" Jackson asked.

"No." I shook my head and gazed up at him. "My best friend's husband was shot in a robbery of some type. I've got to go, can you cover for me?"

"No problem." He reached for my shoulder and squeezed.

Appreciating the gesture, I gave him a quick hug, then grabbed my purse and keys and hurried to get Daniela's kids out of school.

I didn't tell them much, just that there had been an accident with their father. That he was fine, but needed to be checked out at the hospital. The oldest boy didn't buy my lie and ended up sitting up with me and waiting for his parents to get home.

At about one in the morning, Daniela called home to say Fabian was out of surgery and in recovery. That he was fine, but that she was going to wait until he awoke—wanted her face to be the first thing he saw. She spoke with her son and seemed to put his mind at ease, because the boy went right to bed after he disconnected.

I agreed to stay the night, and curled up on the couch to get some sleep. But as I lay all alone in Daniela's house, with her children sleeping in their rooms, I wondered if I'd ever have what Daniela had. Strange thing to think at a time like this, but I couldn't help it. A mortgage payment, children, and a million other responsibilities—people actually volunteered to take on such things?

I closed my eyes and snuggled into the cushions of the comfortable couch. Well, maybe I could see the benefit of a nice, comfortable home and kids who love you so much they don't sleep until they know you're okay. Yeah, that's pretty cool, gotta admit.

Saturday, September 25

❀ Daniela showed up alone about three in the afternoon. I kept the kids busy, playing games and cooking, but their hearts weren't into anything, so I was relieved when Dani walked into the house. The kids ran to her and she tried to hug them all at once, kissing the tops of their heads.

Fabian would be in the hospital another two days. The bullet went under his bottom left rib cage and did a lot of internal damage on its way out. The doctors felt it important to make sure the internal organs healed properly and that there was no bleeding. She told the kids to go get ready, that they would go to the hospital together to visit their father, and they all ran upstairs.

She motioned me to follow her to the patio.

"I feel like God is getting me back," she muttered as we took a seat under her striped blue and white umbrella.

I squinted, trying to block the bright sun from my eyes. "What are you talking about?"

"Remember the guy I told you about? The one who flirted with me? The one I invited to my home?" Daniela looked down at her lap and spoke in quiet, subdued tones.

"Yes." I leaned forward and lowered my voice. "Ballet daddy?"

"It's terrible, Marcela. I was with him when Fabian was shot. I had my cell phone off. Didn't even find out about it until Fabian was in the hospital, in surgery."

"You were *with* him?" What did that mean?

She nodded.

"What did you do?" I feared the answer to that question, but I had to know.

"We had lunch. We flirted. We kissed."

"You kissed? That's . . . all?"

"All? Don't you think that's horrible enough?"

I breathed a sigh of relief. Wasn't anything I'd give her a medal for, but at least she hadn't slept with the guy. "Don't beat yourself up over this."

"You know, this flirtation was exciting and forbidden and dangerous and I loved it. But when I found out Fabian was in the emergency room, I almost passed out. Do you know he got shot trying to convince the thieves to let these two kids, who were crying and scared, go? He was helping some kids and I was debating whether to screw around on him. I'm scum."

"No, Dani. You're not."

"Here I was kissing another man while my husband could have been killed." Tears pooled in her eyes.

"You didn't know."

"I knew I was fucking up. I knew I shouldn't be doing what I was doing." She sniffed. "Marcela, I love my husband. I don't need excitement and danger. I need him."

I nodded. "I know. He's going to be fine." I patted her knee, hurting for her as I watched my best friend torture herself with what might have happened. "What you did isn't as bad as it seems. A kiss was fixable." Whereas what my mom and Paul did was not.

"You really think so?"

"Sure." I smiled and reached across to give her a hug.

"Sometimes," she said as she held on to me, "when I hear about how great and free your life is and all the guys you get to date, I wish I wasn't so . . . attached." She pulled out of my arms and gazed at me through tears. "But I wouldn't give my family up for the world. You think God knows that?"

I never knew she worried so much about what God thought. "Yeah," I whispered. "He knows."

We were silent for a few seconds. "You're not missing out on much, Dani. Being single can be nothing but heartache." I shared my George drama with her.

"You're a fool," she said.

Thanks. That makes me feel better. "Probably."

"Do you really want to be single forever?"

"I don't know."

Daniela leaned back in her seat and put her feet up. *"Mirá, piba,"* she said, taking a deep breath and fortifying herself as she changed roles to the one giving advice. "Marriage isn't perfect, but having someone to count on, someone to share your disappointments and challenges and triumphs with is . . . what makes life complete. It's like a drug. Once you've had it, you can't live without it."

"But I've got people to do that with already. Like you," I said.

"Not enough."

"And my sisters and my parents."

Again Daniela shook her head.

I was glad she was coming around. Fixing me took her mind off her own problems. But she wasn't convincing me. Married women all seemed to find their own "ballet dad" eventually. And if they didn't, their husbands found a ballerina. I couldn't shake the feeling that marriage was nothing but a lifetime of self-inflicted torture.

"Think about it," Daniela said. "It might not be too late to tell George you're sorry and that you *do* love him."

She meant well, but I could *not* face George yet. I still refused to believe that what I felt was love. And if it was, it would go away if I ignored it, wouldn't it? "I can't see him. Besides, love isn't enough. He wants . . . everything. I just can't give up who I am for him. It's over."

My relationship wasn't the issue anyway, hers was. Fabian was a great guy, and I didn't want Daniela to lose him. "But you my dear, have kids and a great life. Don't fuck it up. Call me if you need me again. I need to get into work for a few hours."

"On a Saturday?"

"That's *my* life."

"Work can't hold you on lonely nights," she said.

"True." And neither would George without major strings. But maybe I didn't need anyone to hold me anymore.

Thirty-Seven

Thursday, October 7

🌺 Two weeks later, Fabian was back home. Daniela remembered she was happily married again. And I arranged for a "date" with my mother to discuss my visiting Paul.

Next door to the Panoply studios offices was the best seafood restaurant in Los Angeles. Rather than talking to my mom at her home, I thought this neutral setting would be better.

But to my surprise, I saw George sitting a couple of tables away, apparently in a business meeting with two other Panoply executives.

He looked so good. My handsome, polished, perfect lover. I missed him. In the three weeks since I'd been back from Mexico, I hadn't run into him once. I made a point of not seeking him out, and he probably did the same. But I realized as I watched him that all my feelings were still very much on the surface.

He noticed me too and we sat there staring at each other from across the tables.

"What are you looking at?" My mother looked over her shoulder.

George said something to his lunch partners and stood.

"Hello, Marcela," he said as he approached our table.

"Hi. Business meeting?"

He nodded. "Looks like I'm getting a promotion—executive director of our department."

"Congratulations." Sitting in front of him in such a formal setting, with lush greenery and classical music in the background, discussing our jobs made me feel awkward. He'd held me, kissed me, made love to me. I could never again pretend nothing deeper existed between us.

Apparently neither could he, because he said, "You didn't call me when you got back from Mexico."

My mother cleared her throat. I'd forgotten that she was sitting beside me, probably checking him out.

"Mom, this is George. We work together."

She smiled and extended her hand.

George shook it. "Nice to meet you."

"Do you need a moment?" My mom asked me.

"No," I said.

"Yes, please," George amended, and he held out a hand for me to go with him.

"I'll order for us. You want the Mahi Mahi?" Mom asked.

"Yes." I took the white linen napkin off my lap and placed it on the table as I stood. "Thank you."

Mom nodded and smiled.

"Sorry," George said as we walked in the direction of the bar, "but I didn't want to risk another three weeks going by without talking to you."

I crossed my arms as we stepped off to the side of the bar and faced each other. "What is it?"

He placed his hands in his pockets and tilted back on his heels. "I guess I'm waiting for the verdict."

I shrugged, trying to remain cool and unaffected though I was starting to shake from the inside out. "Nothing's changed."

"Meaning what?"

I lowered my arms. "Too fast. You moved too fast, and I . . ." Looking down to the marble tile floor, I swallowed a lump in my throat. "I don't want what you want."

After an awkward silence, I noticed him nodding sadly.

"I'm happy by myself." A lie. I wasn't all that happy, but I couldn't admit that he'd broken my heart into a million pieces. The truth was, I'd given him all I could—all I was capable of—and it hadn't been enough for him. He still wanted more. How could I ever make him happy?

He looked over my shoulder, out the wall of smoky windows. "Maybe I was going fast because I feared you'd slip away. Maybe I was so stupidly happy to have you, I wanted to put labels on our relationship to keep you with me."

My God, he was going to make me cry. I blinked fast to clear my vision. "I wasn't going anywhere."

He pulled his hands out of his pockets and took a step closer to me. "You don't know where you're going and that bothers me."

It more than bothered him. It scared him. And who could blame him? If it were me, would I put my heart on the line if I thought it might be obliterated? Not likely.

"I'm figuring it out," I managed to say through choking tears that now crept out of my eyes and down my face. I wiped my eyes, hating this. "And damn it, I thought you were going to be by my side while I did."

He sniffed and nodded, looking like he was fighting his own tears. "Marcela," he whispered, regret thick in his voice.

"No, I'm okay. Maybe it's good that you aren't with me. I mean, you were right, our relationship was leading nowhere. You would have wasted months, maybe years, with me, and I'd never have been able to promise you forever. It's not in me."

His gaze penetrated deep into my soul as if challenging the

idea that I wasn't capable of committing. "This is killing me, you know? It's not what I wanted."

Damn him. Did he think it was what I wanted? I wiped under my eyes again and tried to compose myself. "Just know that I've wanted you from day one, George. This isn't about you, okay? If it would have been anyone, it would have been you."

He closed his eyes tight. When he opened them, he reached for me.

I stepped back. "I've really got to go." And I went to face my mother with swollen, red eyes. Wonderful.

❀ My mother reached across the table and took my hand. "So, tell me about George," she said.

George, I definitely didn't want to talk about, but I knew it would be useless to pretend there was nothing to tell. "We . . . didn't work out."

"I didn't know you were seeing anyone seriously."

"I guess I didn't realize it was serious until it was." I blinked away the tears that reappeared in my eyes.

"And what happened?"

"Mom." I gave her a warning look. Couldn't she just let it rest for a little while?

"What?" She released my hand.

I took the opportunity to wrap it around a glass of water. "I can't talk about this." I shakily raised the glass to my lips.

"Why not?"

I sighed and placed the glass back on the table, wanting to leave this restaurant and get away from these questions. "I'm dying inside, okay? My heart feels like someone took a hammer to it and shattered it. Is that what you want to hear?"

"It's the last thing I want to hear. You know that."

We listened to the soft music and silently watched as our lunch was served. How in the world was I going to eat?

As my mother cut into her swordfish steak, she gazed at me. "You love him," she said.

"I don't know. How would I know? How do you ever know?" I was frustrated and angry and hurt, and just didn't know how to deal with all these feelings anymore.

"Well, you just do."

"No." I shook my head. "How?"

"Honey, you mean to tell me you don't know what love feels like?"

Yes and no. "Did you love Paul?"

"We've been through this before."

"Did you?"

"No."

"He loved you. He told his son that he loved you."

My mother's face blanched. "You've talked to him?" she whispered, and looked around the restaurant as if anyone here would care that she'd had an affair.

"To his son. He thinks we should meet."

"*¡Dios mío!*" She put her hand to her forehead. Then she lowered her knife and fork.

Well, at least I got her off the subject of George. "Mom, don't worry. I'm not sure I even want to meet this guy."

"Then why did you track him down?"

"Because I had to." Emotionally exhausted and physically drained, I shook my head and leaned back in my chair. "I needed to know."

"Then I suppose you have to see him. Just know from the start that I have no intention of helping you. I don't want to talk to him."

"You're afraid he's going to be pissed because you didn't tell him about me."

She closed her eyes and lolled her head back. "He's going to want to kill me."

"No."

"Don't be too sure. I'll be lucky if all he does is hate me. I've hated myself for lying to him, and hurting your father, and now you. *Ahi*, Marcela, some mistakes you can't take back and they never go away."

I didn't take that personally. I already knew she didn't regret having me. But she regretted what she'd done, as she should.

The sounds of murmuring voices and silverware suddenly felt intrusive. I got up and sat beside her rather than across from her. "I'll tell him he can't contact you under any circumstances."

She sat in silence, lost somewhere in her own mind. "He told his son he'd loved me?"

I smiled and wondered what really went on between them. "Yep."

"I was still in love with Juan when I met Paul. He was kind and handsome, and made me remember how it felt to be free—to enjoy those first few weeks of infatuation. But . . . in my heart, it was always Juan. My only real love."

I nodded. "So . . . how did you know?"

She laughed and placed an arm around my shoulder. "*Mi'ja*, you just know."

"George told me he loved me and I couldn't say it back, Mom. I feel like if I do, I'll be trapped with him forever."

"And being trapped with him forever doesn't make your heart sing?"

"No. Not really."

"Well, there you have your answer."

Yes, I did. But, not having him at all also sent me into a panicked depression. I wanted him on my terms. Was that unfair? "Is that how you felt with Dad? Trapped?"

"Yes. I was so young and I felt my life was over. No more following my dreams. No more nights out with my girlfriends. My life was set—I would be a man's wife, nothing more."

That would scare the crap out of me too. "Why couldn't you do both, follow your dreams and be married?" I wondered what her dreams had been.

"Different times. Your dad wouldn't have gone for it."

Just like my sister said—Dad ruled with an iron fist. "I heard that Grandma told you you were lucky you put a stop to his macho attitude. Was he that domineering?"

My mother smiled and patted my thigh, and I felt closer to her than I ever had before. We were finally able to really talk.

"Juan was great until he found out about Paul, then he became a controlling, suspicious, jealous tyrant. I couldn't leave the house without reporting back every tiny thing I'd done. It was terrible for years. But it was my fault."

I nodded. How ironic. She feared being trapped in a marriage, and created a situation where she became a virtual prisoner. "So after that, there was no way you were going to have a career or a life outside this house."

"That's right. He would have divorced me if I'd even mentioned wanting anything other than him. Besides, when I found out I was pregnant with you, that was it. I knew I'd never be more than a mother and a wife."

I cringed. "Jeesh, sorry Mom."

She laughed. "Don't be, baby. I had the best job in the world. Today, I wouldn't change it for anything. But back when I was nineteen and pregnant . . ."

"I hear you."

She turned to face me, reaching for both my hands. "But having a family, a child, is . . . oh, indescribable. It makes you feel whole and fulfilled. Watching you all grow and learn, and become beautiful women makes me so proud. When I look at my *familia* I see what really matters. Don't even think of cheating yourself out of that, Marcela."

Here we go. The push for grandkids. The same old speech about family being the most important thing in the world.

"You're not me. You have a career," Mom continued. "And times have changed. You can have both. If you love this man, don't give him up."

But I had. Or he gave me up. I don't know which.

She released my hands and gazed out into space. "And when you meet Paul, tell him I'm sorry."

I reached across and caressed my mother's lovely face, which she took great pains to maintain in youthful, glowing radiance. She still looked like she was in her thirties. I suddenly saw her in a brand new light. She'd given up everything for my father and us girls. She had poured her soul into being the perfect wife, the perfect cook, the perfect housewife, the perfect mom. She'd convinced herself long ago that without family you were nothing, because that was what she herself *had to* believe. "I love you, Mom."

With tears in her eyes, she nodded. "And remember that you are not *his* daughter. You are mine. And Juan's."

"I know that." I hugged her close to me. "I know that."

"Let's get out of here," she said.

And with our meals untouched, we left. She went home, and I returned to work—my one and only love.

Thirty-Eight

Friday, October 15

❀ My flight into Portland took about three hours, but it felt like fifty. My hands shook every time I lifted the bottle of water I bought at the gift shop in LAX. I tried to read my novel, but couldn't concentrate. I tried to close my eyes and think of what I would say when I met Paul face to face, but nothing sounded good.

Hi, I'm Marcela. Unfortunately we seem to be related, because you couldn't keep your pants zipped around a married woman. Want to get a drink? No, that won't work. How about: *Although I have nothing but disdain for you, I'm curious as hell about who you are, so let's chat.* Darn. For the millionth time, I thought maybe I should just catch the first flight back home and forget the whole thing.

But we landed and I walked out of the Jetway into the airport. When I got to the area where nonpassengers were allowed to wait, I spotted the two Pauls right away. Not because of the picture young Paul had emailed me, but because I just knew the moment I saw two men waiting expectantly that they were waiting for me.

The three of us stood facing each other.

Finally the older Paul smiled and said, "Hello."

"Hi." That came out okay.

It was the younger man who finally broke the awkwardness. He took my carry-on and gave me a hug. "If you turn out not to be my sister, how about a date?"

I laughed. "Nice to finally meet you, Paul."

"You know," he said, turning toward the glass doors, "I told my dad, we should have gone to see you. I've never been to Hollywood. You ever meet any movie stars?"

We walked out of the airport. "Lots. Though I usually only meet them at preview parties. I can watch the voice recordings if I want, and sometimes I do, but I have so much of my own work to do that I don't have time."

"Exciting. How did you get into that line of work?"

We walked to the parking structure. My sperm donor didn't say a word, though he watched me intently and listened to young Paul and me talk.

I related my love of animation to my possible younger brother, and he laughed and chatted as easily as he had over the phone. I felt like I'd known him all my life.

When we got to their SUV, the older Paul took my bag from his son. "Okay if I put this in the back for you?" he asked.

"Sure."

Then he took the wheel while the younger man opened my door.

"I can sit in the back with you."

"He won't bite," he whispered in my ear. "Go on."

We drove in silence until we got out of the airport.

"Did you have a good flight?" my sperm donor finally asked.

"Great. Yeah." "Good." He paused. "Your mother know you're here?"

"Of course."

He nodded and remained silent.

"She said to tell you she was sorry."

"For?"

"I guess for not telling you about me."

His jaw worked. "Yes, she should have. This has been a shock."

I didn't know what to say to that. "I might not be your daughter."

He threw me a glance. "You think you are?"

"There are other Paul Peckinpaughs in the country. At least two more that popped up online. Could be more."

"How about other men with different names?"

"Are you suggesting my mom slept with men other than you back then?"

"I'm suggesting nothing. I'm asking."

I should be offended for my mom, but I understood why he would ask. "Well, I wasn't there, so I guess I wouldn't know."

"I'm sorry," he said.

I took pity on the guy. After all, this whole "new daughter" thing had to be a pain in the butt for him too. "That's okay," I said. "I can say pretty confidently that aside from my father, you were the only other man she's ever . . ."

"Right," he said, and reddened.

I watched him, trying not to be too obvious. I didn't look anything like him.

We drove to my hotel. Both men got out and stayed with me as I checked in.

"Ah, I'll go put my bag away and meet you both back here in the lobby?"

They nodded.

When I got into my room I took a deep breath and leaned against the wall. This felt so insane. I don't want to go back down there. I want to go home. This strange man is no one to me. What the hell am I doing?

But since I couldn't keep the men waiting forever, I forced myself to return to the lobby and finish what I'd started.

"Should we get a drink?" I asked them.

"Now you're talking," the twenty-four-year-old man said.

He placed an arm around my waist and we walked to the bar. He smiled once we found a table to claim as our own. "Don't feel like I'm abandoning you, but you two need to talk without me hanging around. I'll be over there at the bar, flirting with whatever girl looks my way."

I wanted to clasp onto his hand and beg him not to leave, but I managed to keep my hands on the table and nod.

Paul slapped his father on the back a couple of times and winked at me as he left.

"He's great," I said, truly liking the idea of having a brother, especially one that cool.

"Yeah. He was born with a smile on his face. I don't even think he cried the day he was born. If I remember correctly, he told the doctor a joke, then asked for a spiked bottle of milk."

I smiled.

"What about you?" he asked.

"What about me?"

"Tell me about yourself."

Tall order. But details of my life didn't matter. Not yet. "I only just found out about you earlier this summer. Came as a big shock."

He tapped his stir straw. "I loved your mother."

I didn't respond.

"Marta was so cute and full of life and miserably unhappy with her husband. I begged her to leave him, and to marry me, but she told me her family would disown her."

"You had no business sleeping with a married woman," I blurted out before I could stop myself. Then I wanted to apologize, but I couldn't.

He looked appropriately remorseful. "You don't plan stuff like that."

"But you knew she was married."

"Of course I knew. She cried on my shoulder every week over the way that bastard treated her."

I felt like he'd slapped me. "You're talking about my father."

He looked away momentarily and I could tell he was battling with his emotions. "You're right. I'm sorry, Marcela." He drew a sharp breath. "So things worked out for her? They . . . stayed married?"

"Of course. They have a great relationship." Okay, so I said that to "show him," but in my eyes they always *had* had a great relationship.

"I'm happy for her. I only wish . . . if you really are my daughter, Marta should have told me. Instead she let another man raise you." He tapped his straw a few more times, then took a long drink. When he put it down, he gazed at me. "I look at you and wonder what might have happened if she had told me."

"My life would have been disrupted. My parents would have divorced. She did what was best for me."

He nodded. "I don't doubt that. Your mother was an amazing woman."

Was? She wasn't dead. But I knew what he meant.

"I'm sure it all turned out for the best," he continued. "You have a good family?"

"The best."

"Me, too. I've got a wonderful wife and great kids."

Great. Can I go home now?

He smiled at me. "So where does all this leave us?"

Hell if I know. "We exchange phone numbers. You tell me any medical issues I should be aware of, and we go on with our lives."

"You contacted me to get medical information?"

"No." I sighed. "To see who you are. To find out about you. To see if I looked like you."

"You don't."

"I know."

"Should we get DNA tested?"

I shrugged. "I don't really care to. You're obviously the man my mother had her affair with."

"So you're sure I'm your father?"

"Let's get this straight, Paul. You're not my father. I hate the fact that I'm a result of one of the scummiest things my mother ever did, and that the man I adore was hurt because of you two." I drew in a deep breath. My hand shook uncontrollably.

"Hey." He reached across and put his warm hand over mine. "I'm sorry, sweetheart. Calm down."

"Don't call me sweetheart." I pulled my hand back. I didn't want him to be nice to me or to treat me like his child. I didn't want to like him.

He nodded. "Okay. Okay." He ran a hand through his hair. "I'm sorry. I really am. All I can say is that I truly loved your mother and if she had wanted to leave her husband, I would have married her."

This didn't make me feel better.

"This is awkward and painful for me too," he said. "Part of me was infuriated to find out that Marta had my child and never let me know. I've thought about you every minute of every day since Paul told me you'd contacted him. I've wondered what you looked like, how you'd turned out, and if you'd had a good life. And no matter how it looks to you, you aren't the result of anything scummy. You are a result of two young kids who shared something special."

I shook my head, refusing to accept that he'd ever meant anything to my mother.

"It was sweet and totally impossible. I see that now. But back then, I was going to gallantly rescue this gorgeous girl and we were going to live on love." He grew quiet. "It just wasn't meant to be."

Our eyes met. "Yet here I am."

"And I don't know what I can do for you now. What to say."

He couldn't do or say anything. He hadn't meant to get my mom pregnant, hadn't abandoned me—didn't even know I existed. His big crime was that he fell in love with a married woman. And what the heck, I've had a great life. And I have a great family. And all of a sudden, I wanted to head back to it, immediately. I stood.

The move was unexpected enough that he stood as well, probably wondering what I was doing.

"Can you take me back to the airport. I don't need to stay any longer."

"But, why? There's no hurry," he said, clearly distressed. "You can at least stay one night."

"I don't think so."

He took a bill out of his wallet and tossed it on the table. "Please." He moved around the table. "Don't leave tonight."

I stared at him, trying to feel something, searching for some connection, but nothing clicked. "Paul, we met. And I'm glad we did. But there's nothing else for us to say or do."

He looked surprisingly sad. Tentatively, he reached across and touched my hair, running his fingers through the dark strands. His gaze followed his hand. Then he touched my face. The intimacy made me only slightly uncomfortable.

"You look so much like her."

"Do I?"

"Yes." As if realizing what he was doing, he pulled his hand back abruptly. "Excuse me."

"It's okay."

We stood in the hotel bar, staring at each other like two alien beings not sure if the other comes in peace.

"Marcela, don't go yet. I want to get to know you better."

I shook my head. "I'm a grown woman, and I already have a father."

He didn't move a muscle, didn't react.

"I don't want anything from you. You don't have to *do* anything, Paul."

"At least spend the night in Portland. Get some rest. And tomorrow, we can have breakfast before I take you to the airport. I never got to do anything for you, but I gave you life. Give me a few more hours to know something about you."

Inside, I began to tremble again. Did this man give me life? Was he the other half of my biology? I nodded. "Breakfast, tomorrow."

"Thank you." He smiled and, though it was a sad sort of smile, I noticed that it was warm and kind. He wasn't the monster I'd made him out to be. And I could see what my mother liked about him.

"See you tomorrow."

The two Pauls left and I took the elevator up to my room. I felt cold and alone in this generic hotel room. I got under the blankets and stared at the wall in front of me for a good hour. This was strange. How could I be related to these people? To a man I've never met before today?

I picked up the phone and started to dial my mom, but before the first ring, I hung up. She said she didn't want to be involved, and if she knew how confused I was, she'd only become distressed herself. So I dialed a different number.

"Hello," George answered.

"Hi. It's me. I'm sorry to bother you, but—"

"Marcela." I could almost see him sitting upright on his couch at the sound of my voice. "No, you're not bothering me. How are you?"

"This is totally unfair to you, I shouldn't be calling, I know, but—"

"Marcela, stop it. What's wrong?"

"I'm in Oregon. I met my birth father," I said with a voice that sounded subdued and young even to my ears.

"What's he like?" George asked.

I loved that George immediately became concerned and that I could share my most painful and insecure thoughts with him and he stood by my side to support me. "Nice, though he seemed pissed at my mom."

"I can imagine."

"Why?"

"Marcela, you were his kid too, and she didn't tell him."

"Yeah, I know."

"You okay?"

"No."

He cursed. "Why didn't you call me before you left? I would have gone with you."

My heart swelled, and I wished I could touch him and see him. "This isn't your problem. I shouldn't even be calling you." I sighed. "Why don't you tell me to leave you the hell alone?"

"Marcela." My name coming from him sounded like a caress even over the phone line. "You're my . . . obsession. Haven't you figured that out yet?"

I pulled my legs up and hugged them close to my chest. "Oh, George. What the hell are we doing? What am I doing? To you. And to me."

"Reaching out to someone who cares about you." He left the L-word out of it.

"I care about you too."

"I know. And I'm hoping that when you check off all the points on your list, you'll come looking for me."

"You're a glutton for punishment, aren't you?"

"Well, I'm only going to wait around for you twenty years or so, so don't think you're going to string me along forever, okay?"

I laughed. "You're crazy."

"Just a little."

And I was crazy about him. I couldn't let him go. As if an invisible tether held me connected to him, I needed some contact. I simply needed him, and one of these days, I'd have to deal with that realization.

"Marcela?"

"I'm here."

"You'll get through this. Just remember that this man, whether he's your father or not—"

"He's not my father."

"Birth father, sperm donor, whatever. Whether he is or not, makes no difference. You are whomever you decide you are."

"You keep telling me that."

"Is it sinking in yet?"

"Yes. A lot is. Thanks for talking to me."

"Any time."

"I'll see you soon," I said.

"I'm counting on it."

I didn't say good-bye and neither did he. After a long pause, I pressed a finger to the button on the cradle and hung up. Then I held the receiver close to my heart and I felt better.

Thirty-Nine

❀ The earliest flight out was in the afternoon, so I met Paul for breakfast, and then he gave me a tour of Portland. I found the city to be nice, but somewhat gray. Perhaps because the sky was overcast, or perhaps because of the man walking beside me through the city streets.

Paul was more animated today, more like his son. I could see what my mom had been attracted to, even if, compared to Juan, Paul appeared bland. My father had a strong, aggressive personality and you knew when he was around. Paul was meeker, gentle, definitely not Latino.

He told me about leaving California and moving to Oregon shortly after he and my mother had split. He bought a small house on five acres of land, started farming and kept buying more land. He now owned about 150 acres and was one of the largest organic vegetable suppliers in his state. He was happily married, adored his children. Being a good Catholic, he wanted more children, but his wife decided to stop at three. In his spare time, he painted landscapes. This I thought interesting and he promised to send me one of his paintings.

I told him about my childhood, and my sisters. I shared pieces of my life, my dreams, my hopes, even a few of my fears. I admitted that this new development had made me question my life and its direction. He held my hand and told me it changed nothing, and that deep inside I already knew who I was and what I wanted.

Here he sounded like George.

We ended the afternoon with a drive to the airport.

"I'm sorry I never got a chance to be your father," he said as he kissed me good-bye.

I wasn't sorry. I love Juan and I love my family, and I can't even imagine not having had the great childhood I shared with my family. If anything had been different, I wouldn't be who I am today. And come to think of it, I like who I am. "You would have been a great father," I said, because I'm sure he would have been.

"Tell your mother I forgive her. She did a good job with you."

I hugged him and walked away through the metal detectors, which detected neither my vague sadness nor my relief to be getting back to my life. I kept increasing the distance between us without turning back, even though I could feel him still watching me.

Life sucks sometimes.

Monday, October 25

❀ I hurried to our financial meeting to go over the budget my feature film, *Aztec Kings*, would be expected to operate under. After pitching my Aztec idea, my colleagues enthusiastically embraced the project. We quickly translated the rough sketches into storyboards sequences, which we managed to sell to our story supervisor and producer. I expected to spend half the day battling with Panoply execs over the budget we'd receive. What I didn't expect was that it would be with George.

"New chief financial director," I said, realizing *what* he'd actually been promoted to recently.

He grinned. "That's me."

Now, he'd be an integral part of my film. And my producer, whose job it was to get the film done within budget, would have regular meetings with George to make sure that happened.

I took a seat beside Jackson. "Did you know about this?"

"Sure. I agreed with Bruce that George would be perfect to keep us on target. Besides, I figured what better place for the guy to learn to loosen up than by working with us?"

"Not to mention keeping him right under my nose."

Jackson leaned back with a mouse-that-ate-the-canary smile. "Great how some things work out, huh?"

I never found out what Jackson and George had said to each other while I was in Mexico, but Jackson's attitude toward George had changed.

"Let's get started," Bruce said.

Jackson, the other three supervising animators, and I stood and walked business executives through the story just as I'd done with my story supervisor, character developers, and animation crew. We brought the story to life with sketches and our voices, describing everything we thought we'd need to create our film. When we finished and got our applause, George and Bruce stood to go over the dull numbers, an initial figure that we'd blow out of the water.

We argued, negotiated, and ended the meeting with everyone pretty much pumped up and ready to start our new project.

I hung back and waited for everyone to filter out. George waited too. Pretty soon it was just the two of us.

"Wow," he said. "This is what you came up with after I left you alone in Mexico?"

I sat on the table and shrugged. "After I'd chased you away, I knew all I had left was my career so I got to work."

He picked up a Magic Marker and tossed it up and down. "You're amazing. I could never do what you do."

"And I could never do what you do, babe."

My attempt to keep things light backfired, because that one word forced us to pause and notice each other. He'd come to work without his suit today. Still well-groomed and clean cut, but in Dockers and a casual top he didn't look stiff and unapproachable. He checked me out too and I wondered what he saw. Did he notice I was wearing the Aztec jewelry I'd picked up in Mexico, and that I'd toned down my make-up, and that my heart was bouncing around in my chest?

"I've got an idea," he said.

"What?"

"Can you take the rest of the day off and spend it with me?"

"Depends. What do you have in mind?" I narrowed my eyes and gave him a sultry look. Then I cringed inwardly. Would I ever be able to stop hiding my feelings behind false bravado?

But luckily, he laughed. "Let's go, and I'll show you."

Did I want to spend the afternoon alone with George? Absolutely. "All right," I said, losing the smile and the pretense. "Let me get my purse."

❀ I found myself in the city of Fontana, sitting in the grandstands of a NASCAR speedway. George had changed into jeans and a T-shirt and his Dodger baseball cap had been replaced by one with the colors of the car he was rooting for.

"No blood here, sweetheart. Just metal, rubber, and lots of adrenaline."

I smiled, no doubt he was referencing the horrible bullfight I'd endured in Mexico. Attending sporting events with George was becoming sort of like a game in itself. New adventures to

challenge my preconception of sports. I was pulled out of my isolated world of animation, movies, and fantasy and exposed to live
action that opened up a world of emotions. Baseball was boring,
bullfighting was distressing, but this race car stuff was . . . exhil-
arating.

We cheered together, jumped up and down as our car took the
lead, or groaned when our car got bumped to the side or took too
long at the pit.

There were quiet moments too when we were able to chat. I
filled George in on how it went in Oregon. He talked about his
new position at work and how he was excited and nervous but was
looking forward to the challenge.

After the race, I found I didn't want the day to end. We stood
to leave, but I stopped him before he merged into the stream of
people exiting into the aisles. "Want to come over for dinner?"

"Over where?"

"My apartment of course."

"Sure you don't want to hit a restaurant on the way home
instead?"

I smiled. "Just because I burned your dinner once, doesn't
mean I'm going to do it again."

He pulled the cap off and rubbed his head, then put the cap
on again, backward. "You promise?" he asked.

Everyone around us continued to empty out and a breeze blew
paper wrappers and popcorn cups around our feet. But all I really
noticed or saw was George. I crossed my heart. "Trust me."

❀ Once we stepped inside my apartment we stood awkwardly in
the living room. I knew I should invite him to sit at the table
while I prepared something, but I couldn't move or say anything.
Finally, I latched my arms around his shoulders, and kissed him.

His arms went around my waist and he hungrily kissed me
back.

"To my bedroom," I said.

He lifted me off the floor, continued to kiss me, and walked to the bedroom.

He lowered me onto the bed and stared down. Questions. Tons of questions begged to be answered, yet I wasn't prepared to answer anything except the fact that I needed to feel him close to me. To connect with the best relationship I'll ever have. I simply wanted him. I care about him and he cares about me, and is there ever a better reason for two people to make love?

Sometimes feelings and emotions can't be explained or wrapped up in pretty little boxes. George seemed to realize this as well, because he dropped butterfly kisses on my lips as he pulled my top over my head and asked me nothing.

Gently, he took my clothes off. I did the same for him. We paused, each on our knees, neither making a move to touch. I wanted to run my hand over his body so badly. I needed to feel his arms around me, and his body close.

When he held out a hand, I put mine in his and he pulled me to him. He lifted me up and I straddled him. Our bodies became one in an agonizingly slow, painfully sweet union. I shuddered and held him close. Oh, I so needed this.

He moaned into my neck. "I don't ever want to let you go."

"Shh," I said. "Please. Don't say anything. Just make love to me."

He bit and kissed my neck, then encouraged me to lean back and he devoured my breasts. Only when I thought I'd die of need did he lower me onto the mattress and begin to move inside me.

"You're beautiful."

"Oh, George," I said, pulling him closer, deeper. "Harder." But he took his time—savoring every moment, driving me insane.

"Don't rush this."

"I'm not." But the feelings were so intense, so on the edge.

"Feel me inside you. Want me there."

"Oh, babe, I do." I kissed all along his face, his neck, his chest, his hardened nipples. He was perfect—as perfect as a man could be, and I couldn't get enough of him. Part of me couldn't believe I was lucky enough to have him in my arms again.

His muscles became taut. I was getting to him. His thrusts became harder, and the deeper he reached into my body, the faster I was sinking into a sensual spiral.

"Mmm." I wrapped my arms tighter around him.

He held me close, his hands moving over my hot skin, touching every part of my body.

"Do it faster, George. Please."

"Marcela," he whispered in my ear. "I love being inside you."

"I love it too."

He moved faster. His hands cupped my bottom and he entered me deeper. "I can't get enough of you."

The feelings inside me were so raw, so intense, I thought I'd really and truly explode. "Ah, I can't . . . take any more," I said.

"Marcela?" He gripped my hair and pulled back, exposing my neck.

"What?"

"Oh, Marcela." He nipped at me. "I needed this."

He was close. "Yes," I said. "Yes, babe, me too."

"You're everything." His lips tugged at my earlobe. "Everything I want, and need, and I—"

"Ah," I screamed as my body gave in to pleasure. "I'm yours. Only yours."

"Oh, sweetheart, I love you," he said. "I love you so much, Marcela."

"I love you too," I gasped, as I floated on a magnificent, sensual cloud.

In a violent thrust, he let go and grunted a release.

I held him close, feeling so wonderful I wanted to close my eyes and never leave this exact spot.

But eventually, the feeling faded and I realized what I'd said. I loved him. I did. No doubt about it.

He didn't move. Didn't talk.

After my heartbeat slowed to normal, I looked up at him.

"I guess you'd like me to get off." He grinned.

"Only if you don't go too far."

He slid beside me. I rubbed his belly.

"How about a bath?" he asked after about five minutes.

"Okay."

I ran the water. We didn't talk. We sank inside facing each other, both tired and spent. He closed his eyes and leaned back. I did the same.

He finally opened his eyes and pulled me onto him. "Straddle me."

I did. Moments later he was hard and he instructed me to take him in.

Not being used to marathon sex sessions, I was a bit sore, but it also felt nice to feel him inside again.

He closed his eyes and leaned back again. Was he kidding?

I kissed his shoulders and moved my hips.

"Mmm, no," he said. "Just hold me."

He meant his penis. Hold it inside me. Didn't he understand things didn't work that way? I *had to* move. But I tried to do what he wanted and rested against his chest, joined together intimately.

"This is nice," he whispered.

"Yes," I said.

"So how did you like racing?" he asked, still looking like he could drift off to sleep at any moment.

"Mmm." The corners of my lips lifted a little as I replayed the afternoon in my brain. "I loved it."

He angled his head to the side so he could look at me without lifting his head. "I knew you'd go for all that power and the huge engines."

I laughed. "I'm a sucker for huge engines."

"Oh, I know."

"So you took me out there as what, foreplay?" I moved my hips and he let me.

His hand ran up and down my back. "I'm buying you season tickets tomorrow."

I laughed.

"Oh, that feels so good," he said.

"You're gorgeous, George." I reached for my sponge and rubbed it along his chest.

"I thought you were the gorgeous one?"

With a sponge, I dripped water on his hair and smiled as it ran down his face.

He pulled me close and kissed my shoulders as his fingers worked their magic on my back—tracing every curve, every dip. The way he loved my back was so damned sexy.

"I wanted to make love to you so bad. No . . . I *needed* to," he said. "I've been dying a little every day without you."

"Me too."

He opened his eyes and looked at me sleepily. Then he pulled me closer and we kissed.

Pretty soon the passion between us had built again and we made love a second time, right there in the tub.

Afterward, we drained the water and turned on the shower. We washed each other then climbed into bed together. We fell asleep wrapped in each other's arms like in the movies and didn't wake up until morning.

George awoke first and when I opened my eyes he was sitting up, leaning on the headboard, staring at me.

"I didn't think you'd ever wake up," he said.

"Well, good morning to you too." I stretched.

"Someone invited me here under false pretense."

I frowned. "What are you talking about?"

"I was promised food."

Oh. "You want me to cook for you?"

He slid down and slipped his hand under the sheet. "Either that or I want you to keep stretching for me. It's turning me on."

I did stretch, enough to give him a peck on the cheek and to get out of bed. "I've got to get to work."

"What?" The mock hurt look in his eyes was almost too adorable to resist.

"There's fruit in the fridge and cereal in the cupboard."

"I've been seriously cheated here. How about I give you a chance to make it up to me tonight?"

I didn't want him to think I was running; for once I wasn't. But slow was the name of the game, and this time I wouldn't let him rush me. "I will prepare a fabulous meal for you someday soon, and I'll invite you over when I do."

He got it and nodded. "Sounds perfect."

I wrapped my arms around his waist. "It will be. I promise."

"I believe you. I always have."

Forty

Monday, November 1

❀ I've barely had time to breathe lately. It's been like an out of control tornado ever since *Aztec Kings* was approved. I've been working twelve-hour days to get the project into production. From start to finish it will take two years, and will require a trip to China to confer with our animators there. Since it's my baby, I've got most of the creative control and most of the responsibilities.

Then the prep for the education center has consumed the rest of my "free" time. I've met with lawyers, building designers, educational consultants, bankers, accountants, financial planners, and my manager, Ryan Nash, who I snagged from a community center in Orange County. He answered my ad and I hired him immediately, because he's fantastic and promised to organize and run everything without me. All I had to do was worry about funding, and it appeared that Panoply had agreed to personally fund this project. I think George's influence in the finance department had a lot to do with their decision to consider donating some money to charity.

If they do, the entire thing will be out of my hands. I don't mind. All I wanted was for kids to have a place to escape the ugliness of the outside world. Panoply likes the idea as well, and sees this as a possible training ground for future employees.

I go to bed tired everyday, but I'm so excited about my life that I don't care.

Friday, November 5

❀ In the filming room, I watched as a couple of the character designers acted out parts of the film. The guys had a great time getting stabbed and falling to the ground, then doing it again. My animators would use this eventually, when it came out right, to simulate movement for the characters.

I laughed as my Aztec prince stood up after being dead and started a sword fight with Cortés. "Hey, that's not in the script," I called out.

But they didn't care, now they were just goofing off and I knew that in the next few minutes I'd get nowhere with them.

"Is this what you all are wasting our money on?" George stood behind me on the sloping floor leading to the filming area, one hand in his pant pocket, the other wrapped around a coffee cup. He was back in a suit, but that was okay, he still looked great.

"Hey, stranger."

He handed me the cup of coffee. "Thought you'd be bonded to your computer and wanted to bring you some fuel in case you decided to pull an all-nighter again.

I took the coffee. "I'll have you know, I've been out of here before eight every night."

He shook his head. "I've heard. So I haven't taken it personally that you haven't called or come down to see me."

Even with my schedule, I thought of him every day, many times during the day, but I had this feeling we were okay. He wasn't going anywhere and neither was I. But I wanted to give him a chance to go if he wanted. "Now you see why I'm a terrible person to date." I waved my arm down to the scene being played out down below. "This is what I live for."

George moved down to my level. He took the coffee out of my hands and sipped some of it. "No, it's not. It's what you love, it's what brings passion and excitement to your life, no doubt about it. But it's not what you live for."

I angled my head. "Go on."

"You live to be happy and secure and your job is only *one* of the ways you achieve that."

Okay, I'd buy that. "My family is another."

"Yep."

I took my coffee back. "And you're most definitely another."

He smiled. "Glad to hear that."

I took a sip of the coffee and it was too strong and too bitter, but hell, I could take it.

"You look more colorful lately," he said.

"I've been shopping with my aunt Lydia. Do you like it?"

"It's different."

"What does that mean?"

"I like it."

I checked my watch. "Shit. I almost forgot. I agreed to have dinner with my aunt tonight." I called out to the guys that I was leaving and that they were doing great. They waved, but didn't really pay too much attention to me as they continued their work.

I met George's gaze. "Do you want to come with me?"

"To dinner with your aunt?" I'd told him all about her and he knew that this was no careless invitation.

I nodded and swallowed down some of my apprehension about what I'd just decided to do. "I'd like you to."

"Sure." He took the coffee back again. "Maybe I'd better drink this."

"Fine. Keep it. I'll order a stiff drink when we get to the restaurant."

Aunt Lydia registered only mild surprise when I walked up to the table at the American Grill with George.

"Sorry I'm late."

She kissed my cheek from across the table. "*Mi'ja*, I know you, I've only just gotten here myself a few minutes ago. And who is this handsome young man?"

"*Tía,* this is George Ramirez. My boyfriend."

She arched an eyebrow at me. "Nice to meet you," she said to him, and reached out a hand.

But George ignored it and leaned across the table as I'd done and kissed my aunt Lydia on the cheek!

"Oh, well, that was nice," she said, blushing. "So, George, what do you do?"

He took the linen napkin and placed it on his lap. "Well, I have the unique privilege of controlling what Marcela spends."

Lydia frowned.

"I'm the finance director at Panoply."

"Oh, I see."

I watched the exchange, knowing she was just starting to rake him over the coals, and I was proud of how he was handling it.

We ordered our meals. Aunt Lydia loved this place because they had the best salads. As Mexican as she was, she rarely ate Mexican food out because it was too fatty for her. George ordered a big, greasy burger.

"Well, you make sure she has all the money she needs for this movie. It's going to be very important to our people."

"What people would that be?"

I called the waiter over and ordered my rum and Coke. "Easy on the Coke," I said.

"Our people, *Mi'jo*. You're Mexican, aren't you?"

"I'm American."

Her back visibly stiffened.

"But I'm finishing up a Spanish class and got a chance to visit Mexico with Marcela recently. Do you get to visit often?"

My *tía* looked a little flustered, but smiled. She began swishing around her water glass. "No."

"Next time we go, you should come along. What do you think, Marcela?" he asked.

Next time? "Sure." I reached across and pried the water glass out of my aunt's hands, because she was driving me crazy. "My aunt doesn't visit often because all our family lives here."

George broke out into a wide smile like he'd just discovered gold. "Oh, so you're American, like me."

Oh, George, what are you doing?

"I'm Chicana," she said.

The food arrived. He picked up the ketchup bottle. "Well, I'm glad we got that straightened out before our food got here. I'm American, you're Chicana, and—" He turned to me. "What are you, honey?"

I stared at him, feeling like Bambi facing a shot gun. I turned to my aunt who also seemed to be awaiting my response as if the answer would change the spin of the earth.

I reached for my rum and Coke and downed the entire thing. My temples pounded and my throat burned. "I'm . . . me," I said finally. "Your lover and friend." I turned to my aunt. "And your niece who loves you and respects you so much sometimes I wish I *were* you."

I drew a deep breath and felt light-headed. "What the hell difference does the rest of it make?"

They both stared at me, then finally Aunt Lydia snapped out of it. "None at all, *Mi'ja*." She called the waiter over. "I'll have a rum and Coke too," she said. "My niece has just introduced me to a boyfriend for the first time ever. I feel like celebrating."

"Yes ma'am," the waiter said.

"I'll take one too," George said.

"And I'll have another," I said.

"So." My aunt smiled. "This is turning out to be quite a dinner."

George covered my hand with his and winked.

I winked back. God, I loved him.

Thursday, November 11

❀ Since everyone had Veteran's Day off, I invited my parents and my sisters to my home for dinner. Alberto had told me on Monday that I had mastered the basics of Mexican cuisine and that I was ready to go on to advanced culinary training if I chose. I'm having so much fun, I decided to go for it and learn Italian dishes next. Besides, I like my cooking nights with Alberto.

But what good is all this cooking if I can't show it off, especially to my mom?

I had a second reason for having my family visit. Katie and I decided it was time to introduce Dad to Gilbert. Despite what we thought, she got back together with her lover. I met him, and he's a nice guy—owns a hot restaurant in Manhattan Beach. I've eaten there and there's usually a two-hour wait to get in. He seems to really adore Katie, and she is totally head over heels about him. Glad my baby sister is not like me about expressing her feelings. Smart girl.

Katie and Gilbert arrived first. I put the finishing touches on the meal, while they set up a second makeshift table out of this pop-together picnic bench thing I bought at Costco. No way would we all fit around my small, round dining table.

Anna arrived next and when we introduced Gilbert, she was instantly charmed.

"I can't believe you didn't tell me about him earlier," she chastised Kate.

"She told me and all I did was confuse her," I said.

"Well, what is she doing asking you for man advice?"

I hopped onto my little decorative corner bar stool. "Because I'm older and wiser." And they've both always come to me for advice since we were kids.

"But I'm much more sensible than you are."

I laughed. "And you're so modest."

"So, Gilbert. Tell me about yourself," she said, ignoring me.

He smiled and began sharing tidbits about himself.

A knock at the door made us all freeze. I bounded off the stool and opened the front door to let Mom and Dad inside.

Everyone stood to make room for them on the futon.

"Dad, this is Gilbert," Katie said. "My boyfriend."

"Nice to meet you, sir." Gilbert extended his hand.

My dad sort of frowned, and raised his hand almost hesitantly.

My mom gave him a hug. "Nice to meet you, *Mi'jo*."

"Gilbert owns a very popular restaurant in Manhattan Beach," I said.

"And a nice house on the beach," Anna threw in.

"He's worked from the time he got out of high school and saved money to start his own business. Isn't that industrious of him?" I asked.

"And he goes to church every Sunday with his *mami* and *papi*. He's Catholic, of course," Anna said.

"He's also—"

"*Bueno, bueno,*" my father waved us all off. "Let the poor man speak for himself. Let's sit."

Gilbert sat beside my father.

"You're dating my baby, huh?"

"Yes, sir. I'm dating Katie."

"She is still in school, you know."

"Yes."

"She's going to finish."

"Of course."

"There will be no wedding and no babies until she's finished."

"Dad!" Katie said, clearly horrified.

Gilbert chuckled, and gazed at my sister. "Better hit those books, *amor*. I'm not getting any younger." Then he turned to my father and nodded. "I won't interfere with her plans."

My father smiled. "Good."

"Well," I said. "Let's eat."

"I can't wait to try your cooking," my mom said, hooking an arm around my waist.

"You're going to love it."

"I'm sure I am. I've always thought you'd be a great cook once you got around to it."

I laughed. "You did not."

"Of course I did."

I shook my head. I forgot—Mom is always right.

So I served my family dinner in my small apartment, and it was fantastic. Yes!

Forty-One

Sunday, November 21

❀ I loosened my hair from its clip and shook it free. Even my scalp was moist with sweat. I had worked my butt off all weekend, and my head was spinning from all the people who'd walked in and out of the building, but as I looked around the small rec room I smiled.

Just one more thing to complete the room. Out of a box I pulled a painting that Paul had sent me. He's a pretty good artist. I hung the painting in a section we'd set aside for kids to practice their artistic talents.

The front door opened and the bells chimed. My dad walked through and scanned the room. "Looks like you're ready for business."

I leaned against a table, resting my hands on my hips. I felt like a limp noodle. "What are you doing back here? You were supposed to go home."

He strolled inside with a box under his arm. "Come on," he said.

He headed into my "office," a small room I'd set aside to keep the financial records my new financial planner advised me to keep. He pulled a ceiling fan out of the box. "The room needs a few finishing touches."

I walked around my desk to check it out. He climbed on my desk and began to install the fan.

"Thanks, Dad." I smiled. How sweet that he went out after working so hard all weekend and found something special for me. "Just what this room needed to make it homey."

He finished and tested it, then looked around. "Still doesn't seem like you have enough light in here."

"Dad, it's fine." I took a seat behind my desk. I crossed my legs, then wondered if that was a good idea. I'd probably be stuck in this position 'til morning.

"I don't know. Seems dark. Maybe you need a window. Rooms look like closets when they don't have windows."

"Dad," I said gently. "It's perfect. Sit down."

He reluctantly sat across from me.

"How can I thank you for all your help?"

"You don't have to thank me. I'm your father."

Never before had those three words held such meaning for me.

"I'm proud of you for doing this, *Mi'ja*."

"I'm exhausted, but I feel good. I'm finally doing something for someone other than myself."

He stared at me strangely.

"What?"

"Nothing." He scratched below his left eye. "You've just become such a beautiful, perfect woman. How did it happen?"

"You're biased, *Papi*."

He stood and leaned across my desk and kissed the top of my head. "I'd better get home to your mother."

I forced myself to stand. The least I could do was walk him to his truck.

"Don't stay here too late. This neighborhood is . . . not the best."

I'm sure he was thinking dangerous. I agreed. "I'll lock up and head home soon."

He opened his truck door. "Why don't you come over and have dinner with us tonight?"

"I'm too tired, *Papi*."

"You're too skinny. Come over and eat."

"Dad, I'm fine. I can cook now, remember?"

I'm not skinny—though I've lost weight since I started cooking more at home. "Almost as good as your mother, but don't tell her I said that."

I smiled. "I wouldn't go that far. But I can make a few things."

He nodded. "Listen, ah . . . I've been wanting to talk to you."

"Okay?"

He sighed and looked down. "Your mother told me something and I think we need to talk about it."

By his serious tone, it couldn't be good. I started to feel sick to my stomach. "What?"

"She told me why you went to Oregon."

Oh, shit. My entire body sagged. I swallowed, but my mouth had suddenly gone dry. And all the blood must have drained from my face because it felt numb. I took a step back, unable to meet his gaze.

"Marcela, it's okay."

But I couldn't talk to him, couldn't look at him. I felt like a traitor. Guilty of betrayal. I kept walking backward.

He leaped after me and took my arm. Walking to the back of his truck, he lowered the tailgate. "Sit," he said.

When I stood there immobile, he picked me up and sat me on the tailgate. "It's okay," he repeated. "But we have to talk about it. We can't continue to pretend the other doesn't know."

I nodded.

"It was your mother's mistake, not yours."

"I know."

"And I'm sorry I never told you about it and that you had to find out from Sonya, but I didn't because you are *my* daughter. You always have been and you always will be."

I met his eyes. "*Papi*, I know what you mean. But I'm actually not and it hurts so much."

He pulled me into a fierce hug. "I love you," he said. "I love you so much." He kissed the top of my head. "I love you, *Mi'ja*." He kept repeating it as if the words would erase the truth and ease my pain. His desperate attempt to shield me from hurt made me cry.

"I love you too, *Papi*," I cried. "And I'm so sorry."

"Shh, don't say that. Ever." He wiped my eyes and sat beside me. "I'm going to tell you something."

I nodded, and wiped at the tears that continued to fall.

"When you were three, I couldn't live with the doubt anymore. My heart kept telling me that you weren't his, that you were mine. After all, I'd slept with your mother too. You didn't look white. I thought . . . maybe. Just maybe, you were mine."

I frowned, but he now had my complete attention.

"I took you in for a blood test. A paternity test. You cried and begged me not to let the lady stick the needle in your tiny arm." He tightened his jaw and I could see his eyes become moist. "But I was obsessed. I had to know the truth. So I forced you to go through it. You kicked and cried and begged me to make them stop. But I held you down as they tied the rubber band around your thin arm and ignored the frightened look in your eyes." He shook his head. "I was such a bastard."

I placed my hand over his. He was silent for a moment, then I saw that he was crying. My strong, macho father was crying and my heart broke.

"But in the end, I had the results of the tests."

My empty stomach turned over on itself, and my heart was beating out of control as if I'd just jogged for ten miles. He had had me tested. I was his. This was why he'd accepted me, why he'd loved me. I was his, not Paul's, after all. "Tell me what the tests said, Dad."

"I don't know."

"What?" I frowned. "How could you not know?"

"I never opened the envelope. The woman told me the result was in the envelope and that we could open it and discuss it, or I could take it and open it in the privacy of my home. I chose to take it with me."

"And you didn't open it?" My voice was loud and abrasive, but I couldn't believe it. How could he keep that envelope all these years and not check?

"No." He leaned across and kissed my forehead. "I realized that if I did, everything would change. You'd either be his and I'd resent it forever, or you'd be mine and I'd walk around like a peacock in full color. But none of it had anything to do with you. *Ahi, Mi'ja*, you were this tiny little girl who was so *hermosa*, so lovely, like your mother, and you loved me and followed me around like I was a king. I realized *that* was all that mattered."

I scooted closer to him and put my arms around him.

"You already were mine. It didn't matter what that paper said." He smiled at me. "You talked like me, you gardened with me, you brought me my coffee and sat on my lap as I read the paper and had my breakfast. You were my world."

"And you were mine."

He kissed my temple and held me close. "I loved you but I hated your mother," he admitted. "I wanted to make her pay, until one day I realized if I lost her I'd lose you too, so I forgave her. And I burned the results of the test. It was over."

"Oh, Dad." I had been hoping he still had them. "Now I'm going to wonder forever."

"We can go and be tested. It's much easier these days with DNA. If it matters to you, we can be tested. But I don't want to know."

"Are you afraid you'll still resent me if it turns out he was the birth father?"

"No. It just makes no difference to me. *I* changed your smelly diapers." He chuckled. "And I got all your sticky kisses. You're *my* baby, and I love you, and I want you to stop trying to become some kind of super Chicana. I like who you are. One Aunt Lydia in the family is enough"

I smiled. "You've got a point."

"So come have dinner with your family. I'll call your sisters and we can all sit at the table together. Make your old *papi* happy, huh?"

How could I refuse? I nodded. "Okay."

That night we all sat around the table, laughing and joking and all talking at once. My father sat at the head of the table, a proud man surrounded by all his women. I caught his eye only once and I knew, fair or not, that he still loved me most.

When I got home, I gently pulled my Becoming Latina list off my desk. I'd accomplished most of it. And I had changed. I had a new appreciation for my culture. Mexicans were beautiful, proud people with a rich heritage. But much of what went on in America, much of what Aunt Lydia was involved with was political, and that wasn't me.

I let the paper go and it floated down into my wastebasket as if in slow motion. It was over. With everything I'd learned, I decided I was right all along; blood meant nothing. *Love* bound me to my family. Responsibility and just a bit of obligation did too. What other reason could there be for my father deciding to love me? And why else would I have fallen in love with Lupe . . . and with George? My heart didn't care about blood, and neither did I.

No matter who my father was, no matter how many organizations I joined, no matter how Mexican my boyfriend was, I'd never become more Latina. And it didn't matter.

In a day or two, I'd call Paul and tell him that it turns out I wasn't his daughter after all. I'd tell him how my real dad had me tested and learned that I was his. After all, that's the truth.

Monday, December 6

✿Today, Lupe got her get-out-of-jail-free card. I made a deal with her mom—Lupe helps out at the center after school and I pay for private schooling, and she makes sure Lupe stays off the streets and is physically safe.

The judge seemed to accept our plan. It's probably to the state's advantage to keep kids out of the already-clogged foster care system.

Lupe appeared happy with our plan, though she made it clear that all teachers were geeks and she preferred to skip the whole school scene. Since that wasn't an option, she agreed to private school.

Tonight, I left work early to dine with Lupe and her family. Her mother was kind enough to invite me for Lupe's celebration dinner. She seemed to have been able to work through her animosity toward me. I think it had something to do with my mother speaking to her while I was in Mexico. Maybe two moms were better able to understand each other, I don't know.

Afterward Lupe walked me to my car.

She reached into her backpack and pulled out her switchblade knife.

I glanced down at the knife she'd threatened me with on various occasions. "Where did you get that? I thought the cops took it?"

"I had a spare."

"Why are you giving it to me?"

"I'm giving it up. Take it."

"Good idea," I said. I held out my hand and she dropped it into my palm.

"I'm never going to be cuffed by a cop again."

I hoped not. "Those damn things hurt," I said, trying not to overplay how thrilled and proud I was at this moment. I wanted to hug and kiss her and jump up and down and dance.

"Think I've got a chance?"

Unable to restrain myself, I reached for her and pulled her into a hug. "Of course you do. You've got your whole life ahead of you, kiddo." I stepped back. "See you at work next month when we open up?"

"See ya." She eased back. "I'm gonna go inside and get more ice cream. All they had at camp was healthy food. Yuck."

I smiled as I got into my car. Lupe was a good kid, and the cool thing was that maybe now she could be just that—a kid.

Forty-two

Today

❀ What is it about Palm Springs that draws my family? In particular, for wedding receptions. *Abuela* and Rogelio had a relatively small ceremony at our family Catholic church. Yep, *Abuela* snagged herself a younger man with her killer chile verde. Apparently Rogelio can't get enough of that spicy, homegrown loving. After the ceremony we drove two and a half hours to the desert to the Marriott Springs Resort for the largest reception I've ever seen in my life.

I thought I was at a Hollywood premiere. Cars kept pulling up and people kept pouring into the hotel. I told my mom I'd hang out in the lobby to direct people to the correct ballroom. My sisters and cousins would help with the seating.

The wedding was spectacular. Rogelio and *Abuela* both held hands like teenagers as Padre Rodriguez had them repeat their marriage vows. The joy in their eyes was evident even from the distance of the pews where I sat with my sisters and parents.

Amazing—to find love again at their age. I smiled. Maybe there was hope for me after all.

"I thought that was you."

I whirled around. "George!" The smile on my face grew. I'd seen him off and on since our lunch with Aunt Lydia and had a couple of dates that ended in hot lovemaking, but we always left blocks of days in between where we neither saw each other nor spoke.

He smiled back and stuffed his hands into his pockets. He was dressed in a suit and tie, and looked like a gift-wrapped present.

"What are you doing here?" I asked, surprised and wildly happy.

"Lydia invited me."

"You're kidding. How did she get ahold of you?"

"She called Panoply and asked for me." He looked over his shoulder as he took three steps closer to me. "Looks like half of L.A. is here so maybe that invitation wasn't as special as I thought."

"Trust me, it was special."

He lifted an eyebrow as if to say "oh really."

"I'm standing here to see if anyone looks lost so I can steer them the right way."

He moved beside me. "Heard you're leaving for China next month."

"Yes. I'm so excited." Was I beaming as much on the outside as I was on the inside, I wondered.

"I can see that. You look amazing, by the way."

"Well, so do you." I purposely looked him over appreciatively, making him chuckle. Then I saw Daniela and her family walk in. "Excuse me a sec."

"Hey, girl," Daniela called as I waved her over.

I gave her and her husband a warm hug and kissed the kids. "This hotel is great," Daniela said.

And it was. A waterfall and river ran down the center of the lobby. Tropical plants and parrots made you feel like you had walked out of the desert and into a tropical oasis. Plus they had the entire place decorated for Christmas—every tree twinkled with colorful lights and all employees wore Santa hats.

"Follow the crowd to the left. We've got the largest ballroom on the left-hand side."

"Great." Daniela looked at George. "Hi. Marcela isn't very good at introductions."

"I'm sorry," I said. "This is George. George, my friend Daniela and her husband Fabian."

They shook hands and both men did the same.

"Okay, I'll see you in there," Daniela said, and gave me a wink when she got behind George. She pointed at him then shook her hand as if she'd burned it, indicating she thought George was hot.

"So when do you leave?" George asked.

"Leave?" I asked, ignoring Daniela and letting George's handsome form block the view of my crazy friend.

"For China."

"Oh." I wasn't sure. I don't really want to go. I'm excited about starting my project and thrilled that they're moving forward with it, but not happy about leaving. "I think I leave in about three weeks. I'll only be gone off and on for the next few months."

He nodded. "Right. I'm happy for you, Marcela."

"Are you?"

"Sure."

I watched him. He didn't sound so sure. "I was hoping you'd be a little sad."

He gave me a strange look, something between a frown and a smile. "Sad?"

"Yeah, sad. Because you're going to miss me."

"Oh." He chuckled. "I am."

"I'll miss you too." I do miss him. Seeing him only occasionally and then going our separate ways sucked. After the last time we made love, I realized he was letting me do it my way. No promises, no commitments. Just sex, a good time, and then he stepped back. I hated it. What the hell was I thinking?

He suddenly looked too serious and stared at me like a man trying to control his emotions. "Are you going to save a dance for me in there? There will be dancing, won't there?"

"We're Latinos, what do you think?" I'd made him smile again, and for that I was happy. "I'll put you down on my list. One dance for George. Maybe two, if you make the first one worth my while."

He leaned across and brushed his lips against the side of my face. "I can't wait." He turned and left, and my legs turned to butter. Had I actually wanted to get rid of him once? I was such a fool.

I stayed in the lobby for another twenty minutes and greeted as many people as I could. I even chatted with Sonya for a while. She had gotten a job as an assistant accountant, and was taking night classes to get her own CPA.

"That's great," I said, and meant it.

"Listen, Marcela. Thanks for what you said to me. Just to prove you wrong, I finally got off my butt and took some action. I'm going to make something of my life."

"I'm glad." She'd even lost weight, I noticed.

"And, I'm sorry about spilling the beans about your mom and—"

"It's okay," I interrupted, knowing what she was going to say. That was all in the past, and I wouldn't discuss it with her. "It's over. It was hard for me to deal with, but I did, and now it's over."

She nodded. We both knew she had meant to hurt me, and she had, but it really was over, and I had to forgive everyone, including Sonya. As difficult as it was to do so, I leaned across and gave her a quick hug.

Then deciding enough people had arrived, I walked to the ballroom with Sonya, commenting on the long drive out here and how we wouldn't allow any more relatives to get married in the desert. I found the table where my family sat and joined them.

After eating the rubber chicken, and drinking too much wine, I got up to socialize and chat with the family and friends I could find. I tried to tell myself I wasn't looking for George, but I kind of was. I scanned the hundred or so tables, each with at least six guests, and drew a breath. Amazing how many people turned out to see the joining of two patriarchs. Some people really made an impression in the lives of others.

My aunt Lydia gave a toast to the happy couple and announced they would now take the dance floor. They received a standing ovation and a few catcalls from Pepe's table.

I laughed and clapped. When your own grandmother beats you to the altar you know you're in trouble. But then again, some women are altar types and some simply aren't.

After the first dance, they were joined by their children. Mom and Dad danced, clinging to each other like they were newlyweds themselves as they moved along the dance floor. Somehow, I found myself at the edge of the ballroom, leaning against royal blue drapes, blending into the sides.

Turning away, I left the reception hall wanting to get some space. Not because anything was bothering me or anyone was annoying me. Quite the contrary. Everything, for once, was perfect. And maybe I needed to reflect on that just for a second.

I headed outside, to the gardens and pool, and felt a chill in the air. December was starting and our California six-month summer was finally winding down.

"Can I join you or is this a private walk?"

George. He'd found me.

I looked over my shoulder, angling my head. "I'll always make room for you on my private walks."

We strolled a few steps. "How about in your private life?"

The hotel had various paths leading to private gazebos. I

pulled George into one. "My unstable, crazy, unpredictable private life?"

"Yep, that one."

"You're there." I let my hand slide down his arm to his hand. "So . . . you going to ask me to dance?"

"There's no music."

I backed away from him, but held onto his fingertips. My heart was doing strange things. First it sped up making me feel dizzy, then it seemed to slow down and I was floating, moving as if in slow motion. "Please."

He stepped forward and took me in his arms. He hummed in my ear and glided his body back and forth. I rested my head on his shoulder.

Okay, *now* everything was perfect.

He caressed my back and stopped humming. Silently, we moved together. I wondered what he was thinking. Did he want me when we stood so close together and our bodies brushed against each other? I tipped my head back to look at him and found him staring ardently at me. Our lips were so close I felt his breath. I inched forward and his lips parted. But he just breathed harder and stared at my mouth.

Then he closed his eyes and swallowed. Gently, he released me, and took a step back. "Nice dance."

My heart had finally decided on its desired speed—the screaming jungle beat of a Latin salsa. I drew a breath and looked away, out of the gazebo, away from him.

"I've been thinking," he said.

"Mmm, about?"

"You. Me."

I hugged my arms across my chest as a breeze touched my arms. "Me too."

"Really?" He moved beside me. "What have you been thinking? You cold?" He took off his coat and draped it across my back.

"Thanks." I sent him an appreciative smile. "I've been thinking that . . ." I decided to lay it all out in the open. It was my turn to take the emotional risk. I drew a breath and promised myself I would be completely serious if it killed me. "I never would have gotten through these past few months without you."

"Not true," he said, leaning a shoulder against the side of the gazebo, crossing his ankles.

"Yes, it is true. You've been there for me. I've leaned on you. I've needed you. And you've never let me down."

His gaze was focused and his expression serious. "Glad I could help."

"But I've let you down."

He shook his head.

"Yes," I said, and placed a hand on his chest, running my fingertips along the cloth-covered buttons of his white shirt. "You're such a great guy and you deserve a great woman. One who will love you and appreciate everything you are."

"Marcela." He looked up over my head as if in deep thought. "If this is your way of telling me good-bye because you're not that woman, please—"

"No," I interrupted. "That isn't even close to what I'm saying."

His eyes lowered and locked with mine. "Then what are you saying?"

"Oh, God. I'm so bad at this." I sighed. "I'm trying to tell you that I'm so deeply and completely in love with you, George."

I inched away from him, dropping my hand from his chest to be able to think clearer.

"This crazy emptiness settles in the pit of my stomach when I think of being without you. I can't even think straight anymore. I try to work and find myself daydreaming about you. I think about some of the sweet things you've said, and cringe when I remember my own responses. I'm so sorry for hurting you."

He drew a breath and reached for my hand. "That's all in the past."

"Exactly. All in the past. All my reservations and all that dumb uncertainty . . . I'm over it all. I'm ready to try a life together with you, George. I love you. I really do, and I'm an idiot for waiting so long to tell you."

"Actually, you did tell me. When we made love after going to the speedway, remember?"

"What? Oh, yeah." Was that all he had to say after I'd spilled my guts?

"I wasn't sure if you really meant it or if, you know, it was the heat of the moment making you say it."

"I, I meant it." Okay, I'm confused. Shouldn't he be responding more positively to what I just said?

"Oh. Good," he said.

Oh good? I just admitted to being in love with him. Wasn't this what he'd been waiting for all this time? I frowned and decided that, no, he'd probably guessed how I felt about him. What he wanted was to know that I was ready to commit to a life with him.

"George, I know I work too much," I said, gazing into his warm eyes. "And now I have the center I'm responsible for too. And my family demands a lot from me. I'm not the best cook in the world, though I'm getting better all the time." I paused, wondering why any guy would want me. "I'm not a great catch," I admitted, defeating myself. "I know all that. But you wanted me to be sure of what I wanted, and now I am. I know what I want and it's you. Forever."

He smiled and placed a hand on the side of my face. One freeze-frame at a time, he leaned forward and brushed his lips lightly against mine.

Moving his lips along my jawline, he dropped another kiss under my earlobe. "Shh, slow down," he whispered in my ear. "I'm crazy in love with you, Marcela. You must know you've got me on a leash just waiting to jump through any hoop you say."

I collapsed against him, never feeling more relieved. I decided

I'd done it, I'd mastered the serious talk. So I gave myself a break and pulled back. "Any hoop?"

"Tell me you don't want to subject me to one of those massage things again?"

I laughed, feeling all giddy inside, and I don't normally use silly words like "giddy." "No, but I can go for years of romantic nights like we had in Mexico. And lots of wild sex of course."

"You got it," he said with a grin.

"And I want you to go with me to China."

"I'll see what I can do."

"And I want you by my side at all company parties and events."

He rolled his eyes. "And you know what I want?"

"Anything. Just say the word."

"I want a ring on your finger."

"This finger?" I wiggled my left ring finger under his nose.

He kissed my knuckles. "That one. Yes. I want you to be mine forever."

"I'm all yours. I promise. All yours."

"So you'll wear a ring?"

"Is this your way of asking me to marry you?"

"I'm trying not to use that word. Last thing I want is to freak you out again. But yes."

I curled my arms around his neck and drew him close. "That isn't going to happen anymore. I'm a new woman, remember? Ask me."

The corners of his lips quirked up and his eyebrows rose as if excited by the opportunity I was offering him. "I realize you're going to put in long hours at work, but at night I want you to come home to me. I want to make love to you every night and wake up to you in the morning."

"I want that too."

"Marcela?"

I arched an eyebrow and waited.

"Will you marry me?"

"Oh, yes."

He took my lips and kissed me. "That was easy."

I nipped at his lower lip. "Yes, easy. That's me. Anything else you want?"

"Just to plan the day, immediately."

"You got it, but let's skip the whole wedding ceremony thing, okay? I hate these things."

"Whatever you want, baby."

I liked the sound of that.

But for now, we returned to the wedding already in progress. There would be plenty of time to discuss our future later. Knowing who I was and what I wanted felt phenomenal and I suddenly wanted to scream it to the world. "Can we tell my family?"

"Of course."

I led George to the table where my family gathered, all laughing and talking at once. "Hey." I waved at everyone so they'd shut up. "Hey!"

They all looked at me with annoyance for interrupting their various conversations.

"I'd like you all to meet George. My fiancé."

It seemed to take a couple of seconds for them to digest what I'd said. "I just got engaged," I clarified.

My sisters screamed and jumped out of their seats to come hug me and George. My mother and father both sat back telegraphing their happiness silently from across the table, then my father stood and embraced George. "*Mi'jo*, that's my first baby. You need my permission to have her."

"Yes, sir," George said. "And I'll do what I have to to be with her."

"Do you love her?"

"More than you can imagine."

My father smiled. "Me too."

Now if this were my movie and I were the director, I would

pull the camera out at this point, widening the angle to include the table where my father made room for George, and everyone shot us one question after another.

I had my family and I had my man. Everything that mattered was here. Everything was as perfect as it could possibly be.

My story will continue, and there will be ups and downs along the way. I say that with a fair amount of certainty. But in my life, today will always go down as the snapshot I will remember forever.

Because today, I wasn't becoming anyone or anything. Today, everyone knew where I stood, especially me. And girls, as long as you know that, you know everything.